The spell . . .

Fanuilh's thought crashed through his own. *Master, there is magic close by.*

The thought was still firm in his head as he jumped to his feet and dashed for the side door . . .

"Ah, gods, make it stop!"

Liam whirled to his left, toward the scream, and then recognized Provyn's voice, distorted by agony. He walked a few steps forward and could just make out the fat quaestor rolling on the ground, tearing at his clothes, clawing at his skin.

It is a spell, Fanuilh explained. *Like the sleeping Guards.* The dragon stepped to Liam's side, its head cocked to examine Provyn's contortions.

Liam knelt down and grabbed the fat quaestor's arms. "Did he go this way?" Provyn's eyes rolled up in his head and he kicked at his own legs, scraping his bootheels down his shins. With a curse, Liam let him go and rose. His eyes adjusted slowly to the dim light of the alley . . . He turned then, to look to his right . . .

SCALES OF JUSTICE

CONTINUING THE THRILLING ADVENTURES BEGUN BY AUTHOR DANIEL HOOD IN *FANUILH*, *WIZARD'S HEIR*, AND *BEGGAR'S BANQUET*

Ace Books by Daniel Hood

SCALES OF JUSTICE

Daniel Hood

ACE BOOKS, NEW YORK

This book is an Ace original edition
and has never been previously published.

SCALES OF JUSTICE

An Ace Book / published by arrangement with
the author

PRINTING HISTORY
Ace edition / March 1998

The Putnam Berkley World Wide Web site address is
http://www.berkley.com

Make sure to check out *PB Plug*,
the science fiction/fantasy newsletter, at
http://www.pbplug.com

ISBN: 0-441-00515-2

ACE®
Ace Books are published by the Berkley Publishing Group,
a member of Penguin Putnam Inc.,
200 Madison Avenue, New York, NY 10016.
ACE and the "A" design are trademarks
belonging to Charter Communications, Inc.

PRINTED IN THE UNITED STATES OF AMERICA

10 9 8 7 6 5 4 3 2 1

CHAPTER 1

ACRASIUS SAFFIAN—SCHOLAR of magic and judge of one of the Duke's circuit courts—went for a walk after a rainstorm and did not return. He made his home in Southwark, a city of steep streets and treacherous cobblestones: no one saw his fall, but no one doubted the result. An old man with brittle bones, Saffian had broken his neck.

Apart from the natural grief at the death of so old and long-serving an official, there was serious concern over the future of the Areopagus, the court over which Saffian had presided, and which was supposed to begin its spring circuit the very next day.

The common assumption in Southwark was that the court's departure would be indefinitely delayed—but Saffian's successor would hear nothing of it. The new Areopage had served for almost two decades as one of the late judge's quaestors, his investigative assistants, and her elevation to the post was universally acclaimed. Her decision that the Areopagus would ride as planned, with only a day's delay for Saffian's funeral rites, met with considerably less approval.

In large part the disapproval was based on the fear that the decision was the result of muddled thinking, the product of a deep but mostly unexpressed grief on the part of the new Areopage—for, in addition to being Saffian's successor, she was also his widow. Milia Saffian discounted the argument entirely, however, ignoring pleas from friends like Thrasa Priscian, a long-time intimate and a prominent merchant in Southwark, and from colleagues like Aedile Coeccias, the city's chief constable.

1

Both begged her to reconsider, to allow more time between funeral rites and legal ones.

The widow stoutly refused, buried her husband in a single day and took up his work the next, arranging the complicated details of the court so quickly that it was able to depart only a day behind schedule. Unwilling to suggest that she was addled by grief—a notion belied by her efficient handling of the Areopagus' affairs—Aedile Coeccias and Mistress Priscian fell back on a more practical argument: with her advancement, the court now lacked a quaestor, and could hardly ride without its full complement of two.

Widow Saffian acknowledged that the court was short a quaestor, but did not seem overly concerned about it. She did, however, agree that if the Aedile or Mistress Priscian could find a suitable candidate and have him ready before the Areopagus departed, she would accept whomever they chose.

Since this was the only point on which she had shown any flexibility, they set about finding a new quaestor.

Toward sunset, Liam Rhenford paused his horse on a rise and considered the town of Warinsford on the banks of the river below. It was much smaller than Southwark, the city from which he had set out three days before, but it seemed a bustling place nonetheless. The town proper was a rectangle of closely packed buildings facing the Warin and surrounded by stout walls of stone, outside of which smaller neighborhoods straggled further north along the riverbank. Liam could make out a large number of ships moving on the water.

Where is the ford?

The thought appeared in Liam's head, but it was not his own—it came from the tiny dragon perched on the front of his saddle. He laughed and reached forward to scratch between his familiar's wings, rubbing his knuckles along the black scales. The scales were strangely soft, ridged like moire-patterned cloth.

I don't know, Fanuilh, Liam thought, deliberately

forming the words in his head and then pushing at them, mentally projecting them at the dragon. *Maybe there was a ford when they named it.* There was certainly no ford now; he could make out a ferry poling away from the town to the far side of the river, and some of the ships looked fairly deep-draughted. Fanuilh snaked its head around on its long neck and peered at him with slit-pupilled eyes.

If there is no ford, they should change the name.

I'll speak to the Duke about it, Liam promised, scratching now at the yellow scales of the dragon's throat and underbelly. Behind them, a jingle of harness and the clop of hooves announced that the Areopagus had caught up to them.

A trio of Southwark Guards on horseback led the way, talking and laughing amongst themselves; their jokes were at the expense of people farther back in the column, a straggle of clerks and servants and packhorses that had only just reached the bottom of the rise, still out of sight of the town.

"Quaestor Provyn's the talk of the courts," one of the Guards said, "for the splendorous contents of his wardrobe."

"His garderobe, more like," a second put in, provoking snickers from his comrades.

"Aye, he's the very cock of the dunghcap," the first agreed. "It's the word bruited around the courts. My wife's brother carries wood for their fires, and all he heard these last two days was of how tricked up the quaestor was. They said he was wont to be jealous of his appearance—off to the baths four and sometimes five times in a sevennight—but now he's the clothes to match his pretensions. The next you know, nothing'll do but he wipe his arse with cloth-of-gold!"

Liam smiled to himself; he had only known Provyn for a few days but their appraisal did not seem far off the mark to him. Looking back over his shoulder, he could just see the quaestor, the vivid red and yellow of his velvet coat picked out from the drab colors of horse and road by the fitful light of the westering sun.

He certainly likes his clothes, Liam thought, steadfastly refusing to think anything worse. They would have to work together in the days ahead and he wanted to keep an open mind, however difficult the quaestor made it. From the moment they had met in Southwark three days before, Provyn had snubbed him rudely. *A remarkable feat, considering we shared a room two nights in a row.* He cut himself off, unwilling to complain any more about the other man, even silently.

In an odd way, he empathized with Provyn, and could not blame him for his antipathy. *He's been with the Areopagus for ten years—worked his way up from clerk to quaestor—and you get the post through favoritism, just because two of your friends have a wildly exaggerated opinion of your skills as a solver of mysteries. What's more, the post is only open because of the death of a man Provyn knew and worked with for years.* Liam frowned; considered in that light, it was no wonder the clothes-conscious quaestor disliked him.

His appointment was not favoritism, he knew. Both Mistress Priscian and Aedile Coeccias honestly believed he was a sort of human bloodhound, and the man best suited to the job. They had told him so, when they came to ask him to join the Areopagus on the night of Acrasius Saffian's funeral rites.

At first he had been of a mind to refuse the offer, if only because he did not want to be given the position solely through the influence of his friends. The more he had considered it, though, the more it had intrigued him. He had until recently been much involved in outfitting Mistress Priscian's merchant fleet for the spring trading season, but the ships had sailed and he now found himself rattling aimlessly around Southwark with nothing to keep him busy. Riding the court circuit would fill his time admirably; more important, it struck him as something of a good deed, and worth doing. If Widow Saffian was brave enough to fulfill her duties in the midst of her mourning, the least he could do was help. And if he had gotten the position through the influence of his friends, he would simply have to prove himself worthy of it.

He had rushed through his preparations for the journey, and joined the Areopagus the next morning, at a caravan marshalling yard on the western outskirts of Southwark. Coeccias had come down to see him off, and they stood together at one side of the dusty yard, watching the column slowly coalesce. Liam had mentioned to the Aedile that it seemed an inordinately large train.

"Truth, that it does," the other man had laughed, "but there it is: the Duke's bounty. Did I not tell you? All who ride with the Areopagus—with any circuit court, for the matter of that—are vouchsafed a brace of horses for their effects, from the Duke's stables. Y'are his officer now. You needs must ride like one—and dine like one and go to bed like one. All will be supplied on your way."

"Well, it's quite a berth you've fixed up for me, my friend," Liam said, smiling his approval of the arrangements.

Coeccias dropped his eyes to his feet and cleared his throat. "Truth, Rhenford, it's not so soft as all that."

"How so?" Liam asked, puzzled.

"Look you," the Aedile said, clearly embarrasssed, "you know I was strong against the court going out at all, as was Mistress Priscian, but Widow Saffian would not listen." Seeing Liam's look of confusion, he hurried on. "It quietened some of our doubts, I'll say, to know that you'd go. If it needs must ride, then we're both comforted to know y'are riding with it, for that . . . for that we have our doubts as to the wisdom of it."

Liam knew they had opposed Widow Saffian's decision, but he could not see why his friend seemed so nervous. *Unless* . . . "Is there something you aren't telling me?"

The Aedile held up his hands in self-defense. "No, no—only that you should take care. There are strange doings in the duchy now, unheard-of crimes. I told you some of the crimes were of black magic, did I not, and that demons had been summoned?''

Liam nodded. ''Yes, you mentioned it last night.'' He indicated his baggage, and the two sword hilts visible there. One of the weapons was a plain blade; the other was enchanted, a gift from a wizard he had once known. ''I've taken some precautions.''

''Well and well,'' Coeccias said. ''Keep your eyes wide for the strange, but softly. Don't let the widow know you suspect aught is amiss.''

She appeared then, her clothes black, a mourning veil covering her face, with Quaestor Provyn in tow. Between introductions and the fact that the column was almost ready to leave—the packhorses' loads secured, the people beginning to mount—Liam did not have a chance to ask his friend what, exactly, he was supposed to suspect was amiss.

Three days later, on the ridge above Warinsford, Liam decided that Coeccias had been overly concerned. He had seen no sign of anything out of the ordinary. *He just likes to worry.* Slapping the reins, he set his horse walking down the hill, only to pull up short when one of the Guards hailed him.

''Ho, Quaestor Rhenford! You'll want to wait there, Quaestor!''

''Eh? Why?'' Of all the members of the Areopagus, the three Guards were the only ones he knew; he had met them through his acquaintance with Coeccias. They had taken him under their wing to a certain extent, including him in their conversation and filling him in on small details of court procedure. *Which is good,* he thought ruefully, *since no one else seems to want to.*

''Y'are to go into the town together,'' the Guard explained, ''you and the Areopage and Quaestor Provyn. It's the way of it.''

Then, from down the eastern side of the rise, he heard a call. ''Quaestor Rhenford! Attend us there, if you will!'' He recognized Widow Saffian's voice.

The Guard nodded. "It's what's proper."

Shrugging, Liam resigned himself to wait while the rest of the column reached the top of the hill. It seemed an age to him—from the beginning the court's pace had struck him as absurdly slow—but soon enough the others caught up, Quaestor Provyn and the Areopage in the lead.

"Y'are eager to start, I see," she said with a curt nod. She wore black, a simple but expensive riding coat and a voluminous dress that looked normal when she was standing but which had been cleverly divided to allow her to ride like a man. She was bony and thin, with a strong beak of a nose and wide gray eyes. "I looked for no less, Quaestor, but for this, we must enter Warinsford together."

"So they were just telling me, Areopage." He gestured at the Guards, who had meanwhile assumed a more professional air, unlimbering their long spears and setting them upright in their stirrups. Attached to the shaft of one was a rolled-up pennon.

"It is mere ceremony," she said, "but it's as well to stand on it. Guards to the fore, then, and Quaestor Rhenford, if you'll to my left?" Though couched as a suggestion, it was unquestionably an order. There was an obvious strength in her voice and her bearing that impressed Liam, all the more so when he considered her recent loss. *Recent!* he marvelled. *It was only four days ago!* In those four days she had managed to arrange both her husband's funeral and all the details of the court— no mean feat, in his estimation.

They started down the hill as the sun slipped beneath the horizon. The banner was unfurled, but in the dusk Liam could not make out what device it bore; he took up his position to Widow Saffian's left, reaching out one hand to steady his familiar. The Areopage had already reimmersed herself in her ongoing conversation with Quaestor Provyn, and the two ignored him. They had spent the days of travel deep in a discussion of the crimes the court was to try, a discussion Liam had tried to follow until he finally realized that they dwelt almost entirely on obscure points of duchy law, referring frequently to past crimes of which he had never heard. Moreover, they did not seem to expect him to pay attention; at one point Widow Saffian had implied—politely but unambiguously—that the discussion was for her benefit as judge, not his as investigator, and that he should not feel compelled to pay attention.

All of which would be fine, Liam decided, *if they would just take a little time to have a discussion that* was *for my benefit.* From working with Aedile Coeccias he had a vague idea of what was expected of a quaestor, but he was completely in the dark as to the specifics; he did not even know what crimes he would be investigating. There had been no time in Southwark to look at the detailed reports sent in by the local authorities, and once they were on the road Quaestor Provyn had made it clear that digging them out of the pack train would be far too much of an inconvenience. He had finally rebuffed Liam's requests with the sneering implication that if he was skilled enough to be chosen quaestor on such short notice, the reports would probably be of little use to him—his natural genius would suffice. Put off by the man's rudeness, Liam had let the matter drop.

So he approached Warinsford with mixed feelings—eagerness to get started, to see the reports and learn the procedural details he needed to know; and apprehension that his days since leaving Southwark had been misspent, that he was woefully ill-prepared.

Time to find out, he thought, as the gates of the town came into view.

By the time the court reached the town's southern gate, the sun had gone down. Flaring torches illuminated the gate, a broad tunnel between two squat towers. The Southwark Guards paused only to exchange a word with the squad of Warinsford Guards on duty, and then the Areopagus swept through, hooves clanging on cobbles now, echoes rebounding in the tunnel of the gate.

They clattered into the streets of the town proper, and

after a few minutes winding through the dark, narrow streets, arrived at their inn. The Guards found their way without hesitation, though Liam would have been hard-pressed to say exactly what route they had taken from the gates. A sign showing three red foxes announced the inn as the Duke's Arms, a five-story stone building with two enormous bay windows looking in on a lively common room. Before they could dismount, the door of the inn burst open and a crowd of servants came boiling out, followed by a blond giant wearing a gray tabard emblazoned with three red foxes.

"Hail the Areopagus!" he bellowed, wading through the milling servants as if they were children to reach Widow Saffian's stirrup. He helped her down, then stood back and bowed deeply. "Milady Areopage, y'are well come to Warinsford—and may I be the first to offer my condolences. We feel the lack of your husband deeply. Villains across the duchy rejoiced when they heard the news."

One of the inn servants appeared at Liam's stirrup, but he brushed the man away and dismounted on his own, keeping hold of the reins in spite of the man's attempts to take them.

"Y'are kind, Aedile Cuspinian," Widow Saffian said in a formal tone, handing her reins over to a hovering servant. "I myself sorely miss him—but he would have it that we carry on his work. Quaestor Provyn is known to you, I believe." The men exchanged bows, and she turned to look for Liam, who stepped forward, still holding his reins. "This is Quaestor Rhenford, who has joined us for our circuit."

"Quaestor Rhenford," Cuspinian said, appraising him with a swift glance that took in the plainness of his travelling coat, as well as its stains. Then he made a slight bow, as if he had judged Liam and found him wanting. He had a manner of easy, open power about him, not just in his broad shoulders and strong hands, but in his hooded eyes and the way his lips seemed perpetually on the verge of twisting into a smirk.

With a wry smile, Liam returned a deeper bow. "Aedile Cuspinian." Coeccias had mentioned some interesting things about his counterpart in Warinsford, few of
which were to his credit.

The two men locked glances for a moment, and then
the Aedile turned to Widow Saffian and offered her his
arm. "We'll in—you'll want to wash the road away, and
then we'll dine. Come along, gentlemen." He strode off,
the Areopage hurrying her stride to keep up. Quaestor
Provyn scurried after, abandoning his horse to the nearest
servant.

Liam lingered, politely but firmly fending off the inn
servant, waiting for his boy to appear from the back of
the column. Both Widow Saffian and Provyn were accompanied by bodyservants, but Liam, not realizing that
he could bring a servant—and not having one to begin
with—had been adopted on the first night by the son of
one of the court's ostlers. The boy, who mumbled un-
intelligibly and toed the ground when asked his name,
had curried Liam's horse and carried his bags faithfully
and with a sort of reverential awe that made him smile.

"Master, if it please you," the inn servant began, just
as the boy arrived and snatched the reins from Liam's
hands.

"I've got him now, Quaestor; you can go in. I've got
him. Easy, Diamond," the boy said, stroking the horse's
nose. "I've got him, and I'll bring your bags up as soon
as ever he's put away."

Liam thanked him, keeping him only long enough to
retrieve Fanuilh and his sabretache. Slinging the bag over
one shoulder and letting the dragon perch on the other,
he made his way into the inn.

Chaos reigned inside, baggage-carrying servants rushing here and there, shouting contradictory orders as they
went, and it took Liam a few minutes to corner a woman
who thought she knew where he was supposed to be staying. With many a fearful glance at Fanuilh, she led him
through the crowded halls of the inn, up three long flights
of steps and then down two shorter ones, and was only

able to deposit him at the right chamber because the door was open, and Liam saw Provyn through it.

The other quaestor sat on a trunk in just his shirt and hose, being shaved by his valet, and barely nodded his head in response to Liam's greeting. Liam was used to this by now, however, and simply acted as if he were alone in the room. It was much larger than the ones they had shared on the road from Southwark, and much cleaner: the wood floor shone with a recent polishing and the bed did not smell musty. Three basins of hot water waited on a stand by the fireplace, in which a fire had just been laid.

He puttered for a while, retrieving a straight razor from his sabretache and then arranging the bag in a corner by the shuttered window. Fanuilh curled up on it, nose to tail, making itself as unobtrusive as possible; from the first Provyn had objected to sleeping in the same room as the dragon, but Liam had stood firm, pointing out that it made no noise, did not smell, and was an excellent guard. The other man gave in reluctantly, but Liam had felt it politic for his familiar to keep a low profile. Once the dragon was settled, he stropped his already-sharp razor and waited for the boy to bring his bags.

"That'll do," Provyn told his valet, his shave finished. "Lay out my clothes for dinner—the blue slashed velvet, I think—and have those from today cleaned. Cleaned well, mind you, not just waved near a bucket of hot water and then hung by the fire. That innkeep's wife lied like a very rogue, and knew not her station." This, Liam had learned, was part of his roommate's evening ritual: ordering his clothes cleaned and then complaining about them.

"In course, master," the valet replied from the depths of Provyn's trunk. Somehow his baggage always arrived in the room before Liam's. "Though fair is fair, master, and that sort of stain is passing hard to out."

"I know another rogue who knows not his station," Provyn said coldly, and turned away from his man's mumbled apology to face Liam. He was a fat man, not tremendously so but flabby, with drooping jowls and a belly that sagged over his belt. His black hair had receded across the top of his head, but it hung to his shoulders in the back and the sides, so that he looked like a lady wearing her veil in reverse. Rubbing idly at his pink, fleshy cheek, he considered Liam for a long moment, then gave a sigh. "I wonder, Quaestor Rhenford, whether y'have another coat. A cleaner coat."

Liam was so startled at being addressed that he dropped his razor; it was one of the longest sentences Provyn had ever spoken to him. "Oh yes," he said, quickly retrieving the razor. He looked down at his worn and travel-stained coat. "I brought some nicer clothes for when the court actually holds sessions."

"May I counsel you to wear your . . . nicer . . . clothes this evening? We're to dine with Aedile Cuspinian and his people at eight bells, and while I'm sure the reputation of the Areopagus can be of little moment to you, who are so newly created a member of it, it is a matter of pride for those of us who have served some time with it."

Liam bit back a sarcastic reply and forced a smile. "Of course, Quaestor Provyn. I'll wear my best—I don't think you'll be disappointed."

"My thoughts were more of whether Areopage Saffian would be disappointed," the other man said, drawing himself up into an indignant pose.

"Oh, I think she'll be pleased too," he replied, privately doubting if she would notice if he came to dinner in a sack. *Probably comment on the magical and criminal applications of sacks.* "Speaking of the Areopage, she said that as soon as we reached Warinsford you would be able to dig through your papers and find those reports for me. If I could have even a moment's glance at them, it would help me do my share in upholding the reputation of the Areopagus."

Provyn's eyes narrowed suspiciously. "She warranted that?"

Liam nodded, trying to make his smile as innocent as

possible. Widow Saffian had vaguely promised that the reports would be forthcoming in Warinsford, though she had said nothing about "as soon as." "Since we're dining at eight, that would give me time for a quick glance at them, and then I won't come across as such an idiot at dinner."

After a moment spent trying to penetrate Liam's ingenuous expression, the quaestor snorted and gestured irritably at his valet. "Find Iorvram, and have him give you the small Warinsford chest. I'll dress myself," he added, as if it were a great sacrifice. The valet darted off.

"I really do appreciate it," Liam assured him, resuming his stropping with vigor to keep from laughing at Provyn's attempts to get into the clothes his servant had laid out. He managed to pull on his shiny satin breeches well enough, but got caught up in the lining of his jacket, which was of a pale blue that showed up well through the slashes in the dark blue outer layer. After watching the fat quaestor struggle to get his arms through the sleeves for over a minute, Liam took pity and held the jacket for him.

Grunting reluctant thanks, Provyn shrugged himself into the jacket and began buttoning it up the front. He sucked in his belly before doing up each button, and by the time he was done he looked much thinner and his face was a frightening mulberry color. Between the slashing and the silver braid that crawled around the hems and buttonholes, the jacket was a monstrosity, but even its garishness had not prepared Liam for the neck ruff the quaestor now pulled from his trunk and, wordlessly, handed to him.

"I haven't seen one of these for quite a while," Liam said, passing it around the other man's neck and searching for the fastener. *And the last time was on a pimp in Torquay.*

"They're no rarity—at least among the fashionable," Provyn sniffed. The ruff formed a plate beneath his head three inches wide.

Liam made a noncommittal noise and finally found the

hook that held the stiff cloth together. "All done." He stepped away just as his boy arrived at the door, weighed down by a set of saddlebags, a writing case, a sailor's dunnage bag and two swords. Liam relieved him of his burden and sent him away with a copper coin as a reward. For his generosity he received a bright grin from the boy and a snort from Provyn.

"Not all rogues are servants," the quaestor opined when the boy had gone, "but all servants are rogues."

"That's why I don't have any," Liam said brightly, searching through his dunnage bag for a good suit of clothes. "Such trouble all the time—stealing the silver, being insolent, always underfoot. They're a curse, plain and simple." He found his green tunic and breeches and laid them out on the bed. They were a little wrinkled, but there was nothing he could do about that.

"Aye," Provyn said suspiciously, not sure if he was being mocked; the arrival of his valet with a heavy wooden chest prevented him from deciding. "On the bed," he ordered, and when the chest had been deposited, the mattress sinking several inches under its weight, he used a key from a pouch on his waist to open it. After a few moments of going through the contents, he pulled out two thin bundles of paper tied with red string, placed them on the bed, and carefully locked the chest. The valet took up the chest again at his gesture and left.

"These are the reports," Provyn explained, tapping them with his index finger. "I pray you to keep them in order, and not to lose any of the pages."

Liam nodded solemnly and picked up the bundles as if they were holy relics. He thought about asking if he should wear gloves while handling them, but decided that would be pushing the quaestor too far. Hesitantly, he asked, "Is this all?" Together the bundles contained no more than thirty pages.

"Aye," the other man said, his mouth twisting in a grimace Liam did not understand. "There're but two capital cases here. Now, we dine at eight, look you, and it would be a disservice to Aedile Cuspinian to be late.

You'll not be too long?'' When he had Liam's promise to be on time, he adjusted his neck ruff and left the room.

''What do you know, familiar mine,'' Liam said, after he had shut the door. ''I've finally got something to sink my teeth into. Now, shall I dress or shall I read?'' He brandished the reports at the dragon.

I do not understand why they could not give them to you earlier.

''Neither do I,'' Liam admitted. He played with the red string for a few seconds, wondering what Provyn meant by capital cases, and why mentioning them had seemed to pain him. ''Well, at least I'll know what I'm looking into,'' he said. ''Now—dress or read?''

Dress, the dragon advised. *You do not want to be late for dinner.*

''Right,'' Liam said absently, running his thumbnail along a length of red string. ''I'll need to shave, too. These can wait.''

He pulled a chair close to the fire, untied the string on the first bundle, and started reading.

CHAPTER 2

SOMEWHERE IN THE town, a bell gave its eighth peal as Liam dashed into the common room of the Duke's Arms, just in time to join the court's migration to the private dining room where they would eat. He had read too long, and only a warning from Fanuilh had allowed him enough time to shave and dress.

Hair and face still wet, he deliberately fell to the back of the procession, as far from Widow Saffian and Cuspinian as possible, and fell in beside a young man who gave him a friendly smile and introduced himself as Vaucan Alasco, Cuspinian's quaestor. "Y'are Quaestor Rhenford?"

"I am," Liam admitted, and shook the proferred hand. Alasco was no more than twenty, ten years Liam's junior, with jet black hair and milk-white skin; a perfect blood-red circle bloomed on each cheek.

"We're to be harnessed as a team, then," the young man said. "I'm glad of it, for that Areopage Saffian's told us y'are passing skilled at this sort of thing."

Liam fought down a grimace. *I wish people would stop spreading that idea,* he thought, and was seeking an appropriate response when they came to the dining room. What he saw inside momentarily—and literally—dazzled him: scores of candles burned in the chandelier and on the table and the sideboard, their light reflecting off a display of crystal and silver that would have pleased an emperor. He froze for a moment, amazed at the many-faceted goblets, the profusion of silver plate, and only snapped out of it when he heard Cuspinian guffaw from the head of the table.

"Why, I'd wager our newest quaestor's never seen a tablecloth ere now!" The Aedile's tone was light, and a ripple of polite laughter spread among those already seated, but he fixed Liam with a challenging look that no one else caught. He held his bulky frame with an unexpected grace, and behind his loud voice and louder laugh lurked a sort of predatory quiet, as if he were listening to how everyone heard him.

"Well," Liam said, remembering something Coeccias had told him about Cuspinian's spending habits, "if I'd known the Duke fed all his officers so extravagantly, I'd have joined up long ago." His tone was as light as the other man's, and was rewarded with much the same polite laughter; only the Aedile frowned, picking up a silver bell by his place and ringing it. A servant entered through a side door, and Cuspinian began giving him instructions.

That was foolish, Liam thought, taking the seat to Widow Saffian's right. *You're not going to make friends that way.* The Areopage sat at the foot of the table, opposite Cuspinian; Liam found himself across from an elderly woman. Alasco sat beside him, facing Provyn.

"I fear me you've not met Mother Haella," Widow Saffian said, touching his arm and indicating the old woman, who was swathed from foot to throat in a shapeless gray dress that reminded him of a shroud. "Mother Haella, this is Quaestor Liam Rhenford, who's joined us for our circuit this year. Mother Haella is Warinsford's ghost witch."

"Quaestor Rhenford," the old woman acknowledged, her voice barely more than a whisper. She hunched in her chair and avoided his eyes as she spoke, her own eyes darting from her lap to her plate to the back of the chair beside her, where Provyn sat.

Liam half-rose and bowed, which startled her so much that she let out a little squeak. "I believe I know your counterpart in Southwark, Mother Japh." *And she certainly wouldn't squeak if someone bowed to her.* He had met her while working with Coeccias, and liked them both for many of the same reasons: Southwark's Aedile

and ghost witch were forthright, honest, and competent—
and he was beginning to wonder if Warinsford was as
well served. *If Cuspinian and this timid creature are any
indication, I doubt it.*

Mother Haella muttered something too quietly for anyone to hear, and before Liam could ask her to repeat it,
a servant appeared at his elbow to pour him a glass of
wine and the Aedile took control of the table.

"I'll make a toast," he said, causing the servant to
leave Liam's glass half-full and hurry around to splash
wine in the crystal goblets he had not yet reached.
"Though it should wait for the end of the meal, I'll toast
to Areopages past and present."

They all raised their glasses solemnly toward Widow
Saffian, who bowed her head in acknowledgement of the
tribute, and from that moment Cuspinian directed the
conversation. At first he appeared merely the affable host,
asking the usual questions about their journey, clucking
over their difficulties—Provyn gave a brief oration on the
shocking inability of country inns to wash clothes properly—but it quickly became clear that there were subjects
he did not want pursued.

Three more servants appeared shortly after the toast,
and while they distributed bowls of steaming fish soup
to each plate, Liam took advantage of the silence to ask,
"I wonder, Aedile Cuspinian, if you can tell me a little
more about this wizard?"

"Wizard?" Cuspinian peered quizzically at him from
around the arm of the servant who was pouring him more
wine. "What wizard is this?"

"The one who was murdered." It had been by far the
more interesting of the two reports: a wizard found dead
in his bedchamber without a mark on him—except for a
grin so wide and so hideous that the man who discovered
the corpse had fainted at the sight.

"You speak of a case, Quaestor Rhenford!"

Liam hesitated, trying to read the other diners' faces
to see how he had transgressed. "Ah, yes, I was. The
wizard from the inn."

"We'll not have cases and sessions this night, Quaestor!" the Aedile said, as if he were chiding a too-serious child. "Tomorrow is time enough for that. More, whyever would you hear of the wizard? It's a capital case, and meat for Quaestor Provyn here."

Capital cases again. What in the name of the Dark are capital cases? He did not want to ask, sure it would expose him to ridicule. Instead, he said, "Quaestor Provyn gave me the reports, so I assumed—"

"The capital cases are his," Provyn said brusquely, snatching a roll from a silver-worked breadbasket and drowning it in his soup.

Cuspinian glanced rapidly back and forth between the two men, then demanded, "Is this so?"

Widow Saffian looked up from her soup, and from her mild expression, Liam guessed that she was not aware of the undercurrent of emotions at other parts of the table. "It is," she answered. "Quaestor Rhenford'll have the capital, and Quaestor Provyn the mundane cases. I apologize—perhaps I did not tell you. Does it change your plans?"

"No," the Aedile said after a moment's glance at Liam. "No, not in the least. Only, I felt sure that . . . it does not signify. Vaucan will go with Quaestor Rhenford." He leaned back in his chair so that a servant could remove his soup bowl, and then leaned forward when the bowl was gone, all trace of uncertainty vanished. "I would know more of Southwark, and what news there is. Y'have had an interesting winter, I hear tell, with this new goddess, this Bellona, walking the streets. It's long and long since a goddess appeared in Taralon."

He directed his request to the Areopage, who deflected it to Liam. "Quaestor Rhenford should know—his name was often on the Duke's lips, for that according to Aedile Coeccias's communications he was in the thick of the thing."

Aedile Coeccias should keep his mouth shut, Liam thought. He had seen more of Bellona than most—far more than he cared to talk about. "I'm sure I can't add much to what you've probably already heard about Bellona," he said. "She appeared to sort out a rivalry among her priests, and to establish her worship more firmly. I can tell you that the temple is quite settled now, and seems to be thriving. I have some business dealings with them."

"Business dealings?" Cuspinian asked.

"When not an officer of the Duke, Quaestor Rhenford is in trade," Provyn explained, laying down his spoon disdainfully. "Y'have funds from Bellona's temple, have you not?"

"We—my partner and I—have an arrangement with them, yes."

"A merchant?" Cuspinian demanded. Servants flocked around the table, removing soup bowls and laying a platter of cutlets before the Aedile.

"What routes do you run?" Alasco asked, genuinely interested.

"New ones, actually, sailing south in the Cauliff."

The young man cocked his head, impressed. "South in the Cauliff? You must crew Freeporters then—no Taralonian'll sail those waters."

"And rightly so," Cuspinian told him, scowling with displeasure. "That way are only devils and endless wastes. But come, trade is no fit subject for dinner, and I'll not have it. It may intrigue your father, Vaucan, but it's of no interest at this table."

Alasco blushed and hung his head; Liam, knowing that the rebuke had been aimed at him as well, merely shrugged. They passed their plates around to the Aedile, who put several cutlets on each and ladled enormous amounts of sauce onto them, all the while extolling the virtues of the Duke's Arms's cook.

The food was good, Liam had to admit, just shy of too rich, all the sauces and gravies—on the cutlets they began with, the poached fish that followed, and the roast goose with which they finished—heavily laced with wine. He counted at least a dozen different serving men and women bringing in and taking away dishes, refilling wine glasses, and fetching extra bottles, not including the innkeeper himself, who made an appearance with the roast goose, beaming and rubbing his hands and receiving Cuspinian's compliments with transparently false humility.

The Aedile kept up a running commentary on the dishes and the wines, lecturing them on the qualities of reds from Riale in Alyecir as opposed to those from the Freeports—subjects that made for the pretence of conversation but allowed him to control it. Provyn smiled, bobbed his head and said "Truly?" or "Is't so?" and Widow Saffian nodded and said, "Very much" each time she was asked how she liked a dish. The others were silent, Mother Haella absorbed in the contents of her plate, and Alasco in the contents of his glass which, by Liam's count, was refilled thirteen times.

For his part, Liam enjoyed the food but could not help thinking that the evening was a waste of time. He knew so very little about what was expected of him, and had hoped that when they arrived in Warinsford he might have a chance to clear up his many questions. *They know what they're doing,* he thought. *It's all very well for them to listen to this ass go on about casks of Oporto.* Mention of the wine—a particularly rare and expensive vintage from the Freeport colony of the same name—reminded him again of Coeccias's description of Cuspinian, and for the remainder of the meal he tried to calculate just how much it was costing the duchy.

By the time the Oporto had been brought out, to go with the cheese and honeyed cakes that were dessert, he was up to at least a hundred crowns. *And that's just the food and the wine,* he realized, savoring a sip of the rare wine. He had carefully limited the number of times his glass was filled and felt remarkably clearheaded, though the room had grown uncomfortably close. *Then there's the extra servers laid on, the rooms, feed for the horses— not to mention room and board for the clerks and servants.* It added up to hundreds and hundreds of crowns chargeable to the Duke's treasury, and of that, Coeccias had said, a significant portion would find its way to Cuspinian's pocket.

But if the Duke doesn't put a limit on spending . . . , Liam thought, and let the idea trail off, taking another sip of wine.

Servants came and cleared away the cheese and the cakes, their rapid passage creating a welcome breeze. Sweat streamed down Provyn's face, sprinkling his ruff, and Mother Haella plucked furtively at her gray shroud, loosening its tight grip on her neck; even Widow Saffian displayed an awareness of the room's heat, shifting uneasily in her seat and glancing hopefully at Cuspinian, who was still holding forth on Oporto, gazing through the side of his glass at the wine's ruby depths. After a few minutes the restlessness of his guests penetrated, and he straightened in his chair.

"I find the room tolerably stifling—it needs must be the many candles. I'll offer another cup, and then perhaps we should all retire."

He rose and they rose with him, hiding their relief in pushing back chairs and lifting glasses.

"Once more, I give you Areopages past and present."

They drank, Widow Saffian thanked him on behalf of the Areopagus for the meal, and then they all started filing out of the little dining room. Liam held back for a moment, waiting for Provyn to round the table.

"I think I'm going to take a walk," he told the sweating quaestor. "I won't be very long."

"Is your beast in the room?"

"Yes."

"I'd not feel safe alone with it. You'd best take it with you."

"Safe?" Liam asked, incredulous; then he stopped and forced himself to adopt a more polite tone. "I promise you, Fanuilh's quite harmless—but if you'll just open the door, he'll leave on his own."

Provyn sniffed as if this was just barely acceptable, then swept through the door. Liam let him go, waiting until he was out of sight before expelling a pent-up breath and shaking his head. *Fanuilh,* he projected, *when Quaestor Provyn arrives, come downstairs and meet me outside.* An image occurred to him of the little dragon wandering into the common room, and of the chaos that would likely ensue. *Try not to be seen, if you can.*

A moment passed, and then the dragon's thought appeared in his head. *Yes, master.*

From behind the service door he heard the innkeeper's voice, a shrill hiss instructing a servant: "And mind you save those candles—they're a copper the one, and plenty of wax left in them!"

Liam made a quick estimate of the number of candles before he left, adding them to his mental tally of the meal's expense.

The cool night air drove the lingering fumes of wine from Liam's head and the heat-induced torpor from his body. He stood on the front steps, breathing deeply and rubbing at his taut belly. *I should have paid less attention to how much I was drinking and more to how much I was eating.* He walked out into the street and looked up to the stars, just barely visible beyond the rooftops.

Master, can you open the door? Warinsford was not going to be one of his favorite places, he decided, walking back to let his familiar out. *If Quaestor Provyn had opened the window I could have flown down,* the dragon told him, claws clicking on the cobbles as it walked into the street.

You know he doesn't like to open the windows. On their first night in a room together, Provyn had made it clear that he considered the night air too dangerous to breathe. *Noxious humors and miasmas and all that.*

In this city he may be right, Fanuilh thought, quartering the street, nose to the ground. Something in a pitch-black alley across the way caught its attention and its body went rigid; then it sprang silently into the darkness. A moment later Liam heard the sound of a scuffle.

Whatever you're hunting, keep it in the alley, he projected.

It is only a cat.

Keep it in the alley! And don't come out until you've finished eating!

The noise of the scuffle crescendoed into a cat's yowl, and then there was silence. *Yes, master.*

Thoroughly disgusted, Liam turned back to the Duke's Arms just as the front door opened to disgorge Cuspinian and Alasco. The two men froze on seeing him, and to his surprise a hesitant smile appeared on the Aedile's face.

"Quaestor Rhenford," he said, coming forward. "Y'are taking the night air?" Alasco came up beside him, unsteady on his feet.

Liam was taken aback by Cuspinian's friendly tone. "Yes," he said, somewhat suspiciously. "A walk after a good dinner helps the digestion."

"A short walk," the Aedile suggested. "The streets are dark. . . ." He let the sentence trail off, and they stood facing one another in an uncomfortable silence. After a few moments, Cuspinian cleared his throat and said, "Come, I fear me we've had an inauspicious beginning. It is my sad fate never to show well on first acquaintance. Let us start afresh, Quaestor Rhenford, and be good friends." In the dim light from the inn's windows, Liam could see that the other man had held out his hand. He hesitated for only a moment, then took it. The Aedile grinned, teeth gleaming in the dark of the street. "Good! We've a clean slate then, and can go from there."

Whatever the reason for this change of heart, Liam decided to exploit it. "A clean slate, I'm afraid, is a perfect description for me," he said ruefully. "Or a blank slate. To be honest, Aedile Cuspinian, I have to admit that I'm a little confused by my position here."

"How so? In Warinsford? Y'are an officer of the Duke, a quaestor, of a level with Provyn and Alasco here." He spared a glance at the young man, who was wobbling on his feet and squinting intensely to follow their conversation. "For now, a level above, perhaps. What you ask will be answered, and what you need done will be done, barring only the approval of myself or Milia—or the Duke himself.''

I had no idea, Liam said to himself. "That's good to know, but my confusion goes a little deeper. You see, I was recruited only a few days ago, and neither the Areopage nor Quaestor Provyn has had much of a chance to explain things to me. I know very little about the Areopagus, and I wonder if you can clear up some things for me."

"In course, in course," the Aedile said expansively. "What would you know?"

"Well, to start, what's the difference between a capital case and a mundane case?"

Cuspinian goggled at him. "These things are basic, man. Were you not quaestor to Coeccias? Milia would have us believe you a tried and tested investigator!"

Spreading his hands, Liam shrugged. "I've solved some mysteries for Coeccias, but in a very . . . informal . . . way. I looked into things on my own, and he handled all the official aspects—arrests, trials, that sort of thing." In fact, only one of his investigations had resulted in a trial, and he had been bedridden during it; the others had been resolved in ways as informal as his investigative methods. "So I'm at sea when it comes to how things are done when they're done properly. I'm not sure Areopage Saffian understood that when she asked me to join the court, and she's been so busy that I haven't been able ask her any questions." And she had made no effort to explain, either; sunk in her discussions with Provyn, she must have assumed he knew what he was supposed to do just as Cuspinian had.

The Aedile frowned. "But y'have some experience? Milia reported you a very bloodhound, on Coeccias's recommendation."

"He must have a good reason to call me that, don't you think?" *I don't know what the reason might be, but . . .* He did not want the other man to think him some kind of neophyte, but neither did he want to brag—particularly since he did not think he had much to brag about. "I mean, I have done this sort of thing before. I've solved mysteries. I just don't know how it's done officially."

"Or how to tell a capital case from a mundane." Cuspinian considered him for a long moment, still frowning; then nodded decisively. "Very well, we'll take you at your own estimation. Come inside—we'll have a cup and educate you."

Liam breathed a sigh of relief. "Thank you."

There was no mistaking the skeptical expression on the Aedile's face as he re-entered the inn, but Liam did not care. *Better to look a fool now than in the middle of a court session.* Alasco followed Cuspinian, and Liam followed him, putting a hand on the young man's shoulder when he wobbled.

Closing time had come while they were outside; drudges were busy sweeping up the sawdust and spilled drink from the common room floor. They knew Cuspinian, however, and did not object when he led the two quaestors to a table and called for a jug of water. In the brighter light Alasco looked greenish, and when the water was brought, the Aedile forced him to drink several glasses of it. When the young man had sobered to the point where he no longer looked like he was on the verge of throwing up, Cuspinian poured himself a glass and turned to Liam.

"Now, sir—what would you know?"

"Everything," Liam said, with a self-deprecating laugh. "But since we have to start somewhere, let's start with the wizard I was asking about earlier, the one who was killed in the inn. I'm not quite sure why he's an Areopagus case at all. Granted, he was a wizard, but that doesn't necessarily mean his death involved magic."

Alasco focussed blearily on Liam and slurred, "Didn't see the smile." Cuspinian nodded.

"Aye, you didn't, or you wouldn't ask. There's nothing shy of magic'd make a man grin so. But look you," he continued, "even if we didn't have that, just that he was a wizard puts it in the Areopagus's bailiwick. First, for that it's hard to kill a wizard other than with magic, and second, one with the court would see more in it than one's not. What seems a plain fustian murder to me might show itself a cloth-of-gold sorcerous death to you. And, in course, the punishments differ.''

''Punishments?''

''For mere murder, it's hanging. For murder with magic, that and burning and quartering.''

Liam grimaced, suitably impressed. ''So that means I not only have to determine who did it, but how they did it?''

The Aedile rapped his knuckles on the table. ''You hit the mark, Quaestor. Your work is much more than the who of a thing. It's also the why, the how and the how much. This wizard, this Passendus, is not a prime example. Y'have read the report on Aldyne Handuit?''

He had. A prominent Warinsford merchant, Handuit had been torn apart by a demon summoned by his brother and sister-in-law. While interesting in a gruesome way, Liam did not think it much of a mystery. ''Yes, but you know who did it already. Why should I look into it?''

''This is a case of the how, and how much,'' Cuspinian answered, jabbing his index finger skyward. ''If the brother and's wife raised the demon to take Handuit off, the punishment is generally far stronger than that for murder with magic. The details escape me—Milia will look to the specifics—but the least of the additions that I can recall is that their tongues be cut out. The Dukes have long frowned on demonology. Look you, though: they claim they were only skrying, and that the demon slipped its bonds against their will. For the accidental death, they might only take a hundred lashes apiece.''

Holding back a comment about split hairs—a hundred lashes would kill any but the strongest man—Liam simply nodded. ''So I have to find out whether they meant to kill him.''

''Ever the how, and the how much. All this the Areopage must know ere she can render her judgement. When y'have them all conned, you present it to her, and she makes use of it to prepare for the session. In the session, then, the accused are brought before her, the facts are read out, and they may plead their case—but's rare that they've aught to add, not if the quaestor's done his work. Then the Areopage renders judgement, ordering such punishment as she sees fit.''

"As she sees fit? You mean she makes it up herself?''

"In course. How else?''

"Well, don't the laws include punishments?''

Cuspinian cocked his head, puzzled. "However could they? There are more crimes than any set of laws may compass, more transgressions than the lawmakers dream of—no code can scope them all. Here's more: were the Areopage in all ways bound by rigid rules, she could not fit the punishment to the crime. See you, one man murders while another merely protects his own life, but the two deaths may look the same. She's guided, to be sure, by the Duke's intent in the law, by certain broad rules, and by past cases, but she must be free to weigh each separately. It's the how and the how much again.''

The how and how much, Liam thought, frowning. *How much hanging, how much burning.* "Well,'' he said at last, "it doesn't sound much more complicated than the work I've done for Aedile Coeccias in Southwark. It was just the uncertainty that bothered me.''

"Milia is much afflicted these past days,'' the other man said, shrugging. "Allowances must be made.''

Liam nodded absently, trying to think if there was anything else he wanted to ask. Nothing occurred to him, though he knew that as soon as they parted a thousand questions would spring to mind. He straightened in his chair and returned his attention to the Aedile. "Certainly, certainly. It's amazing that she decided to hold the court at all, with Master Saffian's death so recent.''

Alasco hiccoughed, then brought his hand to his mouth too late to hide it. Cuspinian scowled at the drunken boy, then turned a stern look on Liam. "The court was their passion, Quaestor Rhenford. I'd wager she needs a passion just now. And it'd ill serve her to have aught go wrong with it—so if y'have doubts, or questions, you'll ask me or Provyn, see you? These sessions'll serve as Master Saffian's monument, if you take me."

"I'll do my best," Liam said. "And I'll ask about anything I'm unsure of."

Cuspinian flashed a warm smile. "Then I'm satisfied," he said, standing and putting out his hand. "The Areopagus's reputation is secure."

Liam rose and they shook hands. "I hope so." He wondered if Cuspinian's reputation was in any way tied to the court's.

"I'll warrant it," the Aedile said, with a good-humored wink. "And now, I needs must see my quaestor to his bed."

Together they got Alasco to his feet and guided him to the door, where they bid each other good night. Liam watched them go, swallowed up by the darkness a few feet from the inn, the young drunk leaning heavily on Cuspinian.

Fanuilh, Liam projected. *You can come in now. I'm going to bed.* Distant bells began tolling twelve, and after the sixth peal, in perfect counterpoint, he heard the flap of his familiar's wings. The dragon appeared out of the darkness and dropped lightly to the ground in front of him.

They went back into the Duke's Arms together, crept quietly up the stairs and along the corridors until they found their room. The raspy sound of Provyn's snoring reached them through the door, and Liam breathed a silent prayer for patience. In his long years of travelling, of sharing beds with complete strangers—a common enough occurrence when inns were crowded, or popular— he had never had a worse roommate than the fat quaestor.

Opening and closing the door as quietly as possible, he slipped inside.

CHAPTER 3

A REDHEADED WOMAN flitted through the halls of Liam's house in Southwark, luxuriant falls of copper down her back, and in the dream he pursued her for what seemed an eternity until she turned to face him and spoke.

"Wake," she said, just once and very softly.

Liam opened his eyes, saw the room he was in, and closed them again, wishing he was elsewhere.

The bells have rung six, master, Fanuilh told him. *You wanted to be woken at six.*

The dragon was pitiless in the morning, so instead of arguing Liam hauled himself out of bed. He spared a glance for Provyn, who was snoring contentedly, and decided he could risk a single candle. By its light he found a linen cloth out of one of his bags and scrubbed himself with the tepid water left in the washbasins, then dressed quickly. His choice of clothes, he was sure, would not reflect poorly on the Areopagus: buff breeches, snow-white shirt, and a long maroon vest of brocade, all clean and respectable, if a little wrinkled from their journey. After a moment's debate he put on his travelling coat; worn and travel-stained it might be, but it was also comfortable and its pockets were enormous, properties he valued above the reputation of the court. From his saddlebags he took a quarto volume which slipped easily into his coat pocket, with room left over for the reports Provyn had given him.

Last, he gathered up his boots and squatted down by his baggage pile, considering the two swords he had brought with him. The first had simple leather wrappings

30

and a businesslike pommel; he put it aside and looked to the second, at the tarnished silver wire on the hilt and the age-encrusted gem set into the butt. He slipped the jewelled sword free of its sheath; the blade was a milky gray, with strange veins of silver running through it. It had belonged to Fanuilh's former master, a wizard of considerable power, and the dragon had told him it was enchanted against all manner of magical beasts, including demons.

For a long minute he stared at the blade, at its silver veins, and then put both swords away with a quick shake of his head—he would not need them in Warinsford. *With any luck, you won't need them at all.* A moment later he slipped out of the room.

Liam paused on the stairs to pull on his boots and then went down to the common room, hoping for a quiet breakfast and some time alone to question Fanuilh about things he had noticed in the reports.

A drudge stood in the center of the room, leaning on her broom and watching through the bay window as the first rays of the sun turned the street outside pink. The girl spun around when Liam coughed, blanched at the sight of Fanuilh, and fled toward the kitchen.

"You have this effect on women," he told the dragon, and settled in at one of the tables. He took the book and the reports from his pocket and started going through the details of Aldyne Handuit's death. *You can read along with me?* he asked.

Yes, master, if you unknot the silver cord. The dragon looked up at him from beside his chair, like a faithful dog.

"That damned cord. . . ." Liam muttered. Visible only in the ethereal plane, the cord was a symbol of their relationship as master and familiar; simple manipulations of the cord allowed them to exchange thoughts and share one another's senses. *Simple manipulations if you're a wizard,* he thought; he had no doubt that real wizards took to the ether like ducks to water and worked their

cords with the greatest of ease, but he was not a wizard—
he had only inherited one's familiar.

Sighing, he closed his eyes and concentrated on calm-
ing his mind. He always found slipping into the semi-
trance easier when he was tired or had just risen; in a
few seconds the luminescent blossoms behind his eyelids
disappeared, and he felt as if he were floating in a black
void. He gave a mental push to a formless thought, imagining it as a comet, trailing clouds of dust. In the ether,
whatever he envisioned strongly enough happened: the
thought began to glow, dripping glowing motes as it
arced away from him. Every time he did this he felt an
urge to crow, to exclaim aloud at the wonder of what he
was doing, but he stifled the urge and concentrated instead on the motes as they drifted down like diamond
dust. They formed a concave layer, coalescing like snow
on a tree limb, and the thing they rested on slowly took
shape, delimitated by the motes.

The cord took shape beneath a layer of comet dust, a
line of silver stretching into the limitless blackness of the
ether, the comet-thought speeding along above it, both
headed toward Fanuilh's ethereal presence. Liam imagined reaching forward, pulling himself along the cord,
and was rewarded by a sensation of movement, of impossible distances traversed in the blink of an eye.
Where's the knot? he wondered, and even as he thought
about it, the knot appeared, an intricate convolution in
the cord, a tangled sphere of looping silver.

Morning light seeped into the common room and
touched his face but he did not notice; nor did he notice
that he was frowning. In the void behind his eyes he was
considering the knot, trying to puzzle it out. He had made
it himself, imagined the constriction in the cord, but making was easier than unmaking, it seemed.

Learning how to enter the ethereal plane—something
wizards learned in a few days early on in their Guild
training—had taken him two months of practice, and he
had wandered in the void for a further two weeks before
he mastered the trick of making the silver cord appear.

The very first time he imagined the knot in the cord, however, it had appeared, looking just like the tangle of ship's rigging he had pictured in his mind. He took Fanuilh's word that it could no longer read his thoughts at will, and had not been back to the ethereal plane since.

Now he wanted to remove the knot, and it was proving as stubborn as a real one. He imagined different sections loosening and they did, loops of silver cord hanging away from the central knot one by one, but each time he let the loops slide back to tightness, unable to proceed. It was a sailor's nightmare of a knot, and after almost a dozen fruitless tries he grew frustrated. *I wish I'd never put the damned thing there in the first place.*

It disappeared, the cord suddenly as smooth as it had been the first time he saw it, a silver umbilicus stretching into the distance.

Liam laughed, jarring himself out of his trance and back into the common room. The sun was warm on his face.

Can you read along with me? he projected.

Yes, master.

I'm getting pretty good at this, aren't I?

Apprentice mages learn to do that in their second week, the dragon told him.

So? That means if I were to become an apprentice, I'd be two weeks ahead of everyone else.

You are too old to be an apprentice.

Liam shook his head, and then noticed that the servant who had fled at his approach was now hovering in the doorway of the kitchen, trying to attract his attention.

"If it please you, my lord," she stammered, "the master says you may go up to the dining room, for that the breakfast is laid out there."

"Breakfast?"

"For the Areopagus, m-m-m-my lord." She threw a glance at Fanuilh, summoned her courage, and added, "I'll show you the way, if it please you."

"No need, no need," Liam said, smiling to himself. The girl had obviously been ordered to guide him; she would never have offered on her own. "I can find it myself, thank you." He unceremoniously scooped up jacket, book, papers and familiar and headed out of the common room. The serving girl sketched a curtsy and fled back into the kitchen.

So we have our own breakfast, he thought, retracing his route of the night before. *Yet another meal to line Cuspinian's pockets.* There were fewer candles lit in the private room but the table settings were as opulent, and silver chafing dishes of food had been laid out on the sideboard. Liam set down his burdens, including Fanuilh, by the seat he had occupied at dinner, and went to examine the fare. Warmed by stubby candles of pure wax were an enormous ham, two mountains of fish—one fried and one smoked—and a bubbling lake of porridge; plates of cheese and baskets of bread flanked the chafing dishes. There was more food on the sideboard than the entire Areopagus, drivers, servants, clerks and all, could eat in a week. A little disgusted, Liam took a hot roll from a basket and returned to the table.

Fanuilh looked up at him from the floor. *Is everything cooked?*

I'm afraid so, he thought back, shredding his roll and popping pieces in his mouth as he did so. *I'd have made you up a plate otherwise. Now, shall we go through these reports? The knot is gone, isn't it?*

Yes. I can read along with you.

"Good," Liam said aloud, and began re-reading the report on Aldyne Handuit's death, searching for the sort of clues that would give him the how and the how much.

Just past midnight one Godsday morning, a trio of Warinsford Guards, attracted to Handuit's house on the riverfront by the sound of screams, arrived at his door just in time to see him thrown out his bedroom window. His body had been severely mutilated, and in the smashed window the Guards caught sight of a "prodigious great black cloud, in the shape of a horned beast, with eyes of fire and iron blades for fingers, with which the beast did grip the sill of the window."

Handuit's housemaid burst from the house at just that moment, calling for the Guards to enter and help her, which they did immediately, showing a courage Liam found commendable. By the time the men reached Handuit's bedchamber on the top floor of the house and broke down the door, the demon was gone, but signs of it were everywhere: deep scores in the wood of the windowsill where it had rested its claws, the wreckage of furniture, the smell of sulfur and other, less pleasant odors, and, finally, the piece of blue chalk and the dead cat which had been used to summon it.

The housemaid—"greatly discomfited" in the words of the report, which Liam guessed probably meant hysterical—insisted on a search for Handuit's brother and sister-in-law, Elsevier and Roviana Handuit, presuming that they, too, had been victims of the demon. Their bedchamber was empty, nor were they discovered in any of the upper rooms. When only the cellar was left to be inspected, the housemaid had grown so "discomfited" that the Guards decided it would be best to remove her from the premises, and when one man had been detailed to do that, the other two went down the steps.

"Which one got to remove her from the premises?" Liam wondered aloud, imagining the two remaining Guards staring fearfully down the stairs to the cellar.

It does not say.

"I know that," he said patiently. "It was a rhetorical—never mind."

Whoever the lucky man was, the other two eventually forced themselves down the stairs, and there they found Elsevier and Roviana busy erasing a pentagram drawn in blue chalk. Naturally, they were arrested—and that, Liam would have thought, was the end of the case.

The Handuits, however, claimed that they had summoned the demon solely in order to question it regarding the future, and that the monster had slipped past their protective circle; they vehemently denied any intention of harming their brother, though they stood to inherit his wealth. When questioned about the source of their demonological knowledge, they would only say that they had come across a piece of parchment describing the necessary ceremony in a batch of old papers bought from a bookseller, and that the demon had taken the parchment along with the corpse of the cat and the blue chalk. Without specifically stating why, the author of the report—Liam assumed it was Cuspinian himself; the same pedantry informed the writing as had characterized the Aedile's talk about wine—implied that this was doubtful.

The Handuits were guilty, but how guilty? Liam set aside the report and steepled his fingers, trying to imagine the scene and formulating questions. What information had they hoped to get from the demon? Why a demon at all? Why in the middle of the night? What could they possibly stand to gain from having Aldyne Handuit noisily torn to pieces?

Master? Fanuilh's thought was tentative, as if it recognized that he was thinking and might not wish to be disturbed.

Hold on, he projected back. The dragon would be able to answer many of his questions—but he needed to ask them properly. *All right, first of all: is there a way to tell why they summoned the demon?*

The return thought came immediately, as if Fanuilh had prepared it in advance: *Yes. The Lords of the Dark are legion, and fall into broad categories, or Spheres. There is a Sphere whose power is prophecy, foretelling, omens and so on, and a Sphere among whose powers are assassination. There are many other Spheres, but they are not pertinent. Lords from each Sphere will only answer one type of call, and perform only one type of service.*

"Only one type of service?" Liam interrupted aloud. "Then they're definitely lying. A demon summoned for fortune-telling couldn't be used for murder, right?"

Unfortunately, no. All Lords—it is the proper term; Lords are the only demons which may be summoned to the terrestrial plane—all Lords will commit murder, given the chance. By their very nature they desire nothing

*more than death, and if given the chance they will in-
dulge themselves.*

Frowning, Liam forced himself to shape his question
as a thought: *So this Lord they summoned could have
been a fortune-teller who slipped his leash?*

*Yes, but there is a way to tell. As I explained, each
Sphere of Lords responds to only one type of call, one
type of conjuration, and the prime difference between the
conjurations are the shape and position of the pentagram
drawn. The report says that the Handuits were caught in
the midst of erasing their pentagram. If enough remains,
we should be able to tell which type of Lord they conjured.*

And you know which circle goes with which?

The dragon gestured with its head toward the table.
They are described in the Dominia Daemonologia.

Liam picked up the quarto volume and examined its
spine and binding. On the night before he left Southwark,
Coeccias had mentioned that a number of the court's
cases involved demons, including one that had caught the
interest of the Duke himself; when Liam relayed the information to Fanuilh, the dragon told him that there was
a book on the subject in the library of its former master,
which Liam had inherited.

The *Dominia Daemonologia* was bound in heavy, red
cloth over thin, wooden boards, without a title, and when
he opened it to the first page he was confronted by a
solid block of tiny handwriting. He read the first paragraph with growing dismay.

> *Daemonology is taught first among the Mages'
> Quadrivium,* it began, *as its quintessence is disci-
> pline both physical and metaphysical. Conscription
> of a Lord Daemon, of whatever Order, Principality,
> Power or Sphere, is an exercise necessitating the
> nicest momentary control of material, attitudinal,
> symbolic and vocal components with the concomi-
> tant maintenance of the Mage's ultimate purpose.*

Liam read the paragraph twice more, then riffled
through the book. After five pages of solid text he came
to the first of several diagrams, each drawn in red ink;
all were circles, bounded by strings of hieroglyphs and
sigyls and bisected by arcs, tangents, chords and various
other geometric shapes.

Which are the ones we're interested in? he asked his
familiar.

*The diagrams are on the twenty-third and fifty-second
pages.* Liam counted through until he had located both
drawings, and spent a few minutes flipping back and
forth between them, noting the differences.

This should be easy enough, he projected. *We'll just
compare the book to the Handuits' drawing, and that will
be that.* Fanuilh made no comment, but a quick glance
showed that it was preening itself, head ducked in false
modesty. Liam smiled. *Have you read all of this?*

Master Tanaquil did. I remember. The late wizard had
always made the dragon read along with him, because its
memory was eidetic.

Good. Explain it to me.

The dragon cocked its head at Liam, and after a moment thought, *It is complicated, master.*

I know that, Liam projected patiently. *I can tell that
from the first paragraph alone. That's why I'm asking
you to explain it to me.* One of his familiar's more ex-
asperating faults was its occasional obtuseness.

As you wish, the dragon thought, settling back on its
haunches and refolding its wings. *Demonology, or Lord
Daemonology, is not actually magic, in the sense that it
is not restricted to mages. It is part of the Quadrivium,
the first four subjects studied by apprentice mages, because its disciplines pertain to many true magics. This
book is made by every apprentice mage as one of their
first spells—a cantrip much like the one I used to make
Master Tanaquil's will.*

"To fake Master Tanaquil's will," Liam corrected.
"What's a cantrip?"

Unfazed by Liam's reference to its forgery, the dragon

explained that a cantrip was simply a small spell not requiring much expertise. *I can cast a number of cantrips, but no higher order spells. The study of cantrips is also part of the Quadrivium.* Included among the cantrips apprentice wizards learned was a spell that duplicated pages, and it was one of the first they cast, in order to produce their own copy of the demonology text. *Master Tanaquil made his* Daemonologia *when he was an apprentice himself, but he did not think much of it. He used to say that the only reason he had ever looked at the text was to copy it, and that since then he had never opened it.* There was a gap in the dragon's thoughts, and then, *I understand the Guild chapter in Torquay hires its apprentices out to duplicate other books.*

Liam had attended a university in Torquay, and remembered the red-robed apprentices in Pamphlet Square, magically producing copies of fables and travelers' tales and monologues from popular plays. "Indeed they do," he said aloud, "though I never knew just why."

In theory it is good practice. Much as simple demonology is. An apprentice will conscript—summon—one of the less powerful Lords under the supervision of a more accomplished mage.

If you're not a Guild apprentice, how do you get one of these books? Can you buy one?

Absolutely not. The Guild is very strict about all of its texts. Its libraries are carefully guarded, and apprentices are never allowed to take books away from the guildhalls.

So how does someone who's not a wizard learn to summon a demon?

The dragon's thought was a long time in forming. *Texts can be . . . pirated. And one does not have to be a mage to summon a Lord. The Guild does not have a monopoly on the knowledge.*

Interesting as the information was, it was superfluous, and Liam found his mind already turning to his second case. He did not think the mystery of the grinning wizard would prove as easy to resolve. Pushing aside the demonology text, he pulled the report on Passendus's death close to him and started reading.

He had scarcely finished the first paragraph when the door to the dining room opened and Provyn entered. The quaestor raked Liam with a disdainful glance and stepped around the table to his seat.

"None's arrived yet?" he asked.

"Just me," Liam said, gathering the pages of his two reports together. "I didn't realize we'd be having a big breakfast. When are we supposed to meet?" He tucked the reports into his coat pocket and reached for Tarquin's book.

"Seven," the other replied absently, his attention caught by the *Daemonologia,* which lay open to the pentagram used for skrying. "What's that?" he demanded, leaning over the table and slapping his hand down on the spread pages.

Startled, Liam stared at the quaestor in bewilderment before he found his tongue. "A book," he said at last. "It's about demons. I . . . I thought it might be useful. It *is* useful—I think I've figured out how to tell what kind of demon the Handuits summoned."

After a long moment of scrutiny, Provyn nodded and removed his hand. "Well and well," he said, as if nothing untoward had happened. "I shouldn't show that to the world, if I were you. Demons are a point of contention this session." He shot his cuffs calmly—he was wearing another slashed coat, black and yellow this time, and his cuffs were adorned with sprays of lace—and turned to the sideboard.

Liam closed the book and found room for it in the pocket that held the reports. "I had heard that about demons," he ventured, and noticed the back of the black-and-yellow coat stiffen. "Aedile Coeccias told me that there were a number of cases that involved demons. That's why I brought the book."

"If y'are wise," Provyn interrupted, still facing away from him, "you'll heed my counsel, and keep the book to yourself. Aedile Coeccias has the right of it—there are more demons abroad than anyone would like, and a man with a *Daemonologia* in's pocket is like to be unpopular.'' Having loaded a plate, he came back to his seat and started eating, dissecting pieces of ham and conveying them to his mouth with fastidious concentration.

''I'm not going to be summoning any demons myself,'' Liam chuckled and then, seeing Provyn's brow wrinkle in consternation, added quickly, ''But I won't let anyone know I have it.''

''See that you don't.'' The quaestor focused on his eating, completely ignoring Liam, who shifted uncomfortably in his seat, trying to properly phrase an idea that had just come into his head.

''Still, I'm glad I brought it with me. It's got quite a lot of information about all different facets of the art.'' He was not sure how many different facets there were to demonology, but he had caught Provyn's attention. ''I was just looking through the book for five minutes, and I've already found a way to solve one of the capital cases here. So I thought, perhaps, if you could find the time, if I might look at the reports from the other sessions— from Crossroads Fair and Deepenmoor—I might be able to start. . . .'' He trailed off, Provyn's studied indifference and the intricacies of his own sentence thwarting him.

''I should think,'' the quaestor said, ''that you'd do well to mind the cases you have here and now, before you go haring off to others.''

''Oh, I'm not going to get ahead of myself, I promise you. But if I knew what the other cases were about, I could be thinking about them in the back of my head, if you see what I mean.''

''I don't.''

Ass! Frustration got the better of him, and he leaned forward, tapping the table in front of the other man's plate with a rigid finger. ''Quaestor Provyn,'' he said, his tone icy, ''I don't think it's too much to ask to be allowed to look at the reports. I'm not even asking you to get them yourself. All you have to do is send a servant and open a chest. Surely that shouldn't require too much effort.''

With a great show of deliberation, Provyn set down his knife and fork, a red flush of anger rising from his jowls up his face and across his scalp. "Quaestor Rhenford," he began, "if you think I'll be talked to in such a tone—" He stopped suddenly, his eyes narrowing and darting to the door, through which Aedile Cuspinian was ushering Widow Saffian, with Vaucan Alasco a few steps behind. There was a chorus of greetings, Liam and Provyn tacitly adopting cheerful faces while the others took their breakfasts from the sideboard.

As he sat down before a plate heaped high with fried fish, Cuspinian noticed that Liam did not have a plate before him. "Quaestor Rhenford," he called, the genial host, "let me help you to some of our fish. They frisked in the Warin only this morning, I promise you." He half rose, ready to go to the sideboard again. Liam waved him back down.

"No, thank you; I've had a roll already. I wasn't very hungry—I'm still full from last night." This drew a grin from Alasco, who was tucking into a bowl of porridge despite his bloodshot eyes and the chalky pallor of his face.

"I wonder," Widow Saffian asked, "since y'are not eating, Quaestor Rhenford, if it'd like you to go down and see that my girl has all arranged for the rite."

Liam cocked his head politely. "The rite?"

"I fear me I mentioned it not," she said, and then shrugged, as if the omission were unimportant. "See you, it is our custom before each session begins to make a small offering. When breakfast is done, we'll to the Pantheon. It's to ensure a good outcome."

Southerners, Liam had found, took their religion far more seriously than the people of the Midlands, where he had grown up. The judge fully expected him to attend, and had probably not even considered the possibility that he might not wish to. He rose hesitantly, casting about for a reason not to leave. As valuable as his talk with

Cuspinian had been, there were still many questions he wanted to ask the Areopage herself.

"Of course," he said, unable to think of a polite excuse. "I'll go and see."

She thanked him and went back to eating while he gathered his coat. Fanuilh followed him out the door, unobserved by the other members of the court.

CHAPTER 4

LIAM HAD NO trouble locating Widow Saffian's maidservant—she nearly bowled him over in the front hall, bursting through the door with a wickerwork basket swinging on her arm. Breathless, she asked if the Areopage was still upstairs, and before he could even nod, she rushed past him and up the stairs.

Fanuilh at his heels, he went outside to wait for the rest of the Areopagus to finish their breakfast and come down. The dragon explored the alley across the street where it had hunted the evening before, but found nothing of interest in the daylight and soon returned. Liam leaned against the wall by the inn door, his face turned to the sun, eyes closed. He was anxious to begin, to finish with the formalities and get down to the job for which he had been brought along. Despite his misgivings, he felt oddly confident, a confidence he attributed to having a way to determine whether Aldyne Handuit's death had been murder or accident. *We've hardly begun, and I'm almost half done,* he congratulated himself. *That ought to show Provyn.*

Frowning, he acknowledged the pettiness of the last thought but did not disown it. The fat quaestor was an ass, and Liam knew he would enjoy proving his competence to the man. More, he looked forward to demonstrating it to Widow Saffian, though for an entirely different reason. They had hardly spoken since she agreed to let him join the court, and he could not help but wonder—though he knew she had much on her mind, between her husband's death and the details of running the court—whether she had come to regret it.

Well, we'll just make sure she doesn't have any cause to, he promised himself, and as he did, the door of the Duke's Arms opened and the rest of the court emerged. As if she had read his thoughts, Widow Saffian let the others pass by and stepped aside to stand with him.

"Attend me, Quaestor Rhenford," she said. "I've neglected you, and must mend my ways." She wore black, but the color made her look more ominous than bereaved; there were no mourning streamers on her dress, and the sleeves were wide and full with cuffs like a monk's robe, so that when she gestured they flapped like a crow's wings. The skirts of the dress covered her feet, and she seemed to glide along.

"You've been very busy, I know," he said, falling into step beside her. The others had already gone on ahead, Provyn and Cuspinian together, Alasco and the maid with the basket after them. He picked up Fanuilh and perched it on his shoulder, then noticed her looking and stopped. "Is it all right? I should have asked—I can leave him at the inn, if it's better."

"Not at all, not at all. It's as well to have him, and he may be useful. It'd be a hard man who could give the lie to a mage and's familiar." They started walking again, turning into a bigger street lined with shops. It was early yet, and a number of oxcarts were trundling along the road, carrying produce to the Warinsford market.

"I'm not a wizard, really," he said. A nearby ox sneezed right after he spoke and then started lowing, as if to contradict him.

"I know it, Quaestor, and you, but will they? The Handuits, now—they'll not know it. The late Areopage was not averse to leaving a misconception uncorrected, perhaps more so than was right. Still, we are not responsible for the assumptions of others. As long as you tell no lies, they may think what they like. If a man thinks you a mage, he'll treat you as one—and who'll lie to a mage?"

Everyone believed him a wizard in Southwark, and Liam had on certain occasions turned that impression to his advantage, so he had no qualms about it. He had, however, noticed a hitch in the judge's voice when she mentioned her husband, and he was anxious to leave the topic behind. "As long as you think it's all right," he said. "And you shouldn't think you've neglected me. I know you have many other things to attend to. But I'm glad to have a moment or two to talk to you—there are some questions I'd like to ask."

The street grew crowded, sidestreets filtering in streams of wagons, horsemen and people with baskets and sacks and barrels, all making their way toward the center of Warinsford. Having Fanuilh with them guaranteed easy passage, and Cuspinian and the rest were somewhere in the press up ahead, but Widow Saffian guided him out of the main road.

"Those mobs like me not," she explained, "and we'll have quiet for your questions. I'll guess you want to know more of your duties."

"Anything you can tell me, please." He did not try to keep the eagerness from his voice, but he smiled to show that things had not yet gotten desperate. "I'm still at sea about how the court works."

She nodded, then tapped the end of her nose a few times, twisting her mouth a little in concentration, as if she was trying to figure out where to begin. "For the main part, you may do as you would if you were working with Aedile Coeccias. The signal difference is that our aims are somewhat narrower than his, more tied to the necessities of the court and the vagaries of the law. An instance: I warrant this with the Handuits perplexes you. We've clapped the villains in, after all."

"Well, Aedile Cuspinian told me that the real question was whether they meant for the demon to get loose or not. He said the punishments are different."

"There is that," she agreed. "For the skrying and the accidental death, they'll be whipped and branded, with the number of lashes at my discretion—though one hundred strokes was the figure used in the most recent case of this sort, some fourteen years ago. If they intentioned their brother's death, though, it's death by ordeal."

"I think I know a way to figure it out," he interposed, pleased to be able to share Fanuilh's information.

"That's to the good," she said, "but not the sum of the case. There is also the question of the source of the conjuration."

"The conjuration?"

"The spell they cast. We needs must know where it is, whether it's been destroyed, and whence it came, for that there is a law against trafficking in such works. Demonological works are proscribed in the duchy, except for those belonging to true mages sanctioned by the Guild. So you must con out the source of the spell. You see how it is complicated?"

"I do," he muttered, but he was not thinking about the case. He was remembering Provyn slapping his hand down on the *Daemonologia,* the book which now seemed terribly heavy in his pocket. *Why didn't he tell me it was illegal?*

She seemed to know Warinsford well, and led him through a maze of less-crowded streets without hesitating, all the while elaborating on his duties. She spoke rapidly, almost breathlessly, as if there was too much to say in too short a time, and she flapped her crow's-wing sleeves constantly for emphasis. After the offering at the Pantheon, the court would go to the town's jail to interview the accused. From there they would split up, and Liam would make whatever inquiries he felt were required. He would have the whole day for his investigations, and most of the next morning, and Alasco would assist him. Before the actual session the next afternoon, Liam and Provyn would present whatever evidence they had acquired to the Areopage, so that she could prepare herself for judging the cases.

Only half-listening, Liam took in what she said but could not really concentrate on it. His eyes kept flicking to the pocket where the *Daemonologia* lay hidden. *Did you know this thing was illegal?* he asked Fanuilh.

I do not know the laws of the duchy, the dragon responded. *Master Tanaquil never considered it. However,*

I would think that, as you are his heir and a member of the Areopagus, no one would object.

The answer soothed Liam a little, and he expanded it until he had justified the book to himself. He had inherited it from a Guild-sanctioned wizard, after all, and it was going to help solve a crime. *And it's not like I'm going to summon up a demon myself.* When he was finally able to turn his full attention back to the judge, she was saying, "In course, you'll have told me beforehand what evidence you'll present, and I'll have a conception of my ruling. Seen thus, it's not so very complex, eh?"

"No, not at all," he said, reassured.

"And where y'are unsure of your way, Quaestor Provyn or I will lead you; y'have but to say the word. Now with this grinning wizard . . ."

Once again, Liam's attention was divided. He had been anxious for just this sort of talk, but now that it was happening he could not keep his mind away from Provyn. *He acted like it was nothing, nothing at all, and he couldn't possibly be unaware of the law.* His natural conclusion was that the quaestor had hoped to trip him up, to make him look bad at some later date, but while he would not put it past the other man, he warned himself that that sort of suspicion bordered on the paranoid. Perhaps Provyn thought it was acceptable for him to have the book because he worked for the Areopagus—or he might believe Liam was a wizard, as so many others did, and thus exempt from the law. Either reason seemed more rational than his first suspicion. *And if he ever brings it up, you can honestly claim ignorance—and the fact that he never said anything about it.* In the meantime, though, he would keep the book out of sight, and not mention it unless it was absolutely necessary.

Widow Saffian only discussed the dead wizard for a few minutes, and the gist of her comments was that Liam need not be overly concerned if nothing turned up. "Cuspinian proposes a magical death, for that there is no obvious cause, and we should like to know if that is the case. Beyond that, though, I harbor no great hopes of

success—the man was a stranger, unknown to any in
Warinsford. His killer may well be long quit of the duchy
by now. So do not tax yourself overmuch with it.''

Her roundabout route brought them abruptly to the
Pantheon, the narrow street they were on opening out into
a little plaza formed by an angle of the building. The
temple was built along the usual design—a central hub
with four projecting wings, each dedicated to three of the
twelve major gods. Warinsford's pantheon differed only
in that it had a tall spire over the center instead of a dome,
and that its wings were slightly taller than usual, with
steeply-pitched slate roofs and long panels of stained
glass visible between straining buttresses. Separate flights
of steps rose between buttresses to each god's door, and
elaborate bas-relief lintels crowned the doors, the carved
figures gilt or painted in bright colors.

Widow Saffian ignored Strife's door, with its stone
warhorses rearing on a carved battlefield, and Fortune's
as well, not even glancing at the statue of the goddess
on her wheel, peeking out from beneath her blindfold.
Liam would have liked a chance to spin one of the two
smaller, wooden wheels mounted on the jambs—it was
considered lucky—but the judge glided along so quickly
he did not have a chance; he had to hurry to keep up as
she went around the Pantheon to the next wing. It was
only then that he realized that he was not sure exactly
which god's favor they would be seeking. The Peacemaker made the most sense, but he had never been able
to keep the various functions of the Taralonian gods
straight, partly because they varied so much. Farmers in
the Midlands prayed to Uris for good harvests and to
Mother Pity for strong children; merchants in the coastal
cities sought Uris's blessing for their trading voyages and
thanked Mother Pity for the food they ate; scholars in
the universities of Torquay considered Uris their patron
and invoked Mother Pity when they threw a coin to a
beggar. Few gods had domains as straightforward as
Strife's.

She stopped at the first door of the next wing, looking

around impatiently, and Liam had a chance to inspect the
lintel and the stained glass windows to either side. He
had guessed right: they stood outside the Peacemaker's
door. The frieze above the lintel showed the god standing
in the middle of a battlefield, his hands held palms out,
a serene smile on his face. Kings knelt in homage beside
him, their armies prostrate behind them while discarded
weapons were thrown by children onto mirrored bonfires
at the far ends of the panel. The scenes in the windows
were difficult to make out, the colors dull and smoky
from the outside.

"At last," Widow Saffian murmured beside him, and
he turned from the decorations to see the rest of the court
approaching. "Come, come, gentlemen," she said,
louder this time. "The day slips away! Thala, you backward girl, have you the gifts?"

"Here, mistress," the girl panted, holding out her basket. "All's in readiness."

The older woman took the basket with a stern nod.
"You'll wait here, Thala." She looked around at the four
men. "Sirs, shall we in?"

Liam lifted Fanuilh from his shoulder and deposited
the dragon on the steps. *Try not to scare Thala off,* he
told it, and followed the court inside.

Twin niches flanked the Peacemaker's door on the inside,
at the first of which they washed their hands and anointed
their mouths from a stoup of blessed water. Liam hung
back to see what the others did, moistening the tips of
his fingers and brushing them across his lips as Alasco
had, his eyes wandering over the window at the back of
the niche. With the morning sun behind them, the scenes
were easier to understand: the god in his many guises—
male and female, husband and wife, parent and child,
servant and lord, and even, though close to the floor and
partially obscured by the stoup, the Peacemaker as judge
and accused.

Widow Saffian stepped up to the stone altar in the
second niche, and bowed her head; the men behind her

knelt, with Liam belatedly following their example.

"A man wears two faces," she intoned, "and the wind blows both ways. A fool may rise up, and a prince be cast down. The man that rises rich goes to his couch a beggar, and the judge stands accused. Who will be ready on that day? Will you receive where once you gave? Will you follow where once you led? Will you find justice where once you dispensed it? To judge as you would be judged, is to judge as the Maker of Peace; to temper just satisfaction with mercy, to know that all may fall—and all may rise again. These are your tasks, and the Maker of Peace is with you, if you will have him."

She spoke the set prayer with evident sincerity, and when Liam sneaked a glance at the kneeling men, he saw that they were mouthing the words along with her, equal belief in their expressions. Both Alasco and Provyn bowed their heads and closed their eyes, while Cuspinian directed his gaze to the stained glass panels above the altar, his eyes wide and his face strangely innocent. Liam hung his head guiltily and tried to pray.

At the altar Widow Saffian removed a loaf of bread and two small jugs from her basket, raising each up for a moment and then laying them out on the cloth. "Would you begrudge another a crust and a drop of wine today? You will hunger and thirst on the morrow. But if it please you to shed light today, it will please the Maker of Peace to illumine all your days." She held up a cruet of oil, and then put it with the bread and the jugs.

"Serve as you would be served, rule as you would be ruled, hold dear as you would be held, and judge as you would be judged. All tales have two endings—seek you both. Let us pray now, that the Maker may find us worthy of his service."

The Areopage knelt at the altar, and the other men prostrated themselves. Liam quickly followed suit, lying on his elbows and resting his cheek on his clasped hands. Silence descended, an interminable one for Liam, who imagined the others' faces screwed up with devotion.

He had never prayed very often, or had much use for

Taralon's organized religions. It was not a question of
believing that the gods were there, though he had met
some people who questioned their existence. He knew
they existed because he had met some of them—he had
stood before Bellona herself only a few months before—
but he had no faith in them. They were bent on their own
ends, with their own inscrutable purposes, and were an
awfully thin reed on which to rely.

Nonetheless, he managed a sort of blanket prayer: *Let
me be good at this,* and repeated it a few times before
giving up and beginning to wonder how long the prayers
of the rest of the court would take. The stones of the
temple leached the warmth from his bones, and he was
eager to get started, to try to recapture some of his earlier
excitement.

At last Widow Saffian stirred, rising to her feet and
brushing off her skirts, and the rest of the court rose as
well, Liam with relief.

"Come, gentlemen," she said, "the morning speeds
away."

For all her haste to be gone, Widow Saffian did not accompany them to Warinsford's jail. On the steps of the
Pantheon she turned to Cuspinian, said "I'll see you
anon," and hurried off around the building, the basket
on her arm. The Aedile merely nodded and led the other
men in the opposite direction, away from the temple and
into the maze of narrow streets. It was only after several
minutes of silent walking that Alasco asked the question
Liam had been wondering about.

"Aedile Cuspinian," the young man asked hesitantly,
"where has Areopage Saffian gone?" The prayer seemed
to have done him good: his face was less chalky, and
bright spots of color had appeared on his cheeks.

Provyn answered the question with a snort. "T'another
fane, boy, where else?"

"I'd wager Laomedon's," Cuspinian added, noticing
Alasco's confused look. "For to offer something for her
husband."

Thoughts of the late Areopage sobered them all, and the resumed silence had a certain introspective gravity. Liam, who had never met the dead man, found himself wondering anew at the widow's determination to go through with the sessions. *Everything she does must remind her of him,* he thought.

Master, the book is showing. Fanuilh was perched on his shoulder again.

With a start, he looked down and saw that the top of the *Daemonologia* was indeed peeking out of his pocket. He quickly covered it and turned his head to raise his eyebrows at the dragon.

I'm going to have to find a safe place for that, he projected.

It would be wise.

Provyn had fallen into step beside the Aedile, and Liam glared at the back of his expensive coat. *Can you imagine that ass not telling me?*

It does seem odd. Perhaps he was not aware of the law.

"Ha!" Liam said aloud, and blushed, checking to see if the other men had noticed, but they were wrapped in their own thoughts. *Don't you believe it. He probably hoped I would pull it out at some point and then he could arrest me.*

Why would he want to arrest you?

Because he's an ass, Liam thought, but he did not elaborate.

They emerged from an alley onto a broad boardwalk facing the Warin, a muddy expanse of water alive with craft of all sizes and descriptions—barges and galleons, launches and lighters, even rafts and tiny, one-man coracles. Piers jutted crazily into the stream, many occupied, cargos being taken aboard or off-loaded into the oxcarts whose wheels rumbled and thundered on the foot-thick planks of the boardwalk. Gulls screamed and dove from the sky, squabbling furiously over the refuse that collected in the odd angles of the piers.

On the landward side were ranged wooden ware-

houses, seedy wineshops and, visible several blocks away
to the south, two large stone buildings, imposing bulks
on the waterfront. Pennons hung from their high facades,
the Duke's red and gray snapping in the breeze off the
river.

People recognized Cuspinian and stepped aside for
him, sometimes with lowered heads and hastily averted
eyes, sometimes with bows and ingratiating smiles or respectful greetings. The Aedile nodded regally but said
nothing, the three men of the court trailing behind him
like a retinue. At first Liam was grateful not to be, with
Fanuilh, the center of attention, but as they made their
way down the boardwalk he began to frown uneasily.
Aediles were the Duke's representatives, charged with
keeping order in his lands; Cuspinian walked through
Warinsford as if he were the Duke himself, and the greetings offered him took on, in Liam's eyes, an almost sub-
servient tone that only deepened his frown.

As they approached the first of the stone buildings he
noticed Alasco staring at him, and forced away his frown.
He gestured toward the nearest, a gray granite edifice
with a long arcade in front, beneath the arches of which
came and went harried-looking merchants, ink-stained
clerks and grimy boys clutching messages. "Are those
the Duke's courts?"

"No, Quaestor," Alasco replied. "That's the Impost
Tower, for the tariffs and the taxes, new-built these three
years past." He indicated the second building. "Those
are the jails. The Water Gate, we call it, for that it opens
on the river, see you." The boardwalk gave way to stone
pavement in front of the jail, and Liam followed the
young man's pointing finger to where a flight of steps
descended to the brown waters of the Warin. "It was a
fortress, formerly," he added.

Liam had no trouble believing that. The Water Gate
was a grim pile of black, age-pitted stone, with massive
crenellations like beetled brows, its few windows mere
slits with thick bars. Cuspinian led the way to the entrance, an arched tunnel complete with murder holes, and

received the salutes of the Guards on duty with a satisfied look. The tunnel ended in a courtyard hardly bigger than Liam's room at the inn, with iron-banded doors of oak on three sides. The sky was a small square of blue high above them.

"Well and well," the Aedile said briskly. "We'll part here. I'll with Quaestor Provyn for to see his knaves, and Vaucan'll take you to see yours, Quaestor Rhenford. Remember, if there's aught you need, y'have but to call." He turned on his heel, beckoning Provyn, and they disappeared through the door on the right, leaving Liam and Alasco alone in the courtyard.

"This way," the young man said, going straight ahead. He knocked on the door, wincing a little as his knuckles struck the hard wood. "We separate our prisoners by crime."

A Guard opened the door, examined Alasco for a long second, and then stepped aside to let them pass. Stairways led up and down from a landing just inside the door, and Alasco paused only to light a lantern, relieve the Guard of his keys, and tell him to bring two chairs to the Handuits' cell before descending.

Beads of moisture glittered on the stone walls and Liam, his long nose wrinkling at the smell of mold and rot, guessed that they had gone beneath the level of the river. Far below, it seemed to him, but the stairs went on, the air growing colder and damper. He trailed his fingers along the wall and quickly withdrew them; the masonry was furry with moss. When they finally reached the bottom he was cold and decidedly uncomfortable— he did not like being that far below ground.

Two corridors stretched away from the stairway, one completely unlit, a yawning black emptiness from which Liam averted his eyes, and the other with a few glimmers of light at its far end. He followed Alasco toward the lights, noting the empty cells on either side as they passed, fully expecting the lantern to reveal a chained skeleton in one of them.

"Quite a cheery place," he muttered. Stagnant

puddles of water had gathered in uneven patches of the floor; he splashed through one.

"Your pardon, Quaestor?"

"Nothing." The moldy smell was worse. *Remind me never to commit a crime in Warinsford,* he told Fanuilh. *Or at least, not to get caught.*

The light came from three cells at the end of the corridor. In the first a man lay on his back, snoring noisily, rusty stains of blood splashed across his clothes; in the second three sailors were playing a game of dice. They barely looked up from their game as Alasco and Liam passed. In the third, the Handuits waited.

"Come awake, Master Handuit," Alasco called, rattling the ring of keys he had taken from the Guard. "The Areopagus is at hand!"

CHAPTER 5

TRICKLES OF RIVER water ran down the walls and gathered in puddles, but where the snoring man slept on the floor and the gaming sailors tossed their dice on the bare, wet flagstones, the Handuits at least had furniture—two fragile-looking cots, a plain table, and two stools.

Elsevier Handuit clutched at the bars of his cell while Alasco unlocked the gate. He had a long, thin face, his nose drooping down almost to his lips, with large, watery eyes that tracked every movement of the young quaestor's hands. He was bundled in an ankle-length cape, a long scarf wound around his neck, and a shapeless cap with ear flaps perched atop his head. "At last, at last," he muttered until the gate opened, and then he rushed to the gap in the bars and fell to his knees, hands raised imploringly at Liam. "Oh, master, master, you must have pity, pity my wife and I, for the gods know we never intentioned any harm—"

He caught sight of Fanuilh and stopped.

"This is Quaestor Rhenford," Alasco said into the sudden silence. "He's here to con out the truth from you, Master Handuit. And you, mistress." His tone left no doubt as to the truth he thought Liam would discover, though it had softened a little when he addressed the woman.

Roviana Handuit lay on one of the cots, peeking out from beneath a mountain of blankets and quilts. There was a slight bluish tinge to her drawn face, and she coughed a papery, rustling cough.

"Quaestor," she whispered, then broke off to cough

again, a hand slipping from beneath the quilts to gesture weakly at Liam.

Her husband found his voice again. "You can see, Quaestor, that my wife's sorely ill—sorely. I've begged and begged, but they'll not move us elsewhere."

"Y'have at most another day here," Alasco said reasonably. "The session's tomorrow."

"Pray you, Quaestor Rhenford—can you do aught for my poor wife?"

Both Elsevier and Alasco were looking expectantly at him, but Liam was speechless for a moment, struck by the sight of the sick woman. He could not believe that she had been forced to stay in the cold, dank cell.

She is under suspicion of murder, Fanuilh reminded him, and he blinked, recalled to his purpose. *It is only another day,* the dragon's thought continued.

"True," Liam said, still staring at the woman on the cot. She would not die in the next day and a half—he hoped—and she had been caught in the act of committing a heinous crime. The dice in the next cell clicked on the flagstones, and one of the sailors cursed. Liam shook himself and turned to Handuit. "True enough. It's just one more day, Master Handuit. In the meantime, I suggest you think more about the crime you have both been accused of."

The look of disappointment in Handuit's eyes almost made him wince, and the whispered cough nagged at him. Perhaps later in the day he could arrange to have a healer visit, or for an apothecary to send some medicines.

"These are serious accusations," he said, deliberately assuming an air of gravity to distance himself from his pity for the sick woman. He pulled the report from his pocket and tapped the top sheet. "According to this, you were caught red-handed summoning the demon who killed your brother. What do you say to that?" There were other questions that he had wanted to ask, better questions, but he needed a moment to collect himself.

"Oh," Handuit wailed, "it was a grievous error, Lord Rhenford, a grievous error, but we intentioned no murder, I swear it. We would only skry, my lord, and knew't was wrong, but thought no harm would come of it. My dear brother's dead for it—is that not punishment enough?''

''So you didn't raise the demon to kill your brother?''

''My lord, how can you even say it? I loved him! My wife—sick here, and not just for the noxious humors of this hole, but in her heart, that we should innocently cause this—she loved him too!''

''And you only meant to try a little fortune-telling?'' The dialect of the duchy sometimes put Liam at a disadvantage, never sure if he completely understood what was said to him, but now Handuit's southern longwindedness gave him time to think. The questions he had worked out at the breakfast table were coming back to him. *Questions . . .*

''Only that, my lord, but how wrong we were t'essay it! If we could only go back—''

''What did you ask the demon?'' Liam interrupted.

Handuit blinked twice. ''My lord?''

''What questions did you have for it? You wished to know something, so you conjured up a demon to tell you. What did you wish to know?''

Handuit goggled, glancing rapidly back and forth between Liam and Alasco.

''Come, Master Handuit,'' Liam said. ''You raised a demon to learn something—surely you knew what it was.''

''My lord,'' he stammered, but could find nothing to say.

''The ship,'' Roviana Handuit whispered, and all three men turned to her in surprise. Her hand slipped from beneath the covers again, and she made a weak rolling gesture at her husband. ''The ship, my love, that we waited on . . .'' Her words trailed away in a fit of soft coughing, and Handuit scrambled to her side, pressing her hand to his lips.

''Don't trouble yourself so,'' he urged her, then addressed Liam. ''She has the right of it, my lord. We sought news of a ship, in which we had invested our all, but which was late returning. It was late, and all our little money was in it, my lord. Surely you can understand what drove us—our future hung on Fortune's blessing and that ship! Our creditors were pressing us something cruel, my lord, and we wished to know when the ship would return.''

''What was the name of the ship?''

''My lord?''

The Guard arrived with the chairs Alasco had requested, and made a fuss of setting them down. Liam flashed him an irritated glance, and when he turned back to the Handuit, the man blurted, ''The *Tiger,* my lord, out of Dordrecht in the Freeports. A spice ship, my lord.''

Liam frowned. Hundreds of *Tigers* roamed the seas, and many of their unimaginative owners would both live in the Freeports and trade in spices. Still, he pressed on: as disturbed as he had been by Mistress Handuit's life in the cell, her husband's faltering had convinced him of the couple's guilt. He only needed to catch the man in a slip, and parley that into some tangible proof.

''Has it come in yet?''

''Unhappily no, my lord, and I fear it lost, and all our hopes were in it.''

''All? Did your brother invest in it too?''

''I—no, my lord, he didn't.''

''I understood he was very wealthy,'' Liam said, pretending an ingenuous confusion. ''Won't you inherit his money, now that he is dead?''

''My lord,'' Handuit protested, rising to his feet, ''even should the truth out, and our innocence be proclaimed from the rooftops, we'd sooner go begging than touch any of Aldyne's money. Why, it is bloody, and we, howsoever unwittingly, were the agents of his death. It would not be right.''

Liam finally sat in the chair the Guard had brought, gesturing for Alasco to sit as well and helping Fanuilh slip from his shoulder to a relatively dry spot on the floor. ''That's a commendable sentiment, though if the court does decide you didn't mean to kill your brother, I'd suggest you spend at least some of your money on regaining your wife's health." He turned to Alasco. "Did Master Handuit leave a will?"

"Why, no," the young quaestor answered, taken by surprise. "I think not."

"So you would inherit his money in the event of his death," Liam continued, turning back to Handuit. "And his house, too, I suppose. It was his house?"

"Aye, my lord—left him by our father."

Liam stretched out his legs, making himself comfortable. "You got along well with him? The household was . . . harmonious?"

Handuit nodded eagerly. "Oh, aye, my lord. Never have brothers been closer, my lord."

"I'm surprised you were so worried about the *Tiger,* then. Surely your brother would have helped you out— a loan, at the very least, between such close brothers."

Once again Handuit fell speechless, unable to answer, and his wife had to wheeze a response from her sickbed. "No . . . loans," she said. "Elsevier . . . tell them. . . ."

Handuit grimaced, then hung his head, as if ashamed. When he finally spoke it was with great reluctance. "Aldyne was strongly against loans, and against the spice trade. He thought it an unnecessary luxury. He was a passing strange man, in his way, always locking himself away in his chambers." Handuit raised his head then, and there were tears in his eyes. "But for all that, he was my brother! He kept us and fed us beneath his own roof! Oh, how I wish he'd never bought those papers!"

"Elsevier!" Mistress Handuit exclaimed sharply, the effort sending her into another coughing fit.

Liam leaned forward, interested. "What papers?"

"Those thrice-damned papers of his! He had them of a bookseller here in Warinsford, a bundle of them. They purported to be from the library of a wizard, and though I warned him, he persisted, and would buy them. Aldyne was ever interested in magic, see you—though he never practiced, I swear!"

"And the spell you used came from this bundle your brother bought?"

"Aye, my lord. Aldyne kept them locked away, but once it chanced that he left them out, and I happened to see them—and I saw the spell for conjuration. Would that I never had!"

Mindful of Widow Saffian's instructions, Liam asked, "Do you know the name of the bookseller? Can he confirm this?"

Handuit lowered his head. "I do—one Relly, that had a shop in Token Alley, where the pawners are."

"And is dead these last five months," Alasco said skeptically. "A great convenience, eh, Master Handuit?"

Indignant, Handuit pointed his chin at the young quaestor. "Not so, sir! If he lived, he could tell that the papers were my brother's, and that I did not buy them intending his murder."

Liam cleared his throat. "Let's leave the bookseller for now, and come back to the spell. You found it among your brother's papers and—what? Copied it?"

"Aye, my lord," Handuit replied, his indignation giving way to shame. "I stole it and copied it out and replaced it, without Aldyne's knowledge. I was desperate, my lord—the *Tiger* still out, our fortune at stake—and I thought it would help."

Tell me if he lies, Liam projected, careful not to look at Fanuilh. "The spell fit on one piece of paper?"

"Aye, my lord. It looked to have been ripped from a volume, for that one edge was ragged. And it said only that the summoned creature would answer questions—nothing on the score of murder, I swear!"

It could have been torn from a copy of the Daemonologia, *Fanuilh supplied. And most of the spells fit on one page.*

"So you performed the spell," Liam went on, "and the demon appeared?"

"A great, fearsome beast he was," Handuit said with a shudder. "And would not answer our questions, but instead rushed from the room and made for the highest part of the house—my brother Aldyne's room.''

''The Guards had to break down your brother's door, you know,'' Liam pointed out, fighting the urge to smile in triumph. ''How do you suppose the demon got into his chamber?'' His urge disappeared when tears began to form in Handuit's eyes.

''I would that I knew, my lord! I would that the beast had taken me in his place!''

Clearing his throat again, Liam gave the man a moment to collect himself. ''The demon took the chalk and the cat and the spell with it?''

''Aye, my lord,'' Handuit sniffled.

If it slipped the confining circle, a demon would attempt to destroy the spell, so as not to be summoned again, Fanuilh explained. *But it would also try to destroy the caster, and I can think of no reason it would be interested in the chalk or the cat.*

It was a reasonably solid story, nonetheless. If he did not have a copy of the *Daemonologia* to compare to the circle in Handuit's cellar, he would have been hard-pressed to prove it false. As it was, however, the comparison would be evidence enough. Better still would be the copy of the spell they used, but since the demon had apparently destroyed that, the comparison would have to do.

''All right, Master Handuit, just one more question. Can you describe the pentagram you drew?''

The man groaned. ''Oh, my lord, ask not that! I have burned the memory from my mind. It is so painful, and so long ago—''

Ask him whether he stood inside the circle or outside. The dragon's thought appeared in his head, and he could not concentrate on the other man's words until it faded.

''I understand, I understand,'' he said quickly, forestalling Handuit with a raised hand. ''Just tell me this: did you stand inside or outside the circle?''

Shaking his head miserably, Handuit turned beseeching eyes on his wife, whose coughing had subsided to a

low rattle in her chest. "I cannot remember," he moaned.
"I've tried so hard to forget. . . ."

"Without," Roviana wheezed. "Without, my love."

That would be right for a Skrying Lord—the conscrip-
tor outside the pentagram, the Lord inside, to prevent it
from escaping. For a Lord Assassin, the conscriptor
would stand inside the pentagram, to protect himself.

"Very well," Liam said, as much to his familiar as to
the other people in the cell, "I think that's all for now.
Unless there was something else you wanted to add, Master Handuit?" He looked expectantly at the man, who
only shook his head.

Mistress Handuit stirred on her cot. "I would . . . say
something, my lord. Come . . . closer, I pray you." The
words, faint as they were, cost her a great deal of effort.
Liam went and knelt apprehensively by her side. She
clasped his hand, hers hot and trembling, and struggled
for breath. "Have pity," she managed at last, then let his
hand fall and slumped back.

Oh, gods, he thought, backing away from the cot as
Handuit hurried to his wife. When they asked him to join
the court, no one had said anything about sending desperately ill women to the gallows. Liam picked up Fanuilh and nodded at Alasco. "Let's go."

Further down the hallway, when he could still hear the
mutters of the gaming sailors and the snores of the sleeping man but not Mistress Handuit's coughing, Liam
paused to take a deep breath. He knew there was nothing
inherently innocent or fragile about women—he had met
enough who were cruel and murderous to belie that notion—but he could not shake the pity he felt for the sick
woman. The way she had rallied to her husband, provid-
ing the answers he could not, had made Liam uneasy, as
if he should be ashamed at forcing her to such lengths.

Alasco paused with him, nodding his head thoughtfully. "Y'are thinking of the wife," he said. "I swear,
ofttimes I think she's more heart and stomach than Handuit, for all her fevers."

"Mmm." They started walking again, heading for the stairs. "How long has she been ill?"

"Only these last few weeks. She's been like that each time I've seen her, and the men who bring their food comment on it. Think you the Areopage'll show mercy, for that she's so ill?"

"I don't know," he said truthfully. He did not know the judge well enough to say, but a sudden suspicion had risen in him. Thinking it a reaction to his own pity, he tried to dismiss it, but it would not go, and when they reached the stairs he stopped and half-turned to face down the corridor. "Those sailors—how long have they been in that cell?"

"A week, no more. They'll be before a judge in another. They killed a waterman and stole his boat, and'll hang soon enough. Why?"

"Can you bring one of them upstairs? Just for a few minutes? I'd like to ask them a question." If they had been in those lightless cells a week, a few minutes in the open air might make them more cooperative—and he did not want the Handuits to hear what he asked.

Alasco gave him a curious look but did not press for explanations; he shrugged and went back down the corridor. Liam climbed the stairs, accepted the salute of the Guard on duty there, and stepped out into the small courtyard.

What are you thinking? Fanuilh asked.

Something ungenerous, he projected back, absently reaching up to scratch the dragon's back. It arched pleasurably under his hand, flexing its claws to maintain its perch on his shoulder.

Ungenerous, certainly, and most likely a false trail, but the suspicion was the sort he knew it was best to lay to rest immediately; otherwise it would nag at him for the rest of the day. Alasco returned shortly with one of the sailors in tow, a weathered old man with a gray pigtail and a dirty smock.

"Here he is," the young quaestor announced, pushing the sailor forward. "Answer what y'are asked, sirrah." The sailor spat reflexively, bobbing his head at Liam and grinning to show his willingness to cooperate.

"The woman in the cell next to yours is very ill," Liam said, and the sailor nodded vigorously.

"Aye, aye, she is, my lord, sore ill, as you say."

"She coughs a great deal."

"Aye, that she does," the sailor agreed, blackened teeth bared in an affable grin. "As you heard, my lord, the cough of the world."

"Does she cough that way all the time?"

The sailor's grin vanished, and he shuffled his feet, perplexed. "Eh, my lord? All the time?"

Liam rephrased his question. "Do you hear her cough at night?"

"I couldn't say, my lord, for that I'm sleeping at night. I'd wager she sleeps then, too," he added, unsure if this was helpful.

Liam tried again. "Have you ever heard her cough when there are no Guards around?"

Screwing up his eyes, the sailor tried to figure out the gist of the question, and then, suddenly, a look of wonder spread across his face. "Why, my lord, it comes to me that I only hear it when they're bringing the meals, and the like. Most times I hardly hear it, now you ask, but for when such as yourself visits."

There are herbs that will counterfeit illness, Fanuilh put in.

"Very good," Liam said, dismissing the sailor. Alasco took the man to the door and handed him over to the Guard there. When he returned, he bore an expression of wonder akin to the sailor's.

"I'd never have credited it," he said, regarding Liam admiringly. "How did you know?"

"Just a bad feeling," Liam said. "Can you find out if they have any medicines? Any herbs or potions or that sort of thing?"

Alasco nodded and hurried back through the door. While he waited Liam paced the courtyard, glancing occasionally at the small square of blue sky high above and pondering his next move.

Feigning illness was not proof of murder, by any stretch of the imagination—it only meant that the Handuits were hoping for mercy. He still had to prove that they had summoned a Lord whose Sphere was assassination. Since the demon had apparently destroyed the piece of paper with the spell on it, he would have to hope that the part of the circle that had not been erased would be sufficient, which meant a trip to Aldyne Handuit's basement. The report had said that the house was on the waterfront, so the trip would not take long. Once he was finished there he could turn his attention to the matter of the grinning wizard, which promised to be far more difficult, and also far more interesting.

Alasco returned then, bursting with news. Prisoners in the Water Gate were allotted a minimal amount of food each day by law—a small loaf of bread of a specific size and weight, water, and a cup of dried peas—but by custom they were allowed to augment this at their own expense, one of the Guards being dispatched to make the purchases. The Handuits had taken advantage of the tradition to arrange for wine and meat and better bread to be brought in. "Cimber—the Guard who markets for them—has been to an apothecary these several times at their request. Mistress Handuit's father was an apothecary, and she had her husband write down what was needful. Cimber hasn't his letters, so he knows not what it was, but we can ask that of the apothecary himself. Shall we to him? It's not far."

"Could we send someone?" Liam asked. He did not want to go off on a tangent that was, after all, of no real significance.

"In course," Alasco replied, though he looked disappointed.

"I'd rather go straight to Handuit's house now," Liam explained. "I want to see what's left of their pentagram. From that we should be able to tell what they intended. . . . What's wrong?"

Bewilderment was written large across Alasco's face. "You would visit Handuit's house?"

"Of course. I need to see their pentagram."

"But it's been sold," the young man blurted. "The circle will be long erased, Quaestor Rhenford."

"Sold?" Liam echoed stupidly. "Sold to whom?"

"Truth, I couldn't say. It was done these four months past, after the murder."

"Four months? This happened four months ago?"

Alasco nodded wordlessly.

"They've been sitting down there for four months? In that pit?"

"They needs must await the Areopagus, Quaestor Rhenford," the other man said, holding out his hands helplessly.

"And the house is sold? The pentagram is gone?" Liam shook his head, incredulous. *Four months!* He could not imagine being imprisoned in the Water Gate for four months, particularly through the winter. More importantly, he could not imagine having to investigate a crime that old. "How am I supposed to figure out . . . if the pentagram is gone . . ." He breathed hard, trying to collect his scattered thoughts. *Four months ago I had hardly even heard of the Areopagus.* Whoever had bought Aldyne Handuit's house would long since have destroyed the pentagram; no one would want such a thing in their house.

"I'm sorry, Quaestor Rhenford," Alasco said unhappily. "We'd no idea that would be of interest to you. Aedile Cuspinian assumed we had all that was needed. They were caught in the act, see you, and—" An idea struck him, and he brightened. "But it may be that the Guards who were there could remember! Could we not ask them? Would that do?"

The idea calmed Liam, and he nodded slowly. "Yes, that might do, if they can remember. Can you arrange that?"

"They work the nights, but I'll send a man to roust them out of their beds presently." He started away but Liam stopped him, a new worry surfacing.

"The wizard—Passendus—how long ago was he killed?"

Alasco smiled, relieved to have good news. "Only a week. And we've everything you could want to see of his, I promise."

"A week," Liam grumbled to himself when Alasco was gone. "A week!" Any good woodsman would say that a week-old trail was too cold to follow.

Gods, he thought. *This is going to be harder than I thought.*

The Guards who had been on duty the night of Aldyne Handuit's murder lived outside of Warinsford, and when Alasco returned from sending a man to fetch them, he apologized that it would take almost an hour for them to arrive. Liam waved away the apology.

"It doesn't matter," he said. "I should have realized that some of these crimes would be months old. While we wait, perhaps we can get started with Passendus." He had hoped to have the merchant's death out of the way before he began investigating the wizard's, but that could not be helped, and he was possessed by a feeling that the morning was slipping away very quickly.

Slipping away without results, he added, and then collected his thoughts.

Alasco accepted his suggestion eagerly. "In course, in course! You'll see there that we've been thorough, Quaestor, I promise. Would you see his corse first, or his belongings?"

"The corpse," he said, used to the odd southern abbreviation of the word. He wanted to see the smile of which so much had been made.

"It's in Mother Haella's cold room," the young man said. "Above." He jerked his head toward the Water Gate's upper stories, and then led the way back into the prison, through the same door they had entered before. They went up now, climbing six long flights of steps. Thin bands of grey light lit every other flight, filtered through barred windows that looked out on the courtyard.

At the top of the last flight was a small landing with a single, low door. Alasco knocked and shouted the ghost witch's name.

"Mother Haella? Are you there, Mother Haella?"

The landing was dark, but Liam could just discern the outline of an enormous spiderweb constructed over the door; the strands were so many and so intricately intertwined that it looked the work of centuries. Mother Haella answered the door after several long minutes, first putting her face in the crack to determine who her visitors were and then opening it wide.

"Good day to you," Alasco shouted, with the sort of cheerfulness reserved for old people whose hearing and sanity are in question. "I've brought Quaestor Rhenford to see the grimacing wizard."

The ghost witch muttered something too faint to hear and beckoned them in. Liam ducked beneath the doorjamb, eyes on the spiderweb, and only when he was safely past it did he examine the room.

Unclaimed bodies were a commonplace of any town or city that brought strangers together. Men and women away from home—or even away from their own neighborhoods—met with accidents, were murdered, or sometimes simply died. Their corpses could not be allowed to rot in the streets, and in the Southern Tier it was the responsibility of the Duke's ghost witches to provide a storage place, where they could be kept until claimed by a relative or, failing that, buried anonymously. The ghost witch in Southwark called her storage room a morgue; Liam had visited it several times while working for Aedile Coeccias, and had never found it unduly unpleasant.

Mother Haella's cold room, on the other hand, immediately sent a chill down his back. A patina of dust lay over everything, even the beams of the low ceiling that he drew his head down to avoid. There were a few windows along one wall, mere arrow slits, but tangled masses of birds' nests had been allowed to accumulate in them, cutting off most of the light.

The bodies in Southwark rested on widely-spaced

stone slabs; in Warinsford they lay on jury-rigged
wooden shelves, lashed together with rope and cobwebs,
piled like goods in a merchant's warehouse. There were
three sets of shelves against the wall opposite the windows, each set with room for four, though there were
only six residents that Liam could see by the flickering
light of Mother Haella's lonely candle.

Six dead *residents,* he thought, suppressing a shudder.
In the corner of the cold room there was a small pallet,
a clothes chest, and a table with a meal set out on it. *She
sleeps in here!* he projected, so amazed by the idea that
he had to share it with Fanuilh. The dragon did not respond.

''He's here,'' Mother Haella, standing by one of the
shelves, her fingers fluttering in the direction of the body.
''He's here.''

Taking a deep breath, Liam accompanied Alasco to the
shelf and looked down on the grinning wizard.

CHAPTER 6

LIAM GAVE A low whistle. "If his smile were any wider, the top of his head would fall off." Alasco giggled, mostly from surprise at the remark, and Mother Haella clucked, her nervous hands fluttering with disapproval.

The dead man's smile exposed his teeth all the way to the gums, and the corners of his mouth were drawn so far back they seemed about to touch his ears. His eyes were closed, the muscles around them tensed by the awful rictus. For several long seconds, Liam could not take his eyes off the distorted face, but finally, fighting his morbid curiosity, he forced himself to examine the rest of the man.

In life, Passendus had been somewhat on the short side, slim and small-boned with long, delicate fingers. His fingernails had been pared and filed smooth, his hair cropped evenly all around, and his mustache and beard shaved and trimmed down to a narrow strip; all the telltale signs of a fastidious man preserved by the charm Mother Haella had placed between his feet. It was an untidy bundle of herbs and twigs Liam did not recognize, held together by a twist of hemp. The ghost witch in Southwark made neater charms, but he guessed it did not matter much to those on whom they were used.

The wizard wore a robe of plain blue wool, cinched at his waist with a tooled leather belt; his shoes were wooden-soled and stout. Liam rubbed the wool of the robe absently between two fingers.

"This is what he was wearing when he was found?" According to the report, the wizard had arrived in Warinsford in the evening, taken a room at an inn, spent the next day on unknown business, returned to the inn, and been found the next morning on his bed.

"Aye," Alasco said. "He had other clothes, some finer, but they were all in his bags. Is it significant?"

"These look like travelling clothes," Liam remarked, "but they're clean."

"He may have had them washed at the inn. I can send a man to ask, if it please you. Shall I?"

"No need," Liam said. The young quaestor still seemed embarrassed about the sale of Aldyne Handuit's house, and was too eager to accommodate him. "I may want to go over there myself, so we'll spare one of your Guards the walk. There were no marks on the body at all?"

"Naught that we could see. Should there be?"

Liam turned to Mother Haella, who hovered nervously nearby, like a glass dealer with a shopful of clumsy clients. "Was there any spirit?" Ghost witches had a spell, he knew, that allowed them to see a person's spirit shortly after death, and by examining the spirit they could often learn important things about how the person died.

Mother Haella's eyes grew round and her hands stopped fluttering. "I did not—did not think to—I did not." She looked stricken; her lips moved soundlessly and her eyes roamed restlessly about the room, as if hoping to find the spirit she should have sought as soon as the body was brought in. Liam sighed, more than ever grateful that he lived in Southwark, where the Aedile was not corrupt and the ghost witch not a fool.

"No matter," he said. "You've, ah, you've taken off his clothes? I mean, you've checked his whole body and found nothing?"

"Naught," Alasco said, but he sounded as if he doubted himself.

Liam clapped his hands together to dispel the gloomy mood brought on by the mistakes he had uncovered. "Good, good, I'm sure you couldn't miss anything. I think we ought to take a look at his things now, don't you?''

Alasco agreed with a heavy nod. Mother Haella hardly even noticed their departure; they left her standing by Passendus's shelf, still casting her gaze around the room as if the spirit was hidden there, and she had only to remember where.

''Was the spirit passing important?'' Alasco asked on the stairs, wincing in anticipation of the answer. ''Mother Haella well knows she should check it, but she's ancient, and forgetful—though the corses never stink; she sees to that well enough.''

''It would have been nice, but it's not that important.'' Liam spoke absently, his mind on other things. *Have you ever heard of a spell that makes a man laugh himself to death?*

No, Fanuilh replied, *but there is a spell that will cause that sort of smile. It is one of the cantrips learned in the Quadrivium, a very simple spell. I have told you about it before—I can cast it myself.*

Liam frowned. *You said you could make a man laugh uncontrollably,* he projected, *not grin himself to death.*

The spell does not kill, and the laughter does not last for very long, a few minutes at most. But it might serve to put a man off balance, if he were taken by surprise.

Let's assume it was your nasty little cantrip. Does that tell us anything?

It tells us there was a wizard involved, and that he or she most likely killed Passendus.

Alasco stopped by a door in the middle of a long hall. ''The armory,'' he said, and opened the door.

Liam gave a noncommittal grunt. *Why a wizard? The Handuits aren't wizards, and yet they conjured up a demon easily enough.*

Racks of weapons and armor filled the room, pikes and bows and long-handled axes, cuirasses of leather and shirts of chain; Liam could see the dull tinge of rust on much of the metal, and the unstrung bows looked warped. The armory was not well-maintained, and he guessed sourly that Cuspinian probably received a sum from the Duke for its upkeep.

Demonology is not magic, as such, Fanuilh explained. *It has many similarities, but in form, not substance—the niceties of control, the elements of ritual. True magic, even the casting of cantrips, requires the manipulation of astral power, which only a wizard may touch. Hence, Passendus was killed by a wizard.*

Or the best jester in Taralon, Liam projected back, and then, before the dragon could respond, added, *Hold on for a moment.*

Alasco pulled a travelling bag from the bottom of one of the racks, and began emptying it onto a small table near the window. Indicating the first things he removed— a small glass bottle held in a silver frame, a gilt stylus, and a scroll of paper—he said, ''These were in his room, on the table. The missive ends abruptly, as though he were interrupted, but of disturbance there was no sign. All was in its place, and he was on his couch. The rest was in his bag.'' He continued to lay out the contents while Liam, curious, picked up the bottle. It held a golden-colored liquid, so thick and viscous that when he tilted the bottle it only sluggishly followed the angle of the container. He replaced the bottle on the table and took up the stylus. Heavy enough to be solid gold, the nib held a far sharper edge than gold could have; it drew a small bead of blood from his finger when he tested it.

Sucking his finger and feeling foolish, he put the pen down and unrolled the scroll. The paper was shiny, as smooth as glass but with a tendency to roll itself up. He held the paper flat and read the golden letters:

Magister Escanes—I am arrived in Warinsford somewhat ahead of schedule, as you can tell. Have almost completed my business here—I sought out our man this afternoon, and he is to come to me here shortly. There will be no trouble, and the Guild elders will see that there was no need to call for the

*Cold Chamber. Once that is disposed of, I shall
move on to my other business. With any luck, I shall
return to Harcourt within a few months.*
  I have misjudged the time. More later.

Liam turned from the window and handed the paper
back to Alasco. ''You've read this?'' The young quaestor
nodded. ''What do you make of it?''

''The man who attended him was his murderer?'' It
was a question, not an answer.

His thoughts elsewhere, Liam hardly heard the
younger man. He had heard of divisions within the Guild,
an impending schism between the so-called Whites, led
by the Harcourt chapter, and the Grays, who tended to
associate with the Torquay chapter. If Passendus, whose
letter indicated that he was in close contact with Escanes,
the Magister of Harcourt and one of the most powerful
wizards in Taralon, had come all the way to Warinsford
to see ''our man,'' it seemed a safe assumption that he
was a wizard as well, and an important one at that. The
real question was, why had Passendus wanted to meet
him at all? Was he on their side of the split, or on the
wrong side, or on no side at all?

''Think you this Passendus meant to take off his guest
but was killed himself ere he could? He writes that
there'll be no trouble.'' Alasco asked. He was re-reading
the wizard's letter. ''Oh—but then he says there'll be no
need for the cold room.''

''No,'' Liam said, thinking it through aloud. ''Passendus might have been sent to sway the man to Harcourt's
side, and expected to succeed. And if they wanted him
on their side, he must be a powerful wizard. That spell—
the laughing cantrip—is an apprentice's spell, but it
might have taken Passendus by surprise. He wouldn't
expect a great wizard to use it.'' *Would he?* he added,
projecting the thought.

Fanuilh's reply came instantly; it had been waiting for
him to ask. *No. And more importantly, if Passendus were
laughing so much he could not speak, there are many*

spells he could not cast. It would be an effective way to disarm him. Furthermore, he did not write that there would be no need for the cold room.

The dragon had read along with him; he had forgotten to reknot the silver cord. Annoyed at his own slip, and at the dragon for taking advantage of it, he spoke aloud. "Cold room, cold chamber—is there a difference that matters?"

Alasco looked puzzled. "None that I know of, Quaestor. But y'are right, it does say 'chamber.'"

There is a difference, Fanuilh told him, its thought once again prepared in advance. *Mage tradition holds that the Guild disciplinary body has a secret arm, called the Cold Chamber, which metes out sentences of death to offending mages. Its members are unknown and their methods a mystery. Master Tanaquil doubted its existence—he called it "the Cold Chamberpot"—but for most wizards it is a sort of bogeyman, fear of which keeps them obedient to the Guild elders. And now, it seems, we have proof that it exists.*

Liam relayed the gist of this to Alasco, mulling it over himself. "Perhaps Passendus held the Cold Chamber over our man's head as a threat. But that still leaves the question of what he wanted from him. What offense would make Passendus come all the way from Harcourt?"

"I couldn't say, Quaestor. Could the murderer have stolen something belonging to the Guild?"

It is possible, Fanuilh told Liam, *but the thing stolen would have to have been very valuable. Crimes requiring the attention of the Cold Chamber are few: killing another mage in an unsanctioned duel, direct disobedience of a Magister, revealing Guild secrets, or abandoning the Guild.*

"If the Whites in Harcourt controlled the Cold Chamber, could they use it to their advantage?" Liam asked aloud.

"What are Whites?"

Liam waved aside Alasco's question, focusing on the

dragon's reply. The three-way conversation was becoming cumbersome, and he did not want to continually interrupt his thoughts to explain things to the other man.

If the members of the Cold Chamber were Whites, certainly. Remember, it is not really a place, but a group of mages. If even half of the stories told about the Cold Chamber are true, then they are very powerful indeed; having them as allies would be a great source of strength for the Whites.

"Are there any wizards that you know of in Warinsford?"

Alasco shook his head. "None. The Duke's no friend to wizards, as you might know."

Liam cocked his head, bemused by the comment. He knew that the Duke had enacted several laws limiting the practice of magic in the Southern Tier, but something in Alasco's tone sounded odd to him, as if he ought to have a special reason for knowing it. After a second he decided to leave it alone, however; he had more important things to think about. The Cold Chamber he put aside as well, deeming it an unproductive tangent. Whatever the Guild's response, or that of its semi-mythical punitive force, the identity of "our man" was the central question.

"All right," he said, "we assume he's a wizard, and that he's concealing himself deliberately. Coeccias says wizards tend to be noticed, that they have a certain air about them that's unmistakable. Warinsford's small enough that if you're not aware of him, it's because he doesn't want you to be."

From the hallway a man called Alasco's name, and he excused himself for a moment. Liam hardly noticed his departure. "Can you keep a lookout for any magic that's performed?" he asked Fanuilh. The dragon could sense the use of magic as a disturbance in the astral plane.

Yes. You should also know that the pen, the letter and the ink are enchanted. What Passendus wrote would immediately appear on a similarly enchanted piece of paper, presumably in Harcourt.

"Very nice," Liam said, "but even less relevant than

the Cold Chamber. We need to know why Passendus was looking for 'our man,' not how he communicated with the Guild.'' He began poking through the contents of the wizard's bag. ''Of course, he might not even be in War-insford anymore. He might have killed Passendus and fled.''

It is possible.

Alasco cleared his throat from the doorway. ''The men are here, Quaestor Rhenford—those who answered the call when Handuit was taken off.''

Hold that thought, Liam told the dragon, and went to interview the Guards.

When they returned to the armory Liam was worried and Alasco was perfectly miserable.

''I can't make sufficient apology, Quaestor Rhenford,'' the young man said. ''I'll not blame the men—it's been four months, when all's said, and memory is a net in which only the biggest fish are caught—but we've done you a great disservice, I fear.''

Neither of the Guards remembered the pentagram in any detail; even with prompting from Fanuilh through Liam, they could offer only the vaguest of descriptions, nowhere near enough to determine which kind of circle the Handuits had drawn. Liam had thanked them and apologized for the inconvenience.

''Stop worrying about it,'' he told the young man, trying to be gracious, though he was beginning to be worried himself. His earlier confidence about the crime was gone, replaced by a grim determination that seemed futile the more he considered it. Unable to disprove the Handuits' story, unable to check the nature of their spell, he racked his brain for alternatives.

Passendus's death nagged at him as well, and his eyes turned constantly to the wizard's belongings, laid out on the small table. Some clothes, a thick spellbook with a lock, and a leather satchel divided into compartments, each containing vials or small bundles of herbs or powder-filled twists of paper that Fanuilh explained were the

requisites of various spells—he could find no clues in
any of them, but he could not stop looking. Widow Saffian's instructions notwithstanding, he did not want to
abandon the search for the wizard's killer to concentrate
on the Handuits. He wanted to solve both mysteries, and
he admitted to himself that it was a question of pride, of
proving himself to the court.

Bells rang somewhere in the town, and with growing
dismay Liam counted the peals. When they reached
twelve he shook his head fiercely to clear it—the morning was gone.

Pride or not, he scolded, *you're not getting anywhere.*
Taking a deep breath, he went to the window and forced
himself to reorder his thinking.

It was a matter of information: he had none of any real
use on either crime, and no promising places to search
for it. Once or twice while working with Coeccias he had
run into similar impasses, and the only way around them
was to look in the unpromising places.

You got a good start with those Guards, he thought
ruefully. *Completely useless. Who else could be as useless as that?* Ideas began to come to him: first the maidservant who had raised the alarm—she might be able to
confirm or deny some of the Handuits' story. And there
was the bookseller who supplied the spell; he was dead,
but if Aldyne Handuit had pursued magical texts, he
might have approached others. Besides, they might shed
some light on the dead bookseller, and where he had
acquired the spell. Beyond that he would be reduced to
talking to people who had known the Handuits in any
capacity—friends, associates, former servants, relatives—
but he hoped it would not go that far.

For Passendus, the field of unpromising places to start
was much smaller. He could jar the memory of the owner
of the inn where the wizard had stayed, in the hope that
something useful might be dislodged. There was a
chance, too, that someone had seen the wizard as he went
about his business in Warinsford, but that was a very long

shot indeed, and would probably require more time than
he had.

On the other hand . . . He turned from the window to
the table, and threw back the flap of Passendus's satchel.
Wizards always needed herbs and powders for their
spells, so it would make sense to check Warinsford's
apothecaries and herbalists. Even if Passendus had not
visited them, "our man" might have, particularly if he
had been in the town for any length of time.

It was a poor start, but a start nonetheless. Energized,
Liam clapped his hands together. "Quaestor Alasco!"
The young man had been observing his silence, half-
respectfully and half-fearfully. "I want to take a tour of
the city, and I want you to lead me. We have a lot of
stops to make, and not much time."

"A tour, Quaestor Rhenford?"

"Why not?" Liam laughed at the younger man's expression of bewilderment, even as he guided him to the
door. "It's a beautiful day in spring, and I've never been
to Warinsford before. Come along, Fanuilh."

The dragon hurried after them, paws clicking on the
floor.

Before they left the Water Gate, Alasco insisted on
checking in with Cuspinian, to let him know where they
were going. By a series of corridors and staircases he led
the way to a dungeon like the one where the Handuits
were kept, except that it was not as far below ground;
tiny windows, set too high in the walls for the prisoners
to reach, allowed a little light to trickle in. There were
men and women in almost half the cells, and their eyes
tracked Liam and Alasco as they walked by. Cuspinian
stood at the door of the second-to-last cell, arms folded
across his chest, glowering at the man Provyn was interrogating.

"I swear to you, my lord," the prisoner said. He was
an ugly youth with unruly black hair curling down to his
shoulders. "I swear that I never used magic in making
love to them. Yes, I seduced them—but I did it like any

man would, and let me tell you, they were all more than willing!''

"The ladies give you the lie," Provyn said haughtily. "They say when you came to them, they fell into slumber, and when they awoke . . . well, it was done. Have you any proof of their prior affections? Letters, sweet words, locks of hair—aught?''

The man shook his head sadly. "We exchanged nothing. If their families found anything like that, we would have been ruined.''

Provyn continued his questioning while the Aedile snorted with disgust and turned away to acknowledge Liam and Alasco. "The rogue ensorcels three young ladies of quality, ravishes them, and calls it love! What would you, Vaucan?''

"I thought to tell you that Quaestor Rhenford would go on a tour of the town.''

"There are some people I want to see," Liam hastily explained. "At the inn where Passendus stayed, some booksellers, that sort of thing. I didn't get much from the Handuits.''

"They're close, and sly," Cuspinian agreed. "Look where you would, and find what you may. Have you seen Milia? No? If you do, then, be so good as to ask her to attend us here when she's time.''

They promised they would and departed up a different staircase, which led to the courtyard, where Liam paused and looked back at Fanuilh. He frowned, trying to decide whether or not to bring the dragon along. Its presence tended to distract whomever he was with, and while that could be useful when interrogating criminals, he was not sure it was the best thing when he only planned to look for information.

Stay here, he told it. *We can't have you upsetting the whole city.*

Yes, master.

He rejoined Alasco, who was waiting at the entrance of the Water Gate. If the quaestor thought it odd that Fanuilh had been left behind, he gave no sign.

"Well, then—where would you go, Quaestor Rhenford?"

First they visited the booksellers. Liam counted off the people he wanted to visit and Alasco decided that they were the closest, a short walk from the riverfront. There were only two, both small shops tucked at the end of Token Alley. The first had recently been replastered, and stood out from the shabby pawn shops that surrounded it.

"That was the shop of the vendor as died of late," Alasco explained. "It was bought up, stock and building together, by a man from Carad Llan, a good man, for all that his accent's atrocious."

"Bought since Aldyne Handuit's death?"

"Aye. Think you there might be a connection?"

"No, we needn't bother him. We'll try the other one."

The second bookshop fit the alley, its plaster cracked and crumbling to reveal the withes beneath, but the interior surprised Liam. It was a tiny, immaculate room, walled with shelves on which the books—predominantly quarto and octavo volumes but with the occasional outsized folio—were laid face out; a table in the center of the room held yet more books. A small man in a smock of gray wool stood over the table, lovingly dusting his stock. He squinted at them, smiling uncertainly.

"Good day, good day, sirs, can I help you? Is there a title you seek? I've a sampling of the latest masques and plays from Torquay."

"Good day, master," Liam said. "We're actually not here—"

"Or it may be you sought devotionals," the bookseller went on, "of which it may be said that I've the finest selection in Warinsford."

"No, thank you, we're not interested in—"

"Philosophies, now, are the jewels of my collection. Priceless wisdom," the old man rhapsodized, his eyes roaming dreamily over the shelves, "put down and

bound up, ever at hand, for consolation in time of trouble
and as a guide to virtue in happiness.''

"Master Corkeran," Alasco said, laying a gentle hand
on the man's arm, "we're here for information, but not
that kind which is written.''

"Is that young master Vaucan?" the bookseller said,
clutching Alasco's hand and squinting at his face. "It is!
Though by right I should say Quaestor Alasco, for which
I apologize. Why just this morning your father was by,
and bought of me a *Geography* of Strabo.''

"My father collects books," Alasco told Liam, blush-
ing unaccountably, then turned back to the bookseller.
"Master Corkeran, I've brought Quaestor Rhenford with
me, who serves with the Areopagus. He would speak
with you.''

"In course, in course," the man said, looking vaguely
in Liam's direction. "Forgive me, Quaestor, for my eyes
are not what they were. Too great a devotion to my children, I fear," he added, sweeping his hand in a broad
gesture that took in all the books in the shop and almost
hit Alasco in the head. "How may I serve you, Quaestor?''

"I was wondering if you knew a man named Aldyne
Handuit.''

"Oh, aye," the bookseller said, his face falling. "A
sad thing, his death, a sad thing, but if you'll play with
fire, you'll be burned.''

"How so?''

"Oh, he was ever seeking out dark knowledges, so
Fortune saw fit to make them his downfall. Why, twice
or thrice a month he came in, asking to know if I'd heard
of any for sale, though I told him many and many a time
that I'd no truck with it. The surprise is that it was his
brother who called up his doom. I'd've thought him the
agent of his own destruction.''

Liam nodded, pleased. While it did not specifically advance the case against the Handuits, it did allow him to
begin separating the truth from the lies in their state-

ments. "So you sold him nothing—but your neighbor did?"

Corkeran harrumphed. "Aye, the gods grant him mercy. My late neighbor, Master Relly, did not scruple to traffic in forbidden works."

"Do you know where he got them?"

"Hedge wizards, cranks, false alchemists, counterfeiting rogues—for that the most of his 'works of magic' were forgeries, look you, and Master Handuit was much practised upon."

"He wasn't killed by a forgery," Liam pointed out, and the bookseller nodded.

"Oh, aye, I only said the most, not all. There were some few that were genuine, or so Relly claimed. Not many, mind you, but some few. How he came by them, I know not—though hold a moment, hold a moment!" He raised a forefinger, commanding silence, and furrowed his brow, trying to remember. "It comes to me, now! There was a man, in the fall of last year, come to me essaying the sale of divers books. He couched his words delicately, but it soon came clear that they were magical, and that he should not have them. I sent him off with a flea in his ear, in course, but I'd wager he went next door, and sold them to Relly!"

Liam shot a look of amazement at Alasco. "Can you describe the man?"

"Alas, no," Corkeran sighed. "These eyes are not what they once were. My fingers do me the service of eyes, now, and I know my books by touch. But I can vouch for this: he was from the west, the Midlands or Harcourt. He'd a tongue like yours, Quaestor Rhenford—and y'are a Midlander, unless I miss my guess."

"That I am," Liam admitted, grinning at Alasco. "You're sure this man was from Harcourt?"

"Or the Midlands. The accents are close."

"And this was at the end of fall, six months or so ago?"

"Just so, just so. Near Uris-tide, I think."

For the sake of thoroughness Liam pressed Master Corkeran for details of the man and his books, but though he was eager to please, he could remember nothing beyond what he had already told them. After a few more minutes they departed, the bookseller seeing them to the door and recommending himself to Alasco's father.

CHAPTER 7

IN THE STREET, Liam laughed out loud for the sheer pleasure of it. Corkeran's revelation had only enlarged the dimensions of the mystery—of both mysteries, Handuit's and Passendus's—without offering any solid clues, but it was information nonetheless, and from such a surprising source that he could not help but consider it good luck.

Alasco smiled happily. "Y'are pleased, Quaestor?"

"Very much so. And please, call me Liam. Now, I want to go to the inn where Passendus was killed."

"The inn? I had thought—that is, Handuit's maidservant is nearby, and with these news of him so fresh, do you not wish to follow it up?"

"We are going to follow it up," Liam explained patiently, though he could not see how the young quaestor had missed the connection. "At the inn."

"In course," Alasco said, too quickly. "It's not a great a distance." He started out of the alley.

"You don't see?" Liam asked, catching up to him.

The other man flushed and spread his hands unhappily. "I fear I don't . . . Liam. And you'd honor me by calling me Vaucan."

As they walked, Liam explained. "The two deaths are linked, you see. 'Our man' sold Relly the spell that he sold to Aldyne Handuit, which Elsevier and Roviana used to kill him. And he's from Harcourt, which is where Passendus is from. Now do you see?"

It was midday, and the streets they walked were thronged with people buying and selling and tending their business. They separated to get around a fishwife arguing with a customer, and when they came together again, Alasco was still perplexed.

"I see the parts, but not the whole. Did our man kill Aldyne Handuit?"

Liam took a deep breath and started from the beginning, as far as he saw it. In a way it was useful to him, forcing him to order the events, skeletal as they were, in his own head.

Six months before, his hypothesis ran, a man from Harcourt arrived in Warinsford with some books of magic to sell, books that he was not supposed to have. "We'll have to make a number of assumptions here, but that's all right. First assumption: he sold them to Relly. Second assumption: Aldyne Handuit bought some of the books, or at least pages from them, individual spells." Handuit was interested in that sort of thing, so the assumption seemed valid, and it was certainly true that around two months later his brother and sister-in-law cast a spell that they claimed to have found among his papers. "The demon they summoned killed him, but we're not sure if that was an accident or not. To find that out, we need to know what sort of spell they cast."

"Which you'd know, if we'd kept that cursed circle," Alasco burst out. Liam waved the interruption aside and continued.

"Who would know best what sort of spell they cast?"

Alasco brightened, but he still phrased his answer as a question. "The man who sold it to them?"

"Exactly!" Liam said, and then qualified, "Which is Relly, who's dead. Second best, though, would be the man who sold it to Relly. Now, Aldyne Handuit is dead, and we skip forward to last week."

Passendus arrived in Warinsford from Harcourt, searching for a man who had done something to make him a candidate for the attentions of the Cold Chamber. He found and arranged a meeting with the man—almost definitely the same man who sold Relly the books of magic. "Now we assume that 'our man' killed Passendus, but I think that's safe. So, he can tell us what sort of spells he sold. All we have to do is find him, and make him talk.''

Comprehension dawned on the young quaestor's face, and then, suddenly, he frowned. ''Won't he be a great wizard?''

''Ah, yes. Yes, that seems likely.'' Liam frowned too, realizing the implications of his own train of thought. How were they supposed to arrest a wizard powerful enough to kill Passendus? ''Maybe Areopage Saffian will have an idea. Anyway, we can cross that bridge when we come to it. We have to find him before we can arrest him.''

Alasco digested this somberly, as if it were a piece of great wisdom, and they walked a while in silence.

Passendus had lodged at the Riverman, an inn on a busy street that fed into Warinsford's market square near the Pantheon. Even in the afternoon it was a busy place; tables in the street accommodated the overflow from the common room. Liam and Alasco threaded their way through the densely packed clientele into the cool, cavernous interior.

''I'll fetch the innkeep,'' Alasco said, and disappeared into the crowd, leaving Liam to inspect the Riverman. The common room was twice the size of the one at the Duke's Arms, and the men behind the bar seemed less like tapsters than soldiers on the barricades, determined to protect their barrels and casks from the siege of the thirsty. It was not the sort of place he would have expected Passendus to choose—too loud and too popular, ill-suited to the clandestine business of the Mages' Guild.

And an awfully public place for a murder, he reflected, *even in the middle of the night.* Of course, for all he knew the place might be as quiet as a tomb after dark, but it still struck him as odd that no one had seen Passendus's killer entering the inn. *Unless he never came in—* He cut the thought off and rapidly projected another one. *Fanuilh, can the laughing cantrip be cast at a distance?*

No, the dragon replied after a moment. *The person to*

be enchanted must be in view. It is so for all the apprentices' cantrips—causing laughter or itching, putting a man to sleep, stanching the flow of blood from a wound—all require proximity.

All right. Liam rolled his eyes and muttered, "Itching."

Alasco returned, the reluctant innkeeper in tow. "This is Quaestor Rhenford, who would—"

"Your servant," the innkeeper interrupted, sketching an ungracious bow. "If you'll with me, we'll to the room." Before Liam could reply the man whirled away, plowing through the crowd. They hurried after him, catching the running flow of commentary he tossed back at them as he led the way upstairs to the room in which Passendus had died. "Though on my life it seems hard, cruel hard, as if I hadn't already lost so much custom on the score of this cursed wizard, now I must be taken from my station. At the end, see you, where he asked, though curse his asking, I say, and his dying as well," the innkeeper growled. "And he would have his own, wouldn't share—and now I've a room I cannot let, for the stench. And if the stench grows any worse, how'll I let these others?" There was a faint smell in the corridor, an unpleasant odor that Liam could not name. "My beer's not watered, my rates are paid, I give the gods their due, and yet my guests are taken off in their chambers, and leave a foul smell behind. A visitation, it is, and none of my drudges'll even enter the place to clean it." He made to leave but Liam stopped him with a hand on his arm.

"I'm sorry to keep you," he said, his commiseration bordering on the sarcastic, "but I need to ask you just a few questions. Very brief ones. The night the wizard was killed, were you busy?"

"Busy? Gods, Quaestor, I'm ever busy with the cooking, the cleaning—"

"Customers. Did you have many customers? Was the common room full?"

"Aye," the innkeeper said, recognizing Liam's impatience.

"And how many rooms had you let?"

"On this floor but two, the wizard's and another, to a man I'll vouch for."

"Good," Liam said. "Is that man around? Can we speak with him?"

"He's a rider-out for the Duke's wool, Quaestor—he's gone on to the north."

"We spoke with him the morning after," Alasco put in. "He'd heard naught."

"All right, just one more question—the wizard went out in the morning, didn't he? Did he give any indication where he went? Ask directions of anyone?"

The innkeeper gave it some honest thought, then shook his head. "Not that I know of, Quaestor, and I brought him his bread and ale myself. He held converse with none ere he went out, nor after he returned."

Liam smiled and let go of his arm. "Thank you very much. We'll let you get back to your work." While the innkeeper stalked back down the hall, Liam opened the door of Passendus's room and beckoned for Alasco to follow him in.

The smell was much stronger inside the room, and instantly identifiable: rotten flesh. Alasco gagged into his palm; Liam cursed and pinched his nose shut. "Gods! If I hadn't seen the body in the cold room, I'd swear it'd been left here." Even as he said it, though, Liam knew it was not true: the smell was powerful, but not powerful enough for a whole corpse. *Part of a corpse,* he thought, and winced at the image that rose in his mind.

"Think you," Alasco coughed, his eyes watering, "think you it's some haunting? A visitation?"

"It's probably a rat in the walls," Liam said grimly, determined to drive away the picture he had conjured up. The wizard's body had been whole in the cold room, he reminded himself. "A rat or a cat that got behind the walls, that's all it is."

Apart from the smell, the room was unremarkable: a large canopied bed, a table and chair, a stand for a wash-basin. There was a single window, and Liam squeezed past the bed to open it. Warm spring air immediately cut the stench of decomposition, and he let go of his nose. The window looked out on the main street, and at such an angle that no one below could look in.

"Amazing what a little fresh air will do."

"But at night," Alasco pointed out, "the vapors and humors would—"

"So Passendus was found on the bed?" Liam interrupted, not interested in hearing any more about the harmful effects of night air. He knelt down and lifted the blanket out of the way; there was nothing underneath the bed but dust.

"Aye, in all his clothes, and atop the covers."

He stood up and examined the canopy; its top was a good foot beneath the ceiling, and the center of the material hung down over the bed. "A cat," he murmured, "or a rat," and tapped the sagging canopy with the back of his hand. Something bounced against his knuckles, and he flinched.

"Quaestor?"

Liam had once met a wizard with a cat for a familiar, and he had a tiny dragon; he wondered what other kinds of animals could be familiars. He squeezed past the bed again, pulled the chair over and climbed up on it to peer over the top of the canopy. In the pool of shadow in the center of the cloth lay an animal that might have been a very small fox in an advanced state of decay; from the way its muzzle pointed one direction and its stiff legs another, he guessed that its neck had been wrung.

With a little shudder, he climbed down from the chair. "I should've brought gloves, but I think our friend the innkeeper should probably clean that out himself."

Alasco's eyes were wide with wonder. "What is it?"

"A fox cub, I think. I'd guess it was Passendus's familiar and that 'our man' killed it and tossed its body up there."

"A fox cub? Whyever would he do such a thing?"

"Familiars are much more than pets, you know. And

they can be . . . unpleasant . . . when their masters are
killed.''

"It seems a vicious thing, still. Perhaps it gives us the
measure of the man, eh?''

Liam made a noncommittal noise; he was not convinced that the dead familiar told them anything concrete.
That the killer used his hands, and that he hid the corpse,
seemed important to him, but he could not figure out
why.

Despite the open window, the smell was still unpleasant. ''Well,'' he said, ''I think we've learned all we can
here. Let's go tell the innkeeper about his unwanted
guest.''

The innkeeper eyed them skeptically while Liam described the source of the smell, but as soon as they turned
for the door he dashed for the stairs, shouting for his
drudges as he went.

Out in the street Alasco waited patiently for Liam to
make up his mind.

If he had been in Southwark, Liam would have asked
Coeccias to send Guards around to all the apothecaries
and herbalists, trusting the Aedile to instruct them properly as to what information to seek. He would not do that
here, however; the mistakes already made aside, he did
not know any of the Warinsford Guards, and was sure
that he would second-guess whatever news they brought
back. *Which means making the rounds yourself. And after
that, we'll see. . . .*

''Why don't we get something to eat,'' he suggested,
''and then we'll start looking at apothecaries.''

Alasco shrugged agreeably and started back into the
Riverman. Liam stopped him and pointed toward the
market square a block away. The bulk of the Pantheon
hovered beyond the collection of stalls and booths, its
spire sharp and distinct against the clear blue sky. ''We
can get a roll or something.''

The market sprawled in a disorderly way across the

square, completely without plan or organization, though those selling the same things tended to cluster together. They searched among the twisting alleys and odd, circling paths created by the random erection of tents, scaffolded booths and wooden stalls, and finally found a stall selling sausages at the far end of the square. Liam bought two in rolls and began eating even as he led the way to the point where the market met the Pantheon. A fountain stood in the gap between the squares, surrounded by stone benches. Alasco followed, eyeing his own greasy sandwich with suspicion.

Liam chuckled, his mouth full. "You don't eat outside much, eh?"

"My father's cook . . ." Alasco began, and let the sentence trail away.

"You live with your parents?"

"Aye, with my family. My father is a merchant here."

"Would he have heard of the *Tiger*?"

They found an open spot on one of the benches and sat. The sun warmed them but not too much, and the fountain was a cool presence at their backs; Liam bit into his lunch happily.

It took Alasco a moment to remember the Handuits' supposed investment, and then he shook his head. "No, I fear not. He's not much in the Freeport trade. He deals far more in that with the Suevi Principalities." He nibbled at his lunch, decided that it would not kill him, and then added, "To the northwest, see you, beyond Alyecir."

Liam nodded; the Principalities were one of the few places he had never visited, but he knew where they were. "So you're a second son, I take it?"

In the middle of another tiny bite, Alasco cocked his head quizzically. "No, nor a third or fourth, but first. Why?"

"Nothing, nothing," Liam said quickly. "It's just that most first sons follow their fathers, and the later ones seek out . . . careers."

"Oh, aye, it's mostly so. Truth, my father was sore

hurt when he learned my determination to join the Guard, even as quaestor. But I tell you, it appeared to me much the more interesting of the two paths at the time—and so I've found it. You must know of what I speak: bringing justice to th'affairs of men, and righting what's wrong, watching and warding the city.''

"I'm actually more of a merchant, myself," Liam said. "I'm only a temporary quaestor—but I think I understand you." In truth, he did not, but he tried to sound as if he did. Alasco blushed and addressed himself to his lunch.

"It must seem a small thing, the Guard of Warinsford, after that of Southwark."

"Oh, it's not very different," Liam said. *Except that the Aedile in Southwark doesn't line his pockets quite so much.*

"Still and all, I'd warrant it a real challenge to be of Southwark's Guard. To stand so close to the Duke! Pray, tell me, what sort of man is he?''

He's a nice enough fellow, but he's got an awful grasp of geography. "I'm afraid I don't know. I've lived in Southwark for less than a year, and he doesn't come there much. Not that I'd meet him if he did, but there you are.''

The young quaestor jerked his head back as if Liam had struck at him. "Never met him?" he asked, incredulous. "But surely you—that is—you say you've never met him?''

"I've never seen him," Liam said, puzzled by the other man's reaction. "Eight months ago I'd never even been in the duchy."

Alasco stammered, his face red with embarrassment. "Your pardon, Quaestor. It's only that Aedile Cuspinian said— Forgive me, I mistook some words of his. It is nothing."

"What words?"

"Only that he guessed you were in well with the Duke, or something like, from some words he'd had of the Areopage, and of Quaestor Provyn. I beg you, forget I

spoke, and breathe not of word of it to the Aedile. It's
my error, not his.''

*That would explain Cuspinian's sudden change in at-
titude,* Liam reflected, smiling to himself. *And if it required a little misconception, who am I to disabuse him
of it?*

''Don't worry about it,'' he told Alasco, and wondered
how many more times he would have to say those words
in Warinsford. ''I'm finished—we should get back to
work.''

They washed their hands in the fountain, and were
about to go back into the market when they heard Widow
Saffian calling them.

''Quaestor Rhenford!'' She approached them from the
Pantheon, the offering basket on her arm, surprise and
displeasure on her face. ''What do you here? Did you
never reach the Water Gate?''

For no reason he could discover, Liam felt guilty in
the face of her disapproving stare. ''We took a few
minutes for lunch, Areopage, but now we're going on.''

She frowned heavily at Alasco. ''And could you find
no food more convenient to the prison?'' Bright spots of
red had sprung up on Alasco's cheeks over his earlier
misunderstanding; now they grew darker, and his mouth
moved without producing a sound.

''We were nearby—at the inn where Passendus
stayed,'' Liam said, his inexplicable feeling of guilt ebbing fast. ''We weren't at the prison.''

''And whyever not? Is not Passendus there? Are not
the Handuits there? Whatever could you want at the
inn?'' She crossed her arms awkwardly, the basket getting in the way, and glared at him.

''I've already spoken with the Handuits, and Passendus isn't saying much, Areopage. I needed some more
information, so we came out to speak to the innkeeper—''

''And the bookseller,'' Alasco added timidly.

''—and the bookseller, who told us some very interesting things.'' Liam briefly outlined what they had

learned about "our man" and the connection he proposed between the two deaths. As he spoke the Areopage's stern expression loosened somewhat, and by the time he finished she was nodding grudgingly. "So now I thought we would talk to some apothecaries—wizards often deal with them, you know."

"Aye, aye, for material components." She spoke distractedly, as if something else had just occurred to her. "It is well-conceived. I was merely startled to see you out of the Water Gate. We rarely felt the need of going out, in past years."

"Ah." *How did she expect me to learn anything if I didn't leave the prison? How did* she *ever learn anything without leaving the prison?* It struck him as singularly bizarre to travel all the way to Warinsford just to sit in the dungeon of the Water Gate. And then he realized that she had not come to the prison all morning—as far as he could tell, she had been in the Pantheon since they left her, hours before.

She frowned in concentration, fretting at her lower lip. "It's well-conceived, but this with the Cold Chamber likes me not. I'd thought it a story."

Where she was praying for her husband, Liam reminded himself. *She's allowed to be a little odd.* "Apparently not."

"No," she muttered. "No, so it seems. I'll leave you to it then, Quaestor Rhenford. I needs must consult with— I needs must consult. I'll see you back at the Water Gate."

She walked off into the market, caught up in her own thoughts, leaving Liam to wonder with whom she wanted to consult. Only when she was out of sight did he snap his fingers and curse. "I should have asked her about arresting wizards," he said, and then shrugged. "Not that I think she'd have an answer."

"I fear not," Alasco agreed. "She is much preoccupied."

"Hm. Yes. Well—those apothecaries won't come to us. Where's the closest?"

Alasco considered a moment, then followed Widow Saffian's path into the market.

Liam listened to the town's bells toll six, and cursed all apothecaries, druggists and herbalists with great feeling. Intellectually, he had known that it was not the most promising way to look for "our man," but their success with the bookseller and at the Riverman had inflated his hopes. They started in the market, talking with the hawkers of herbs and spices, home remedies and harmless potions, but none of them remembered meeting or selling anything unusual to a Harcourter in the past six months.

"That's all right," he said confidently as they left the market. "He probably wouldn't want to deal out in the open. Let's try the shops." Alasco, buoyed by his confidence, eagerly led the way.

By six they had visited every establishment in Warinsford, ranging all over the town from the riverfront to the walls and once, briefly, beyond them. Both confidence and eagerness were gone; a sour frown had etched itself on Liam's face, and a look of apprehensive dismay on Alasco's. None of the shop-owning apothecaries and herbalists knew anything of a man with a Harcourt accent looking to buy supplies. Even the man whose sign boasted an appointment from something called "The Royal Guild of Wizards" could tell them nothing—he dealt with middlemen, transhipping the occasional package to a factor in Torquay.

As the afternoon wore on, Liam's frustration grew, and so did the length of time he spent in each shop, pestering the owners with questions he knew were pointless. He could not help himself, however; if "our man" was as powerful a wizard as Liam imagined him, then he would need the powders and herbs and odds and ends that only an apothecary could offer.

"And that damned blind bookseller!" he exclaimed as the last bell of six shivered in the air.

They were back on the riverfront, not far to the south of the Water Gate, outside of the very last shop, a dingy

place run by a quack who catered to the strange medic-
inal ideas of sailors and bargemen. Alasco began to say
something—undoubtedly an apology—and Liam cut him
off, certain that he would be obliged to throw the young
quaestor into the Warin if he expressed his heartfelt sorrow one more time.

"I'm afraid I've wasted your time," he said, beating
Alasco to the apology-punch, and taking a small amount
of pleasure from it. "I'm very sorry. We'll just have to
go back to the Water Gate. Maybe the Areopage or Aedile Cuspinian will have an idea."

The sun was westering in the sky but the boardwalk
was still busy with stevedores and wagons. Ships slipped
by in the river, their sails silhouetted against the golden
glow, and the surface of the water glittered prettily. Liam
ignored it, thrust his hands in his pockets and started
slouching back to the prison, regretting the loss of the
afternoon in what he now was forced to recognize as a
fruitless search.

He took some small consolation from their visit to the
druggist who provided the husband and wife with their
"medicines": the herbs they bought were meant for
grinding into liniments; eaten, they produced just the
symptoms Roviana Handuit exhibited. Liam had ordered
the druggist to send along a harmless substitute with the
day's order. *Mistress Handuit will make a remarkable
recovery, I think.* Still, it was a vindictive sort of consolation, and showing that she had deliberately made herself sick to elicit pity was not quite the same as showing
that she and her husband had summoned up a demon to
tear their brother to pieces.

Children suddenly surrounded them, dragging Liam
from his brown study with their shouts and screams as
they fiercely contested possession of a ball. The game
swept past him like a rain squall, and he paused to watch
it recede down the boardwalk, a slight smile twitching
over his lips.

"Merchants' children," Alasco volunteered, gesturing
to the houses that lined that section of the waterfront.

"They should play elsewhere, but their homes are here."
He hesitated, then pointed out a neat and cheerful-looking
house with an elaborate brick facade. "That's Aldyne
Handuit's, as was."

"That?" It did not match its image in his mind; he
had pictured an abandoned wreck, shutters swinging in
the breeze, red eyes peering out from darkened windows.
And so it might have looked, he reflected ruefully, *four
months ago, when the murder was new.* He squared his
shoulders, took a deep breath, and touched Alasco's
shoulder. "Come along—we don't want Aedile Cuspinian to wait dinner for us."

They walked on in the lengthening shadows, leaving
the cheerful house behind, the dark bulk of the Water
Gate growing before them.

CHAPTER 8

FROM THE GUARD on duty at the Water Gate, they learned that the other members of the court had returned to the Duke's Arms, and that they were expected there at eight for dinner. Alasco offered to accompany him back to the inn, but Liam assured him he could find his own way; he wanted some time alone, to order his thoughts and play with the few pieces of information they had discovered. They shook hands and Alasco hurried off down the riverfront.

Fanuilh, Liam projected, when the young man was out of sight. *Go back to the inn and wait for me there.*

Yes, master.

He stared up at the roofline of the Water Gate, and a few moments later saw his familiar rise above it and disappear to the east. Then he began retracing his route to the Pantheon, and from there to the inn; while he walked, chin sunk down on his chest and eyes focused on his feet, he brooded over his cases.

With the outline he had given the Areopage as his starting point, he began poking and prodding for weak spots in the argument, hoping to find avenues of investigation he had not yet explored. The structure held together well—the flaws were all in the details. If "our man" was a wizard, why had he not gone to the apothecaries? It was possible that there was nothing he needed from them, but that rang false to Liam; in six months a real wizard would need *something*. Fanuilh had told him that its former master visited the apothecaries in Southwark once or twice a month simply to keep abreast of what was available.

He briefly considered the possibility that "our man" was not a wizard at all, but rejected it. How else could he have killed Passendus, if not with magic? No joke was funny enough to have engraved that smile on the corpse's face.

Then he's a wizard who performs very little magic, which still leaves you nothing to go on beyond his accent. And Harcourt accents were not that uncommon, since the city dominated Taralon's trade, and sent out its merchants and sailors all around the kingdom.

With a scowl, Liam put thoughts of "our man" aside and concentrated on the Handuits. The single missing detail—the nature of the spell cast—irritated him immensely. One irksome oversight on the part of the Warinsford Guards had robbed him of the chance to settle the matter easily, and while he was convinced of the couple's guilt, his certainty was not proof.

Passing the Pantheon, the streets now in shadow and the sun sunk below the buildings to the west, he began to question that certainty. The Handuits based their defense on the claim that they had raised the demon in order to foretell the future, and that its murderous rampage was purely accidental. *But if that's not true—if they're as guilty as you think—why use a demon? It's like dropping a boulder on an ant.* "Our man" used magic to kill Passendus because he was a wizard, but the Handuits were not wizards; neither magic nor demonology was natural to them. If they wanted their brother dead, why not stab him, or poison him, or push him out a window?

The answer came to him with surprising ease, just as he arrived at the Duke's Arms, and he stopped outside the door, afraid that if he entered the noisy inn he would lose hold of it.

Master?

Wait, he commanded, not even looking around to see where Fanuilh was.

People knew Aldyne Handuit collected forbidden manuscripts. People knew he had an interest in magic, and that he was a solitary, secretive man who locked himself

up in his chambers at night. And if, one night, he conjured a demon which escaped his control and killed him,
who would question it? Liam imagined the grieving
brother and sister-in-law, tearfully shaking their heads.
*"Poor brother Aldyne—always meddling with things best
left alone!"*

The theory also made sense of some stray facts about
which he had been curious. The blue chalk and the dead
cat were in the upstairs room because the demon was
supposed to leave them there, as proof that Aldyne himself had cast the spell. The Handuits were caught in the
middle of erasing their pentagram not because they were
trying to hide the lesser offense of skrying, but because
they had not expected their brother to scream. *They didn't
think the demon would be so vicious, so careless—they
expected to have plenty of time to clean up before the
body was discovered.* Instead, Aldyne Handuit's screams
and his attempts to flee the demon had roused the housemaid and alerted the Guard, and they were caught in the
act.

A slow smile of comprehension crept across Liam's
face, and when it was complete, he projected the idea
and a question: *What do you think of all that?*

Fanuilh dropped out of the sky right before him. *It fits
together,* the dragon admitted.

Scooping up the dragon, Liam entered the inn and
headed for his room. *You think it makes sense?*

*Yes—but it does not tell what they did with the spell
when they were done. And it is possible for a wizard to
go a long time without visiting an apothecary. Unlikely,
but possible.*

Liam frowned. *Forget Passendus for now. I want to
talk about the Handuits. I assume they couldn't give the
spell to the demon to plant in Aldyne's room, right? The
demon would destroy it?*

To his relief, Provyn was not in the room. He shut the
door and locked it, then took one of his travelling bags
from the corner and started unpacking it, all the while

continuing his conversation with Fanuilh, slipping into speaking aloud from time to time.

Yes, it would. If they meant to lay the blame on Aldyne Handuit, they would have had to put the spell in his room after they had dismissed the Lord.

"And if they gave it to him before dismissing him?"

That is impossible. They would need the spell to do that. You can see for yourself—it is in the book.

He took the *Daemonologia* from his pocket and flipped through to the page Fanuilh specified. At the top it said "A Lord Assassin" in large letters, and below that was the text of the spell. Much of it was gibberish to him, chants in some guttural, half-unpronounceable language, but what he could read was fairly clear. The pentagram was drawn, the demon summoned and told who to kill. Only when the person was dead could the demon be dismissed, and that only from within the confines of the protective circle. The dismissal was complicated, and included a long line of the ugly language to be spoken aloud. After the last line of the spell there was a space, and then a warning:

> *Few calamities equal that of a Lord Assassin loose in the earthly plane, unchecked by a controlling Mage. Remember the fate of Ryssel of House Severn, who failed to dismiss the Lord Assassin he released on House Jaffadwyn, and whose lands, as well as those of his enemies, were devastated thereby.*

The book is very old, Fanuilh explained. *The reference is from before the Seventeen Houses came to Taralon.*

"Ah." Tracing the diagram of the pentagram with his forefinger, he projected, *We can assume they dismissed the Lord, right?*

If they had not, there would not be a person alive in Warinsford today.

He imagined the Handuits in their cellar, safe within the pentagram, dismissing the demon they had sum-

moned and listening fearfully while the Guards searched
the house, calling out their names. They would dismiss
the demon, and then what? They tried to get rid of the
pentagram, but what did they do with the spell?

They would destroy it, he thought. *Or would they?* In
the picture in his mind, they were using the book he
himself was holding. One of them—Elsevier in his imagination—was erasing the pentagram, while Roviana held
the book. *And how? Burn it?* The *Daemonologia* was
heavy in his hands. There would be no fireplace in the
cellar, so they would have to light it from a candle or a
lantern. It would take forever to burn.

They were not using a Dominia Daemonologia, *master. They were using just the single spell.*

"How do we know that? They've lied before—they
could have lied about this." *Think about it,* he continued
silently, still following the outline of the pentagram with
his finger. *"Our man" comes from Harcourt, a powerful
wizard. He doesn't need his copy. It's a book for apprentices, after all. Why would he tear it up? Why not
just sell it whole?*

The bookseller, Relly, might have torn out the pages.

*No. Aldyne Handuit would have bought the whole
thing.* The more Liam thought about it, the more the idea
grew on him. It appealed to him for its neatness, the way
it told him something more about "our man" and tied
him in with the Handuits, and because it matched the
image in his head of Roviana Handuit rushing around the
cellar, desperate to get rid of the incriminating book.

We cannot know that, Fanuilh reminded him. *We cannot even know "our man" supplied the spell, whether in
a book or as a separate piece of paper.*

"Yes, yes," Liam said, waving at the dragon to be
still. *She could not burn it, so what would she do with
it? Hide it! She must have hidden it somewhere in the
cellar!*

We cannot know that, Fanuilh repeated, ever cautious.

"No," Liam admitted, grinning, "but we can find
out."

• • •

Freshly shaved and dressed in his best clothes, Liam descended to dinner at eight o'clock, immensely pleased with himself. The *Daemonologia* was tucked safely out of view at the bottom of one of his bags with Fanuilh to guard it, and he was sure again that he had a way to prove the Handuits' guilt.

Although he was not late, he was the last to arrive at the private dining room, and they sat down to eat as soon as he came in. Cuspinian announced that Mother Haella would not be joining them and rang a bell for the first course to be served.

It was altogether a different meal from the one the night before. At first it seemed as if the Aedile meant to hold forth just as much, but he directed a number of his comments to Liam, and allowed him an opportunity to agree with some of his own opinions on wine and the proper presentation of game.

"Oh, of course," Liam said, when Cuspinian asked him with a beneficent smile whether he did not prefer his meat as cutlets rather than in stews. Since the servants had only a moment before laid a platter of cutlets on the table, it struck him as the diplomatic thing to say. *How close does he think the Duke and I are?* Liam wondered.

"A cutlet is a perfect thing," the Aedile said happily. "Allow me to help you to one." Liam held out his plate for the proffered piece of meat.

Widow Saffian, who had sat through the first few courses with a quiet air of preoccupation, suddenly laid down her knife and fork and cleared her throat. "I wonder, Aedile Cuspinian, if we might break our rule, and discourse on pressing matters."

Carefully depositing the cutlet on Liam's plate, Cuspinian gestured with the serving fork as if it made no difference to him. "As you will, Areopage. It may be that heavy thought will breed appetite. Go to, if you will."

"My thanks." She put her elbows on the table and began kneading her knuckles as if they pained her. "This business with the Cold Chamber oppresses me, and I wonder if we should meddle in it.''

Provyn gulped heavily at her words, but Cuspinian only looked puzzled. "The Cold Chamber?''

"A most powerful arm of the Mages' Guild,'' she explained. "It is entangled in the matter of the wizard's death. I would not trespass in Guild business without better knowledge than we can glean before the session tomorrow. I wonder if we might close the matter.''

"The Guild's not to be trifled with,'' Cuspinian ventured mildly.

"Nor the Cold Chamber!'' Provyn was so agitated he could hardly bring himself to say the words. "I think y'have the right of it, Areopage. We'll leave this among wizards.''

Liam glanced around the table as if they had all lost their minds. "Forgive me, but what does the Guild have to do with it? A man's been murdered—the law's been broken—why should the Guild be involved?''

"The man was a wizard,'' Cuspinian pointed out.

"And not even of the duchy,'' Provyn added, sniffing. "Why should we bother ourselves about him, if it's the Cold Chamber's business?''

"It's not,'' Liam said, suppressing the urge to tell the fat quaestor not to speak of things about which he was ignorant. Instead, he turned to Widow Saffian. "Passendus's letter specifically said that the Cold Chamber need not be involved.''

Alasco, who had been silent until now, spoke up hesitantly. "Wouldn't it like the Guild if we conned and caught the man who'd taken off one of their own?''

"Exactly!'' Liam could not believe what he was hearing; that they should officially ignore a murder for fear of offending the Guild—or because the victim was not from the duchy—struck him as close to cowardice.

The Areopage shook her head. "It likes the Guild not to have others meddling in their affairs. What's more, Quaestor Rhenford, you needs must admit that we've not made much progress on that front.'' Liam would have protested, but she gently forestalled him. "No, I think it best to let the matter lie. You'll concentrate your efforts on the Handuits."

"Aye," Provyn said, leaning back with a smug expression. "When y'have proved the obvious, then you may meddle with the Cold Chamber."

Liam's mouth twitched, but he kept control of himself. "Very well," he said, through gritted teeth. "If you wish it, Areopage Saffian."

"I do. And I wouldn't have you think it a reproof," she went on, with a meaningful glance at Provyn. "The case was deep, Quaestor Rhenford, and yet y'have delved far into it. Alas, not far enough, I fear. I think it best to let it lie."

Somewhat mollified, Liam bowed his head. "As you wish."

An uncomfortable silence shrouded the table; only the judge was unaware of it. She returned to her meal with an air of satisfaction while the others fidgeted uncomfortably in their chairs.

"Come, sirs," Cuspinian burst out after a minute or two, "this is too much. Banish this heaviness, and have a glass of wine with me." He snapped his fingers and a servant made the rounds of the table, filling glasses.

Toying with his glass, not drinking, Liam turned again to Widow Saffian, adopting a nonchalant tone. "I wonder, Areopage, will I have time tomorrow morning before the session to do some looking around?"

Cuspinian answered for her. "Why, in course! The session'll not start till after noon. You'll have the whole morning." He stopped, glancing at Widow Saffian. "Unless, it may be, that the Areopage has aught else planned."

"No," she said. "You may spend the morning as you wish. Quaestor Provyn has still some inquiries to make as well, do you not?"

"I do," the fat quaestor admitted. "The matter of Lons Kammer is most delicate, and I must to the young ladies in question in their homes. It would not do for them to have to appear before the court. And there are some other, trifling matters—that Muskerry, and's false potions, wants but a moment of attention to clear up. As for the rest, they're all well in hand.'' The dig at Liam and his unsolved mysteries was unmistakable, but he did not rise to the bait. He would have the Handuits "well in hand" by noon, he was sure, and if he was ordered not to pursue Passendus's killer, he could hardly be blamed for not finding the man.

''These cutlets are excellent,'' he said, smiling cheerfully at Provyn. ''Don't you think so?''

There was no point in getting into a sparring match with his roommate, much as he disliked the man. He tried, and for the most part succeeded, to view the whole thing philosophically. Provyn was an ass and Widow Saffian was shying away from non-existent dangers, but the Areopagus was their concern, not his. He was only along to do what was asked of him.

In that frame of mind, and with Cuspinian's help, he managed to enjoy the rest of the meal. The Aedile, trying to recover his own festive mood, plied them all with wine and new dishes, eliciting Liam's opinion of each. He even went so far as to gradually expand his circle, asking what Provyn thought of the partridge pie, and how Alasco liked the cheese.

Slowly, the conversation grew more general and more genial, Cuspinian carefully directing the flow of talk but allowing everyone to participate, so that by the time the table was cleared and the Oporto brought, they were all in a far better mood. Liam admired the skill with which the Aedile had drawn them out—he had even managed to make Provyn say something sensible, if only about partridge pie—but though he was comfortable, he could not help but imagine some ulterior motive on the part of the man at the head of the table. After every witticism, every telling point and every generous remark, the Aedile looked either to him or Widow Saffian, as if to gauge their reaction. And as the meal wore on and the unpleasant discussion of court business receded, it seemed more and more to Liam that Cuspinian was only barely suppressing a wink, that with the increase in good feeling he was trying to establish some bond between them, to get across some message.

And it's not just that he's a good host, Liam reflected. *There's more than that. He wants something from me.*

His stomach ached from too much food, and his head spun from a glass too many, so it was a moment before he made the connection: *Because he thinks I'm a friend of the Duke.* Exactly what the Aedile might want he did not know, but he was simultaneously amused by the idea and embarrassed at letting the misconception continue, both in a comfortably hazy way. The wine whirled through him, preventing him from taking the whole thing too seriously.

Luckily, whatever he wanted, Cuspinian did not choose to discuss it that evening, and when the dinner was over, simply bade them all good night with a promise to see them at breakfast. Alasco went with him, after bowing several times to the room at large, and the Areopage took a candle and set off for her own room. Left alone with Provyn, Liam muzzily recollected his roommate's cutting remarks from earlier in the night, and the two walked the halls enveloped in a frigid silence.

A fire had been laid in their room, and to Liam it was unbearably hot. They prepared for bed in silence, though Liam sighed heavily from time to time and projected occasional stray thoughts to Fanuilh.

Can you believe that ridiculous cap? Provyn wore a long, tasselled nightcap to bed, pulled low down over his ears. *He must sweat away most of his brains while he sleeps.*

Yes, master.

He took off his boots, grunting as each one came free, and stripped down to his smallclothes. *What do you think of the Aedile, eh?*

He certainly behaved oddly.

He wants something.

Is it wise not to disabuse him of the notion that you are an intimate of the Duke?

Liam climbed into bed, covering himself with the lightest blanket he could find. *Can't hurt.* He was suddenly very sleepy. *You're watching that book?*

Yes, master. It is safe.

Wake me early. Drifting away, he hardly noticed the explosive breath with which Provyn blew out the candle, and when the fat quaestor got in on his side of the bed, Liam did not stir.

As always when he drank too much, Liam had vivid dreams. For most of the night he was at sea, on a ship out of the Freeports in which he had once served as surgeon. The weather was fine, a not-too-stiff wind out of the west, but the ship had no crew and he had to run between the masts and the rudder, trimming sails and checking the course, constantly back and forth, back and forth, never tiring but never quite catching up with all the work that needed doing.

Later the crew appeared and he simply stood at the rail, staring at the horizon, not even remembering how he had worked the ship single-handed; then he was watching the ship from a distance as it flew over the waves.

Finally something came from the ship, a tiny speck that grew larger and larger until he could see that it was Fanuilh.

Wake.

Stifling a groan, Liam forced himself to rise and stumble over to the washstand. He washed his eyes and felt a little more awake, but it seemed to him as if the night had been too short. The sky outside was still dark, and the only light in the room came from the banked fire.

Are you sure it's morning?

It is the same time as yesterday, Fanuilh replied from its spot by his bags.

He was not hung over, just tired, so tired that all he wanted to do was crawl back into his bed, even if he had to share it with Provyn. Frowning sourly at the sleeping man's bulk, he stretched his arms over his head. *You have to get past that,* he scolded himself. *He's just a sorry little man who thinks too much of himself and his position. Get past him.*

Resolving to do just that, he began dressing.

CHAPTER 9

LIAM HAD THE dining room to himself: no one from the court had arrived yet, and the three serving girls who were laying out the breakfast curtseyed and disappeared at his entrance. After a brief survey of the sideboard, he took his usual seat at the empty table with a bowl of honey-laced oatmeal.

First things first. Massaging his temples and clearing his head as much as he could, he closed his eyes and put himself into the trance. It was harder this time, but he managed it finally, shoulders slumping and breath slowing, and the silver cord materialized in the void, sprinkled with dew like a ship's line in the morning. He half-remembered his dream and imagined a complicated sailor's knot in the cord. When he was satisfied, he slid easily out of the trance and back to the world, confident that Fanuilh was now barred from his mind.

He had left the dragon on guard by his bags, not for fear of any petty thieving, but because he was nervous about leaving the *Daemonologia* unprotected. The book weighed heavily on his mind, as did its erstwhile owner. Widow Saffian had closed the case, and he had reconciled himself to that, but he could not help thinking about "our man."

As he ate, he reflected how much easier the investigation would have been at home. If Warinsford were more like Southwark—if Cuspinian and his men were more like Coeccias and his—his course would have been clear: send Guards to talk to ship captains and caravan masters, asking about a lone Harcourter who had arrived six months before. Innkeepers, too, because "our man"

113

would have had to stay somewhere when he first arrived,
and wizards were not notorious for their low profiles. A
kitchenmaid or a potboy might remember a mysterious
Harcourter, and Liam did not think they would have to
check all the inns; he could not imagine the man he
sought staying in a sailors' dive. He would have stayed
in one of the better inns, if only for a few days, and after
that he would have rented or bought more permanent
lodgings in the same style.

The more Liam thought about it, the more easily he
could picture the man in his head: an imposing figure,
physically like Cuspinian but with the dangerous aura of
deep wisdom and deeper power associated with wizards.
He would make an impression, Liam was sure: people
would notice him.

Immediately after thinking that, he realized the problem: no one *had* noticed. He was wrestling with this con-
tradiction—that, while Liam imagined him a highly
conspicuous character, "our man" had apparently
slipped into Warinsford without anyone taking notice—
when Alasco came in. Happy to put aside the thorny
question, Liam bid him a good morning.

"And to you, Liam. You passed the night well?"
Alasco's complexion was back to its normal milk white,
and a barely-restrained excitement danced in his eyes. He
wore a tabard of grey velvet with the Duke's foxes
worked on it in red, fine black hose, and tall boots of
leather so highly polished they looked like obsidian.

"Very, thanks. You're ready for the sessions, I see."
Bright red spots bloomed on Alasco's cheeks, and he
hurried to the sideboard to hide his embarrassment. "My
clothes, aye. My father'll be there, and my good mother
would have me the glass of fashion, to make him think
the better of me. She'd the livery ordered especially for
appearing in court, and at official functions. But come,"
he went on, returning to the table with a full plate, "pray
tell, what have you in store this morning?"

"A visit to the Handuits' old house, first of all." Liam
explained his hope that the spell might have been hidden

somewhere in the cellar, and though Alasco did not seem convinced, he nodded as if he were.

"And what then?"

"Then? Then I thought I would come back here and change for the session." He had only brought two sets of good clothes with him, so he was wearing the same clothes as the day before, having changed only his shirt and his smallclothes. They were clean enough, he judged; he did not smell, at least, and there were no obvious stains.

"Hm." Alasco picked at his food for a few moments, gathering the courage to say what was on his mind. "The session is not truly open til noon. I wonder, Quaestor—"

"Liam."

The young man's blush deepened. "Aye, Liam. I wonder, then, what might be made of this with Passendus, if the morning is not all run out after the Handuits' cellar."

Liam caught his meaning immediately and wagged his finger at the other man. "Oh, no, my friend. I know what you're thinking, and it's not a good idea. The Areopage has warned us off that, and whether we like it or not, she's in charge."

"But does it like you?" Alasco demanded.

"No, but it's not our place to question here. We had our chance, and she decided against us." Recalling the idle thoughts he had indulged in before the quaestor's arrival, he was a little surprised at the indifference he heard in his own voice.

"But it's not just," Alasco blurted. "A man's taken off, and we're not to con him out for that this Cold Chamber may be involved? You said yourself that there must be law!"

"Well, yes," Liam admitted, liking the young man afresh for the passionate way he clung to abstract principles, but at the same time taking a slightly cynical pleasure from pointing out the way things were. "But there must be law in all things, and the law here consists in obeying the Areopage."

Alasco held up a finger, smiling craftily. "Ah! You'll pardon me, but it doesn't. There is no written law for it. The Areopagus is a creation of the Duke, with a commission to try such cases as are brought before it by the Aediles of the towns in which it sits. We bow to Areopage Saffian, as we did to her late husband, out of custom and respect—the deepest respect, see you, the deepest— but she doesn't command us. If we bring a man before her, she needs must try him!"

From their reception in Warinsford and the way Cuspinian deferred to Widow Saffian, Liam had formed the idea that the Areopagus was above the local authorities; the news put him off balance. "Fine, so you can make her try him. But we'd still have to catch him, and we can't do that in one morning. Besides, are you going to keep a man like that in a cell?" Liam asked, recalling his mental picture of a powerful wizard. "I doubt it. That was probably part of her decision. Look at what he did to Passendus—do you want him doing that to you, or to one of your men? No, the more I think about it, the more I think she was right. We should just let it go."

"For that it's dangerous? Are we to shrink from our duty for that? There are no qualifiers in the oath, that we may put aside our duty when it grows too hot for us."

Liam, who had not sworn any kind of oath on joining the Areopagus, smiled. "Maybe so, but there's a difference between 'too hot' and 'certain death.' You can die in the Duke's service, if you want, but at least have it count for something."

They cut short their conversation when Provyn entered the dining room. The fat quaestor did not notice Liam's guilty look, nor the defiant blush on Alasco's cheeks; he dropped a sheaf of paper on the table and went straight to the sideboard.

"The report you requested," he said over his shoulder. "From Deepenmoor. It seems there're no capital cases at the Fair."

Liam eagerly picked it up; given their angry words the morning before, he had not expected to see anything for days. "Thank you, Quaestor, thank you very much."

"Don't think of it," Provyn said grudgingly, coming back to the table. He carefully spread a napkin across the front of his jacket, royal purple with spills of lace at throat and cuffs, and ate a few bites from his plate, all the while looking Liam up and down. "I trust y'are not going to wear that at the session."

With the report in hand, Liam could not take offense. "I'm going to change."

Grunting his reluctant approval, Provyn focused on his breakfast, and for a time the only sound in the room was that of his chewing. Liam flipped through the pages, not really reading, his eyes lighting on the occasional random phrase or name. Demons were involved, he could tell, and he had resolved to read the report carefully to find out just how when Widow Saffian came in, escorted by Cuspinian.

"Good morrow, sirs." She went to the sideboard and filled a plate without really noticing what she took, then came back to the table and launched into a discussion of the day's work. "The number of mundane cases is so great, we needs must not dawdle. I rely on you, Quaestor Provyn, to provide all that is necessary for speeding through your cases. Tell me the details beforehand, and we'll keep the exposition to a minimum. In fine, we'll take them all a great clip, and hope to be through them by sundown. Quaestor Rhenford, as we've dispensed with Passendus, we'll spend a bit more time with the Handuits. Think you you can uncover some proof against them this morning?"

"I hope so, Areopage." He wanted to ask her what she meant by exposition, but she hurried on.

"That's well. Should you not, we've the lesser charge to fall back on. It'd like me to settle the matter, but if needs be the flogging will suffice."

She turned back to Provyn and began questioning him about the details of his cases, which ones he considered closed, which he was in doubt about, and Liam listened carefully, trying to glean more details of how the court session would actually run. Provyn assessed his cases mainly in terms of how long they would take to present, and seemed to think that most of them would go smoothly, qualifying several, however, with the proviso that they were "without interruption or outburst."

Sensing a way of learning more without seeming too ignorant, Liam waited for a pause in the other man's monologue and asked, "Pardon me, but what does that mean? 'Without interruption or outburst?' Can the prisoners raise objections?"

Cuspinian chuckled and shook his fist meaningfully. "Only if they would be thrashed."

"Oh no," Widow Saffian said. "They've a chance to speak, but only at the proper time. See you, the courts're open here, for that the charter requires it." Noting Liam's puzzled look, and guessing at his greater confusion, she continued, "The town has a charter, granted these three years past by the Duke. In the main it speaks of tariffs and rates, but not the smallest part of its import is that courts and trials such as ours must be open to all. In fine," she concluded, "they may act much as the chartered merchants of Southwark, treating justice as so much theater for their amusement. Here's more: any man may declare himself a Friend of Truth, and force a statement on the court."

"A Friend of Truth," Provyn snorted. "Ha!"

"Come now," Cuspinian said, "we're not so small a place that we may be ridiculed. If they may have these rights in Southwark, why may we not have them here?"

"Oh, I grudge you not the right," Widow Saffian replied. "There may be Friends of Truth here as anywhere. It's only that they stand not so much upon their rights in Southwark as you do here, perhaps for that they are yet new to you. I recall to you that man two years ago, so drunk he could scarce stand, who tried to get that hedge-witch off by claiming he'd lain with her on the night of her crime."

The Aedile grinned. "Aye, aye, and she gave him the lie in his face, and begged for her punishment rather than confess to relations with him. I'll warrant you we overuse the privilege, but I promise you there'll be no drunks this year. I caused word to be spread that none but honest statements'll be taken, and I've not heard of any who would stand up this session.''

Alasco quickly agreed. ''Truth, Areopage, it's like to be quiet and peaceful. There's none'll stand up for those we're bringing before you.''

Liam almost regretted their assurances; the session had begun to sound like more fun than he had anticipated. Now that he had a better idea of what it would be like, however, he was aware of the morning slipping away, and he was anxious to get started. ''I should be about my work, if I may. And if you're finished,'' he added, turning to Alasco, who jumped to his feet, ready to go.

''As you will. Do not be late to the sessions—Quaestor Alasco knows the place.''

With bows all around, Liam gathered up the report and went out, Alasco on his heels.

Bright and warm, it was a perfect spring day, with a fresh breeze and a beautiful, cloudless blue sky. Liam sauntered happily along, one hand in his jacket pocket, touching the report to make sure it was really there.

As he left the inn, he sent Fanuilh a thought to stay by his bags. He was not much worried about the book, but he did not want his familiar along. They were going to a private house, the home of people with no connection to the crime he was investigating; there was no reason to scare them with the dragon.

Soon enough he began to wish he had left Alasco behind as well; the young man breathlessly pleaded his case throughout the whole walk to the riverfront.

''Only listen, Liam! We've the morning before us— who knows what we might not learn! Surely y'are not indifferent to this murderer?''

''It's not that at all. I'd be happy to catch him.'' He would, too, if only because it would be something to hold up to Provyn. There was more, though: he really did not

like the idea of a man getting away with murder just
because he was somehow associated with the Guild.
Nonetheless, he was deterred by his own mental image
of "our man." Liam had built him up in his mind until
he was impossibly powerful, the kind of wizard who lev-
eled mountains and dried up seas. *What could we do with
a man like that? What jail would hold him? Who would
arrest him?* He tried to explain, drawing horrifying pic-
tures of what the enraged wizard might do until he began
to get through to Alasco.

"You think he'd do those things?" the young quaestor
asked skeptically.

"Smash the town? Lay waste the duchy? Vaucan, if
he's half the wizard I imagine, he could do much worse.
Say you put him in the Water Gate, eh? Do you think it
would hold him? He'd pull it down around your ears,
and then boil the blood in your veins for your audacity.
Think it through, my friend—it's not worth the trouble
of finding him if he's just going to kill you when you
do."

In a way he was scaring himself, but Alasco did not
press him any more, and they finished the walk to Aldyne
Handuit's old house in silence. The boardwalk was just
as busy as the day before, rumbling with carts and echoing with the calls of gulls and sailors. A serving maid
answered the door at their knock, and the sight of
Alasco's official tabard sent her running for her master,
calling "The Guard! The Guard!" before they could state
their business.

While they waited on the doorstep Liam found his eyes
drawn to the top floor, where the building narrowed and
there was only one window. *Handuit fell from there,* he
thought, and then corrected himself: *Not fell, was pushed.
Or he might have thrown himself out, to get away from
the demon.* When the master of the house finally arrived,
he recoiled a little from Liam's grim expression, and addressed himself to Alasco.

"Good morrow, sir," he said, rubbing his hands nervously on the front of his tunic. He was a slight, pock-

marked man with thinning hair and a drooping mustache. "In what may I serve you?"

Alasco smiled disarmingly. "I beg your pardon for disturbing you, master, but we've a small favor to ask of you. Y'are perhaps aware that there was a death in this house ere you came to live in it?"

The pock-marked man gave up rubbing his tunic and began brushing his mustache, glancing from time to time over his shoulder. "Aye, that I have—but've kept it from my wife and get, to spare them the worry. As it is, she wonders that we got the house so cheaply."

"I understand," Alasco said, in a confidential tone, "and we needn't involve her. But Quaestor Rhenford here is with the Areopagus, of which you may have heard?" The man nodded. "Ah, good. The court is sitting now, and we're looking into the death that was here, and Quaestor Rhenford and I would spend but a few moments in your cellar. We guess there may've been something left behind, some clue, that'll help us find the truth."

"The cellar?" He chewed uncertainly at his lower lip. "I think not, sirs. I keep some stock there, what'll not be harmed by the damp and the wet, and've been through it thoroughly."

"You say thoroughly?"

"From top to bottom," he swore solemnly.

"It'll just take a minute," Liam said, determined to get into the cellar. "We'd very much appreciate it, master."

Recoiling again, the man hastily agreed and led them through the house, fretting at his mustache. As they went into the kitchen, they heard people moving about upstairs and he grew frantic, tugging at the bolt of a trapdoor in the floor. "Please, masters, descend, descend—and should my wife come, not a word about the murder, I beg you!" The door came open with a crash, and from upstairs a sweet voice called out, "Rafe? Is it you?"

He lit a candle at the hearth, thrust it at them and

gestured them down. "Aye, my love! I'm with some gentlemen now, but I'll come to you anon!"

Liam hurried down the steps to the cellar, unhappy at putting Rafe out but seized with anxiety. *It's got to be here,* he told himself, *it's got to be here, got to be here.* He chanted the words over and over to himself, peering around the cellar, waiting for the candle in Alasco's hand to stop flickering.

"Is this all?" he asked when the light had steadied and spread, disappointment lurking at the back of his mind. They were in a single large room, entirely open except for two or three supporting beams. The ceiling was low, and he had to stoop, but he could clearly see that there was nothing there but barrels.

"So it seems," Alasco said.

Barrels of all sizes, from giant hogsheads to small firkins, marched in serried ranks to the walls. There were no nooks, no niches, no convenient hiding spaces; the floor was solid stone, the walls plastered a dull grey. Liam moved slowly among the barrels, his eyes desperately jumping from place to place, hoping and fighting back his burgeoning disappointment.

"Wine, do you guess?" Alasco asked.

"Oil of the leviathan," Rafe hissed from the stairs, and when they turned to look at him, he looked up to the kitchen and raised his voice: "And of the finest quality, good sirs, the finest! The men of Caer Urdoch brave the Cauliff Ocean and the terrifying beasts there to bring it out. Like a star for purity of light, with none of your stenches and smokes! But come, sirs, perhaps y'are perfumers? You'll know then what else the leviathan gives, and I've that as well." He rambled on, mentioning prices and amounts, and Liam ignored him, glaring angrily around the room.

It has to be here! Nearest the stairs were the biggest barrels, and he imagined them fat-bellied men, Provyns, laughing at him; behind them, stacked one on top of the other, were the smaller barrels, diminishing into the corners.

". . . sealed tight, and of proven worth. I'll stake my name on any of them. This lot's fresh from Caer Urdoch, and bought and paid for in Caernarvon, but I expect more anon—it's the season now, when the leviathans swarm that coast. . . ."

Except in one corner which was all big barrels, clustered around a small stack of casks. Liam squeezed through, pushing himself far into the corner, leaning over the top of the last barrels, and saw the shelf.

"What's this?" he called.

Hidden by the height of the large barrels was a wooden platform about a yard square fitted into the corner. The shelf rested on a pedestal of what looked like solid stone, and smaller barrels had been stacked on top of it.

"Ah—the ambergris! Y'have a hawk's nose, sir, a hawk's nose!"

Liam started yanking the small casks off the shelf, resting them on their bigger cousins, and Rafe hurried over just in time to catch one as it rolled away.

"That's but a cistern, sir," he whispered, taking the casks Liam handed him, stacking them gently, and keeping an eye on the stairs. "It filled from the roof, but the water had a foul taste, so I boarded it up."

Alasco moved forward to help but Liam waved him off, handing the casks in a steady rhythm to Rafe. "They're dirty." The wood felt moldy beneath his fingers, and had been smeared liberally with pitch. "We're almost there."

When the last cask was gone, he lay on his belly on top of the big barrels and pulled at the shelf. It slid away easily, and for a moment, he could not bring himself to look. He closed his eyes and prayed: *Let it be here.*

"But's just a cistern," Rafe began, puzzled, and then his tone changed. "Ah, it's dried up. Fo, the smell!!"

Liam opened his eyes and wiggled forward on the barrel until he could look into the cistern, ignoring the foul odor that rose up from it. "The light! Bring up the light!" Alasco handed him the candle and he dipped it down over the lip.

Hung with a green beard of moss, the mouth of a pipe jutted into the cistern a few feet down, and several feet beyond that, below the floor of the cellar, a film of muck and scummy mud coated the bottom of the tank. Atop the film, like a poisonous white mushroom, lay the bloated, moldy remains of a book.

While Rafe ran off to fetch something with which to fish out the book, Liam rested his elbows on the lip of the cistern and frowned.

Alasco thumped him on the back. "It's there! It's truly there! I'd not've credited it, Liam, but there it is! Gods, that's brilliant!"

"It's certainly there," he muttered. "And it's been there for four months." The smell from the bottom of the cistern wafted up to him—stagnant water and general rot—but he did not want to move away, as if by simply staring at the remains of the book long enough he could make it become what he needed.

From upstairs came Rafe's voice, shouting excuses to his wife, and then he skipped down the steps, a long-handled net in his hands.

"Four months?" Alasco echoed, the significance dawning on him as Liam took the net and, awkwardly leaning over the barrels, tried to snare the book. "Four months in the water?"

"Four months." Liam slipped the net around the sodden pages and lifted. A bubble of rank gas burst from the disturbed muck and he averted his head, but he kept his grip on the net and brought up his prize. "Four damned months."

Greenish-brown drops fell from the thing in the net, the boards of its cover warped and bent, its pages mashed together and unrecognizable.

They found a box, and Liam laid the ruined book in it as gently as he could. Rafe waited until his wife was out of the way and ushered them out quickly, closing the door on them with an unmistakable expression of relief.

In the bright sunshine, the box tucked under his arm, Liam suddenly noticed how dirty he was—pitch and muck on his hands, mud and dust and dark spatters of cistern-water on his shirt and jacket. "I'm a mess," he grumbled, shifting the box to a more convenient position and brushing ineffectually at his clothes with his free hand.

"Think you it's beyond help?" Alasco asked anxiously. "Is there naught we can do?"

"I can change," Liam joked feebly, but the young quaestor was too distraught to recognize the attempt.

"But the book, Liam, the book? Is it truly of no use?"

Liam sighed heavily, and started trudging toward the Water Gate. "I don't think so. We'll take a closer look once we're off the street—maybe try to dry it out—but I don't think so. I'll just tell the Areopage I couldn't do it."

He was not thinking of the Areopage, however; he was thinking of Provyn, and the fat quaestor's smug face.

CHAPTER 10

THEY FOUND THE Areopage in the Water Gate, arranging the order of the cases with Cuspinian and the chief clerk, and asked her to join them in the courtyard, where they had laid the wet book out in a square of sunlight. She glanced back and forth between Liam and the sodden mess of paper, as if trying to gauge which was less presentable.

"This is all that remains?" she asked. Liam nodded, and she leaned her head down on her shoulder, as if seeing the book from a different angle would help. "It could be a spellbook."

"Oh, it is," Liam assured her. He had convinced himself of that, and when Fanuilh saw the book it confirmed his belief. The dragon, at least, had no doubts that they had recovered a copy of the *Dominia*.

Widow Saffian was not so sure. "It *might* be a spellbook, Quaestor Rhenford. I would not doubt it, but as Areopage I must. You can see that it does not constitute proof?"

He nodded ruefully. He took some satisfaction from the fact that his guess had been correct, but it was not enough against the bitterness of having failed at his second case. *Ordered off the first, and failed at the second; quite a record, my boy, quite a record.* He made an effort to shrug and smile. "I suppose we should be happy just to have found it. If Rafe hadn't closed off that pipe, there wouldn't even be this much left."

"Could we not confront them with it?" Alasco ventured. "They know we know what it is—it may be that'll shake them, and they'll confess."

126

"But we don't know what it is," Widow Saffian pointed out with elaborate patience, and Liam added, "They won't confess for that." He kicked the book, which gave off a squelching noise. The others heard the bitterness in his voice and tactfully said nothing, staring with mournful eyes at the print of his boot in the wet pages.

Not for that, they won't, Liam thought to himself. *You don't hold to your story for four months in that miserable cell, dosing yourself blue all the while, and then fold because some fool dredges that up and shoves it under your nose. If it had been the real thing, now . . .*

The idea came upon him so suddenly that he opened his mouth to blurt it out, but then he snapped it shut, and forced himself to think it through. When he had, he turned to Widow Saffian and asked, "A confession would be proof, wouldn't it? I mean, without any other evidence?"

She looked askance at him, taken aback by the question. "In course it would! Confession is best—why, if they'd all confess, there'd scarcely be any call for a court at all! And if these'd confess, I'll let them hang first and finally, and then visit the ordeal on their corses." Then, seeing the thoughtful way he digested this, she spoke sternly. "But it must be freely given, Quaestor Rhenford. We've no truck with the question, the boot, the rack. The Areopagus has no need of such things."

"I wasn't thinking of torture," Liam said. "I was thinking about what Quaestor Alasco said, about confronting them with it. If it could be done in such a way that they didn't know that the book was useless to us . . ."

Crossing her arms on her chest, she frowned doubtfully. "It smacks of deceit, Quaestor, and a confession gotten by lies does not like me. And here's more—what when they see that the book is not proof? They'll recant, cry 'trickery,' and they'll have the right of it."

Liam winced; he had hoped she would not read quite so much into his idea. "It doesn't have to be trickery,"

he said. "I wouldn't lie to them, just mislead them a
little, let them infer things, you see? Let them trick themselves, as it were. You said yourself we weren't responsible for their assumptions."

"It still smacks of deceit," she said, but he could tell
she was wavering. "Allowing a prisoner to form an idea
is far different from forcing that assumption on him. And
there is the honor of the court to consider."

He folded his hands over his heart. "Areopage, I
promise you, the court's honor will be safe."

"And your own?" she asked, one eyebrow raised.

"Mine as well," he promised. "No lies, just the
truth—carefully prepared, but the truth, and all of it.
They'll hang themselves, I guarantee it."

His sincerity must have shown on his face, because
after a brief moment's consideration, she gave her assent.
"But be sure, Quaestor Rhenford, be sure that the Handuits do not cry foul in my court!"

Liam swore that they would not and started for the
prison exit at a trot, only to spin on his heel and called
out a question. "Areopage, what happens to illegal works
of magic? What do you do with them when you confis-
cate them?"

"They're burnt," she answered, "destroyed utterly."

"An excellent law," he said, and ran down the tunnel
to the riverfront.

The bells were tolling nine o'clock when Liam reached
the Duke's Arms, Alasco panting behind him, and he
went straight to his room, ignoring the looks he gathered
from the serving maids and drudges he passed. *Plenty of
time to get thoroughly cleaned up,* he thought; he was
eager to get back to the Water Gate to talk to the Handuits, but he did not begrudge the time. To make the
impression he wanted he would have to look the part.

He stripped off his dirty clothes and scrubbed his
hands and face clean with the lukewarm water left in the
washbasin. Alasco made a small noise of surprise at the
sight of his scarred torso, but Liam did not explain the

long-healed wounds and the young quaestor did not ask, leaving him in peace to plan.

Better to talk to them separately, he thought, *Elsevier first.* Apart, they would not be able to support one another, and Roviana could not feed her husband answers. If Elsevier broke, then he could confront her with that and have them both. Bringing the book was a risk: he could not lie and say it was the one they found in the cistern, which meant that the Handuits would know he had a copy of an illegal text. He doubted they would mention it to anyone, but the chance remained.

From his bag he took his best clothes and put them on, wishing that he had something more impressive, more wizardly—something like the flowing robes he imagined "our man" wearing, spangled with symbols and sigyls of power, like the caricatures of wizards in stage plays and puppet shows. *Might as well wish for a long gray beard while you're at it,* he thought, *and a glowing wand.* He had Fanuilh, though, and the book, and judged that they would be enough.

When he was clean and dressed, he gathered up his dirty clothes and turned to Alasco with the bundle. "Would you do me a great favor, Vaucan, and call a servant to take these away? I'd like to have them cleaned before we leave tomorrow."

"In course." When the young man was gone, Liam dropped the bundle and began scrambling through his bags, digging for the *Daemonologia.* He transferred the book to his sabretache, the smallest of his bags, and had that slung over his shoulder by the time Alasco returned with a drudge. The servant snatched the bundle of clothes from the floor and hurried out, carefully avoiding even a glance at Fanuilh.

"Shall we go?" Liam asked, tapping his shoulder for his familiar.

Alasco nodded, and Fanuilh leapt gently to its perch. *Where are we going, master?*

To the prison, he replied. *I want you to scare someone.*

*I do not understand why people are afraid of me. I do
not think I am very frightening.*

Try to be, Liam urged the dragon. *Try.*

On the way back to the Water Gate, Liam studiously
avoided catching Alasco's eye, sensing the questions the
other man was waiting for an opportunity to ask. He
could not guess which the quaestor would be more interested in—his scars or his plan for the Handuits—but
he did not have much to say about either. The scars were
just scars, most mementos of carelessness or bad luck
from his brief days as a mercenary, and he was still formulating his plan. Assuming an expression of deep
thought he hoped would discourage talk, Liam tried to
imagine his way through the imminent interview.

He did not consider himself skilled in the art of interrogation; Coeccias credited him with a genius for it, but
the Aedile did not recognize the difference between asking a great many random questions and asking a single
perfect one. That was the art, Liam knew; it need not
even be spoken, but the right question, properly presented, could unlock a mystery where a barrage would
fail.

They passed through the prison entrance, through the
courtyard, and down into the dungeon, relieving the
Guard of his keys and two candles as they went. Liam
chose a cell near the stairs, and had Alasco open it for
him. "Bring Master Handuit to me here, and then go
back and stay with his wife. Keep an eye on her, and
don't answer any questions she asks. And take your time
bringing him down here."

"As you wish," Alasco said, masking his disappointment at not being included in the interview. When he had
gone, Liam found a niche in the wall, fixed the candle
there, and then stood in front of it. Satisfied with the way
it threw his shadow over the cell, he opened his sabretache and pulled out the *Daemonologia.*

Subtlety was the key, he decided, combined with confidence in what he was saying. Bluster and threats were

effective for some men, but Liam believed himself singularly unthreatening, while a show of kindness would only serve to put the Handuits even more on their guard. And given that he was restricted to telling the truth, his misdirection would have to be very delicate, and his story would have to carry conviction.

He had the book open to the spell for summoning a Lord Assassin when Alasco returned, leading a reluctant Elsevier Handuit.

"Thank you, Quaestor," Liam said. "If you'd leave us alone for a few moments?"

Alasco ushered Handuit into the cell, paused for a moment, and then disappeared down the corridor, shaking his head. Liam returned his gaze to the book, holding it almost upright so that Handuit could see the binding. With the candle behind him the book was in shadow, but he moved his eyes as if he were reading.

Remember, look frightening.

Yes, master.

And when I tell you, can you make a noise—growl or something?

There was a pause while the dragon considered. *I think so.*

Good.

He looked up from the book and smiled pleasantly at Handuit. "Good morning, Master Handuit. I apologize for disturbing you, but there are a few things we need to clear up."

"As you will, my lord," Handuit stammered. He had had a while to look at the book, but beyond the stammer and the wary way he regarded Liam out of the corner of his eye, he gave no sign of recognizing it. He held his cap and the ends of his long scarf in his hands, twisting and untwisting them.

Liam reversed the book in his hands so that Handuit could see the pages. "Could you tell me, was this the spell you used that night?" He had his fingers over the title. Handuit shuffled forward, mashing his cap, and peered at the pages for a second.

"Oh no, master, I'm sure it wasn't, sure."

Now.

Fanuilh arched its back and hissed, a thin whisper of sound that sent Handuit skipping backward until he hit the bars of the cell. Liam was only a little less surprised, and realized that in all the months he had known the dragon, he had never heard it make a sound.

Good, he projected and, quickly recovering his composure, he held the open book out again.

"Take another look. You understand that I'm speaking only of the text? I know your spell was just a single sheet of paper."

Handuit quickly agreed, waving away the book. "No more, my lord, just the one, I swear it, and that's not it."

Liam closed the book and put it under his arm. "And the demon took that?"

"Aye."

Now. Fanuilh hissed again, and Handuit jumped.

"And the chalk and the cat, too?"

"Aye, my lord."

Liam nodded thoughtfully. "That's my problem, you see. We found the chalk and the cat, but not the spell. That's to be expected, of course—did you know that demons will make a point of destroying that sort of thing, so as not to be summoned again?"

"I did not, my lord," Handuit said, his sad, fearful eyes moving back and forth between Liam and Fanuilh.

"Well, they will. If they get loose, that is—as yours did."

Handuit picked up on this eagerly. "Aye, my lord, the beast did rip the paper from us in a passing great rage!"

Fanuilh hissed again, unprompted, and Handuit yelped and cringed. "Hush," Liam told it aloud, and silently, *Nicely done.* "This is where our trouble is, Master Handuit. You see, demons are very thorough about that sort of thing, because they hate to be summoned." He tapped the *Daemonologia*. "This, for instance. A demon would destroy something like this in an instant, given the chance."

"As it did our spell!"

Fanuilh raised its head, and Handuit bit off whatever he was going to say next.

"Now this one," Liam went on, as if there had been no interruption, "this book belonged to a wizard—they're allowed to have them, by law, while no one else is."

Handuit hung his head. "I know that, Quaestor Rhenford, and feel my crime heavily."

Liam paused, half-expecting Fanuilh to interrupt, but it did not. "Anyway, this belonged to a wizard, and thus is not subject to confiscation and burning, as all other writings related to demonology are. Your spell, for instance, would have been burned, had the demon not taken it." He smiled, letting that thought sink in. "That's where our problem is, you see."

Twisting his cap almost in half, Handuit shook his head at his feet. "I would help you, my lord, but I cannot see your problem. My wife and I've confessed to skrying, but there was only the one spell, the which was utterly destroyed by the demon."

"That's just it," Liam said, as if Handuit had made a telling point. "You see, we were looking around your house, and we found a book of spells—a book much like the one I've got here." He paused, ordering his words carefully, aware that he had reached the weakest part of his plan. He could not see the other man's face because Handuit was still staring at the floor, but he had stopped twisting his cap. "It was in the cistern in your cellar, and I wonder to myself, how could it have come to be there? When the demon you summoned got loose, it should have taken the book as well as your single page, don't you think?"

"I couldn't say," Handuit muttered, belatedly adding, "my lord."

It was the kind of answer Liam had hoped for, and the reason he had spoken to Elsevier Handuit first. His wife might have come up with an explanation, but Elsevier was not fast enough on his feet. "The only explanation

I can think of, Master Handuit, is that your demon didn't destroy the book because you had it with you in the pentagram. A pentagram that looked much like this, eh?" He crossed the cell to Handuit, opening the book to the proper page and pushing it at the man, who tried to avoid looking at it. "Come, Master Handuit, wasn't this the spell you used?"

For several seconds, Handuit kept perfectly still, his eyes steadfastly averted. Then, in a slow arc, he raised his head to stare Liam in the face, suspicion and hope flaring in his eyes.

"Pray, my lord, how could a book last in a cistern for four months?"

Liam let a slow grin spread across his face, masking his panic. He had prepared answers to any number of questions, but not this one—and then Fanuilh's thought appeared in his head: *It is magic.*

"Master Handuit," he said, "these books are made by wizards. I ask you, would a wizard make a book that couldn't stand a little dunking?"

Watching the other man's mouth twist, and seeing the hope die out of his eyes, Liam knew that it was almost over. *Carefully, now,* he warned himself. "In fact, they're quite hard to burn, as well, but we'll do our best with yours."

"I—I—"

"Hush just a moment," Liam interrupted gently. "Let me explain something. Right now, you're facing a lashing which, if you're very lucky, won't kill you. Cripple you, certainly, but there is a very small chance you'll live through it. You've been very careful, and told a very good story—and your wife's illness has been very convincing. We all feel quite sorry for her, though I think the medicine she's taking is only making matters worse." A look of horror swept over Handuit's face, and he began to stammer again, but Liam cut him off. "Things don't look very good for you, do they? Your wife takes a medicine that makes her look sick, bidding for pity. This book turns up. You've told a few lies, haven't you, Mas-

ter Handuit? And if you've lied once, how much of your
story do you think the court is going to believe?''.

''We—that is, the medicine—''

Liam leaned forward and whispered in Handuit's ear,
''The punishment for your crime is death by ordeal—
that's hanging, drawing, quartering, burning and whatever else they can think of. If you confess, the hanging
will be first and final. You'll be dead before they do the
rest. Do you understand?'' He forced the other man to
meet his eyes, and saw a swell of desperation rising there.
''You summoned that demon to kill your brother, didn't
you?''

Handuit fell back against the bars, a choking noise rising from his throat. He could not tear his eyes away from
Liam's, and what Liam saw there—the slow ebbing of
hope—was a depressing surprise. In accepting the position with the Areopagus, he had never imagined that it
would fall to him to crush a man like this, to drive out
all hope of life and to watch it go.

''Aye,'' Handuit said, his voice hoarse and unsteady,
and then he buried his face in his cap, like a child hiding
from a bad dream. Long moments passed while Liam
waited for more, but the other man just stood there, face
deep in his cap, motionless. Finally, Liam stepped quietly
from the cell and went to fetch Alasco, slipping the *Daemonologia* into his sabretache before he reached the end
of the corridor.

Roviana Handuit, the bluish tinge almost gone from her
face and her cough much less in evidence, flung a string
of questions at him when he appeared, but Liam ignored
them, beckoning for the young quaestor to join him outside the cell.

''Get a clerk,'' he whispered when they were some
way down the corridor. ''He'll confess.''

Alasco brightened and his mouth opened in a broad
smile, then closed with an expression of concern. ''And's
all open? The Areopage'll be satisfied?''

''Completely,'' Liam said. He had told no lies, and the

few truths he had twisted were minor. "We'll want it written and signed, though, so if you'd get a clerk..."

The broad smile reappeared, and Alasco ran off down the corridor. Liam went back to the cell to find Elsevier Handuit still standing motionless, face hidden. Tears would not have surprised him, or anger, but the man's rigidity and his silence disconcerted Liam. He knew he should be happy to have gotten at the truth, but Handuit's reaction was so odd that it robbed him of his satisfaction, and left him baffled and ill at ease. Folding his arms, he leaned back against the wall of the cell and waited.

At least it's done, he projected after a while.

Yes, Fanuilh replied. *My throat hurts.*

I'm sorry about that. But at least it's done.

It was not done, however. When Alasco returned with one of the court clerks, Liam had to lead Handuit through his confession. The man refused to raise his head or to speak more than a few words, and after several minutes of fruitless prodding, Liam simply outlined what he had pieced together of the crime, letting Handuit confirm his guesses at every step. The clerk, who had brought a stool and lap desk, arranged himself by the single candle and took it all down, glancing irritably up at the feeble light from time to time. The scratching of his pen and Liam's voice were the only sounds in the cell for over half an hour, by the end of which they had a rough draft of the confession.

The clerk left, promising to return with a clean draft. "I needs must have more light," he said, taking only his portable desk and leaving the stool behind. When he was gone, Handuit at last took his cap away from his face and looked at Alasco, who had listened to the confession with undisguised excitement. "May I go to my wife now, Quaestor?" The question came out in a sepulchral monotone. Alasco referred it to Liam.

"In a few minutes," Liam said, "I promise. I'll need a word with her first. Vaucan, if you'd stay here?" He took the keys and went down the corridor, praying that it would be his last trip.

Roviana Handuit clung furiously to the bars of her cell. "What've you done, you bastard? What words've you put in his mouth?"

This was the sort of reaction for which Liam had prepared himself, and he gave a wan smile. "You're looking much better, Mistress Handuit. We found the book you threw in the cistern, and your husband has confessed." Her eyes went wide; she tried to speak but rage blocked her throat. "I suggest you do the same. Your hanging will be first and final." She shrieked then, and lunged so fiercely at the bars that Liam jumped back a step. The sailors in the next cell stirred, coming to the bars to see what was going on.

Her shriek resolved itself into a string of vicious curses, in the course of which Liam regained some of his satisfaction. When she paused to draw breath in a shuddering sob, he spoke firmly. "We know the truth, Mistress Handuit, and with your husband's confession we have you both. Make it easier on yourself."

Torn, she hung on the bars, and he could see her wavering between cursing him again and giving up. He waited, staring imperturbably into her uncertain eyes. She hesitated for long seconds and then, stiffening, pried her fingers from the bars.

"Aldyne Handuit was a demon," she spat, "far worse than aught we summoned. I'll go to my grave cursing his name—and yours as well."

A thousand replies occurred to him, but he put them aside and said instead, "They'll bring the confession to you. Sign it."

Liam left Alasco to arrange the signing of the confession, accepting the young man's hearty congratulations with a weary nod, and climbed out of the dungeons to the little courtyard. He hoped to have a moment to himself, to puzzle out his conflicting emotions, but he found Widow Saffian and Cuspinian there amid a crowd of clerks and Guards. The Areopage motioned for him to stay while she finished rapping out a series of instructions regarding the afternoon's court session.

He waited by the tunnel to the riverfront, and only when she was done and approaching him did he think to look around for the ruined book they had left there.

"It's been put away," she told him, seeing his glance around the courtyard. "Y'have it, I guess—the Handuits've confessed?"

"Yes."

Peering up at his face, she frowned quizzically. "And yet y'are unhappy, Quaestor Rhenford. Is there aught questionable in the confession?"

"No, nothing. The honor of the court is safe. I'm tired, I think. I've never had to do anything like that to someone before."

"Hm." She gave him an assessing look, as if he had confirmed some suspicion of hers, then took his arm formally and put into his free hand a writing case she had slung over her shoulder. "Come, we'll to the courts, and talk as we go. It's past eleven, and the session is at noon." They left the Water Gate and headed away from the river, into the narrow streets. Arm in arm, Liam noticed for the first time how short she was: her head barely reached his shoulder.

"Y'have a different conceit than we, Quaestor Rhenford. Our researches are just that—researches. Quaestor Provyn and I, we go into a cell as to a library, and hope to come out again with our answers. But y'are more a hunter than a scholar, I think, and seek quarry, not answers. Thus your ranging round the town entire, while Provyn has hardly left the Water Gate, and thus, as well, your discomfort now—for what hunter but has some feeling for his prey, eh?"

Liam stared thoughtfully at his feet. In Southwark Coeccias often called him a human bloodhound, but he rejected the idea; he did not think of himself as a hunter, and he was not sure his odd mood was prompted by pity for the Handuits. Nonetheless, Widow Saffian's good intent cheered him a little; she meant well and it would be rude to contradict her. He made a noncommittal noise.

"You'd do well to remember that these are not beasts of the field, Quaestor, noble stags or proud lions. They're but men, and criminal men, villains. Your heart is wasted on them." She paused for a moment, and then went on in a different tone. "Ere I joined him, my husband had as quaestor a man much like you—a hunter. The catching was all with him, and he would fain leave the dispatching to others. He's an Aedile now, and happier in the post, for that he leaves the punishing to others."

"Coeccias?" Liam asked, trying and failing to imagine his friend as a hunter.

Widow Saffian shook her head, frowning at the idea. "No, no, it's Gratian, whom you'll meet in Deepenmoor. No, Coeccias would never shy from seeing a just punishment inflicted. In that he is the better man, though Gratian has many points in his favor. Indeed, he was one of my husband's favorites. It is only that he shies from blood."

They walked in silence for a while, and Liam pondered her comments, trying to determine if the fact that he reminded her of Gratian was good or not. Before he could decide, she pressed his arm, and indicated a nearby building, in front of which a crowd was gathered.

"We're here," she said, a small frown creasing her forehead. "The Duke's courthouse. See you, the mob's here before us."

CHAPTER 11

LIAM WOULD NOT have characterized the waiting men and women as a mob. There were as many fine cloaks and brocaded jackets as there were plain smocks and fustian tunics—and all were conducting themselves well, mingling quietly in the street and on the steps of the Duke's courthouse. The first story reminded Liam of a temple, with double-leaved doors twice his height that met in a pointed arch, but above that it might have been any merchant's house, four short stories of small-paned windows.

Widow Saffian pushed her way impatiently through the crowd, a murmur starting in her wake as people recognized her. The murmur grew when they caught sight of Liam and Fanuilh trailing along in her wake, and he was glad she moved quickly, striding up to the two Guards on duty at the entrance. One hurried to open the doors and the other bowed awkwardly around his pike. "My lady Areopage, are we to let them in?" He inclined his head at the crowd, the bolder members of which were already pressing forward. The judge glared irritably around.

"When the clerks've arrived," she snapped, "and not before!" She slipped inside, beckoning Liam along, and the Guards slammed the doors behind them. They passed through a dark antechamber and into a long hall where servants were busy laying out trestle tables and lighting the candles in two enormous iron chandeliers. The men who saw the Areopage first stopped their work to bow, and then those behind them caught sight of her, and to Liam it looked like a breeze blowing over wheat—a ripple of bows spreading through the hall, servants bending low from the doors and then down the room's length all the way to the dais at the far end.

"Go to!" Widow Saffian ordered, her voice loud in the sudden hush. "The session is almost upon us—go to!"

The servants resumed their work with a will as she swept through the hall to the dais. She hopped lightly onto the raised platform. A servant was draping a linen cloth on the table there; she scowled at him and he fled, but when she was seated she accepted her case from Liam with a gracious nod. While she laid out the contents— quills, sharpener, inkpot, sheaves of paper tied with red string—he surreptitiously straightened a corner of the tablecloth left rumpled by the frightened servant.

Widow Saffian seemed preoccupied with arranging her things, so Liam slipped off the dais and sat in one of the four chairs arranged against the wall to the judge's right. He chose the one closest to the corner, and settled Fanuilh on the floor at his feet before glancing around the hall. A group of men were hauling the chains of the lit chandeliers, raising them to the ceiling, while another group of men tiptoed behind the Areopage, shushing each other and wincing at each noise that might disturb her, to hang a pair of banners on the wall behind the dais. The first showed the Duke's foxes; the second, hung several feet lower, showed a ship, a set of balances and two coins worked in silver on a green field—Warinsford's symbols, Liam presumed.

Chandeliers secured and banners in place, the workmen filed quickly out of a door at the rear of the hall, and a moment later the front doors opened to let in the court clerks, six men in black robes who bowed to the Areopage and then took their places at a low trestle table to her left. They began sharpening their quills and laying out sheets of blank paper, whispering among themselves, and for the first time Liam wondered why there were so many of them. *Six seems a little excessive,* he thought.

One man ought to be able to get it all; two would make sure of it.

Cuspinian entered the hall flanked by Provyn and Alasco; behind them, hemmed in and guided by half a dozen Guards, came the crowd from the street. The three men bowed to the dais and then joined Liam. The Aedile put his boot on the seat next to Liam's and grinned down at him.

"So, y'have conned out both the how and the how much, I hear?"

"Yes, I think so." Liam looked around Cuspinian to Alasco. "They both signed?"

The young quaestor nodded happily. "Master Elsevier as meek as a lamb, Mistress Roviana somewhat less so, but both signed and confirmed and resigned to their fate."

"I give you joy," the Aedile said, clapping Liam on the shoulder. "It was no small thing—a difficult case." He brushed at the seat where his boot had rested and then sat, exhaling loudly to show his satisfaction. "It'll be a good session, if that mob'll keep their peace."

A buzz of talk rose from the spectators behind the line of Guards, but otherwise Liam thought they were well-behaved enough. "They seem all right to me."

"Gods, Rhenford, you can't conceive the trouble they'd cause, given half the chance. Most especially the merchants, now—" He did not finish his thought; Widow Saffian rapped her knuckles sharply several times on the tabletop. The buzz died, and all eyes turned to her.

"Aedile Cuspinian, is all ready?"

Cuspinian rose and offered her a courtly bow. Before he spoke, he swept the assembled crowd with a stern glance. "Aye, my lady Areopage." His voice filled the hall as easily as hers, but with a theatrical overtone. In fact, the Aedile reminded Liam of an actor he had seen once in Torquay; he thrust out his right leg and hooked his thumbs in his belt with the same dramatic air.

Widow Saffian turned then to signal the clerks' table, and an old man with arthritic, ink-stained hands and a long beard rose. "Harken now," he called, staring at some ill-defined point in space near the rafters of the hall, "harken now! These sessions of the Areopagus, by grace of the gods and our lord, Lyndower Vespasianus, Duke of the Southern Tier, Master Steward of Southwark and Warinsford, Knight Marshall of the Order of Edara and loyal servant of the King, are declared begun. Search your hearts, for justice is at hand! The first matter calls Penna, daughter of Rora, of Coopers' Court in the Chartered City of Warinsford. The crime alleged is that of using witchcraft to sour beer. Penna, daughter of Rora, approach and be judged." He gave the whole speech in a rushed monotone, then sat and started writing furiously. The other clerks had been scribbling while he spoke and now waited, pens poised.

Two Guards escorted a pretty, blond-haired young woman into the hall and led her before Widow Saffian. Standing between the two armored men she looked like a child, but she held herself erect and waited calmly for the Areopage to begin. Widow Saffian peered down her nose at the papers before her for a few seconds, then raised her eyes to meet the prisoner's.

"Y'are accused of the following," she began, and then, without referring to her papers even once, recounted the crime in detail. Liam listened carefully, leaning forward on the edge of his seat. Beside him, Cuspinian leaned back in his, his legs stretched in front of him and crossed at the ankles. The Aedile's eyes were blank, gazing blindly at the metal caps on the toes of his boots.

Penna had worked as a serving maid in a tavern, but had been dismissed late in the fall of the past year. Two weeks after her dismissal, several of the tavern's customers fell ill as a result of drinking bad beer, something which had never happened before at that particular tavern, or so the owner claimed. The accusation Widow Saffian recounted was his, and it was his opinion that Penna had soured the beer through witchcraft. As proof, he had included several of her comments on being dismissed— the judge knew even these by heart—as well as the fact that she had been seen a number of times near the inn late at night.

"In fine," the Areopage summed up, steepling her hands, "y'are accused of revenging your hurts on this man through witchcraft, and with causing grievous hurts to those who drank his beer. Do you understand the accusation?"

Penna started to speak and then stopped, considering Widow Saffian suspiciously out of the corner of her eye. Her dress was plain but clean, and she had clearly taken some pains in washing and arranging her hair. Liam felt sorry for her, hauled before the court and faced with the flood of jargon and ceremony. "I do, my lady," she said at last, "but I—"

A single raised finger from the Areopage silenced her. "Are you guilty of these crimes?"

The young woman shook her head, confused by the proceedings. "No, my lady."

"The court agrees. Further, we order the tavernkeeper to pay two months' wages, one month to the accused and one to the Duke for false accusation. Y'are free," she told the girl, "but we urge you to curb your tongue from this day on."

Hesitantly, Penna took a step away from the Guards and then, seeing that no one meant to stop her, laughed happily and melted into the crowd, which murmured appreciatively at her delight.

Widow Saffian rapped her knuckles on the table, stilling the murmur. "Let this stand as warning: this court is a sharp sword, and cuts the hand that would use it ill. We are not here that some may besmirch the names of others. And know also, the commonest punishment for cursing another with affect is a dunking and such a number of lashes as shall please the court, to say nothing of reparations. Clerk?" She looked to the old man and he rose again to announce the next case.

"That's it?" Liam asked Cuspinian in a whisper. "She says she didn't do it so she goes free?"

From two chairs over Provyn hissed at him to be quiet;

the Aedile gave a smug smile and arched one eyebrow. "The facts are hers, Rhenford, not yours. The girl was dismissed for that she wouldn't lie with the tavernkeeper. The beer was sour for that the brewer's a rogue and a knave, but a rich one, so when's customers complained, the tavernkeeper blamed the girl, crying 'Witchcraft!' It was known the town around."

Liam frowned. Even knowing the whole story, he still felt that the trial had been unsatisfactory. If the accusation was well-known to be false, why bring the girl before the court at all? Moreover, he thought Widow Saffian's curt "The court agrees" lacking; she should at least have outlined the reasoning behind the decision. He wanted to ask Cuspinian several questions, but the old clerk was already sitting down and the next case had begun.

It was a man this time, a hedge-magician who was paid a sum of money by a draper to magically dye some bolts of cloth in such a way that the color would never fade. On the way back from picking up the freshly-dyed cloth, however, the draper was caught in the rain and all the color had promptly run out of the material. A titter ran through the audience when Widow Saffian described it, which she immediately quelled with a glance.

The hedge-magician pleaded that he was innocent, and the Areopage asked him rather sharply to defend himself. He claimed he had warned the draper not to take the cloth out in the rain, provoking a storm of catcalls and hoots from the back of the watching crowd.

"Guards, anyone who speaks without our recognition is to be expelled," Widow Saffian ordered, and then declared the hedge-magician guilty. He was sentenced to a dunking and a day in the stocks, and forbidden to perform any sort of magic in the duchy. "As for the draper, he has his cloth, undyed, and is wiser for the experience. Honest toil will set a color firmer than any magic. The money he paid will go to the priests of Mother Pity, for clothing the poor." Silent smiles and nods rippled through the crowd.

Once again, Liam was disappointed. The draper ought

to have gotten his money back, he felt, even if he had been a fool, and he was not entirely sure what the hedge-magician's crime had been. Was the magic itself illegal, or was he being punished for doing it poorly? Or was it that he had promised magic and not delivered? He knew that Widow Saffian was not making her decisions arbitrarily—*I hope she isn't!*—but from time to time it seemed to him like there were gaps in the trials, as if he had fallen asleep and missed important pieces of evidence, or crucial statements that would have made things clearer. It was like watching a play with missing scenes.

The crowd, on the other hand, seemed to know exactly what was going on, and Liam found himself paying as much attention to them as to the Areopage and the prisoners. He watched them nod and whisper furtively among themselves as each case was called, and noted their expressions of approval or disagreement as the sentences were handed down. *They live here,* he realized, remembering Cuspinian's comment. *They know the stories behind each case, and the people involved.*

A man was given fifty lashes for selling a magical amulet to an invalid who eventually died of the disease the amulet was supposed to cure, and Liam saw grim nods in the crowd. Another man was given twenty lashes and a day in the stocks for using an enchanted lute to ensorcel and rob a rich merchant and his wife; the stolen goods were returned and the lute ordered destroyed. The townsfolk apparently did not like the merchant, though, and a sly-looking man in a mechanic's smock was expelled for making a sarcastic comment when they were given back their goods. Moreover, the crowd liked the lutist's nonchalant manner and his witty remarks; Widow Saffian had to silence their laughter several times.

Only Penna was found innocent. Another man was released because there was not enough evidence against him, and in the five other mundane cases the accused was declared guilty. The crowd disagreed with two of the five sentences: the lutist's and that of an old woman given a dunking and a day in the stocks for selling love potions. Liam could see heads shaking throughout the hall; they thought the sentence too severe, and did not listen to the Areopage's explanation of the seriousness of the crime. She ended each case that way, even those where she let the accused go—describing the crime and the punishment she had assigned in a little sermon, as a sort of warning to those watching.

"Of all the parts of a man or a woman, we must hold the mind and the affections inviolate," she explained, ignoring the crowd's mulish refusal to listen. "To force a man to love where he does not is to hold him in an invisible prison, and we won't allow it."

Sobbing quietly, the potion-seller had caught the audience's pity, and Liam saw some actually turn away, disgusted that an old woman was to be punished for something as harmless as a love potion. The more he thought about it, though, the more he was convinced that the Areopage was right, and that in view of her explanation the sentence was rather light. Her arguments made no headway with the crowd, however, and he saw her lips quirk with irritation before she called for the last mundane case.

Her two Guards hastily escorted the old potion-seller to one of the side doors while the head clerk stood and announced the case. Again he focused his eyes on a spot high on the wall, speaking to no one, but he did raise his voice to be heard above the restless murmur of the crowd, still unhappy with the sentence of the potion-seller.

"This matter calls Lons Kammer of Broad Street in the Chartered City of Warinsford, on the charge of using magic to seduce and despoil three several maidens."

Kammer scuttled into the hall, two Guards hurrying to keep up, and the murmur in the crowd died down at once, replaced with a sort of gleeful anticipation.

It'd take more than magic for him to bed a girl, Liam thought, recognizing the prisoner from the day before. Kammer was an ugly young man with a sallow, moon-shaped face and a lumpy nose. His black hair stuck up in unruly spikes all over his head, and he stooped so

much that he barely reached his Guards' shoulders. He
writhed uncomfortably while Widow Saffian described
the case against him, as if each word were a stroke of
the lash.

The crowd drank in the story with a sort of morbid
fascination that Liam had to admit it merited. Early in
the preceding winter, Kammer had set himself up as a
tutor for young women of quality, and managed to gain
positions in a number of prominent households in Warinsford. From then until the time the alleged crimes were
discovered he had enjoyed a certain vogue, teaching the
daughters of the wealthy. No one thought ill of him until,
less than two weeks earlier, one of his pupils told her
father that Kammer had put her into an enchanted sleep
and then taken advantage of her. The father made discreet
inquiries and found two other girls with whom Kammer
had taken "liberties"; the tutor had been arrested only
four days before the Areopagus arrived.

Liam cringed at each of Widow Saffian's euphemisms,
and glared at the ugly tutor. *The toad's a rapist,* he
thought. *Hang him.* The crowd hung greedily on each
word of the case.

"Each accusation's the same," the Areopage said, her
tone revealing the disgust her dry words did not. "That
the victim, in the course of a lesson, fell into a profound
slumber, from the which she awaked alone in her proper
bed, dishonored but with no knowledge of how it happened. They match in all particulars. Do you understand
the accusation?"

Kammer averted his eyes from her glare. "Yes, Areopage."

Liam cocked his head. There was something odd about
the tutor's voice, but he could not place it. He had heard
it once before, in the dungeons beneath the Water Gate,
but had not paid it any attention then.

"And are you guilty of these?"

"No, Areopage."

"You needs must prove it," she said, tensing in her
chair like a cat about to spring. "And I'll warn you,

we've other evidence than these statements.''

Suddenly, strangely, Kammer smiled, an ingratiating smile that only served to make his face even uglier. ''I guess my friends have been talking,'' he said, and the judge's face fell, ''telling you I bragged. Well, Areopage, I did brag. I know it's not gentlemanly, but I couldn't help myself. It's not often that three beautiful women throw themselves at my feet, after all.''

There were a few uncertain laughs from the crowd, but Widow Saffian did not call for silence; Kammer had thrown her off balance, and her jaw worked busily as she tried to marshal her thoughts.

''The rogue,'' Cuspinian whispered, the epithet tinged with admiration. ''He lies boldly. Threw themselves at his feet—ha!''

Liam hardly heard him; his eyes were rivetted to the tutor, and he strained to hear his next words.

''You confess, then, to airing your seductions about the town?'' Widow Saffian asked.

''Oh yes,'' Kammer replied. ''I told some friends— but I never said anything about magic. These women let me into their beds of their own free will, and they'd tell you that, if their parents hadn't forced this made-up story on them.''

He's from Harcourt, Liam thought, at one and the same time leaping to and rejecting the next conclusion: *He can't be! He's nothing like him!*

Widow Saffian glared at the tutor. ''What are you saying?''

''These ladies love me, Areopage, hard as that may be to believe, with a face like mine.'' The laughs from the crowd were stronger this time, and Kammer took confidence from them, standing a little straighter and daring to meet the judge's eyes. ''But they do, and I love them, too. Their parents, though, would never consent to that sort of thing, and when they discovered what was going on, they cooked up this story to discredit me. What am I, after all? A young man, only eighteen, with nothing but my knowledge to offer; that, and my love, of course.''

''Our man'' would not be—could not be—an ugly eighteen-year-old, a tutor-turned-rapist. Liam could not fit Kammer to the mold in his head, the picture of a powerful wizard with a long gray beard. That he had begun teaching roughly five months earlier and that his accent was right might both be coincidences . . . but there was something, something in the way he held himself, in the way he smirked at Widow Saffian's discomfort, that refused to let Liam dismiss the idea.

''Y'are giving these ladies the lie?'' the Areopage demanded.

''Not the ladies,'' Kammer said, raising a finger to make his point. ''No, not the ladies. Their parents, though, yes. Their parents have forced them to tell these lies about me, and about our love. If they could speak openly, without fear, just once, they'd tell the truth. Their parents know this, though, and that's why they won't let them appear here!''

''They're not required to appear here. We've their statements.''

''Statements they were forced to swear to. Bring them forward,'' Kammer dared. ''They won't be able to condemn me face to face. Our love is too strong.''

Widow Saffian ground her teeth, and then turned abruptly. ''Quaestor Provyn, come here!''

Provyn, visibly dismayed by the exchange, jumped to his feet and hurried over to the dais for a whispered conference. The crowd buzzed with excitement.

Could he be ''our man''? Liam projected.

He is too young to be anything more than an apprentice, Fanuilh replied. *But then, we do not know that he cast anything more than an apprentice's spells.*

And the book—that's an apprentice's book.

The dragon answered, *Yes, master,* but Liam had already turned to Cuspinian and tapped him urgently on the knee. ''What do you know about him?''

"He's a bold rogue," the Aedile said. "She'd do well just to sentence him and have done."

"He's but a tutor," Alasco supplied. "Some elements of music, some of philosophy, history, mathematics, calligraphy."

An apprentice is taught all those subjects, Fanuilh thought.

"And he hasn't caused you any trouble?"

"Since we clapped him in, mean you?" the young quaestor asked. "No, not a whit. He's been quiet as a mouse."

"What are you getting at?" the Aedile demanded.

"Where did he live? What was it like?"

Cuspinian repeated his question, but Alasco said, "A set of rooms, somewhat better than most but not by much. He was much in demand as a tutor, if you see, and had the wherewithal to live modestly well. Why do you ask, Liam?"

Why would the Guild dispatch a wizard like Passendus just for a runaway apprentice? And how could an apprentice have killed him? It's a coincidence, he told himself, *just a coincidence.*

The spell they accuse him of using is an apprentice's spell, Fanuilh pointed out, as if it wanted to contradict him. *A more powerful wizard could have taken those women without their ever remembering it.*

And a less powerful one couldn't have killed Passendus, Liam shot back.

We do not know that, the dragon thought, and Liam sensed an irritating edge of patient lecturing. *The laughing spell might have been used to render Passendus helpless. Then no other spell would be required.*

But there were no marks on the body! It had to be a spell.

"Gods!" Alasco burst out, his eyes wide with revelation. "He's a Harcourt tongue!"

Liam hushed him fiercely, a quick glance reassuring him that the rest of the hall, and particularly Kammer, were focused on Widow Saffian and Provyn. "It's just a guess."

"Think you it's him?" the young quaestor asked, his voice lowered and his eyes sparkling with excitement. "We should clap him in presently!"

Cuspinian glanced back and forth between them, confused. "Clap him in, woodenhead? He's ours already. Why clap him in again?"

"For taking off Passendus," Alasco said, before Liam could stop him. "He's a Harcourt tongue, and's a wizard as well, and he arrived here just at the right time!"

"We don't know that," Liam cautioned, anxious to keep the overzealous quaestor under control. "It could be just a coincidence." *What do you think?* he asked his familiar.

Is it a coincidence? It could be—there are other places in Harcourt beside the Mages' Guild that teach philosophy and mathematics.

A minute ago you were arguing just the opposite!

I am only answering your questions.

"Keep still," Cuspinian ordered Alasco, then gripped Liam's shoulder. "Go tell Areopage Saffian what you suspect."

"Tell her what? It's just a guess."

"Go to," the Aedile insisted, pushing Liam to his feet. "Ere she finishes with Provyn—go to! Would you have her sentence him, when only yesterday she wanted nothing to do with him?"

Hesitantly, shooed on by the Aedile, Liam left his seat and crossed the open floor to the dais, throwing thoughts back at Fanuilh all the way.

He couldn't be anything more than an apprentice, right?

No, master. He could not cast anything very complicated even if he were, because he has none of the material components with him.

And you would know if he did, wouldn't you? Fanuilh could sense magic, like a burst of warmth or light nearby.

Yes.

Could you do anything about it? He stopped at the edge of the dais, and caught some of what Widow Saffian was saying.

". . . didn't speak with them, even?" she demanded, her face rigid, her noise aimed at the fat quaestor like a spearpoint.

Perhaps.

"I spoke with their parents, Areopage," Provyn said, practically wailing. "It seemed unkind to make them recount their stories."

"Unkinder still to let this man go, after they've come forward! Now we needs must have them parade their shame in public! We'll put this matter aside, and go to Quaestor Rhenford's case, and you'll bring those poor maids here."

"Aye, Areopage," Provyn said. Head hanging miserably, he skulked off toward the door through which they had brought the prisoners.

Widow Saffian addressed the hall again. "We'll put this matter aside for now, and return to it anon." She told the Guards to take the prisoner away, and signalled the chief clerk for the next case. As the clerk rose Kammer's Guards led him after Provyn, and Liam hurried to Widow Saffian's side.

"Areopage," he whispered, even as the clerk called out the Handuits' names, "Kammer may be 'our man.' "

She glared up at him for a moment, displeased at the interruption, and then caught his meaning. Reflexively, she looked over her shoulder toward the side door. Liam followed her gaze. "Him? I can scarce credit it."

There was an impasse at the prisoners' entrance: the Handuits' Guards, hearing the clerk call their case, were bringing the couple in, while Kammer's Guards were trying to take him out. The tutor was watching the dais, and for a moment his eyes met Liam's—and then the Handuits cleared the way and his Guards led him out.

"He's got a Harcourt accent, he arrived in Warinsford less than six months ago, and the spell he used on those girls is the same sort of spell that was used on Passendus.

It's just a guess, but the Aedile thought you should know.'' *A good guess,* he thought, *but still a guess.* More importantly, what would the Areopage do with it?

Passendus's death could be overlooked—he was a stranger, after all, and despite the gruesome nature of his death mask, there was every reason to believe that it was a matter of self-defense for "our man.'' What Kammer had done to the merchants' daughters, however, could not be ignored, particularly since it had been aired publicly.

Master, Kammer looked at me very oddly before he left, Fanuilh projected.

Oddly? How?

"Thank you for these news, Quaestor,'' she said, in a grave and slightly formal tone. "I must think them through. First, let us dispose of the Handuits, and then we'll have time ere Quaestor Provyn returns to make our plans.''

Liam bowed his way off the dais.

Oddly, Fanuilh repeated. *As if he recognized me.*

He probably mistook you for some other dragon.

"What did she say?'' Cuspinian asked him as he took his seat.

"She said she needed to think about it. Anyway, she doesn't need to make a decision until Provyn gets back.''

Widow Saffian began to give the case against the Handuits, this time reading directly from the signed confession. "She should leave him go,'' Cuspinian murmured, "order him out of the town, and leave it at that.'' Liam wanted to hear if Roviana had added anything to the confession, but it would have been rude to hush the Aedile. "It'd not like me to have another wizard come visiting, wondering how we came to try one of his fellows.''

And Vaucan over there will just arrest him again, Liam thought. Trying Kammer should not be a problem. The simple fact that he had allowed his own arrest indicated that there was less to him than they feared—a real wizard would never have tolerated being kept in one of the Water Gate's cells. As for another wizard coming to Warinsford, Liam did not think it was something to worry about; whoever it was would be more interested in Passendus than in Kammer. *If Kammer really is "our man,"* he reminded himself. *There's no proof, only coincidences.*

A new thought struck him as Widow Saffian was finishing up the Handuits' confession. Everyone looked oddly at Fanuilh; normal dragons were not all that common, after all, let alone miniature ones. Liam bent down and tapped his familiar on the back.

Could he have recognized you?

The dragon twisted its long neck to stare up at him, its slit-pupiled eyes devoid of expression. *I have never seen him before—but he would recognize me as a familiar.*

Everyone looked oddly at Fanuilh, and everyone thought he was a wizard. If Kammer did also, what would he do about it? He had killed one wizard; what would he think now that a second one had apparently shown up at his trial? Liam fidgeted in his seat, staring anxiously at the prisoners' entrance. *What would he do?*

Fanuilh's thought crashed through his own. *Master, there is magic close by.*

The thought was still firm in his head as he jumped to his feet and dashed for the side door.

CHAPTER 12

LIAM HARDLY HEARD the commotion that broke out in the hall at his hasty departure—he was already through the prisoner's entrance and running down the short corridor beyond. He burst through the door at the end, and immediately tripped headlong over the Guard who lay asleep by the doorway. Picking himself up from the floor, he saw a second Guard sprawled at the feet of the first. There was a door in the far wall; he lurched toward it, wincing at the new pain in his knee.

He found himself behind the courthouse, a narrow, high-walled alley. The session had lasted longer than he thought and the alley was thick with late-afternoon shadows, though the sky far overhead was still light. The sudden darkness disoriented him.

"Ah, gods, make it stop!"

Liam whirled to his left, toward the scream, and then recognized Provyn's voice, distorted by agony. He limped a few steps forward and could just make out the fat quaestor rolling on the ground, tearing at his clothes, clawing at his skin.

It is a cantrip, Fanuilh explained. *Like the sleeping Guards.* The dragon stepped to Liam's side, its head cocked to examine Provyn's contortions.

Liam knelt down and grabbed the fat quaestor's arms. "Did he go this way?" Provyn's eyes rolled up in his head and he kicked at his own legs, scraping his bootheels down his shins. With a curse, Liam let him go and rose. His eyes adjusted slowly to the dim light of the alley; to his left it gave out on a larger street, in the mouth of which he could see the silhouettes of passersby.

He turned then, to look to his right, and laughed.

His eyes watered at once, and his sides ached, a deep ache as if he had been laughing for hours. The laughter exploded out of him, torn from his throat; his cheeks felt twisted, as if a strong hand were wrenching them away from his teeth in an impossible grin. He collapsed to his hands and knees, buffeted by laughter like storm winds, so strong he could barely raise his head to see Kammer step out of the shadows.

The tutor kicked Fanuilh out of the way and the little dragon rolled to the side, contorted by its own throes of laughter.

It will not last, it thought at him, and Liam received the thought perfectly. His mind was clear, only his body was helpless, racked with hysteria, refusing to answer as Kammer bent over and grabbed him by the hair, yanked his head up. In his free hand was a dagger.

"If I had a pillow, Master Mage," he said, "I'd smother you like I did Passendus. But—"

The knife fell away, and Liam distinctly heard it clatter on the cobblestones in the second before Kammer stumbled backward. Through his tears, as he, too, fell, Liam saw the halberd blade pulled from the tutor's side, and the spatter of dark drops.

Wracked by spasms of hysteria, he laughed on.

It will not last long, Fanuilh told him over and over, but it seemed like an eternity. When the laughter stopped, all at once and completely, he vomited, and barely had the strength to roll his body away from the puddle. The dragon lay trembling a few feet from him, its breath coming in rapid, shallow gasps.

Alasco helped Liam up, supporting him by the shoulders until he felt steady enough to stand on his own. "Was it he, then?" the young quaestor asked, nodding grimly at Kammer's crumpled body.

Liam nodded and mumbled something, too weak to raise his voice. He felt as if he had been beaten—his ribs throbbed painfully, his stomach ached, and stars swam lazily at the edges of his vision. He rubbed his face gingerly, wiping away the tears.

It looks like a tavern brawl, he thought, leaning against the alley wall for balance and surveying the scene. Cuspinian knelt beside the fat quaestor, chafing his hands and talking to him in a low voice as his whimpering gradually died away. Most of the Guards stood by the back door of the courthouse, six or seven of them with torches in their hands. Two others stood by Kammer, the eyes of one jumping nervously back and forth between the bloody blade of his halberd and the Aedile's back.

"Go to," Alasco commanded the Guards by the door. "Get you within! Who watches the Areopage? Who watches the prisoners? Go to! And bring water and linens for the quaestors!"

Liam shuffled over to Fanuilh and, bending carefully, scooped the dragon up. Alasco came to his side but Liam waved him off. "I'm fine. Go help with Provyn." There was blood on the other man's face where he had scratched himself; he seemed incapable of rising on his own, and was too heavy for Cuspinian alone.

The Guards had lingered despite Alasco's order, but the sight of Liam shambling toward them with Fanuilh in his arms spurred them to action; they had cleared the waiting room by the time he made his way in and slumped down onto one of the prisoners' benches. Cuspinian and Alasco followed, carrying Provyn between them. "Bring him as well," the Aedile called over his shoulder, and a few moments later the last two Guards entered, dragging Kammer by his legs. "Leave him on the floor," Cuspinian ordered, when they made to lift the corpse onto a bench. With Provyn seated and Alasco fussing over him, the Aedile gazed around the room and snorted angrily.

"A pretty pass, this," he said, levelling his glance at the Guard with the bloody halberd. "The man's dead."

"But he'd a knife," the Guard protested.

Liam spoke up, though it was an effort even to lift his head. "He was going to kill me." The image was blurry in his head, strangely remote, as if it were some memory from his childhood—but he could remember Kammer's words distinctly. "Did you hear what he was saying?" he asked the Guard, who screwed up his face doubtfully.

"A pillow, it may be?" he asked.

"A pillow," Liam confirmed. He stroked Fanuilh's back, feeling the dragon's shaking diminish beneath his palm. "Kammer cast that . . . spell, and then smothered Passendus with a pillow." He shuddered and then stilled himself, afraid the laughter might start again.

Alasco looked up eagerly, forgetting Provyn. "So it was he!"

"So it seems." *You didn't tell me it was like that.*

The spell? I did not know myself. I have never seen it cast before. Fanuilh settled itself more comfortably in his lap, boneless with exhaustion.

A Guard came with rags and a basin of water. Liam wet a cloth and held it to his forehead while the others saw to Provyn. The worst of his fear past, the fat quaestor started babbling as Alasco washed the blood from his pale face. "You cannot conceive it, Aedile Cuspinian— the same as swimming through a sea of bees, or stinging ants. You cannot conceive it!" The scratches on his face were shallow, but he winced at each touch of the cloth. "The villain called to me—take *care,* Quaestor!—and I turned. You cannot conceive my shock to see him, but ere I could raise a hand—a lighter hand, if it please you!—he'd ensorcelled me. And look you what I've done in my fit." He pushed Alasco away and began straightening his clothes.

These cantrips of yours are nasty, Liam projected. He sympathized with Provyn, but a small voice in his head whispered that the man could at least wipe his own face.

Laughter, Itch and Sleep are meant for self-defense. They are among the oldest spells known.

Fascinating. Physically he felt better, but Provyn's whining, which had shifted to the subject of his disordered clothes, irritated him. He deposited Fanuilh on the

bench, rose gingerly to his feet and made his way toward
the outside door.

"Where to, Quaestor?" Cuspinian asked.

"I was wondering why Kammer came back." He
stood in the doorway, looking both ways down the alley.
Kammer had caught Provyn to the left, then gone back
to the right, and then returned. "I wanted to see what's
down there." He pointed to the right, but could see nothing in the gathering gloom.

"It's a dead end," the Aedile told him. "There's no
way out there. But tell, Quaestor Rhenford, how knew
you he'd essay an escape? One moment we're talking,
viewing the session, and the next y'are gone, *poof*, like
magic." He snapped his fingers to show how quick it
had been.

"A fine question," Widow Saffian said from the inner
door. "The answer to which it'd like me to hear." She
dismissed the remaining Guards with a wave of her hand
and went over to Kammer's body. "I trust this was necessary?" she asked, after a moment's examination.

All four men tried to speak at once, but she silenced
them with a gesture and indicated Liam.

"He had cast spells on his Guards, on Quaestor Provyn
and on myself, Areopage. He was going to kill me. And
he was 'our man'—he told me how he killed Passendus."

She pointed to the broad wound in Kammer's side.
"He'd have killed you else?" At Liam's nod, her frown
turned thoughtful. "It likes me not, though it can't be
helped. We'll never know what else he sold, what mag-
icks he gave to that Relly to spread."

For her, Liam knew, these were legitimate concerns.
Kammer's *Daemonologia* had already cost one life, and
would take two more when the Handuits were executed;
who knew what else he might have unleashed on the
duchy? Her concern was legitimate, but he could not
share it. In his opinion the ugly tutor had met the end he
deserved, even if it was without the benefit of an official
trial. *And we saved the hangman a noose,* he thought.

Provyn stirred himself on his bench. "He'd have killed us else, Areopage." He sounded like a child trying to excuse an accident.

"Oh, I doubt it not," she said with a distracted air. After a moment, she recollected herself and squared her shoulders. "Well and well, gentlemen, there's no help for it. This'll finish the session, I think, though not perhaps as one might wish it finished. We'll enter into the record that he attacked members of the court, and thus confessed his guilt." Her lips pressed tight for a moment; she was clearly displeased with how things had turned out. With an effort, she said, "It could not be helped. Well. Aedile Cuspinian has invited us to dine again, and I think we may go to our meal with clear consciences. My thanks, gentlemen."

She bowed her head to each man, then turned and went back down the corridor. In the silence she left behind, Liam thought he heard the echo of mad laughter, but it was only his, and only in his head.

Only Alasco seemed genuinely happy as they walked back to the Duke's Arms, but he held himself in check, sensing the other men's desire for quiet. Provyn strode stiffly along, his lips set in an indignant pout, the furrows from his fingernails like stripes of paint on his face. Cuspinian walked with his arms crossed, lost in thought, occasionally throwing troubled, speculative glances at Liam.

For his part, Liam was not so much disinclined to talk as simply exhausted. Drained and sore, he wanted nothing more than to crawl back to the inn and go to bed. *And never was a rest better earned.* All things considered, he was satisfied with his performance. The Handuits had confessed, and he had caught a man he was not even supposed to be looking for. *Well, caught isn't the right word.* On the other hand, Kammer would have escaped if he had not gone to the alley. *Do you think he ran because he saw you?* he projected.

The dragon stirred in his arms. *It seems likely. Of*

course, he may have done so because Quaestor Provyn was going to bring in those women to give statements. However, the fact is that he did run. Whether he did so because he saw me or because he feared their statements is irrelevant. It is idle speculation.

Idle speculation or not, Fanuilh's idea cheered him. It could have been the statements that made Kammer run, and not the sight of his familiar. And the tutor's death had provided a straightforward solution to Widow Saffian's dilemma over whether to try him or not—a straightforward and rather just solution, he thought, if not strictly orthodox.

His mood improved considerably as they walked through the darkening streets. A faint glow on the rooftops to the west heralded the final end of the day, and as they straggled up the steps of the Duke's Arms, he discovered that he was hungry.

Alasco and Cuspinian said they would wait in the common room until dinner; Provyn strode upstairs without a word, but Liam stayed long enough to promise to join them. With his appetite, he felt some strength returning to his body, and he followed a vision of a glass of wine up to his room.

An innservant was building up a roaring fire while Provyn's valet helped him undress and endured a harangue. "None of your excuses, sirrah! Hang the hour! I want poultices and plasters—can't you see I've been foully attacked? Go to, go to!" He shoved the man aside and finished undressing himself. Both servants scurried out, bowing hastily to Liam.

Ass, Liam thought, and went about settling Fanuilh comfortably on top of his bags. *Do you want anything to eat?*

No. I think I will sleep. I did not realize the spell would be like that. Liam chucked it under the chin, and it arched its neck to accommodate the scratching.

"I'll not dine downstairs this night," Provyn announced. "If you'd give my regrets to the Aedile?"

Liam stretched elaborately before replying; his muscles

were stiffening up. *It'd be polite to press him to join us,*
he realized, but he could not muster the energy to be
polite. "I'll tell him."

Between the red nightcap he wore and the scratches
on his face, Provyn's attempt at a dignified pose struck
Liam as ridiculous. "I take it y'are leaving your beast in
the room? You'll vouch for its behavior?"

"Quaestor Provyn," Liam said, allowing his weariness
to show in his voice, "he's in no shape to cause anyone
any trouble."

The fat quaestor snorted as he settled his bulk onto the
bed. "Ha! What's magic to him? A dragon—spells are
nothing to him. I've been tortured!"

Biting off a sarcastic reply, Liam bid the other man
good night and went downstairs.

Three glasses of wine in the common room rebuilt much
of Liam's strength; he sat at a table with the Aedile and
Alasco, draining the first two glasses with single-minded
determination. The other two men discussed small bits of
local business—patrol rosters, a pickpocket captured in
the market, an upcoming festival that would require extra
men to police—and left Liam to his own thoughts.

He had none, really, he nursed his third glass of wine
and let his mind go blank. It was something of a relief
after the past two days, and he felt he had earned it. From
time to time one or the other of his companions would
glance his way as if to include him in the conversation,
but he deliberately avoided their eyes. Alasco in particular seemed anxious to talk to him, but was too polite to
let loose the stream of questions that obviously plagued
him.

They went up to dinner at eight and found Widow
Saffian waiting for them in the dining room. Beside her
sat the chief clerk of the court; an old man with a long
grey beard, he rose and bowed low to Cuspinian as they
entered.

"I've asked Clerk Iorvram to dine with us, Aedile
Cuspinian," the judge said. "I hope it's not amiss."

Cuspinian smiled warmly at the nervous clerk and urged him to take his seat. "I'd like nothing more, Areopage." He bowed to her, and took his own seat.

The Areopagus's third dinner was by far the most pleasant, in Liam's opinion. Apart from urging them to try this wine or that dish, Cuspinian was mostly silent, and let the conversation run where it would. By tacit agreement, no mention was made of the sessions earlier that day, and the talk turned to general subjects. Iorvram, though older than everyone at the table, was ill-at-ease at first, but several quickly-gulped glasses of wine loosened his tongue and he proved to have a fund of gently amusing anecdotes about the Crossroads Fair. Liam had asked about it, and much of the dinner passed with the clerk's stories.

When the servants came to remove the last course and lay on the Oporto, they had moved beyond the Crossroads Fair to markets in general. Alasco recounted a visit made with his father to Metalcross Market in Caernarvon, where the teams of oxen eighteen-strong pulled tiny carts piled high with gold, and Liam told about the caravan grounds in the pass at Carad Llan, which stretched for nearly a mile. From there, the conversation moved on to the northlands in general. Both Alasco and Iorvram had many stories to tell about the lands beyond the King's Range, where the people lived on snow and daily encountered ferocious monsters made of ice. Most of what they claimed as truth Liam knew for fable, or at the very least exaggeration, but he refrained from correcting them, even when Alasco started describing how giants rode fire-breathing dragons into battle. The wine getting the better of him, the young man waxed rhapsodic over the wonders of giant wars, where the battle lines might stretch for a thousand miles on each side. "They're awesome creatures," he said, "and their span of years is enormous, like their mounts! A dragon'll live for centuries. How old is your dragon, Liam?"

The question took Liam by surprise. "I don't know," he stammered after a moment. "I have no idea."

"Quaestor Rhenford's is not a dragon like those the giants ride," Widow Saffian put in, and the slight, amused crinkling at the corners of her eyes made Liam think she knew better about the riding habits of giants. "It is a familiar, a magical conjuration whose span of years is tied to that of its master. And now," she went on, changing her tone, "it's late, and we must part Warinsford early. Aedile Cuspinian, my thanks for your hospitality, and I drink your health."

Following her example, they all drank to the Aedile, who thanked them and in turn proposed a toast to the Duke. The entire table stood and drank, and the dinner was over. Iorvram, ill-at-ease once more, tried to pull out Widow Saffian's chair, open the door, and thank Cuspinian all at once; he ended up stumbling over his own feet in the doorway, and fled. The others filed out at a more leisurely pace. The judge went off to her room, but Liam found himself between Alasco and Cuspinian in the corridor. The younger man took his arm.

"Pray, stay a moment, Liam. I would talk a while with you, if you would. We should talk. I feel strongly that y'have much to teach." His words were not slurred, but his normal earnestness had been exaggerated by too much wine.

Liam tried to disengage his arm without success. "We have an early day, I'm afraid."

From behind them, Cuspinian spoke sternly. "You can speak to Quaestor Rhenford on the morrow."

"But he parts Warinsford then!"

"You may have half the day from your duties, Vaucan, and attend him on the road." When Alasco opened his mouth to protest, Cuspinian repeated "On the morrow" in a heavy tone, and his meaning finally penetrated.

"In course, in course," the young man said quickly, letting go Liam's arm. "If I may wait on you in the morning?"

Liam shrugged helplessly. "If you wish." Alasco nodded several times and hurried off, leaving him alone with the Aedile. Cuspinian clapped him on the back and then left his hand there, guiding him firmly down the corridor that led to the common room.

"I wonder if you can spare me a moment?"

"Of course, Aedile." *Does everyone in this town have to touch me? And what does he want?* Alasco's talk he could guess at—more harebrained schemes to arrest people his superiors wanted left alone—but not Cuspinian's.

"You must excuse Vaucan," the Aedile said, directing Liam to a table in the almost-empty common room. "He can be an importunate pup, at times."

"He means well," Liam responded, feeling the criticism unwarranted. "It's good for a young man to be so eager. He's very . . . innocent." The word had simply occurred to him as he spoke, and as soon as he said it he wished he had not. It sounded pompous in his own ears, as if he were some world-weary sophisticate.

Cuspinian, however, seemed pleased by the phrase. "So innocent," he echoed, "and very eager. Aye, that's our Alasco." His smile faded, and he grew serious. "Y'are somewhat in trade, are you not, Quaestor Rhenford?"

Given the Aedile's low opinion of trade, the shift in topics threw Liam off balance. "A little, yes. More than a little, really. I'm in partnership with a family in Southwark—we have seven ships out this season."

"And do any of your ships touch here in Warinsford?"

"No, they're blue water—the Cauliff and Rushcutter's Bay—not river ships."

"Ah, but it may be that some of the goods you sell come through here?"

"Some," Liam agreed guardedly. In fact, a great deal of the trade goods on his ships filtered through Warinsford—metals from Caernarvon, glassware from the small manufactories along the upper Warin—and when his ships came back, many of the spices and carpets they brought would go through the town on their way to points north and west.

"And're taxed, eh? To say nothing of the costs of the

thieving rogues on the waterfront, with their handling rates and 'spoilage,' eh?''

His partner often complained of the prices charged by the middlemen in Warinsford, and she had mentioned that some were notorious for skimming off a percentage of any lot of goods for themselves, and reporting it ruined or spoiled. It was a custom Liam had seen in dozens of ports, though, and much as it irked him, he had accounted for it in his planning.

"The handling charges are high," he admitted.

Cuspinian nodded sympathetically, and then squared his shoulders and leaned forward to speak in confidence. The gesture reminded Liam once again of how impressive a figure the Aedile cut: the man loomed over him, his broad shoulders and leonine head creating an imposing presence. "My resources in Warinsford are not inconsiderable," he said, "and it'd be my pleasure to succor you and your partners in whatever way I may. I am not much in the way of trade, but I might keep an eye on your factors to see that they deal fairly with you. And surely, if the Duke's custommsen here were to treat you as a friend, that'd be to the good, eh?"

It took Liam a moment to understand the circuitous offer, and even then he doubted his comprehension. *He can't be bribing me. How could he bribe me?* Why *would he bribe me?*

Cuspinian, seeing his hesitation and misunderstanding it, spread his hands and assumed an ingenuous pose. "Such things are only the natural due of one of the Duke's intimates. A man with his ear . . . pray tell me, Quaestor Rhenford, how have you found things here in Warinsford?"

"Fine," Liam managed to say, and then snapped his mouth closed: the Aedile was not asking what he thought of Warinsford, but what he would tell the Duke about how the town was run in his name. Cuspinian still believed that he knew the Duke; he had never corrected the misconception.

A scowl flashed across the Aedile's face and was

quickly suppressed. "Only 'fine'?" he asked, trying for a light tone. "The customsmen your friends, and me to police your factors, and Warinsford is only 'fine'?"

Only two days before, he had decided that Cuspinian's corruption was none of his business. If the Duke could not find better men, that was his worry. Now, though, with an offer on the table, the idea both repelled and attracted him. Explaining at this stage that he had never met the Duke would be extraordinarily awkward. He could, without saying a word, with only a nod, save himself and his partner a fair sum of money. He would not even have to lie to the Duke about the state of affairs in Warinsford, because the Duke would never ask him. *You'd be lying to the Aedile, in a sense—but then, there's no honor among thieves.*

On the other hand, appealing as the idea was, it was illegal. *You're a member of a court,* he reprimanded himself. *How can you even consider it?*

A small voice in the back of his head sneered at that. *You've done worse,* it reminded him, and he knew it was true. Theft had more than once put money in his pocket when he had none, and food in his stomach.

That was different, he protested. *I had to. This—I don't need the money. I don't need it.*

In the end, that fact made the decision for him. It was not a moral question, but a practical one: he did not need the money. Still, he had been Cuspinian's guest, and that counted for something. "I think fine will do," he said, meeting the Aedile's impatient gaze. "Should the Duke ask me, that's what I will tell him. And please, don't trouble yourself about my factors. I'm sure they're quite reliable. As for the Duke's taxes, I'll be happy to pay the proper amounts, no more—and most definitely no less." He paused to let his words sink in, noting the way Cuspinian drew back from him and cocked his head. "Do we understand each other?"

The Aedile squinted at him, as if trying to see him through a fog, and finally cleared his throat. "I fear me you mistook my meaning, Quaestor Rhenford. I meant only that—''

''I'm sure whatever you meant, you meant well, Aedile Cuspinian, but I think we should leave things as they stand. My goods will receive no special treatment. You have nothing to fear from me, and I wish to gain nothing from you. Thank you for dinner.''

Liam rose, bowed, and left the common room. As he walked, he half-expected to hear Cuspinian calling after him, but the Aedile did not come, and he arrived at his room alone.

With Provyn snoring beside him, Liam lay still on top of the blankets in the stifling room, staring into the blackness of the canopy, aimlessly replaying his conversation with Cuspinian.

The thing that struck him most about the incident was not that the bribe had been offered—Coeccias had warned him about the Aedile's corruption—but that he had found it so tempting. *What if the Handuits had tried the same thing? Offered you a handful of gold and said, "Don't try so hard."* It would have been easy not to visit their cellar, not to find the ruined *Daemonologia*. It would have been easy, and Widow Saffian would have had to sentence them for the lesser charge.

Embers popped in the fireplace.

He winced at the idea, but could not drive it from his head. What would it take? How much would someone have to offer? *More than anyone in the Southern Tier has,* he assured himself, and managed to fall asleep before having any second thoughts about his price.

CHAPTER 13

A POUNDING AT the door woke Liam, and by the time he opened his eyes the ostler's son had entered the room, bawling that he had come for the bags. Seeing Liam still in bed, the boy exclaimed, "Why, master, y'are not ready! And the train to part presently! I'll see to your baggage while you dress!"

An energetic whirlwind, the boy raced around the room, gathering clothes and stuffing them randomly into bags. It took Liam a moment to realize that Provyn's things were nowhere to be seen, and then he had to jump out of bed to rescue the clothes he needed from his self-proclaimed valet's indiscriminate hands. The boy pleaded that court was about to leave, but a gentle shaking silenced him, and Liam set about washing and dressing as quickly as he could, darting glances at the boy to make sure he did not try to stuff Fanuilh into a convenient pouch.

When he was dressed he packed his bags himself, handing them over to the boy's custody when each was full. His packing was hardly more expert than the boy's, but at least he managed to keep the clean clothes separate from the dirty. "Take those," he said, "and tell the court I'll be down in a moment." The boy staggered off, and Liam threw on his coat and walked over to Fanuilh. *Why didn't you wake me?* he projected, picking the dragon up from the middle, like a cat, and placing it on his shoulder. He grabbed the strap of his sabretache and headed for the door.

You did not ask me to, master.

"Excuses, excuses," he muttered, taking the stairs two

170

at a time. "That boy would make a better familiar than you."

He knows no magic.

"He can carry more bags."

The court caravan was still forming up when Liam swung into his saddle, so he held back the apologies he had prepared. He settled for an angry glare at Provyn's velvet-coated back, and spent a few minutes arranging his sabretache and his swords.

Diamond danced a little in the street before the Duke's Arms, and Liam cursed half-heartedly, shortening the reins. The roan was in good spirits and looked well; when the boy ran up to report that his bags were all stowed on the packhorses, Liam received the report with a salute and tossed him a silver coin. "There's another for you when we reach Crossroads Fair, if you keep an eye on the horse."

Awestruck, the boy stared at the coin in his hand, and was still staring at it when Widow Saffian signalled the court to begin its day's ride. Liam buttoned up his coat against the chill, predawn air. He rode beside the Areopage, third in the column behind two Warinsford Guards bearing the town's colors and those of the Duke, and then a third Guard and Provyn. The fat quaestor held himself aloof from the conversation of the Guards, who were chatting noisily amongst themselves.

Widow Saffian rode well; the reins hung loosely from her confident hands, and she swayed in rhythm with her horse's gait as they turned onto a broader street. "Quaestor Rhenford, there's a question I would ask you."

"Yes?"

Her eyes faced straight ahead, and for a long moment she rode in silence. Then, "Yesterday, in the sessions, how knew you Kammer was escaping?" She finally looked at him, and gestured at Fanuilh. "Was it through your familiar?"

"Yes. He can sense when magic is being used nearby." He had the feeling it was not the question she had originally meant to ask, but she merely nodded, her face a placid mask.

Warinsford woke up around them as they rode through the dark streets—bakers opening their shops, servants sweeping doorsteps and emptying chamberpots into the gutters, farmers guiding their creaking wagons to the market—and Liam found himself breathing deeply, looking around with heightened appreciation of the early morning hours. He got a baker to toss him a hot roll and threw back a coin.

Alasco waited for them at the edge of the town, sitting his horse by the north gate. He bowed to Provyn and Widow Saffian, and drew abreast of Liam.

"Good morrow." He wore a sickly grin, and looked pale.

"Good morning. You didn't have to come see us off."

"Oh, you know. . . ." Alasco flopped his hand as if it were nothing. "I only thought . . ." He let the sentence trail off, shrugging sheepishly, as they passed through the gate and onto the road. Liam waited for the inevitable flood of questions, but the young quaestor had to concentrate on keeping his seat, and made no mention of the talk that had seemed so pressing the night before.

So pressing with a bellyful of wine, Liam thought to himself, grinning at his hungover companion. "Wouldn't you be happier in bed?" he asked at last. "You can't have had much sleep."

"Truth," the young man confessed, slouching in his saddle, "it'd like me. Pray, don't think it a mark of disrespect."

"Not at all," Liam said, chuckling

"I would that my stomach was quieter—I would that we'd more time together. I feel I could learn more from you than from all the scholars in Torquay."

Where do people get these insane ideas about me? "Well, I can't cure a hangover." He turned Diamond to the side, cutting Alasco out of the column, and offered him his hand. "I appreciate you're coming out, Vaucan. It's been a pleasure working with you. If you ever come to Southwark, look me up. Aedile Coeccias will know where to find me.''

Alasco brightened at the invitation. ''That'd like me, Liam. And, should I come across some mystery I cannot fathom, I wonder if I might write of it to you? There're ever couriers between here and Southwark, and words fly.''

''Certainly—but don't expect me to be able to solve every crime that comes your way,'' he added, anticipating a spate of letters from Warinsford. *On the other hand, there is a lot he could learn, even from me, and Cuspinian's not likely to teach it to him. What harm can it do?*

The young quaestor thanked him, wrung his hand again, and rode up to the head of the train to say goodbye to the Areopage. Liam waited on the grassy margin, watching the court train pass by, and waved to him as he returned to the town. The sun, just clearing the horizon, threw a pinkish light onto Warinsford's walls, and for a few minutes it looked fresh and clean—and then he remembered Kammer and the Handuits, and his conversation with Cuspinian, and decided he was not sorry to be putting the town behind him. Spurring Diamond into a trot, he resumed his place in the column.

Growing up in the Midlands, spring had been Liam's favorite season, when the land ran riot with green and the air was rich with the smell—and sometimes, he had thought as a child, with the sound—of things growing. The Southern Tier reacted with less exuberance to the warmth and the sunshine than the Midlands, but he detected echoes of it as they passed beyond the outskirts of Warinsford. The rolling turf was a deeper, more vibrant shade of green, all the more so for the brilliant whiteness of the sheep that grazed the hillsides. Leaves blurred the outlines of the occasional copse, and from time to time he caught the faint trill of birdsong.

The day passed pleasantly enough; their road paralleled the Warin and they took it at an easy pace. Diamond followed the other horses without guidance and Liam barely held the reins, slouched comfortably in his saddle. He surveyed the countryside or watched the traffic of boats on the river, and thought very little.

Fanuilh flew off around noon to hunt, and returned an hour later to settle heavily on Diamond's withers.

There are many rabbits here, it thought.

"Mmm," Liam replied. He had shed his coat, and raised his face with eyes closed to the sun. *That's nice.*

What will you do with the Dominia Daemonologia?

Reluctantly, Liam opened his eyes and looked down at the dragon. *I don't know. Keep it, I suppose. It might come in handy.*

It is illegal for you to have it.

Provyn thought it was all right, as long as I kept it quiet. He wanted to return to his pleasant torpor. *Anyway, I inherited it from a Guild-sanctioned wizard, didn't I?*

There was a long pause, and Liam was about to start sunning himself again when the dragon thought, *That would not mean that you are entitled to keep it.*

No, Liam agreed, and forced himself to consider the question in more depth. He was not a wizard, regardless of what some might think, and he did not doubt that his possession of the book was technically illegal. On the other hand, Provyn had not made much of it, and it had proved useful in Warinsford. *We'll wait until I read the Deepenmoor report more carefully. If it looks like the book will come in handy, I'll keep it until the circuit is finished, and then destroy it. If not, I'll destroy it right away. All right?*

It would be reasonable, the dragon replied.

Liam went back to sunning himself.

The Areopagus stopped that night at an inn on the banks of the river, where the road north from Warinsford met the road east to Crossroads Fair. Provyn, who had not spoken to Liam all day, not even during the court's stop for lunch, made a fuss about finding a separate room for himself, and only grudgingly accepted the innkeeper's apologies that none were available.

Liam rolled his eyes at the transparent insult, but said nothing. With his fop's clothes and the scratchmarks on his face, the fat quaestor cut too ridiculous a figure to take seriously.

Widow Saffian, however, finally took note of the situation, and Liam could see that it troubled her. When she invited Iorvram to eat at her table with the two quaestors, Liam assumed that she hoped the clerk would act as a buffer between them. It was a partial success: he and Liam talked animatedly throughout the meal, undeterred by Provyn's frigid silence. When the dishes were removed, the fat quaestor rose, bowed stiffly to Widow Saffian, and retired. Iorvram—overly conscious of his lower status with the court, in Liam's opinion, and anxious not to overstay his welcome—took his leave as well.

When Liam made to go the Areopage stopped him, and then looked into the fireplace for a moment, composing her thoughts. Liam waited patiently.

"The court is much disordered this year," she began at last, her eyes focused on the fireplace. "It is to be expected, I suppose, with my husband's death coming so close to the commencement of the circuit. Things are misplaced, overlooked, out of joint. Were my husband here, I doubt not that all would be well." She cleared her throat, and met Liam's eyes.

He had expected to see tears, perhaps, or at the very least some sign of sorrow; instead, her face was calm, and her eyes held his with a strong gaze.

"Master Saffian is not with us, however, and so there are flaws. That with Kammer, as an instance: my husband would have plumbed the depth of that as soon as ever he read the cases, and seen the strands of truth in the web of coincidence. He had a genius for that, as he had a genius for organization. He saw *through* things, as he saw *to* things. We feel the lack of his parts, as we feel the lack of them in me."

She paused again, pinching the bridge of her nose and waving her hand impatiently, as if she was unhappy with how she had expressed herself. For his part, Liam could think of nothing to say—he had no idea where she was going. After a moment she clasped her hands in her lap and started again.

"What I mean to say is this, Quaestor Rhenford: there is friction in the court. I see that you and Quaestor Provyn are oil and water. Look you, with my husband's death, he had the expectation of the capital cases, and the loss of them rankles. What's more, he can be . . . prickly. I would ask your patience with him, Quaestor Rhenford."

"Of course," he said, and then cut himself off when he saw that she was not finished.

"On the other hand," the Areopage continued, fixing him with a stern glance, "you must know that we are somewhat disordered, and so not all things may be ordered as we might wish. If a report is a few days late, what does it matter, so that it is in your hands ere the case comes up?"

This time she was finished, and clearly expected a reply, but Liam could only gape. *Has that ass been complaining about me?* "Forgive me, Areopage," he managed at last, "but if you're referring to the reports I asked Quaestor Provyn for—"

"I am," she said. "Y'have been pressing him hard, when he is bearing the greater part of the court's burden. It is the common misconception that the capital cases are the more weighty, for that they involve life and death. But you must remember that there are far more mundane cases, and it is rare that they are as clear in their outlines. I gave you the capital for that there are the fewer of them, Quaestor Rhenford, not for that I considered you the better man."

Swallowing a retort, Liam paused and thought a moment before speaking. "I'm aware of that, Areopage, and I wouldn't pretend to be more experienced in court matters than Quaestor Provyn." *All other matters, yes, but not court matters.* "That's precisely why I wanted the reports so much—because I have so little experience."

Widow Saffian drew back her head with a skeptical

expression, and then waved the argument aside. "The point is moot, in course, for that y'have the report now. It would merely like me if you would do your best not to trouble Quaestor Provyn. He's much to do."

Liam spread his hands in surrender, not willing to push the matter further. "As you wish, Areopage."

With a satisfied nod, she moved on to other business. "There're no capital cases at the Crossroads Fair. Were you aware of that?"

"I was, yes. Quaestor Provyn told me."

"Good. I had thought of pairing you with him, so that you might learn something of the mundane cases, but I see that that would not be wise."

Liam offered a silent prayer of thanks.

"So it seems that you will be free the while we are there. It would like me if you could prepare a statement as to the necessity of Kammer's death, and all the chain of events that led up to it, with your thoughts and methods of investigation included. For the records, look you, for that his end was outside the court and . . . unusual."

A hint of reproach lay hid in the way she pronounced the last word, as if Liam were solely responsible for the unusual nature of Kammer's death. He considered asking her to explain, but then decided against it. If she wanted a statement, he would give her one, and he felt sure it would not redound to his discredit.

"As you wish, Areopage." *After all, I wasn't the one who stuck a spear in his side. I was the one writhing in the alley, whose throat he was going to slit.* A chill ran up his back, but he kept himself still.

"My thanks," she said, and then nodded in dismissal. "Sleep well, Quaestor Rhenford."

"Sleep well, Areopage."

Liam had meant to read the Deepenmoor report that night, to get a head start on the case; instead, he went up to his room and began composing his statement in his head.

• • •

The court left early the next morning, heading now away from the Warin. The road climbed out of the river valley into the gently rolling hills to the northeast, and throughout the morning the Areopage again set an easy pace. As the sun rose higher, what Liam had taken for a distant line of clouds on the northern horizon slowly resolved themselves into mountains.

Fanuilh asked him whether he had come to a decision about the *Daemonologia,* and he confessed that he had not had time to read the report. *The Areopage and I had a little . . . chat,* he projected. *I didn't have a chance.*

You should make up your mind, it told him.

Since the dragon's thoughts always came in the same uninflected, emotionless manner, Liam often found it difficult to determine how seriously to take it—and in this case he was not inclined to take it very seriously at all. The day was beautiful, Diamond was stepping well, and the likelihood of his being arrested for possessing an illicit book seemed very distant.

I'll decide tonight, I promise. But really, now, why are you so concerned?

It is not something that should be put off.

"Make hay while the sun shines"—is that it? Nothing more? Are you sure you're not worried I might take it into my head to summon a demon?

You would not do that.

Oh, I don't know. It might be fun.

The dragon, sitting on Diamond's withers with its back to him, snaked its head over its shoulder to stare at him. *It would not be fun.*

So you say . . . , he projected, and chuckled.

When it saw that he was joking, Fanuilh turned its head forward and thought nothing more on the subject.

Heavy, black clouds gathered with remarkable speed while the court stopped for lunch, and an hour later broke in a fierce rainstorm. Despite the ditches to either side, the road quickly became swampy and the column stretched out, each rider trying to avoid the splashing hooves of the horse in front of him.

The rain slackened to a dull pounding after the first wild squall, and followed them for the rest of the afternoon, chasing them into the inn where they planned to spend the night. The common room filled with dripping, miserable clerks and servants, and Liam was glad when Provyn's complaints got them separate rooms. He gathered his bags and followed the serving maid to his, a little garret under the thatched roof.

"It's hardly a room for such as yourself, my lord," the girl told him, "but the roof's stout, and doesn't leak."

"What more could you ask for?"

She could think of nothing and curtseyed her way out, promising to return for his wet clothes. While Liam changed, Fanuilh shook itself like a dog, an operation so unsuccessful that he finally tried to dry it with a blanket.

"If you were a real dragon, you would breathe a little fire and we'd all be warm and toasty."

Please, the dragon protested, struggling out of his lap as he wiped at its leathery wings. *I think I am dry enough.*

"Suit yourself," he told it, heading for the door. "Just don't drip on the bed."

At the bottom of the stairs, the serving maid scolded him for bringing down his own clothes, and then offered to send his dinner up to his room, informing him that both Widow Saffian and Provyn would be dining privately. The rest of the court was already sitting around a single long table in the common room, sipping at bowls of soup and complaining about the weather. Clouds of steam rose from their drying clothes, hung on racks and the backs of chairs, from roofbeams and hooks by the roaring fireplace.

"No," he said, handing the girl his wet clothes, "I'll eat here." Apart from Iorvram and the boy who looked after his baggage, he had yet to meet any of the Areopagus's long train of servants and clerks. He found a spot at the table next to the chief clerk.

Talk around the table died away when Liam first sat down, but slowly revived when Iorvram began chatting amiably with him; soon enough he learned a great many of the men's names and their positions. They groused about the weather, the consensus being that it was a little worse than on past spring circuits, but not much, and then they fell to comparing cases; the consensus there was that for sheer villainy Lons Kammer beat any prisoner in the last ten years, while the rest were merely average, including the Handuits. One clerk took the logical step and began comparing the sentences handed down, but he was quickly silenced by his comrades. Liam could tell they were on their best behavior, friendly in a deferential way because he was a quaestor, and not a little pleased that he had come to sit at their table rather than dine alone in his room.

"If it please you, Quaestor," one clerk inquired politely, "how does service with the Areopagus like you?"

"I like it very much," he said. "Except you meet an awful lot of villains."

At first they did not understand—Liam even saw the beginnings of an affronted expression on one man's face—and then Iorvram started laughing. As chief clerk, the other men accepted his interpretation of the comment, and a ripple of laughter spread around the table; from that point their attitude toward Liam grew friendlier, more relaxed. Once he saw two of the ostlers, heads together, repeating the joke quietly and sharing a moment of awed amusement. The main point, he gathered, was not that the joke had been funny, but that it had been made at all.

He ate three bowls of the thin soup, and when he rose to go the men stood with a scraping of benches and stools.

"Thank you, gentlemen. I'm off to bed." He felt absurd, as if he were pretending to be some lord or captain bidding his men good night. If they saw anything odd in it, however, it did not show; a babble of polite good wishes followed him up the stairs.

• • •

As promised, the roof did not leak; rain pattered distractingly on the thatch but did not come through. The rough bed was a plain wooden frame with thick, sagging ropes strung like a net between the boards, and Liam shifted constantly in search of a comfortable position in which to read. Fanuilh crouched on the thin edge of the bedframe, craning its neck to keep its eye on the pages through its master's contortions—Liam had refused to unknot the silver cord.

He was reading the report from Deepenmoor, and finding it particularly slow going. *This Gratian doesn't do much writing,* he guessed, as he went over a particularly thorny paragraph for the third time. Widow Saffian had likened him to the Aedile of Deepenmoor, and Liam was not sure now whether it was a compliment. *This makes no sense!* He rubbed his eyes and tried the paragraph again, but it alluded to something that had not been mentioned previously. He folded over the corner of the page and read on.

By the time he had formed a rudimentary idea of the case, his candle was burned down almost to the stub. As near as he could tell, three small children, two girls and a boy, had disappeared over a three-month period from the fishing village of Hounes, in the domain of Galba, Earl Raius. No mention was made in the report of their bodies being discovered, but a shift belonging to one of the girls and the boy's knife were found in a grotto near the village. Both shift and knife were spattered with blood, and traces of a circle "inscribed in blue chalk" were found on the floor of the grotto.

So we keep the book, Liam projected.

It might prove useful, Fanuilh admitted.

Those few facts were certain from the report; beyond that, however, things became hazy. He gathered that the grotto served as a crypt, though it was never stated, and he had no idea whose dead were buried there, though the report mentioned that "none of the corses were disturbed." References were made to keys, one in the possession of a local priest named Kortenaer and another belonging to the ghost witch of Deepenmoor, a Mother Aspatria. From the tone of the report, he guessed they were both suspected of the murder of the children, but he could not be sure, and the uncertainty frustrated him to the point where he cursed aloud.

"What is wrong with this man?" he asked Fanuilh.

It is as if he wrote the report at many sittings.

"With months between each sitting," Liam grumbled. The dragon was right: there was a disjointed quality to the narrative, gaps and sudden changes of topic that made it maddening to read. Even the handwriting was sloppy, a far cry from the neat block writing of the other reports he had read.

Were the priest and the ghost witch accomplices? The report did not say. Was there any real evidence against them, besides their owning keys to the crypt-grotto? At times the report alluded to evidence as if it had already been presented, but Liam could find no trace of it. Did anyone else have keys? No answer.

And how in the world do you put a lock on a cave? he demanded of Fanuilh, tossing the report to the floor and slumping back on the bed. *You'd think that in a case that involves a priest and one of the Duke's officers, they'd take a little more care with the details.*

Perhaps Aedile Gratian can explain when we arrive at Deepenmoor.

I have a sneaking suspicion that Aedile Gratian is a drooling idiot.

The candle began to gutter, drowning in its own wax. Scowling, Liam climbed from the sagging mattress and undressed quickly, then threw himself into bed.

"Put that out, will you? And wake me early. I want to ask the Areopage about this report."

Fanuilh hopped off the edge of the bed and approached the candle. Liam lay back and watched its shadow, grotesque and flickering on the thatch of the ceiling. It stood by the candle for a while, head cocked, then flared its wings and swept them forward to create a breeze.

The candle went out.

In his dream, Liam stood in the Handuits' basement and watched the cistern. From the low ceiling drops of rain as fat as leeches fell, one by one, into the scummy water that lapped at the rim of the cistern, threatening to overflow.

Wake. After each splash, the word rang out.

Drip. *Wake.* Drip. *Wake.* Drip. *Wake.*

He woke to the patter of rain on the thatch. It was pitch dark in the room.

"Isn't there a cantrip for lighting a fire?" he called, and a moment later the candle burst alight, illuminating his familiar.

It will not last long.

Liam dressed quickly and had his bags gathered by the time the candle finally died. He found the door in the darkness and went downstairs. The clerks and servants sat around the single table as if they had spent the night there, and greeted him with smiles and inquiries about his sleep.

"Wonderful," he replied as he sat next to Iorvram. A twinge in his lower back said otherwise, but he smiled to cover it. "Is the Areopage down yet?"

The serving maid slid a wooden platter of bacon, bread and cheese in front of him. "The lady's taking her breakfast in her rooms, my lord."

"She'll be down betimes," Iorvram promised him. "It's a long day's ride to Crossroads Fair."

Busy making a sandwich, Liam only nodded. He had hoped to talk to her about Gratian's report before they left, but it was probably just as well. There was sleep in his eyes and his hair stuck up in clumps. *A little ride in the rain will take care of that,* he thought ruefully. Through the inn's single window he could see a curtain of gray drizzle.

That the men around the table were no cleaner was something of a consolation until Provyn came down the stairs, fresh-scrubbed and clean-shaven, having apparently arranged to wash. *Which you should have done,* Liam scolded himself. *But then, you're just going to get dirty again, aren't you?* He swallowed the last of his sandwich, scooped up Fanuilh, and headed for the door as the fat quaestor called his servant over and began badgering him about the packing of his bags.

Outside, Liam put his familiar down under the eaves of the inn and stepped into the drizzle. Cold rain sluiced away the sleep and slicked down his hair. He stepped back to the shelter of the eaves, spluttering, and found his self-appointed servant at his side, holding out his coat.

"It's dry, Quaestor."

He put it on over his wet tunic and thanked the boy.

"Shall I fetch your bags? We'll be leaving presently." The door of the inn opened, disgorging court servants who ran, hunched against the rain, to the inn's large barn.

"Yes. But get someone to help you," he added as the boy dashed off. An image of the overloaded boy collapsing into the mud of the innyard flashed through his head.

Water dripped from his wet hair down under his collar. Frowning, he walked out into the rain toward the barn. There was no point in keeping dry—a few minutes' riding would soak him as thoroughly as a bath. *The people who enjoy travelling the most,* he reflected, *are the ones who stay at home.*

CHAPTER 14

IT RAINED ALL day, a numbing drizzle that lent a jelly-like consistency to the mud thrown up by the horses' hooves, and every member of the Areopagus—from Widow Saffian down to Liam's servant boy—was covered head to toe in cold, viscous muck. They had ridden since morning without a stop, and were still several hours late in arriving at Crossroads Fair.

Slumped in his saddle, Liam wiped a handful of mud from his face as he passed through the arch of the marshalling yard. He blinked in tired disbelief, unconsciously pulling back on the reins until the horse behind him nudged Diamond, eager to get under cover. Urging the roan on, he stared about him.

Torches flared in the soaring space as Guards ran out to meet the court; the flames cast long shadows around the enclosed yard, showing long rows of columns supporting the massive beams of a peaked roof. Gusts of wind rattled canvas screens stretched between the columns, and the riders of the Areopagus instinctively pressed toward the center of the yard, flinching from the miserable weather they had endured all day. Liam alone strayed to the fringes of the incredible space, marvelling.

"It's as big as the Flying Stair in Torquay," he told Fanuilh, and then added silently, *But roofed!* He looked at the court, huddling together to dismount, and estimated the yard could easily hold ten times as many people—almost two hundred men and their mounts. *It's enormous!*

The Flying Stair is magical, the dragon reminded him. Too tired to think of a suitably cutting reply, Liam simply shook his head and dismounted, wincing at the squelching noise that came from his boots. His boy appeared from nowhere to take the reins, enthusiasm undimmed even by a thick coating of mud, and promised to have his bags delivered immediately.

In the far wall of the yard were two doors, from one of which spilled light and the promise of warmth; Widow Saffian and Provyn stood in front of the door, talking with two women and a man Liam did not know. He tucked Fanuilh under his arm and hurried over, trying to figure out a polite way to request a bath.

"And this is Quaestor Rhenford," the judge said as he approached. "Our newest. Quaestor Rhenford, this is Aedile Tarpeia, Father Enghave, the ghost warlock of the quarter, and Quaestor Casotte."

Liam bowed to the Aedile, a stocky woman in her forties with incongruously wispy blond hair pulled back from a broad, pleasant face. Enghave, tall and thin and wavering like a reed, grasped at his long beard as if he required the extra leverage to bend into his bow.

"Ghost witch, if it please you," he corrected. "Welcome to Crossroads Fair, Quaestor Rhenford."

"Welcome," the Aedile said.

"Welcome, Quaestor Rhenford," Quaestor Casotte said, bowing as Liam turned to her. When she rose, he momentarily forgot his desire for a bath, and immediately after regretted that he had not taken one already. She was his age or a little younger, with a beautiful smile full of small white teeth and long chestnut hair that spilled over the shoulders of her sleeveless leather jerkin.

"Thank you," he said, straining against the idiotic grin that threatened to spread across his face. "It's nice to be here."

For some reason that struck Father Enghave as funny.

An hour later, Liam found himself the sole representative of the Areopagus at the Aedile's table. Bathed and dressed in dry clothes, he felt a new man, and was glad of the chance to learn more about Tarpeia and her subordinates. Both Provyn and Widow Saffian had opted for bed, the judge with a polite excuse and the quaestor with a request that his clothes be washed and returned to him by the next morning.

"Y'have never seen so much slashing and satin and silver thread," Father Enghave said, nudging Quaestor Casotte with his elbow. "He was ever the dandy, but now he's the money to play the role. Has he come into a legacy, Quaestor Rhenford?"

"Not that I know of," Liam replied, "but I only met him a week or so ago."

Casotte shared a grin with the ghost witch. "He does not improve upon acquaintance."

"That is quite enough," Tarpeia scolded. "Quaestor Provyn is an officer of the Duke, as are we, and warrants the same respect." The younger woman bowed her head in acknowledgement of the rebuke—a gesture Liam thought very pretty.

It was an informal dinner, a far cry from Cuspinian's grand affairs. They sat around a much-scarred table, cutting meat from a communal haunch of venison and making inconsequential chatter, and Liam felt less like a visiting official and more like a guest in the home of some strange family. He took an instant liking to Father Enghave's eccentric and boisterous sense of humor, while Aedile Tarpeia was pleasant in a distracted, motherly way. *And Quaestor Casotte is very easy to look upon. . . .* All through the meal they peppered him with questions, eager to know the news from Southwark and from Warinsford, how he had come to join the court, how the circuit had gone thus far, whether he enjoyed his work. When they heard that he had been given the capital cases, Father Enghave and Casotte both burst out laughing.

"Oh, how that must have galled Provyn!" The ghost witch twirled the end of his beard around his finger, happily contemplating the idea.

"And he in his silks and satins," Casotte chimed in, "ever clearing the mundane cases!"

Tarpeia frowned disapprovingly at them, but they ignored her. "See you," she said, turning to Liam, "we thought, well, it'd seem only natural that with Widow Saffian created Areopage, he'd take the capital cases."

Recalling the judge's words on the subject, Liam shrugged uncomfortably. "She gave them to me because there were fewer of them, and she thought they would be easier for a newcomer to handle."

"Easier!" Casotte laughed. "Easier, he says! And with the late Areopage giving them the majority of his attention, and ever calling them the thorniest of crimes! Oh, no, Quaestor Rhenford, mark you: y'have the capital cases for that that knave Provyn's—"

The Aedile slapped her hand down on the table, making the cups dance. "Enough, I say!" The younger woman assumed a fragile expression of sobriety. "We'll have no more on it—still your gossiping tongues. Father Enghave, you'll show Quaestor Rhenford his room now."

Her angry outburst was more like that of a mother scolding unruly children than of an officer disciplining her underlings, and while Casotte remained silent and the ghost witch jumped up to escort Liam, neither seemed overly concerned or frightened. Liam thanked them for the meal and bowed his way out of the room after Enghave.

The rain stopped sometime during the night, and the first rays of the sun falling squarely on Liam's face woke him. He got out of bed and padded to the window. A forest well into the first bloom of spring stretched out before him, marching eastward over the hills. Only the tops of the trees were lit, sparkling with dew and shining over the dark understory; as he watched, birds wheeled and dove above the forest, chattering and calling among themselves.

His room—almost a cell, with bare stone walls and floor, a single narrow bed and a washstand—was at the rear of the barracks on the second floor, and by leaning

out the window he could look along the back wall of the
Fair. The sheer size of it amazed him; it reached almost
two hundred yards to the north, an expanse of stone dot-
ted with windows for its whole length. He stood there
for a few minutes, watching the sunlight creep down
from the roof, and then washed and dressed.

The servants must have worked all night, since the
clothes he had handed over the evening before were
piled, clean and neatly folded, on the washstand beside
the basin. He chose a blue tunic and gray breeches, put
them on, and woke Fanuilh.

"Come on, we're going to have a look at this place."

The dragon trotted willingly behind him through the
long corridors of the barracks, and between the two of
them they found a route out into the marshalling yard.
Guards were busy taking down the canvas screens and
he could see through the columns; to the south lay the
same forest he had seen from his window, and to the
west was the road they had come in on the night before,
a muddy ribbon through the trees. To the north lay the
rest of the Fair.

Father Enghave had given him a brief history of the
place the night before, while guiding him to his room.
Built as the home base of a King's Legion some five
hundred years before, in the reign of Auric the Great, it
had fallen into the care of the dukes of the Southern Tier
with the disbanding of the Legions and the waning of
royal power. The dukes garrisoned it with a force a tenth
the size of the one it was meant to accommodate and
used the rest of the space as a trading fair. The ghost
witch had described the soldiers and merchants who lived
and worked there as children squatting in a crypt of giants.

Liam slipped between the columns onto a broad plaza
of chipped and crumbling stone, at the center of which
was a dry fountain. Beyond that, on the far side of the
plaza, was what looked like another marshalling yard.
The wind came from that direction, and he could make
out the smell of fresh-baked bread. He set off with long

strides to track down its source. The flags of the plaza were uneven, with broad borders of moss running around their edges, and he saw as he approached the fountain that it too was gradually falling apart.

Still, he projected, *it's not bad for something that's five hundred years old.*

No, Fanuilh agreed.

The central building fronted the eastern side of the plaza with a wide, shadowy arcade, above which was an open platform. Liam pointed toward the platform. *The Legion commander could address his soldiers from up there—give orders, make speeches, hold an inspection.*

It would not make a very good fortress, the dragon observed.

No, but it wasn't supposed to. It was a staging area, the home base of a Legion. Most of the fortresses in those days would have been on the coast. There was less fighting within the kingdom. Taralonians didn't set upon one another with quite the same glee as they do now.

The smell of bread was stronger and he moved on, crossing the second half of the plaza. The northern marshalling yard was the Fair proper, and the space inside had been partitioned off into stalls and booths. It was still early in the trading season, so many of them were boarded up, and the few that were open were empty. Their owners were inside the northern barracks, where an enterprising baker had set up shop in the military kitchens. Liam bought a fresh loaf of bread and retreated to the central plaza, aware of the strange looks Fanuilh was drawing, and ate his breakfast sitting on the edge of the empty fountain.

He had brought along his writing case, meaning to find a table somewhere to compose his report, but the warm sunshine was so welcome after yesterday's rain that he decided to do his writing where he was. That was how Widow Saffian found him an hour later, his back to the fountain, the writing case propped up on his knees, stylus in his mouth as he wrestled with a phrase. He did not notice her approach until she spoke.

"Good morrow to you, Quaestor Rhenford." Startled, he scrambled awkwardly to his feet, juggling case and papers and stylus and trying to bow.

"We missed you at our meeting," she went on, and there was no mistaking her rebuke. With her black robes and her beaked nose, she reminded him of a stern crow.

"Meeting?"

"Much as we had in Warinsford, to learn what we must of the cases at hand. We waited on you, and you did not come."

"Ah," Liam said, seeing a defense. "I assumed that since I had no cases, I wouldn't be needed, so I took the time to start my report on Kammer." He held up his writings as proof.

She regarded the papers for a moment, then nodded. "It'd like me if you'd attend us at the next meeting."

"As you wish, Areopage." He bowed, and by the time he rose she was gliding away, her footsteps hidden by the skirts of her mourning robes.

For the rest of the morning Liam sat by the fountain, trying to finish his report, but Widow Saffian's visit continually intruded on his thoughts, spoiling his concentration. The sun was warm on his legs and face, and the songs of birds echoed merrily in the nearby forest, but his mood refused to match the day.

She thinks I'm some sort of truant, he projected, chewing on his stylus. *A stray she needs to keep rounding up.*

Fanuilh lay at his feet; it blinked one sleepy eye at him. *You did not know about the meeting. How can she blame you?*

How can she blame me for wanting the Deepenmoor report? Liam responded. *But she seems to think I badgered Provyn unmercifully.* He had no doubt where that idea had come from, and knew there was nothing he could do about it. The fat quaestor was too firmly entrenched in the court; in a case of his word against Liam's, he would win. Frustrated, Liam rattled a piece of paper at his familiar. *And even this hasn't earned me*

*any respect. As if Provyn could have figured out that
Kammer was "our man"—or the Areopage, for that
matter!*

The dragon made no reply, and Liam fell to musing
about the Deepenmoor case. It seemed more complicated
than either of the crimes from Warinsford, particularly
given the confused nature of Gratian's report. Unless the
Aedile could provide much more coherent information
when they arrived, he was afraid he might not get anywhere with it. *And if you can't solve it,* he thought privately, *no one with the court can.* He had little faith in
his abilities, but more than he had in Provyn's or Widow
Saffian's.

Until then, he had not really appreciated how great a
blow to the court the loss of Acrasius Saffian had been.
*If he was half as brilliant as people say, he could have
settled these cases without getting out of bed in the morning. He's not here, of course, which leaves only Provyn
and Widow Saffian—and me.* Cuspinian's words echoed
in Liam's head: *Villains across the duchy rejoiced when
they heard he was dead.*

With that gloomy thought, he put his writing materials
back in the case and decided to take a walk.

Spring was busy in the forest around the Fair, noisy with
birds and breezes and the rustlings of small animals. Fanuilh did not help, alternately soaring up to the cathedral
canopy of trees to scatter a flock of wheeling starlings,
and swooping down to the understory to flush hares and
squirrels. Twice in his long ramble Liam startled groups
of deer as they silently made their way along the forest
paths, and he watched them bound away with a pleased
smile. Neither master nor familiar gave any thought to
the Areopagus.

Mostly they kept to the wood, skirting the occasional
cleared field and clusters of cottages. Late in the afternoon, when the sun's beams struck through the trees at
sharp westerly angles, they stumbled on a large road running out of the north, and followed it back to the Fair.

That was nice, Liam projected, as they approached the southern marshalling yard, and became aware that he was dragging his feet, unwilling to return to court business. *Back to work.*

If you do not need me, I will fly some more.

Help yourself, he thought. *Only leave the Duke's rabbits in peace.*

Fanuilh banked away and disappeared into the forest, and Liam trudged on to the Fair alone.

A caravan had come in, and he could see them making camp beyond the northern marshalling yard. He would have liked to learn where they came from, and what they were carrying, but his report on Kammer's death was unfinished, and a nagging sense of duty sent him to his room.

The walk had cleared his mind, and he had completed a rough draft and was halfway through copying it out when Father Enghave appeared at his door.

"I've come to bid you to dinner," the ghost witch said, "for that we feel sadly neglected by the Areopagus. You fail us at breakfast, and leave us to Provyn's tender mercies, and he and the Areopage fail us at dinner. How do we offend? Our manners are rude, I know, but for all that we don't smell. Or at least I think we don't smell. Tarpeia and Casotte, perhaps, after a long day's riding, I'll grant you so much, but I never smell, that I know. I'm a veritable flower. Come, Quaestor, will you dine with us?"

Liam tossed aside his half-copied report. "I will, and you don't smell at all."

Feigning confusion, the ghost witch led the way to the room where they had eaten the night before. "If we don't smell, then I confess I cannot see why the court snubs us so. I know it cannot be me—so perhaps it is Casotte. Ah, yes, I see it now! You fear her! You mistake her for a troll, a monster, or a trained bear, perhaps, and will not sit down to eat with her, for fear she will run wild. For all that she is a quaestor at the Fair, she is not a fair quaestor, if you take me, no, not fair at all." He contin-

ued the string of abuse even after they reached the dining
room, where Tarpeia and Casotte had already begun eating. "Ah, my dear, I was just telling Quaestor Rhenford
how very ugly you are, and how y'have been known to
sour milk with a glance."

"Go to, sirrah," Casotte said, with an indulgent smile,
and then addressed Liam. "I'll strike a bargain with you,
Quaestor. If you'll not give his ravings credit, I'll dis-
count what I've heard of you."

"Anyone can see he's mad," Liam said, taking his
seat and hoping the compliment was clear.

Enghave hooted and thumped the table with his fist.
"Gallant, too? Did you hear, Tarpeia? The man's gallant!"

"Hush," the Aedile chided, but the ghost witch ignored her, tugging excitedly at his beard.

"Now tell, who has been slandering the gallant quaestor? What rogue has impugned his name?"

"Can you not guess?" Casotte asked, glancing around
the table, and Liam did. She went on quickly to confirm
his suspicion. "Why, Quaestor Provyn, whom I had the
pleasure of attending today. He would have Quaestor
Rhenford an untried timeserver, a subverter of justice, a
dangerous novice, hasty, impetuous, rude and knavish.
Come, Quaestor, are these things true?"

Liam spread his hands in surrender. "They are—as
true as what Father Enghave has said of you." The words
came out pleasantly, even as he silently cursed the fat
quaestor.

It took a moment for the second compliment to reg-
ister, but when it did, it produced quite a reaction. Casotte
blushed fiercely and bowed her head, while Father Enghave hooted again and nudged her in the ribs with his
elbow. "Did you hear?" he demanded. "Did you hear?"

"We heard," Tarpeia said, who had grown more and
more uncomfortable as the conversation went on. "But
let's have less of personalities, shall we? Quaestor
Provyn isn't here to answer for his words, so let's not
discuss them. Let's eat, instead."

She passed a jug of wine around the table, alert for signs of dissent, and when the jug had returned to her in silence she nodded with relief. "That's good, then. Did you see the caravan that came in today?"

They all had, and while they ate the Fair officials discussed the upcoming trading season. Liam listened with interest, curious to know more about the goods that passed through the Fair, and what prices they brought.

"They say Lons Cullum's to arrive on the morrow," Father Enghave pointed out with a significant look at Casotte, who grinned and clapped her hands.

"Cullum? Then we'll have a dance!"

"A merchant from Caernarvon," Tarpeia explained, seeing Liam's bemused look. "He ever travels with musicians."

"Not the best," Casotte put in, "but they'll play through the night, and there'll be dancing til daybreak! Oh, Quaestor Rhenford, y'are in luck!"

Liam smiled. He was not a very good dancer and knew it, but on seeing her happy smile, he decided not to mention it. *And who knows?* he thought, considering the pretty quaestor. *Maybe your feet will grow wings.*

The others had spent the day on court business or engaged in their usual tasks, and retired immediately after dinner, while Liam, who had done nothing more strenuous than take a walk, went out onto the plaza. There was a chill in the air, so he paced, hugging his arms and gazing up to count the stars, which shone clear and hard in the sky. He had been up since dawn, but was not tired, and when Fanuilh returned from the forest, he showed no inclination to go to bed.

"Have a nice time?" he asked, kneeling down to scratch the dragon's back.

There are owls in the wood, it told him. *Quite fierce creatures.*

"Fierce, eh? Not so fierce as the ones we have here." Silently, then, he projected what Provyn had told Casotte about him. *Can you believe that?*

He seems to dislike you a great deal.

"Hang 'dislike'—he hates me, and all because he thinks I took the position he should have had, which I didn't even want."

You have it nonetheless.

He could not argue with that, so he shrugged and re-sumed his pacing and stargazing. "I don't suppose you know a spell that will turn an ass into a dove, do you?"

There is such a spell, the dragon replied after a few moments' thought. *It would turn an ass into an entire flock of doves, actually—the mass of the ass must be conserved—but what does that have to do with Quaestor Provyn?*

Liam laughed out loud. "Never mind."

They walked awhile in silence, pacing out the perim-eter of the plaza. Fanuilh's claws clicked on the paving stones, but otherwise Liam was hardly aware of its pres-ence. He was wrapped in his own thoughts about Provyn and Widow Saffian, the court and Casotte.

If that's what he said to Casotte, the Dark alone knows what he says to the Areopage. Despite himself, he was anxious to have the Areopage's good opinion. He had no desire to join the court on a permanent basis, particularly if it meant serving with Provyn again, and he did not think his friends in Southwark would believe a bad report of him—and yet he wanted to do well, to successfully accomplish the task given him. *It's pure pride,* he told himself, *and the proud man stumbles, because he doesn't watch his feet. You'll just have to work harder.*

There were things he could do, he knew, to show his competence: completing the report on Kammer's death, for instance, and following up on the questions that had occurred to him while reading the Deepenmoor case. He could show himself sober and conscientious. *You could arrive on time for that meeting tomorrow morning,* he reminded himself, and decided it was time for bed. "Come along," he told Fanuilh. "We have to get up early."

Infrequent candles in widely separated niches provided

the only light in the barracks, and Liam and Fanuilh quickly became lost in the maze of hallways. They wandered aimlessly for a quarter of an hour before recognizing the corridor that led to their room, and that only because they caught sight of Quaestor Provyn as he turned a distant corner. There was no mistaking his red nightcap and portly figure, and Liam knew their rooms were near each other.

He may be a backbiting, bitter little man, Liam thought, *but he makes a good landmark.*

The next morning, Liam rose early and finished copying out his report on Kammer's death, and then spent the time before breakfast re-reading the Deepenmoor case and making a mental list of the questions he wanted to ask Widow Saffian. Feeling more than prepared, he arrived first at the court's breakfast meeting, and waited as the others straggled in. When the Areopage finally arrived and asked Provyn to report on the few mundane cases to be presented at the day's sessions, Liam listened attentively to what the fat quaestor had to say. He managed to ignore Provyn's pompous, solemn tone of voice, and his frequent references to the many similar crimes he had encountered in his long service with the court, and concentrated instead on the actual details.

Gods, no wonder he wants the capital cases. Mundane is too kind a word. They were even duller than those presented in Warinsford.

Eventually, Provyn wound up his summation and Widow Saffian declared the meeting at an end. Liam waited until everyone had started for the door and then approached the judge, holding out the pages he had written on Kammer's death.

"The report you asked for, Areopage."

She regarded the pieces of paper for a long moment, as if unsure what he was offering, and then nodded. "Oh, aye. I didn't look for it so soon, Quaestor." She took the papers. "My thanks."

"And if you could spare me some time today—maybe

after the sessions—I'd like to ask you a few questions about the case in Deepenmoor.''

The others had already filed out of the room, and Widow Saffian gestured him back to his seat. ''I can spare you the time presently, Quaestor. What would you know?''

''Well,'' Liam said, when they were both seated, ''I have to admit I found Aedile Gratian's report very confusing. First, I don't understand if the priest and the ghost witch are being accused together or separately, and I'm not sure I understand which had keys to the grotto. As for that, I couldn't tell from the report if that was just a cave, or some kind of cemetery, and I was wondering—''

He stopped when she held up a hand and began shaking her head. ''Hold a moment, hold a moment. Are these not in the report?''

''Not as far as I can tell, and that's another problem—''

''I haven't read the report,'' she interrupted, ''and am only vaguely aware of the case. It was somewhat infamous in Deepenmoor during the winter, and many fantastic rumors arose about it. The late Areopage took a great personal interest in it, and held much private discourse on it with Aedile Gratian, to which I was not privy.''

Liam opened his mouth to say something, and then snapped it shut. ''Ah.''

Widow Saffian continued as if she had not heard him. ''I do know, however, that's a delicate case. A hierarch and a ghost witch accused—well, you can see it's delicate. Earl Raius came twice to Deepenmoor ere we left for Southwark, to speak with my husband on the matter, and in course the Duke's shown an interest. I'd meant to look into it myself, but since the circuit's begun I've not had the time.'' She paused, as if a new thought had occurred to her, and then abruptly clapped her hands together. ''I shall have a copy of the report from Quaestor Provyn, and go over it as soon as I may. Then we can talk profitably of it. Will that suit?''

"Oh, certainly, certainly. That would be fine."

"Excellent." She rose. "I shall see you at the session."

He bowed and watched her go, the hem of her black robes whispering on the floorstones.

For the rest of the morning Liam wandered around the Fair, exploring the southern barracks and marvelling at the facilities the ancient Legions enjoyed. There were stalls for more than two hundred horses, with an ingenious system of pulleys and hooks and pipes to send feed and water to each stall, and the enormous, echoing armory would have been the envy of an Alyeciri warlord. The tiles in the bath hall were dingy with age and pieces were missing from the decorative mosaics, but a Guard informed him that the hypocaust still worked, and was fired up three times a week for the garrison, to heat the water in the central pool and provide the atmosphere of the steam room.

Fascinating as the place was, he made sure to allow himself enough time to dig a good set of clean clothes out of his bag and change for the sessions. When he was dressed, he commandeered a Guard to guide him to the hall where the court was sitting, and was gratified to see that he was early.

CHAPTER 15

AFTER THE EXCITEMENT in Warinsford, the session at the Fair was anticlimactic, and try as he might, Liam found it difficult to pay attention. The cases were dull to begin with, and he had also made the mistake of sitting next to Father Enghave, who whispered a scandalous—and often hilarious—running commentary to him on the background of each crime. In the second case, in which a woman had accused another of rendering a third's husband impotent with a spell, the ghost witch's explanation of the extramarital escapades involved caused Liam to burst out laughing, for which he received a stern glance from Widow Saffian.

Despite Father Enghave's best efforts, the rest of the cases passed without incident, and the Areopage declared the session closed after only a few hours. Liam lingered in his seat after the adjournment, half-expecting a rebuke for his outburst; the judge, however, immediately left the courtroom, pausing only to tell Aedile Tarpeia that she would spend the few hours before dinner in her room.

Relieved to have avoided the scolding he knew he deserved, Liam accepted Father Enghave's invitation to take a look at the caravan which had arrived during the session. It was Lons Cullum's, and the ghost witch knew many of the carters and drivers, for each of whom he had a nickname or a shared joke. They, in turn, promised that Cullum's musicians would play that night, and were happy to answer Liam's questions about the sort of goods they had brought, and what they hoped to carry back with them. He listened carefully, hoping to turn the information into profit when he returned to Southwark. Between taking mental notes, laughing at Father Enghave's off-kilter wit, and getting caught up in the general excitement of the impending dance, he almost forgot the Areopagus; when Quaestor Casotte came to summon him and the ghost witch to dinner, he hoped the meal would not last too long.

A bonfire blazed in the central plaza, piled high in the bowl of the dry fountain, and people danced and drank around it, the flames painting their faces red and orange. A dozen men battered out a tune with horns, pipes, lutes and drums, their pace ragged and their playing atrocious, a fact that did not seem to bother the dancers, who kept their own separate pace. The baker Liam had met that morning presided over a row of trestle tables, dispensing enormous draughts of beer. Casotte disappeared the minute they reached the plaza, in search of a cloth merchant from Torquay to whom she had promised a dance. Tarpeia headed straight to the nearest keg, drawing Liam and Father Enghave after her.

Once again, Liam was the only representative of the Areopagus. Dinner had been a quick and quiet affair, devoted entirely to eating. When the trenchers were empty, the Aedile—perhaps noting the barely restrained eagerness to be gone on the part of both Casotte and Father Enghave—mentioned Cullum's musicians, and invited the court officials to join the festivities. Widow Saffian had begged off, rubbing a fold of her black dress between thumb and forefinger. "It'd not do," she had said, "and I was never much of a dancer." Provyn had not even offered an excuse, marching off to his room with his mouth fixed in a thin line of disapproval.

Now Tarpeia pressed mugs on Liam and Enghave, and they moved away from the baker's tables. Standing at the edge of the crowd, they surveyed the party for a few minutes.

"Quite a gathering," Liam said, raising his voice to be heard. There were at least a hundred people on the plaza.

"That's word of Cullum," Tarpeia told him. "The cottagers from all around come, for to hear his minstrels." The musicians straggled to the end of their song and immediately started another. Enghave shouted for joy, thrust his mug into Liam's hands and leapt into the crowd of dancers, his patched robe swirling around his ankles.

"It is a favorite of his," the Aedile explained, and Liam nodded his understanding, though he could not tell the difference between this song and the one the musicians had just finished. He craned his neck and caught a glimpse of Casotte as she dragged a befuddled man half a head shorter than she through the steps of a fast-paced dance. He saw her thus a few times, as song followed song; much more often he saw the ghost witch, circling the bonfire with hair and beard flying wildly, dancing reels and jigs, faerie rings and stomp cuts with a glee that was almost maniacal. Some of the clerks and court servants were there as well, mingling happily with the merchants and the Guards and the locals.

Tarpeia stayed with him for a while, then strode out to separate two men who were close to blows over the right to a dance with a local girl, and did not return. Alone, he sipped at his beer and watched the increasingly drunken celebration, working up the courage to go find Casotte. *This is silly,* he told himself. *Go out and find her, you fool.*

Even as he finished the thought, she emerged from the mad crowd of dancers to face him. Her face glowed and she paused only long enough to push an errant strand of hair off her cheek.

"Quaestor Rhenford! Wherever have you been?"

Giving him no time to answer, she dragged him toward the fire as the musicians started butchering another song. He tried to explain that he was not a very good dancer but she would not listen, clasping his hands and forcing him through a series of steps.

For a hectic, exhausting hour, Liam danced. If she noticed how bad a dancer he was, Casotte made no comment; but then, he reflected, so many of the other men around the fire were blind drunk and tripping over themselves that he probably seemed a model of grace. At least he never fell and dragged her to the ground, as four drunken Guards did to him when they impressed him into a group stomp cut. She rescued him from the tangled mass of men, setting him on his feet and whirling him off into the next dance.

An unguessable number of dances later, Liam finally called a halt. He had a stitch in his side and his leg was sore from his fall among the Guards. Casotte followed him away from the bonfire to his seat on the steps of the arcade; she grinned down at him as he slumped, panting, to the ground.

"Y'are not much of a dancer," she teased. "The others'll dance til dawn, and then to their booths and stalls for the day." Apart from the flush on her cheeks and her dishevelled hair, she looked none the worse for her evening, and she had been at it longer than he. She hopped from foot to foot, still full of energy.

"I don't get much practice."

"Are there no dances in Southwark?"

"No one to dance with," he corrected and, somehow finding boldness in his exhaustion, added, "No one as pretty as you."

She grew still, regarding him with a sly smile, then stooped quickly and kissed him. It was awkward—her lips brushed his nose before they found his mouth—so she pulled him to his feet and kissed him again, more expertly this time.

Nothing like a country dance, he thought, and started to slip his arms around her waist. She stopped him, though, skipping backward and grinning at him. "A dance for a kiss, Quaestor Rhenford—that's my bargain."

Liam groaned. "I think I've stored up more than just two kisses already, don't you?"

"We count from now," she said, then turned and dashed back toward the bonfire. Finding his second wind with surprising ease, Liam caught up to her on the far side of the circle of dancers. He was halfway through earning his next kiss, careering around the bonfire, when he suddenly collided with someone and lost his footing.

He scrambled up, afraid he was going to be at the bottom of another pile of Guards, and saw the reason for the interruption: the two men he had seen earlier, arguing over the right to dance with a girl, were at it again, only now they were much drunker, and using fists and tankards instead of words. The other revellers took the whole thing in stride—they simply danced around the two men—and Liam was about to turn away when he saw Casotte leap into the fight, trying to separate the brawlers.

She ducked gracefully under a backhanded blow from the larger of the two men and rose in between them, just in time for the second man's tankard to shatter on the back of her neck. She dropped to her knees and the two men, oblivious, lunged at each other again.

With a snarl, Liam rushed forward and slammed his shoulder into the back of the nearest man, sending both brawlers flying. Ignoring them, he knelt anxiously at Casotte's side, and heard her whisper an astounded curse.

Someone grabbed his hair and jerked his head back—he heard laughter; saw something bright and thought it was a knife, but it was only the fire—and then one of the brawlers was punching him in the face, once, twice, and he hardly felt the pain, only a fearful and indignant astonishment. He lashed out wildly with his fists and must have connected somewhere, because the hand left his head and there were no more punches.

Master?

''What!'' Liam shouted, jumping to his feet and glaring around, at the crowd of wide-eyed dancers, at the Guards pummeling the brawlers into submission, at Father Enghave gently pulling Casotte to her feet. His face was numb, a situation he knew was temporary, and he went forward to help the ghost witch.

Master? Are you all right?

I suppose so, he thought, though at the moment he was not sure.

Liam's cheek and the orbit of his right eye were tender and puffy when Fanuilh woke him, though not as swollen as he had expected. *At least I can see,* he projected. *I was sure it'd be swollen shut.* Father Enghave had smeared a cold and vile-smelling salve on it the night before, after tending to Casotte. She had taken most of the blow on her back, and the ghost witch had stitched up the few cuts on her neck and sent her to bed.

Slowly, with infinite care, Liam got to his feet and started washing.

I am sorry I was not there to help you, Fanuilh projected. The dragon had been full of apologies the night before, and had spent the night perched at the foot of his bed, on guard.

"Don't worry about it," Liam said aloud. Standing had started an ache in his head, and he did not feel up to projecting. "Nothing a hard day's ride won't cure."

His headache faded mercifully as he dressed and packed, and by the time he went to the marshalling yard he had only his bruises to remind him of his part in the brawl. Ostlers and clerks hurried to and fro, saddling the court's horses and loading baggage; Liam found his self-appointed servant and sent him to fetch his bags. The boy gaped at his face for a moment and then dashed off. Shaking his head, Liam went in search of Father Enghave and found him, beard in his fist, grinning, as he watched four servants try to load a mass of baggage onto a recalcitrant packhorse.

"Come now, sirrah," the ghost witch called, "are you not proud to carry Quaestor Provyn's fineries upon your back? Or perhaps it is that you feel yourself unworthy of the honor?" The horse pranced back and forth, dragging the servants along in an ungainly dance. "The feeling does you credit—y'are a brave horse, a horse of parts!" It reared and plunged, scattering servants and chests. "I applaud you!" Enghave shouted.

"Good morning, Father Enghave."

"And to you, Quaestor Rhenford. Y'have a pretty face this morning. The look of your eye likes me—I feared it would have to come out."

"That won't be necessary," Liam said, then yanked the other man out of the way as the packhorse gave one last kick before subsiding.

"Bravely, bravely done! Know you this horse, Quaestor Rhenford? A passing uncommon horse, with acute perceptions. It declines the honor of Quaestor Provyn's bags. You should feel lucky to ride with such a creature."

"I'm sure I am, but I was wondering if you had any more of that salve you used last night."

"Did it like you? The aroma, I imagine. You wish to use it as perfume, I imagine?"

Liam smiled and touched his cheek. "Well, yes, but also for this."

The ghost witch gave Liam's eye a critical glance. "It is a most remarkable blue-black, most remarkable. You look quite the tavern brawler. Alas, the salve will do you no more good. The rest must be the work of time." The packhorse snorted and twitched, sending a chest to the ground; Enghave hooted. "Oh, it's a brave beast, Quaestor Rhenford, a brave horse. You and that horse are well-matched. Tell me, is there no way you can ride him? He was not made for carrying a fat man's laces. No? Then speak to him from time to time, I ask you, and see if you can't loose him some night. Such a brave beast should go free."

"I'm afraid they've broken his spirit," Liam said, pointing to where the servants were tying on the last bag. The rest of the packtrain was assembled, and as he spoke Widow Saffian came out of the barracks with Provyn and Tarpeia. The two women exchanged a few words and then the Areopage mounted, scanning the yard for something.

"She looks for you," Enghave told Liam, who could see Diamond saddled beside the Areopage. He bid the ghost witch a hasty goodbye, asked to be remembered to Casotte, and trotted over to his horse.

"Good morning, Areopage," he said as he mounted. "Quaestor Provyn."

Her eyes widened when she saw his bruise, and she frowned. "Good morrow to you, Quaestor Rhenford." Provyn said nothing. She raised her hand and spurred her horse. As the court began another day's travel, Liam heard Enghave shouting in the marshalling yard, urging him to free the horse and scatter its burden to the winds.

The three Guards from Warinsford had gone home the day before; three of Tarpeia's Guards headed up the column, bearing the Duke's banner. Behind them, Liam rode in company with Widow Saffian and Provyn, aware of a chilly silence but unwilling to let it spoil his appreciation of the weather and the day. It was perfect for riding and he concentrated on it, enjoying the sunshine and the cool breeze, the smell of the forest around them.

After an hour, the silence became oppressive, and he wondered if he was the reason for it. The Areopage still wore a frown, and kept her eyes focused narrowly on the road ahead, steadfastly refusing to acknowledge his presence. He recalled his laughter during the session the day before, and then dismissed the idea.

That's ridiculous, he thought. *She can't be upset about that.* He cleared his throat. "Ah, Areopage Saffian, I wonder if you've had a chance to look at that report from Deepenmoor. The capital case."

She gazed coolly at him for a moment, then looked forward at the space between her horse's ears. "What of it?"

"Well, I'd like to discuss it with you. There are a number of things in it that puzzle me."

"I have as yet to read it, but Quaestor Provyn has. Quaestor, did you note aught that was puzzling in it?"

"Not a thing, Areopage." The quaestor made a disparaging gesture with his hand. "I copied it out myself, and thought it quite straightforward."

*If that's straightforward, I'm more of an ass than you
are,* Liam thought, but he kept his tone equable, striving
to sound like the soul of reason. "Really? I wouldn't
have called it straightforward, but then, I've much less
experience in this sort of thing. Doesn't it strike you as
odd that two different people are accused of the same
crime?"

"There are complications," Provyn said, stressing the
last word to imply that they were beyond Liam's understanding.

"So it's not that straightforward?" It slipped out with
an undeniably sarcastic edge, but the other man did not
rise to it. He shrugged and addressed the Areopage.

"The complications are of a political nature."

"I know that," she said, and something passed between them, some tacit understanding that Liam did not
catch. "I'm aware of some of the complications. It is a
thorny matter, Quaestor Rhenford, as I have told you, and
of some concern to the Duke himself. And so I have
decided to give the case into Quaestor Provyn's hands.
He has more experience with both our court and the
Duke's." The announcement left Liam momentarily
speechless, his only comment the height his eyebrows
attained and the fluttery blinking of his eyes. "You and
I will take the mundane cases," she went on blithely. "It
will be good for you to learn more of them, don't you
think?"

With a shake of his head, Liam tried to recover his
composure. "I'm not sure I understand—"

"The Duke's court is no place for fisticuffs," Provyn
interrupted, leering at him over Widow Saffian's shoulder. "We can't have you brawling in Deepenmoor, while
you investigate a case so much in the Duke's mind."

"Brawling? What are you talking about? I haven't
been brawling."

Both judge and quaestor gave him knowing looks.
"Come," Widow Saffian said, "your face belies you,
Quaestor."

Provyn smiled smugly. "A hundred men saw you fighting at the revels."

"I wasn't fighting," Liam told him. "They were fighting—I was just trying to stop them."

"Are there no Guards for that sort of thing?" Provyn asked. "A quaestor is no mere constable, to police the rabble and separate drunken louts. We are more than that, though it would not seem so from your behavior."

Liam decided to ignore the man, afraid he would say something irretrievable, and addressed himself to Widow Saffian. She listened to his explanation of what had happened, but he could see from her expression that she was discounting everything he said, and when he was finished she shook her head.

"Quaestor Provyn has the right of it. You ought to've commanded the Guards to stop the men. No, Quaestor Rhenford, y'are in your way an excellent investigator—it is only that your way is rash and hasty, lacking in reflection and maturity. You act, rather than think, you confront where confrontation is uncalled for."

She paused then, as if to give him a chance to reply, but he had too much to say, and could not even think of where to begin. She waited, and then went on: "Y'are young yet, and do not consider your own dignity—nor that of the court—sufficiently. I doubt not that you'll grow into the role, but for this in Deepenmoor, I needs must have a cooler head, one more sensible of the necessary delicacies."

A cooler head, Liam thought, taking a deep breath. "As you will, Areopage," he said, speaking through gritted teeth. "If Quaestor Provyn will be good enough to give me the mundane reports from Deepenmoor this evening, I'll acquaint myself with them. And I'll give you my copy of the capital report."

"There's no need for that," Provyn said hastily. "It may be that something was left out of yours, since you say it was confusing. I'll make a new one from the original."

"Very well." Liam bared his teeth in a grim smile.

Try to write more neatly this time, you sycophantic toad.
He was sure Provyn was behind the sudden shift in cases,
that he had talked the Areopage into it. *And she listened!
She's addled with grief, that's all. She shouldn't have
been allowed to head the court.* ''Very well. If you don't
mind, I'm going to ride on ahead a little bit.''

Without giving them time to answer, he spurred Diamond into a faster trot, then a gallop, racing ahead of the
Guards and down the road.

The rest of the day he fumed, riding apart from the column, plotting petty revenges and stinging speeches. His
demotion—and there was no doubt in his mind that it
was a demotion—was only part of it; he also had a general sense of being unappreciated that galled him. After
all, he had put aside his legitimate business as a merchant
to come along on the circuit. Being an officer of the Duke
held no attraction for him: he was only there as a vol-
unteer, helping where he could.

Twice he rode down the train, looking for the packhorse with Provyn's clothes, half-intent on following Enghave's advice. He stopped himself, however,
remembering Widow Saffian's words about cooler heads.
His anger cooled in the afternoon, and he began to re-
prove himself for his childishness. *You're whining like
the hero in a bad saga,* he thought, a wry smile playing
on his lips. *''The Lay of Liam the Self-Important.''*

There were more important things to consider than his
own bruised feelings, after all; the court's business was
to dispense justice, not to make him feel good. And the
mundane cases called for as much care in their handling
as the capital cases, if the justice dispensed was to be
true. *Now you sound like Alasco,* he mocked, but that did
not change his opinion. The work was valuable, and he
would not throw up his hands just because he was set to
a less interesting task.

Out of fairness, he retracted his criticism of Widow
Saffian. He could not think of a single judgement handed
down by her that he disagreed with, and if he found her

punishments harsh and her sermons unnecessary, no one else seemed to think them in any way extraordinary. He could not fault her performance in any respect except where he himself was concerned, and even there, he had to admit, her action was reasonable. His alleyway scuffle with Kammer and his black eye were not calculated to give the impression of a sober, decorous, tactful young man, which was exactly what the Deepenmoor case would require.

Seen from that perspective, it made sense to hand the case over to Provyn. The Areopage had never given any indication that she doubted the other man's competence, and her late husband had apparently trusted Provyn. Given the choice of someone she had known and worked with for years and a reckless near-stranger, how could she have done otherwise?

Because he's an ass, and a fop, and an idiot. That opinion he would not change.

At dusk they reached that night's inn, a half-timbered building tucked snugly into the woods by the side of the road, and Liam blessed his luck when Provyn's obnoxious badgering revealed that they would not have to share a room. Both Widow Saffian and the other quaestor took their meals in their rooms, so Liam ate with Iorvram and his clerks.

Early on it came out that Liam had never met Acrasius Saffian and knew very little about him; the clerks, unable to remedy the former, spent the rest of the meal dealing with the latter deficiency. They shared a store of anecdotes and memories of the dead judge, and recalled for Liam a wise and careful man with a sharp-edged sense of humor and occasional flashes of judicial inspiration. One of them went so far as to liken Acrasius to Ascelin Edara, an ancient king of Taralon famed for his wisdom. Even granting that the stories were a sort of eulogy, they nonetheless formed a picture of an impressive man.

When the dinner was over, Liam went to his room mulling over what he had heard, and as he shut the door it occurred to him that the clerks had scrupulously avoided comparisons between the late judge and his widow. *She may not be the new Ascelin,* he thought, firm in his determination to be fair, *but she is doing very well.*

A knock came at the door and before he could answer it Provyn stuck his head in. "Ah, Quaestor Rhenford, I'm glad to find you in. Have you that report?"

"Have you the mundane reports?"

The quaestor held up a sheaf of papers. Liam took them and turned away.

"Ah—the report?"

Liam glanced at Fanuilh, ensconced in the corner on top of his bags, and gave in to a mean impulse. "I'm afraid it's packed away," he said. "I'll dig it out tomorrow, I promise. Goodnight." He moved to shut the door, but Provyn was in the way, his fingers fluttering over the jamb.

"Could you not look now?"

"Really, Quaestor Provyn, it's very late. I promise, it's perfectly safe here. Besides, I thought you had the original. What do you need with mine?"

For a long moment Provyn hung in the doorway, indecisive, and then bobbed his head. "Y'have the right of it, aye, the right." He retreated into the hall and Liam closed the door, a little disappointed—he had hoped to get a rise out of the other man.

A man can only be so reasonable, he thought as he prepared for bed.

The next day Liam mounted Diamond in his accustomed position near the head of the column, bid Widow Saffian a pleasant good morning, and turned his horse back to the middle of the train. He rode with Iorvram and his clerks in the morning, lunched with them when the court stopped, and spent the afternoon riding ahead of the court. The forest slowly petered out into occasional copses of oak and expanses of flowering meadow, and he enjoyed the chance to let Diamond race, pounding along the dirt road at a flat-out gallop.

He arrived at that night's inn an hour before the Areopagus, and was waiting for them in the innyard, nursing a mug of beer and watching the sun set. He saw Provyn whisper to Widow Saffian as they rode up, but resolved to ignore it. *It's only a few more days,* he told himself, *and then back to Southwark.* In the meantime he would handle the work assigned to him, and otherwise do as he pleased.

Once again meals were brought up to the Areopage and Provyn, and Liam ate with the clerks. They were a little more guarded in their conversation, having sensed the discord among the officers of the court, but no less friendly, and when the meal was over Liam went to his room content with the day. Then Provyn knocked at his door.

"Yes?" He blocked the doorway, not allowing the quaestor to enter the room.

"Have you had a chance to find that report?" There was something obsequious in Provyn's manner that set Liam's teeth on edge, and he went to his bags and quickly found the garbled report.

"There you are," he said, thrusting it at the other man, and then, prompted by no reason he could name, added, "I've already made a copy for myself, so you're welcome to this one."

"A copy?" Provyn burst out, bug-eyed. "Y'have a copy?"

"Yes. Is that a problem?"

"Oh, aye, it is," the other man stammered, "for that there should be only one—that is, the records, for the protection—not everything in them is fact—should a man be innocent—for the court alone, see you—"

Liam cut Provyn's incoherent rambling short with an exasperated sigh. "It was a joke, Quaestor. I don't have a copy." *What is wrong with him?*

"You don't?"

"No. It was a joke."

"Ah." Provyn mopped his gleaming scalp and forced out some weak laughter. "I see. I see. Well and well.

Goodnight, Quaestor Rhenford.'' He hurried away,
clutching the report.

Ass, Liam thought, and shook his head as he closed
the door.

CHAPTER 16

DEEPENMOOR LAY AT the end of their journey the next day, and Liam rode ahead of the column as he had the afternoon before, eager to see the Duke's castle in the daylight. As he passed the Guards, they warned him not to travel too far from the court; he laughed and promised he would not, then went on as he pleased.

He had the road to himself and raced Diamond intermittently, revelling in the wind and the speed. While the roan cooled off between bouts of galloping, Liam admired the countryside, once or twice climbing nearby hills for a fuller view. It reminded him of the Midlands of his youth—the rich green expanses of turf, the shady copses, the sound of fast-flowing water—although there were far more hills here, around the bases of which the water rushed in little streams, rather than in the broad rivers beside which he had grown up. To the east he could see the hazy outlines of low mountains; Deepenmoor lay on this side, he knew, and beyond was the sea.

Around noon he rejoined the Areopagus, nodded at Widow Saffian, and ate lunch a little apart from everyone amid the gnarled roots of an ancient oak. He tossed pieces of cold meat to Fanuilh, who snapped them up hungrily; much to the dragon's dismay, Liam had forbidden its daily hunting, on the grounds that they were getting closer and closer to Deepenmoor, and he did not want his familiar running afoul of one of the Duke's gameskeepers.

After lunch he resumed his position far in advance, pushing Diamond until he was a good mile in front of the slow-moving column and then letting the roan relax to an ambling walk. Fanuilh disappeared into the sky, ranging to the north.

Liam found his thoughts turning more and more to Deepenmoor and the Duke, and his powerful presence throughout the duchy. The Southern Tier was one of the few large, coherent fiefdoms left in the old kingdom of Taralon. Elsewhere, and particularly in the Midlands, a lord's authority rarely reached further than a day's ride from his castle, but the Duke's extended all the way to Warinsford, a week of travel. In a time when the king was more cypher than ruler, when noblemen fought wars over fields hardly big enough to graze a single horse, House Vespasianus had preserved its lands from the decay endemic elsewhere. Isolated and protected by the Warin in the west, mountains in the north and the sea to the east and south, the Duke's courts and laws, his rate-collectors and Guards operated relatively efficiently. All told, it was a remarkable achievement in an era of chaos.

The Duke himself was an odd figure, a traditionalist who clung to old forms and older titles—quaestor, aedile and areopage would be meaningless terms in lands with shorter memories and less devotion to the past—yet he managed to make them work in the present. He was said to believe in the sanctity of the duel and the field of honor, yet his courts were held to strict standards of proof and evidence. He remitted the proper taxes and tributes to the king in Torquay, observed all the outward forms of obedience and homage, yet ruled his lands independently and as he saw fit. As a lord he was both paradox and paragon, and Liam looked forward to meeting him.

Chin sunk on his breast, musing about the Duke and the lord's unique position in Taralon, Liam did not see the two men blocking the road until they were less than a dozen yards away. He reined Diamond in sharp and reached instinctively for his sword.

Fanuilh, come back now.

They glowered at him, hunting spears levelled. Their tunics were ragged and their faces dirty, the epitome of banditry, but Liam noticed the quality of their saddles and the way their horses stood stock-still, calm and steady in the air of electric tension that set Diamond pawing the ground nervously.

I am coming, master.

"Good afternoon," Liam called. With Diamond tired, he could not hope to outrun them. "I'm Quaestor Rhenford, an officer of the Duke, and there's a troop of Guards following a short ways behind me."

The bandit on the left hawked and spat. The other grinned, a gleam of white teeth amid his black beard and dirt-smeared face.

"Stand and deliver, Quaestor Rhenford."

They charged even before the challenge was finished, and a moment later Liam was spurring Diamond cruelly and drawing his sword. Shouting at the top of his voice, he had time to aim the roan to the right side of the road and pray for luck. Then the gap closed.

The grinning bandit had not expected him to react so quickly, nor to ride to the right; he fumbled to bring his spear over his horse's neck, and had it in position just in time for Liam to cut through the haft a foot below the head. Liam stiffened his elbow and smashed the pommel of his sword into the man's face, and then Diamond swept past.

Wiser, the second bandit had held back, turning behind his companion to cut Liam off, and they almost collided, Diamond shying violently at the last moment so that the second spear whistled over Liam's ducking head. He yanked savagely on his reins, turning the roan back to the fight, and swung backhanded at the second bandit. The sword had twisted in his grip, the flat smacked the bandit on the side of the head as the man spurred his horse.

A better horse than a bandit should have, it responded to its rider's insane command and jumped forward into Diamond's rump, staggering the roan and throwing Liam off balance, and the second bandit managed to touch him in the back with the butt of his spear. A touch, no more, but it was enough to send him sprawling onto Diamond's neck, losing a stirrup and pounding with both heels to stay on and get the horse away.

Diamond ran and Liam regained his stirrup and his balance and wheeled to face the bandits. The first clutched the haft of his spear, blood gushing from his broken nose; the second was gesturing angrily with his whole spear, telling his companion to circle around, so they could surround their prey. Then, while Liam was still drawing breath, preparing a shout and a charge, Fanuilh shot down out of the sky and crashed into the first bandit, clawing and snapping at his face. The man flailed madly with his broken spear, dropped it, swept the dragon away with one outthrust arm and bolted.

Fanuilh! The cantrip, the sleep cantrip, stop him! Liam projected, but the dragon had already launched itself at the second bandit. More by luck than skill the terrified man snapped up the butt of his spear, caught the dragon in the stomach, and then fled after his companion, not even waiting to see Fanuilh flutter back and drop heavily to the ground.

Liam jumped down and ran to cradle his familiar in his arms. The creature's eyes were wide and disoriented, and its head wobbled back and forth on its long neck.

"Are you all right?" he asked. It was not bleeding, and had no broken bones that he could tell.

I feel dizzy.

"Where does it hurt?"

My stomach. I should have left the rabbits alone.

Liam laughed weakly. His heart was still pounding and his arms felt leaden, a normal aftermath to a fight. Slowly, holding Fanuilh gently to his chest, he rose and hoisted himself into Diamond's saddle. With the dragon nestled in his lap, he looked to the east, saw no sign of his attackers, and urged Diamond into a slow walk west.

The Guards clucked their tongues at him, coming close but not quite saying that they had told him so. "It's rare that there's bandits this close to Deepenmoor," one said, "but it's been a long winter—they could have come down from the north."

"They were the best-fed bandits I've ever seen," Liam pointed out. "And I'd swear those were trained war-horses. They'd been shoed recently, too."

"Stolen, most like," said another, shrugging. "You'll do better to stay close by the column, Quaestor."

He nodded, scratching Fanuilh under the chin. The dragon seemed fully recovered. "There's no need to tell Areopage Saffian about this, is there?"

The Guards exchanged a series of glances and shrugs. "I don't see as how it's necessary," said the first. "They'd never come after a party as large as this."

For the rest of the day he stayed with the Guards, mulling over the attack and wondering if Widow Saffian had not been right about him. Perhaps he was too rash, too hasty; he had been warned not to ride alone, after all, and if he had come through the attack unscathed that was due more to luck and Fanuilh's timely arrival than to any skill or ability on his part. On the other hand, he had great faith in luck, Luck capitalized and personified, faith that while it might not solve all his problems, his Luck would see him through to the point where he could solve them himself.

Sighing, he offered a prayer that it always would.

The luminous gray of dusk had settled on the road before they reached Deepenmoor, and Liam could see torches and lanterns and candles being lit by the great gates of the barbican and in the windows of the tall central tower. It was a strong place, built on a low hill with massive blocks of stone, unadorned except for the flickering lights and the single pennon drooping from the top of the tower.

Soldiers formally challenged the Areopagus at the barbican, one of the Guards responded in turn, and they waited while a superior was summoned. Then the portcullis creaked upward and the column rode into a torchlit courtyard. Servants and soldiers rushed in, holding reins and helping to unload the weary horses, dogs barked and got underfoot, and a fussy steward was everywhere at once, full of peevish directions. He shooed Liam off his mount and out of the way, leaving him to loiter near Widow Saffian and Provyn, looking for his boy. A tall, thin man in the Duke's livery pushed his way through the crowd and bowed to the Areopage.

"Milia," he said, stooping down to kiss her on both cheeks. He wore his thinning hair pulled back in a short braid. "We've heard your news. The Duke's ordered sacrifices and duties for him, and I would have you know that we all grieve with you."

"My thanks, Gratian," she began, and Liam missed the rest because someone tugged at his coat. He turned to find a young girl in a simple shift looking up at him.

"Who are you?" she asked. "I've not seen you with the Areopagus ere now."

"I'm Liam Rhenford," he said, taken aback by her composure and the seriousness in her eyes. They were a green that sparkled in the torchlight.

"The new quaestor." She nodded as if this confirmed a suspicion she had held, and was about to go on when Liam heard Widow Saffian say his name. He turned back to be introduced.

"This is Aedile Gratian," the Areopage said, and Liam bowed.

Gratian returned the bow. The ends of his long black mustache drooped down below his chin, waggling as he smiled. "We've heard much of you, Quaestor Rhenford. Coeccias says y'are part bloodhound—is it true?"

"Yes," Liam said, warming to the man immediately, "but not the part that hunts, unfortunately."

"Quaestor Rhenford has been a great help to us," Widow Saffian said in a flat tone and then, arching an eyebrow, added, "He is cut from your old pattern, Gratian."

"An impudent wretch, is he?" the Aedile laughed, and then caught sight of the young girl over Liam's shoulder. "You there, my lady—shouldn't you be within, at your prayers or your lessons or some such?"

The girl blinked, unconcerned. "Aye, Master Aedile." She turned to Liam. "Good even, Quaestor Rhenford." She curtseyed gravely and walked off.

"Lady Lascelle grows apace," Widow Saffian observed when the girl was out of earshot.

"She misses a mother's guidance," Gratian explained. "But come, you'll be tired and hungry, and I keep you without. Torquato will see you to your rooms, and I'll see you at dinner." Like magic the fussy steward appeared before them, and with imperious subservience ushered them out of the courtyard and into the corridors of the castle.

Torquato led them to Widow Saffian's room first, then Provyn's, and finally it was just the steward and Liam, moving through a maze of hallways and stairways and half-stairways.

"I've had to put you in a separate wing," the steward said. "By rights you should be nearer the Areopagus, but with Earl Raius and's suite here, I've not the room. I trust you'll be comfortable."

"Earl Raius is here?" He remembered the name from the Deepenmoor report—the lord in whose lands the crime had occurred.

Torquato was a small man with thin arms and legs and a tidy little potbelly. He tented his fingers over his stomach and cocked his head. "Have you not heard, Quaestor? The earl's here for the session, to stand for Mother Aspatria in the matter of the murdered children."

"Ah," Liam said. "Then he thinks the hierarch did it?"

The steward waggled a cautionary finger at him. "Oh no, no, no, no, Quaestor. Earl Raius says nothing against the hierarch, and lets the world know it. He only says that Mother Aspatria didn't do it. A most circumspect and honorable man, is Earl Raius." His words were loud and distinct, as if he thought the earl could hear him.

"Well," Liam said, dismissing the subject, "I won't be handling that case. I'll be doing the mundane cases."

"Very good, Quaestor," Torquato murmured, and

stopped at a door indistinguishable from a dozen others
they had already passed. ''These are your chambers.'' He
flung open the door onto a spacious bedroom, and
pointed out the doors to a sitting room and a bathroom,
in which Liam could see a large copper tub. ''Hot water
will be along presently, and I can send a man to shave
you, if you wish.'' Liam's bags were already piled neatly
at the foot of the bed.

Liam scratched guiltily at the stubble on his cheeks.
He had not shaved since leaving the Fair. ''No thank you,
I'll shave myself.''

''Very well. And will your companion require aught?''
The steward smiled expectantly at Fanuilh, perched on
Liam's shoulder, as if he was long accustomed to serving
the needs of miniature dragons.

''No, thank you.''

''As you wish. The Duke expects the Areopagus to
dine with him.'' Torquato bowed himself out, leaving
Liam to wander around the chamber, testing the softness
of the mattress, peering into the other rooms of the suite.

''Not bad,'' he said to no one in particular, thinking
of the stuffy rooms he had shared with Provyn, and his
tiny cell at the Fair, and innumerable thatch-roofed inns.
''Not bad at all.''

Servants came to fill his tub and empty his bags, men
carrying bucket after bucket of hot water and women
stowing his few clean clothes in the wardrobe and whisk-
ing away his dirty ones. Fanuilh sat atop Liam's sabretache, guarding the *Daemonologia*, and if the servants
noticed the dragon's presence they gave no sign; Liam
guessed that Torquato had warned them what to expect.

When they were gone he shaved and took a quick bath,
dressed in the clothes they had left out for him—his
green tunic with white piping, and the matching
breeches—and installed himself at the desk in the little
study. Fanuilh crouched on the arm of his chair and together they flipped desultorily through the reports Provyn
had given him.

Liam was determined to treat the mundane cases with the same seriousness he had accorded the capital cases, but after reading the first three he had to admit that they were even more boring than he had feared. A fisherman paid to have his nets charmed, and complained that his catches were no bigger. One woman was accused of selling love potions, another of casting a hex that rendered her sister-in-law barren. *And those are the interesting ones,* Liam projected, pinching the bridge of his long nose and sighing. *I get sleepy just thinking about the other six.*

They are well-written, Fanuilh pointed out, and Liam began a gesture of dismissal, then stopped.

They are, aren't they? He chose one at random and read it through with a critical eye. It described the case of the woman who had cursed her sister-in-law, and laid out the barren woman's accusations and the sister's replies in a clear and concise manner. There was even a brief summary at the end, suggesting possible lines of investigation, friends and family members who should be questioned, and the author's opinion.

He checked a few other reports, and found them all equally lucid, equally intelligent. They were nothing like the report on the single capital case. Liam tilted his head back, considering the ceiling and the differences between the reports. The obvious explanation was that they were not written by the same person: Aedile Gratian might have written the capital report, and left the mundane cases to his quaestor. Given the stature of the accused and the complicated nature of the case, Liam could easily see the Aedile devoting more time to it, though it disappointed him to think that Gratian should have produced something so sloppy. He had taken an instant liking to the lanky Aedile.

A servant came to fetch him for dinner, and Liam followed the silent man through the twisting byways of Deepenmoor to the Duke's private apartments. They passed through a scriptorium where even at this late hour clerks were busy scratching away at their high desks, and then into a room empty except for four large tapestries. Each showed a different scene from the duchy—Liam recognized Southwark at once and stopped to look at the others—but the servant gave him no time to linger, holding open a door in the far wall and coughing discreetly behind his fist. Liam jumped and hurried through into the Duke's private dining room.

Silver and crystal gleamed molten in the flare of the fireplace behind the head of the table, the only source of light; it was not as ostentatious as Cuspinian's display, but there was a feeling of age in the room, in the heavy furniture, the massive table black with years of polishing, the soot deep in the pores of the hearthstones, the creak and give of his chair when he sat. The orange glow of the fire left shadows in the far corners of the room, shadows older than Liam, older than any of the guests, as old as the castle.

He had to rise again to be introduced to Earl Raius, who accepted his bow with a graceful wave of the hand and then resumed talking to Widow Saffian, and to Tasso, Gratian's quaestor, a well-scrubbed young man who sat opposite Liam at the foot of the table.

"A pleasure, Quaestor Rhenford," Tasso whispered after their mutual bow, and then dropped his eyes to the tabletop and said nothing more for the rest of the evening. He had a blunt, square face and a neck so thick that his collar cut deeply into it, giving the impression that he was being strangled by his own clothes; he watched the conversation in an agony of apprehension, clearly terrified at the prospect of being called upon to speak.

Earl Raius, on the other hand, spoke freely from his position at the right hand of the Duke's empty chair. He planted his elbows on the table, sharp chin resting on a single knuckle, and questioned Widow Saffian intently.

"You understand the delicacy of the situation," the earl said. "I would help her, but I can say nothing of him. And yet by my help I seem to accuse him." He was in his forties, Liam guessed, his age showing only in the few fine wrinkles around his eyes and the touches of gray at his temples; otherwise his sharp-featured face was unlined and handsome. His velvet coat was slashed and picked out with spills of lace much like Provyn's, but he managed to look elegant while the fat quaestor looked like a garishly-costumed bear.

"It may be," Gratian suggested, his mustaches drooping respectfully, "that the Areopage has not had time to consider the matter."

The earl gave an apologetic smile. "In course, in course. You must excuse my pressing you so."

The Areopage plucked at her widow's weeds. "Not at all, my lord. We've had a surfeit of mundane cases, and I've been concentrating my energies on those. Yet I have Quaestor Provyn's summary of the matter, and I can well see that it's trickish for you."

"Then you'll not object if I declare myself a Friend of Truth?"

"We must look deeply into the matter," she said diplomatically, and was saved from committing herself further by the entrance of the steward Torquato to announce the arrival of the Duke, at which they all rose.

For all that he had heard of the man, for all that he knew of his policies and his laws, Liam had never formed a picture of the Duke, and the sight of the man himself inspired a sort of awe, as if he were a historical figure—an Auric the Great, an Ascelin Edara—risen from the pages of some dusty tome. Lyndower Vespasianus was strong, for one thing: broad across the shoulders like a blacksmith, with heavy arms held away from his sides by thick pads of muscle and legs like tree trunks. But he also looked old, not laden with years but ennobled by them: his face carved from stone, immobile and impassive, gray hair and beard chiseled by the hand of a master craftsman. He could have been a statue of a hero, except for his remarkable green eyes, deep and penetrating eyes that swept the table and rested on Liam's own for a moment, widening slightly.

When he gestured for them to sit, Liam realized that he had seen the Duke's eyes before, in the little girl from the courtyard. *His daughter? Granddaughter?* They both had the same gravity, the same self-possession.

"Y'have my sympathies, Milia," the Duke intoned. "On the morrow we'll have offerings for your husband." Widow Saffian murmured her thanks, and Vespasianus accepted them with a slight movement of his head which might have been a nod. "It is a shrewd blow," he went on. "Acrasius was a faithful and a valuable friend. We shall all miss him."

"The more so with this thorny issue before us," the earl said, when the Duke appeared to have stopped. "His wisdom would be a great guide."

"Thorny issue?"

"Earl Raius refers to the capital case, my lord," Gratian explained. "We were just discussing it, and his proposals regarding it."

The Duke compressed his lips slightly, conveying infinite displeasure in the tiny motion. "I would think that a matter more suited to the session, Galba."

Unfazed, the earl shrugged. "Perhaps so, my lord. I thought merely that since the court was here . . ."

Silent servants slipped into the room and began distributing bowls of soup.

"Your interest is noted, Galba. Let us have another subject. Quaestor Tasso, I've not had the pleasure of dining with you ere now."

Tasso stammered something incoherent about the pleasure being his, and then addressed his beet-red face to his soup bowl.

"And Quaestor Rhenford, y'are new to Deepenmoor entirely. Y'are well come, sir."

Unsure of the proper response, Liam rose and bowed quickly. "It is an honor, my lord." The Duke approved with the same slight movement of his head.

"Y'are a Midlander."

"Yes, my lord."

"Only recently come to the Southern Tier."

"Yes, my lord."

The interrogation lasted through the soup, the Duke

making brief statements and Liam confirming them. Vespasianus displayed a disconcerting familiarity with his doings, including his trading ventures, in which he seemed especially interested.

"And you think the Cauliff Ocean may be safely plied."

"I have done so myself, my lord."

"Not plagued by hellish storms, sea serpents, monstrous leviathans and the like."

"Not in my experience, my lord."

"With profitable routes."

"Yes, my lord."

"And new lands and ports worth the visiting."

"A great many of them, my lord."

The servants returned and replaced Liam's still-full soup bowl with a baked fish. He eyed the fish hungrily, wondering if the Duke would give him a chance to eat more than one or two bites.

"It is interesting," Vespasianus mused, touching his lips with a single finger. "Aedile Coeccias speaks often and highly of you, and I find he is right to do so. You give me much to think on. Now, Milia, tell us of the court."

Released from questioning, Liam made short work of his fish while the Areopage briefly described their stops in Warinsford and at the Crossroads Fair. To Liam's surprise, she was more than generous in her praise of her assistants. "Quaestor Provyn has been an invaluable support to me, and Quaestor Rhenford has lived up to the good name he has achieved in Southwark. Without them, I doubt me the sessions would have gone as well as they did."

The Duke put her to the same sort of interrogation as he had Liam, eliciting details of various cases with short, declarative sentences. Somehow, she managed to answer and eat her fish at the same time, a trick Liam envied. *As long as he doesn't talk to me again. . . .* The Duke's presence set all the guests except Raius straining for their best behavior: they sat stiffly upright in their chairs, cutting their fish with delicate strokes, sipping their wine as quietly as possible. The earl did the same things, but with an air of casual grace that showed that his best behavior was his only behavior.

Mutton was brought in after the fish, carved at the table by Torquato, and through most of the course the table was silent—because the Duke said nothing.

It was not a comfortable meal by any stretch of the imagination, and the food was by no means special, but Liam was overwhelmed by a feeling that this was an important event, an experience to be stored up in his memory and, if not cherished, at least kept bright and well-polished. The Duke was responsible, of course. Liam had met and dined with many noblemen in his life, and none of them had possessed a tenth of the man's sheer presence, his gravity of demeanor, the inexorable force of his personality. *And he barely moves,* Liam marvelled. *He hardly speaks!*

After the mutton there were platters of cheese and fruit, and when they were removed the Duke proposed two simple toasts, one to the memory of Acrasius Saffian and the other to the continued good work of the Areopagus. "Y'are all to be congratulated," he finished.

Raius rose and the other guests followed his example, raising their goblets to the Duke. "Your health, my lord," the earl said.

"Thank you, Galba. And now I'll retire. Milia, I would see you early, ere you breakfast." Vespasianus rose from his seat and made to leave the room, then turned back. "And Quaestor Rhenford, I would speak more with you. Torquato will arrange a suitable hour."

He left without waiting for Liam's reply. *What does he want from me?*

They all stood by their chairs, waiting for some unknown signal, and then Gratian sighed. "I'm for bed too. Would you meet after you see the Duke, to plan the day?"

Widow Saffian nodded. "If you would join Quaestor Provyn and I for breakfast in my chambers, that'd like me. Quaestor Rhenford and Quaestor Tasso can meet elsewhere.''

The Aedile frowned. "Would it not be easier for us all to gather in one place? Tasso knows many of the mundane cases, but there are one or two I looked into myself.''

"Perhaps you could speak with Quaestor Rhenford when we're done.''

"I wonder if I might come as well, Areopage,'' Raius said, toying with the lace at his cuffs.

"I gather the Areopage would prefer to keep the circle close in the matter, Earl Raius,'' Gratian interrupted quickly. "I'm afraid her point is well-taken.''

Liam watched the faces around the table, trying to decipher the strange web of cross-purposes. Widow Saffian wanted him kept away from the capital case; Gratian did not understand why but was willing to turn it into a pretext for excluding the earl. They were all elaborately casual, masking their intentions with polite smiles and expressions of regret, but the Aedile and the Areopage, at least, were inflexible.

The question was why: why did she care if he attended their meeting on the case? At their other stops she had freely discussed the cases with both quaestors, and besides, he had already read the report. What did she expect to learn from Gratian that should not be general knowledge?

He watched the faces, seeing the calculations behind their smiles, and then, suddenly, Raius broke, his smile becoming real, spreading his hands in surrender.

"I press you, I know. It is only that I've a concern that the truth come out.''

Gratian bobbed his head. "It does you credit, Earl Raius, but this is best left to us. The truth will out.''

They all began to move then, heading for the doors, confirming their arrangements for the morning. Tasso and Liam were the last out, and the young man shyly detained him for a moment to set a time to meet in the morning. They agreed on an hour after sunup, and the young

quaestor hurried away, leaving Liam alone in the sitting
room. He watched the young man go, his mind turning
to other things.

Liam eventually corralled a servant into leading him back
to his rooms; the halls of Deepenmoor were a hundred
times more complicated than those of the Crossroads
Fair.

He did not begrudge the time, however, which he spent
mulling over the odd contretemps at dinner. He dismissed
Widow Saffian's part—if she did not want him to attend,
what did it matter? It was a sensitive case, and she did
not think he had the tact or the judgment for it. Perhaps
she thought Gratian had new information to relate, information that was not in the report, the nature of which
should not be spread further than necessary. So be it: he
had the mundane cases to occupy him. More interesting
were the two men.

Earl Raius's interest was easily explained, his zeal in
pursuing it far less so. If he had something to contribute,
why not just say what it was? Why try to push his way
into the investigation? Equally puzzling was Gratian's
quickness to shut him out. Granted that the earl was not
a member of the Areopagus, he was still a high-ranking
nobleman, a close vassal of the Duke and a man whose
lands had been affected by the crimes. What harm could
it do to include him?

By the time he reached his rooms, he was ready to
throw up his hands. He knew too little about the earl,
about Gratian, about the politics of Deepenmoor, to come
to any useful conclusions. *Besides,* he reminded himself,
*any conclusions you come to won't be useful. It's not
your case.*

Fanuilh was asleep, curled up on the floor with its head
resting on his sabretache. Liam tiptoed about the room,
undressing and climbing into bed. *Not your case,* he
thought, and this time he smiled. It went beyond missing
children and pieces of blue chalk; beyond even accusations against a prominent priest and one of the Duke's

officers. It must, or it would not have sparked so much interest.

The more he considered his demotion, the happier he was.

CHAPTER 17

IN HIS DREAM Liam flew over the sea, gliding effortlessly over the vast expanse of the Cauliff, paralleling a line of purple storm clouds from which jagged shards of lightning lanced to the whitecaps below. As he flew, Fanuilh appeared beside him, keeping pace with long sweeps of its leathery wings.

Wake.

The smell woke him more than the thought, a stench of rotten eggs that puffed up from the ocean each time the lightning struck.

Wake. WAKE.

The smell struck his nostrils again and again, and he jerked awake, coughing, to discover that the smell was in the room with him, an acid stink clinging to his blankets and the back of his throat. He groped blindly in the dark for the shuttered window, found it and flung it open. It was still night outside; starlight only faintly illuminated the room, but it was enough to find and light a candle. The smell began to dissipate, swirled in sluggish coils by the night breeze.

"What in the Dark is it?"

I do not know.

A scream rose somewhere in the castle, soaring high, and was overtaken and subsumed by an immense bass bellow. Liam jumped, his skin going cold all at once, and the candle guttered out. He cursed and fumbled with the striker, got the candle lit, and cast about the room until he saw his swords, stowed away in a corner by the servants. Tucking them both under his arm, he hurried out into the corridor, shielding the candleflame.

The bellow stopped for a second, then resumed. Liam guessed the direction and trotted toward it, cursing the weak candleflame. Fanuilh trotted beside him.

Master, is this wise?

They came to a spiral staircase, and Liam led the way down.

Do you notice anything? Any magic?

No. But I would not detect the conjuration of a demon.

"It's a demon?"

The staircase ended, and the bellowing was louder now. The creature that made it did not seem to need to pause for breath.

If it were magical, I would have known.

Liam growled at the tautology, then decided the finer points of the dragon's analysis could wait. The bellowing went on and he followed it, drawn through the maze of hallways. Shielding the candle slowed him and he was on the point of throwing it away when they rounded a corner and came to a long hallway lit with lanterns. He recognized the broad staircase that led to the floor where Widow Saffian and Provyn had their rooms; beneath the bellowing he could hear shouting. He dropped the candle and sprinted down the hallway, bare feet slapping on the cold flagstones, pounded up the stairs with a sword in each hand and slid to a stop.

Doors were open all along the darkened corridor at the head of the stairs, frightened faces peering out and down the length of the hall to the far end. Liam saw Widow Saffian and Tasso frozen by the last door, their faces lit by a nacreous glow from within, and ran to join them, dropping his normal sword as he went. The bellowing continued unabated.

Liam dodged past them, drawing the enchanted sword as he entered the room—and froze, the bellowing washing over him in a physical wave.

Gods.

The demon hunched in the center of the room, its knotty shoulders brushing the ceiling, its head—a bull's head, with curved and gleaming horns—lowered to its chest. It had a man's body covered in a sleek pelt of white fur, backward-bent legs braced far apart, one hoof planted firmly on the ground, the other entangled in the wreckage of the bed. Limned in a pearly glow, it roared down at the broken corpse between its legs, three-fingered hands thrust out behind its back.

It stopped roaring and raised its head as much as it could, horns striking sparks from the ceiling, black tongue moistening its milk-white muzzle as it considered Liam. It blew out a breath, heavy with the stink of lightning and sulfur, and stepped toward him, reaching out.

Liam gulped, prayed *Luck, please!* and brought his sword up, the silver of the blade catching the demon's glow. One enormous arm swung out at him and he ducked; then Fanuilh flew past the creature, distracting it, and he lunged forward, expecting to drive his point through the demon's exposed side.

He met no resistance and sprawled to the ground, the room suddenly dark.

He was on his feet again in an instant, sure that he was dead, swinging the sword in wide arcs—but the demon was gone.

"Quaestor Rhenford?" It was Tasso's voice, quavering and close to tears.

"Fetch a candle!" *Where is it?*

It is gone, master.

His hands shook, and he gripped the hilt of the enchanted sword more firmly. *Damn.*

Candles were brought, and the room filled with people in various states of disarray: Provyn in his nightshirt and cap, Tasso in a long tunic, Widow Saffian in a dressing gown of black linen, two appalled soldiers in chain armor, a gaggle of whispering servants. The Duke himself appeared and shouldered his way in to where Liam knelt by Aedile Gratian's corpse. Vespasianus wore only a pair of breeches and held a naked broadsword in one hand.

"Gratian."

Liam nodded, wincing anew at the sight of the corpse.

The demon had crushed the Aedile's long throat with one hand, and snapped his limbs so the white bones poked through.

Vespasianus stared down at the body, eyes half-lidded, and then turned to the people behind him. "Who did this?"

No one answered. The two men in armor hung their heads.

"Who?" he repeated, the single word sounding dangerous.

"I know!" Provyn suddenly shouted. "And I'll prove it!" He ran from the room. The Duke ignored him, raising a clenched fist at the soldiers.

"It was a demon, my lord," Liam said quietly, going to the Duke's side.

"A demon." Vespasianus paused for only a moment, then began rapping out orders. "You!" He singled out the soldiers. "Go down to the dungeons, find Mother Aspatria and Hierarch Kortenaer, and hail them before me. Quaestor Tasso!" He had to call twice—the young man's eyes were rivetted on Gratian's mangled body. "Rouse the Guard. Scour the castle. Find it. Hear you? Find it!"

Take a look outside, see if you can find any trace of it, Liam projected to Fanuilh.

I believe it is gone, master. Returned to its plane.

Look anyway, please.

There was an open window behind the shattered bed; Fanuilh hopped to the sill and disappeared.

The Duke turned to Liam. "You saw it."

"Yes, my lord. But I think it's gone now."

Widow Saffian joined them, eyeing Liam suspiciously. "Why do you say that?"

He shrugged, confused by the question. "It's gone. You saw it disappear."

"Aye, I saw it vanish, but that is not the same as saying it's gone."

What in the world is she talking about? "I'm sorry, Areopage, I don't understand—"

"We'll search nonetheless," the Duke interrupted, his voice like the crack of a whip. He glared at the gaping servants at the door. "Fetch binding cloths, herbs, a shroud. The Aedile needs must be prepared for burial. Find Torquato, have him sent to me. Go to!" The servants fled and Earl Raius took their place, somewhat baffled by the commotion.

"Whatever—" he started to ask, then caught sight of Gratian's body and blanched.

"Y'have taken the time to dress," Vespasianus observed. The earl wore the same jacket he had had on at dinner. "Your chambers are but a few doors down, Galba." His implication—and his reproof—were clear.

"Forgive me, my lord," Raius whispered, his hand over his mouth. "The castle was abuzz with something, but I knew not this. I was belowstairs, visiting with Mother Aspatria."

The Duke's eyes narrowed. "You were with Mother Aspatria?"

"Aye, my lord—as I have been these past several nights."

"How long?"

"An hour, more perhaps. Why?"

Provyn appeared in the doorway, doubled over and panting. His face was deep purple with exertion, and his words came out in short bursts. "Wait! Wait! I have it!—the murderer—I have it!" He flapped a hand to command attention, cradling something to his chest with the other. "Wait!" Widow Saffian moved to his side, but he waved her away and straightened. "The murderer," he said, his breath coming back. "I have it!"

"Speak, man!" the Duke demanded. "What have you got?"

Snarling, the fat quaestor drew a deep breath and jabbed a forefinger at Liam. "Rhenford! It's Rhenford!"

His harsh breathing echoed in the silence that followed.

Liam gaped, shook his head, gathered his wits.

"You're mad!" Even as he said it, though, a horrible idea struck him.

"No," Provyn said, a cunning smile sliding across his face. "No. If I'm mad, what's this?" He held out the thing he had cradled to his chest, and Liam mouthed a single, silent curse.

It was his copy of the *Dominia Daemonologia*.

Punching and shoving him till he staggered, a trio of Guards herded Liam down into the bowels of the castle. Raius followed behind, urging them on, telling them that Liam had murdered Gratian.

"That's madness," Liam protested, and received a backhanded slap across the face for his trouble. At first he had been too stunned to reply to Provyn's accusations, and it was only after the Duke disarmed him and ordered him taken to the dungeons, only in the hallway and on the stairs that he had recovered enough to speak. Now, when he did, the Guards kicked and punched him.

His mind raced futilely, spinning in circles, grabbing at and recoiling from stray thoughts. He should have burned the book, knew it, cursed himself for not—*But the chalk!* "Earl Raius, that chalk's not mine!" Provyn had produced it from his pocket, a thumb-sized stub of blue chalk, and claimed to have found it with the *Daemonologia*. That was when the Duke had turned to him and knocked the sword from his nerveless fingers. "My lord, you must listen to me!"

They were on a staircase and he half-turned, meaning to plead his case, to speak reasonably, and one of the Guards punched him full in the face. He lost his balance and tumbled down the steps, cracking his head at the bottom. Fireflies danced in his vision when the Guards hauled him to his feet, and the earl's voice was a tinny whisper through the ringing in his ears.

"Don't kill him—we'll want something left to hang!"

His legs were rubber and there was blood in his eyes, and when he stumbled they yanked him upright by his arms and his hair, disorienting him further.

Master? Where are you?

"Fanuilh!" His outburst was met with a vicious cuff. *Fanuilh, stay away!* he managed to project. *Stay outside!*

Where are you? What has happened?

Just stay outside! It's mad—they think I killed Gratian. Provyn showed them the book. I'll clear it up, just stay outside!

Even as he sent the thought, though, he knew it was not true. How could he clear it up? A Guard took hold of his arm and twisted it behind his back, and he screwed up his eyes against the pain. He walked blindly from there, stumbling down steps, pushed and punched when he went too slow, yanked back by his arm when he went too fast.

Finally Raius barked another order, and the punishment stopped. The man behind him let go of his arm, and Liam reluctantly opened his eyes, straightening slowly. They had come to the castle's dungeon, a long curving hallway of oaken doors bound and braced with blackened iron, each inset with a tiny, barred window. At the first he saw the white blur of a face, and heard a woman's voice call out to know what was going on. As the soldiers dragged him further on, he heard the earl talking to the woman.

"Your release, Mother Aspatria, in the form of this foul murderer."

"How so?"

The hallway curved, and Liam lost the rest of their conversation. The soldier behind him took advantage of the earl's absence to twist his arm again, and then Raius rejoined them.

"My lord," one of the soldiers asked, "where shall we put him? The cells are full, waiting the session."

"Put him in with Kortenaer: let the fiends stew together."

The plan appealed to the Guards; they waited impatiently while a cell midway down the hall was unlocked, and then threw him in. There were three steps going

down into the cell, and a man at the bottom: Liam
crashed into him and the two went sprawling to the stone
floor. The door slammed shut.

"Y'are in luck, Quaestor Rhenford," Raius called
through the gate. "Y'have a priest in with you. It may
be he can smooth your way with the gods when we've
hung you—if he's not overbusy smoothing his own way
into the Gray Lands."

Liam twisted around and flung a curse at the door.

"I pray you," whispered the man beneath him, when
the earl's face had disappeared from the grate. "Y'are
crushing me."

Liam helped Hierarch Kortenaer to his feet and then lay
back himself on the low cot that was the cell's only furniture, gingerly probing the cut on his forehead. The
priest timidly offered to help and, when Liam nodded,
tore a strip from the already tattered blanket and began
swabbing away the blood.

"So y'are Quaestor Rhenford," Kortenaer said after a
moment.

"You've heard of me?"

The priest stepped back, nodding nervously. He was
stooped and thin, the apple of his throat prominent and
prone to bobbing when he moved his head. He wore a
dirty white robe with a cowl, and his sparse black hair
was shaved in a tonsure. "I have. Aedile Gratian speaks
much of you—had heard of you from the Aedile of
Southwark." He waved a hand to indicate Liam's con-
dition. "But he said nothing of . . . this."

"I imagine not." With a grunt, Liam sat up on the cot.
His head was clearing, but slowly. "Gratian's dead."

"Dead?"

"Murdered by a demon." *Why should he care?* Liam
wondered. There was no mistaking the depth of Kortenaer's shock, however, nor its sincerity. The blood drained
from the priest's face and his jaw hung slack, his throat
bobbing up and down as if there were a frog trapped
inside.

"Oh goddess," he gulped at last and dropped to his knees, head bowed, hands clasped, muttering incoherent prayers. Liam eyed him skeptically for a few moments, still wondering at his response to the news. The logical assumption—so obvious that Liam adopted it without a moment's thought—was that Gratian had been killed to stop the investigation of the capital case. Yet the priest acted as if his last hope in the world had been extinguished. Why?

Who cares? He shook his head, turned his eyes to the ceiling and his thoughts to his own predicament. Immediately he saw Provyn, holding up the *Daemonologia,* and his mouth twisted bitterly. *The bastard. I'm going to kill him when I get out of here. I'm going to cut him into tiny pieces. I'm going to rip out his fat heart and crush it while he watches.*

He allowed himself almost a full minute to imagine what he would do, then forced himself to think calmly. Hatred was clouding his judgement, and he tried to see around it, to view the situation objectively. He leaned back against the wall and closed his eyes. *You're assuming Provyn trapped you, that he knows you didn't do it. Is that necessarily so?* The idea struck him as stupid, but he forced himself to consider it, clinging to rigorous logic in the face of an eminently illogical situation. Provyn had known about the *Daemonologia* since that morning in Warinsford, and had passed up any number of chances to take advantage of the knowledge. To believe that he had held a piece of blue chalk handy just in case someone happened to summon a demon was beyond belief. Far easier to simply reveal that Liam had the book early on, and remove him that way.

So he trapped me, but that wasn't the main goal. If they wanted to get rid of me, there were easier ways. For a moment he remembered the two bandits who rode trained warhorses, and then pushed them aside. The main goal had to be to remove Gratian; blaming Liam was a convenient way of shifting suspicion from the two people being held in the dungeons.

His unruly mind leapt ahead of itself, and he realized that only Mother Aspatria had a perfect excuse: Earl Raius had been with her during the hours when the demon was summoned. *He's been with her for the past several nights,* Liam remembered, and thought of Provyn, roaming the halls of the Fair, up later than usual. *What was he doing—receiving instructions?* His speculations were getting away from him, running in too many directions. He opened his eyes and called out to the priest.

"Hierarch, did anyone visit you this evening?"

Kortenaer looked up, eyes vacant, the last words of a prayer trailing from his lips. Brusquely, Liam repeated his question.

"None," the hierarch answered, his voice sad. "I am alone among wolves. Mother Pity has deserted me." He hung his head again.

"Me as well," Liam muttered, and went back to his thinking.

Having gone to the trouble to blame him, would they fail to safeguard themselves on other fronts? His "they" was not as nebulous as "our man" had been—he meant Provyn and Mother Aspatria, and though he had no concrete proof he felt sure that it was a safe assumption. Earl Raius he would not consider for the moment.

Regardless, the implications were staggering and he recoiled from them, seeking refuge in a careful recitation of what he knew and what he could safely assume, building up an edifice of thought brick by brick and refusing to look at the entire structure.

Provyn had been bribed, and early on. *How many people commented on his new clothes? How many, and you didn't notice?* With Acrasius Saffian's untimely death—one of the salient structures Liam refused to consider—the fat quaestor had expected to handle the capital cases, and had been very upset when the Areopage unexpectedly gave them to Liam. He had delayed handing over Gratian's report, and then delivered a document so mangled in the copying as to be useless. He had played on Widow Saffian's own displeasure with Liam to persuade her to turn the capital cases over to him, and, finally, produced the *Daemonologia* and the chalk as proof that Liam had murdered Gratian.

So much was certain. That Mother Aspatria was Provyn's employer was only slightly less certain, and the longer Hierarch Kortenaer prayed, the more Liam's uncertainty diminished. As to why they had killed the Aedile, he could only guess that Gratian had found some new piece of evidence, one that pointed strongly to the ghost witch's guilt. What it might have been, he had no idea, as he had no firm recollection of the details of the case—he had been more concerned with the confusion of the report than its contents.

Fine, he thought. *Fine. That's what you know. Now, what do you do with it?* He glanced around the cell, at the massive stone blocks, the inches-thick door, the tiny grill with its iron bars, and stifled a sigh.

There was nothing he could do. Even if he could think of a way to prove his innocence, there was no way to execute it. No one would listen to him—a stranger to the Areopagus and to Deepenmoor, not even born in the duchy, a man who travelled with a dragon and a book for summoning demons. Provyn had ridden the court circuit for more than a decade, and was an old and trusted servant. *A fool rises up and a prince is cast down,* Liam thought, recalling the prayer from the Warinsford Pantheon. *You're not a prince, but he's definitely a fool.* As he remembered, the prayer continued with something about all men falling—and rising again.

You could escape. He examined the cell again, shook the cot to see how sturdy it was. It wobbled, poorly put together, but the legs and the slats were all solid pieces of wood. *Fanuilh!*

The response came immediately; the dragon had been waiting for his call. *Yes, master?*

Liam had escaped from two separate prisons, one in Alyecir and one in the Freeports. In neither case had he had an accomplice like Fanuilh. *Where are you?*

I am on the roof of the tower. I saw no sign of the demon. How are you going to get out?

That's what I want to discuss with you, he projected, already formulating a plan. He would need a horse. *I want you to find the stables.*

I can do that.

Good. After that . . . He let the thought trail off, trying to decide what should come next. He could see himself on Diamond, riding into the night, but the steps in between, from his cell to the roan's back, those were crucial. Obstinately, the image refused to budge, himself escaping, disappearing, fleeing, and it slowly dawned on him that he did not want to run away.

Putting Alyecir behind him had been a positive pleasure, and if there was one Freeport he could not set foot in, there were four that he could; he had no ties to either place, and no desire to return. But if he escaped from Deepenmoor he would have to leave the duchy entirely, and here he did have ties, the first he had achieved in years: a business, friends, a home. He would not abandon them.

Master?

Moreover, there was Provyn. If he escaped, he could come back in secret and deal with the fat quaestor—he had done as much to the man who killed his father. *And what did that earn you? A price on your head and ten years of exile.* Better, far better, to stay, to find a way to bring Provyn down in full view of those he had betrayed, to redeem his own name now, if he could. And if that was impossible, if he tried his best and failed, then and only then would he think of escape.

Fanuilh, he projected, *forget the stables. Go back to Gratian's room, to the window. Go along the wall from there, and check the other windows. Find out which one is Provyn's, if you can.*

Yes, master.

From there, he would have to make it up as he went along.

• • • •

A lantern hung high overhead, bolted to the ceiling and far out of reach, lightening the shadows rather than illuminating the room. Liam stared at it, his mind far away, following Fanuilh around the walls of Deepenmoor.

After a long bout of prayer, Kortenaer stood and took a few awkward paces around the cell. Finally, he stopped in front of the cot and coughed to catch Liam's attention. The priest looked worn and haggard, far worse off than when Liam had first joined him, as if his prayers had exhausted him.

"Quaestor Rhenford, can you tell me, did Aedile Gratian say aught ere he died?"

"No." He pulled himself forward to the edge of the cot, intrigued by the priest's wistful tone. "Why? Did you expect him to?"

"Aye," Kortenaer began, then pulled himself up short, belated realization dawning. "Y'are in here for it! They've taken you for the killer!" Liam spread his hands, prepared to defend himself, but the priest did not give him a chance, raising his clenched fists above his head. "Oh, the villains! The damnable villains!"

"Who?" He had expected Kortenaer to lash out at him. "What villains?"

"The witch," the priest shouted, "the witch and her hellhound! Oh, Mother Pity, look down on us and weep, to see us beset by evil men!" Sudden tears streamed down his face, and his throat bobbed uncontrollably.

Liam stood and shook the other man by the shoulders. "What are you talking about? What do you know?"

"Oh, she is a foul one, a servant of the Dark—see you how she has ensorcelled him? And now he does her bidding, laying yet more false accusations!"

"Provyn, you mean?"

"Provyn?" the priest asked. "Who is this? Is he another of her minions?"

"Never mind. Who are you talking about?"

Kortenaer lowered his voice, casting a precautionary glance at the grill in the door. "Can it be that you don't know? Earl Raius, in course! Did he not accuse you?"

Liam did not want to confuse things by explaining, so he nodded. "Yes, but I don't know why. What do you know about them? Why are they working together? What can you prove?"

At the last question the priest deflated, knuckling tears from his face like a tired child. "Naught. I can prove naught. All is guess and fancy. I am not so clever-cunning as they, to make proofs where there are none."

"Well," Liam said, "suppose you tell me what you guess, and we'll see what proof we can find."

It took a few minutes and all of Liam's patience to induce the priest to talk; he had swung from manic rage far into melancholy, and was close to tears again. His days in prison had weakened him—Liam guessed he had never been strong to start with—but with a great deal of encouragement and much prompting he began haltingly to tell what he knew.

"I was raised in the duchy," he said, huddling on the edge of the cot, "but left it early to join a temple in Torquay, to follow our Mother Pity, to do her honor and service. It was my honor to rise high in her priesthood, and when it chanced that there was a hierarch needed here, my brethren put me forward. It pleased the Duke to take me on, and I came home over a year past, to minister to the people hereabouts."

In addition to propagating the rites of his own goddess, Kortenaer was also supposed to see to the interests of the other gods, maintaining their shrines and offering more universal rites than those of his own cult. The previous hierarch for the eastern duchy had been a devotee of Strife, the war-god, and as he spoke of him, Kortenaer flushed with indignation.

"A lazy man, a limited man, Quaestor Rhenford; you cannot imagine the state of the shrines up and down the coast! A shambles and a shame, a blot upon the landscape and a stinking offense to the gods."

Liam, sure none of this was relevant, urged Kortenaer to get to the point.

"I stray—but the shrines!—never mind. I took up my

post in Hounes, the village of my youth, and set myself
to repairing the shrines and calling the inhabitants of the
coast back to grace with the gods. They had fallen sadly
from the way, and needed much cajoling. It pains me to
say that it did not like them to be called to their duties,
and so I was not well-liked.

"They listened, though, and heard, and came back to
the ways, tithing and making the proper sacrifices, observing the proper rites. In all this Earl Raius was my
helper, for at the time he was not only lord of the coast
under our Duke, but also a godly and a good man, an
upright man."

Sensing that the point was near, Liam nodded eagerly.
"So what happened?"

Kortenaer sighed. "These six months ago, the earl fell
ill with the colic. His innards griped fiercely, he complained of hot irons in his stomach, he was feverish and
burning hot to the touch. You'd scarce guess it to see
him now, but he was as close to the Gray Lands as a
man may come and not pass over, and he lingered there
for a full month. Healers were called, and herbwives with
their simples, and chirurgeons with their leeches. Hedge-
wizards were consulted, and barbers and the like. Nothing seemed to help. I attended him daily, praying for him
and urging him to reconcile himself with the gods, and
till the very end he heard me gladly." He covered his
eyes with his hand, pained by the memory.

"And then she came to him—Mother Aspatria. I'd had
no business with her, and knew her not. She came when
we feared he was presently to die, and was closeted with
him for many hours. When she left, he barred his door
to me and to his servants, and lay alone for a day and a
night. We feared for him and were near many times to
breaking down the door, but he forbade us in a voice
much stronger than we had heard from him in many
weeks.

"Come the morning he emerged, hale and hearty and
as well as could be hoped. He sent gifts to the witch and
rode to a tourney, and seemed as ever he had—a good

man, and a strong, a righteous lord to all his people, saving only me. Me he would not see, and he would not help me in my work nor listen to my prayers. I was banned his keep and retired to Hounes to work alone.

" 'Should have' are a weak man's words, but I'm weak, humble, and lowly. I should have seen, should have guessed—but I did not. I thought only that he was bitter with the gods, for having let him suffered so. It is a common complaint, and I thought to wean him from it by and by.'' His head hung low, almost between his knees. ''And yet I should have seen!''

Master, I think I have found Quaestor Provyn.

Good, Liam projected hastily. *Watch him, listen if you can. Let me know if he does anything.* ''Seen what?''

Kortenaer raised his head, his stare sad and pitying. ''Is it not obvious? He sold himself to the Dark for his miserable life, and Mother Aspatria made the bargain. Now she leads him as her slave, and through her his soul grows blacker by the day.''

''All right,'' Liam said slowly, adding the story to his structure but still shying away from considering the whole edifice, ''where does the grotto come in? And the missing children?''

With a groan, the priest raised his face to the ceiling, eyes closed and throat bobbing. Just when Liam feared he was going to break into prayer, he hitched his shoulders and took control of himself. ''Ah, the poor innocents! I doubt not they were part of his bargain, though I can prove naught. The Dark delights in the blood of innocents!''

The grotto in Hounes was both a burying ground and a shrine to Laomedon, the god of death. Kortenaer had a key because of his position, Mother Aspatria because of hers as ghost witch: she used the place to store unidentified bodies, corpses washed ashore for the most part.

''The sea is hungry, Quaestor Rhenford, and when the three children were missed, the sea was blamed. After a time, I planned a service, as fishermen will, a false interment for a body lost beneath the waves. We went into

the grotto and found their bones, the bloody knife and
the foul circle. I sent word to Aedile Gratian, whom I
had never met but of whom I had heard much good. I
didn't think of Mother Aspatria and her key, but when
Earl Raius saw the Aedile, he waxed wroth and rated me
for meddling, and my suspicions were born.''

Gratian came to Hounes and made a brief investigation. Kortenaer did not tell him his suspicions, but the
Aedile fairly quickly developed his own and arrested
Mother Aspatria. On the day he was to take her back to
Deepenmoor, however, a troop of Raius's soldiers broke
into Kortenaer's cottage and found a stub of blue chalk
and a drawing of a pentagram.

''The earl'd been protesting the witch's innocence all
the while, look you, and made as if this were but further
proof. Aedile Gratian—Mother, enfold him in Your
arms!—took it otherwise, clapping me in but reluctantly.
Had I not called him? What murderer calls for his captor?
And had I not led the service to the grotto? Why, if I
had fouled it so? He saw it all, and clearly, but was chary
of offending the earl, and said that he would take us both,
as we both had keys. Earl Raius was passing angry, but
the Aedile would not be swayed—said it was for the
Areopagus to decide upon. So we were brought here and
locked away from light and life for these months. And
now the good Gratian is dead, and our hope is gone,
yours and mine alike.''

''No,'' Liam said. ''Not entirely. What did Raius say
when Gratian mentioned the Areopagus? Did he say anything?''

Kortenaer shrugged, indifferent. Telling the story had
brought back to him the hopelessness of his position. ''I
was not there. I would not know.''

Turning from the priest Liam began to pace. Widow
Saffian had mentioned that Earl Raius approached her
husband about the case—undoubtedly to plead Mother
Aspatria's side. And when Acrasius Saffian proved un-
helpful, Liam assumed, the earl had gone on to Provyn.

Fanuilh! What's he doing?

Dressing, master. I think he is coming to see you. A servant came only a moment ago, and said the Areopage would be waiting for him at the entrance to the dungeons.

Liam looked to the door, as if expecting them to appear that instant. *They're coming to see me now? In the middle of the night?*

The sun has already risen, master. It is morning.

He ran up the steps and clung to the bars of the grill. Nothing stirred in the dark corridor.

CHAPTER 18

TWO SOLDIERS CAME first, with a bucket of cold water, Liam's boots and one of his tunics. They replaced the almost-spent lantern and ordered him to make himself ready for the Areopage's visit.

Liam cleaned the blood from his face as well as he could and slicked down his hair. He had only the tattered blanket to dry himself, but Kortenaer, sitting listlessly on the side of the cot, made no objection.

The soldiers returned while Liam was pulling on his tunic and hustled the priest out of the cell. Tasso came in a moment later, followed by Widow Saffian and Provyn. The young quaestor stared fixedly at him, his expression an uneasy mix of hatred and confusion. Liam did not spare him a glance, nor did he look at the Areopage. From the instant Provyn entered the cell, Liam looked straight at him, his gaze as cold as he could make it.

Fanuilh, see if you can find Earl Raius's room. It should be along the same corridor.

Yes, master.

"Master Rhenford." The Areopage's voice rang out, too loud in the confines of the cell. She stood behind and to the left of Tasso, using the bull-necked man as a shield.

"Good morning," Liam said, eyes still on Provyn. The quaestor quailed a little under his glance, then stiffened into a belligerent stance, thrusting out his jaw. "You've made a great mistake." The important thing, Liam decided, was to remain calm. "You've been tricked and misled."

"Master Rhenford, you stand accused of two separate charges. One, the first, of possessing a proscribed book, specifically the *Dominia Daemonologia*. Two, the second, of using said book to conjure a demon with which you affected the murder of Aedile Gratian. Do you understand these charges?" She spoke formally, as if she were in court, ignoring his answers unless they addressed her questions.

"The man you want is right next to you. The book is mine, but he put the chalk in my room. I'm not sure who he's working for—I think I know, but I'm not sure—but he has definitely been bribed to undermine the workings of the court."

Provyn made a scoffing noise in the back of his throat. Liam suppressed the urge to leap at him.

"You admit possession of the book?"

"The book is mine. He saw that I had it in Warinsford and said nothing about it. He wanted to use it against me, to make me a scapegoat."

"The punishment for possession of such a book is severe, and y'are aware of it," Widow Saffian went on. She stood erect, hands stiff at her sides. "I told you of it myself. And yet you kept it. Have you any defense to offer?"

"I inherited it from a wizard in good standing with the Guild. Since Provyn made no objection to it, I assumed I could keep it, as his lawful heir. It was useful in convicting the Handuits, and I thought it would be useful elsewhere. Ask him if he saw it, and what he said." He pointed at the quaestor, who shook his head sorrowfully, as if the whole business was pathetic.

"Y'are not a member of the Mages' Guild?"

"I am not. Ask him."

"You knew it was proscribed."

"I did. Ask him."

"These questions are for you, Master Rhenford, not Quaestor Provyn." She stressed the different titles to make his new position clear to him, and Provyn sneered.

"Did you summon the demon that killed Aedile Gratian?"

Liam shook his head, his patience ebbing. "No. I swear on my soul I did not. I was the first person into the room, wasn't I? I tried to fight the thing, didn't I?"

Barking a laugh, Provyn interrupted, "You fought your own creature! You knew it would not harm you, for that you yourself had summoned it!"

A red rage swelled up Liam's chest, and out of the corner of his eye he saw Tasso tense. He took a deep breath and regained his calm. "That's not true. Areopage Saffian, please listen to me. Provyn is working for Earl Raius, trying to free Mother Aspatria." She stirred, indignant at the suggestion, but he overrode her protest. "Please listen! Has he ever had such clothes before? How many people have commented on how well-dressed he suddenly is? Where did he get the money for it? He saw the book, but he said nothing—why not? Ask him, please! And the report, what about the report? Do you remember how upset he was about it, how desperate he was to keep my copy away from you? That's because he had cut pieces out of it, and he knew you would see it at once. Why was he so anxious to have me removed from this last case? Eh? You have to listen to me!"

It was clear, however, that she would not. He was aware of her stony silence, of the way she moved a little closer to Provyn, to show her support. For his part, the quaestor rolled his eyes and scoffed all through the speech, and when Liam ran out of breath he grunted his disdain.

"This is madness, Areopage. Did I not say he would spin some tangled skein of lies? The man's as Dark as night, I say. We've proof enough."

Biting back a vicious retort and struggling to control his own anger, Liam spoke through gritted teeth. "You have nothing of the kind and you know it. Yes, you have the book, and you can lash me if you want. But the chalk and the book are not enough to prove I killed Gratian, because I didn't. There's no reason for it. Why would I want him dead? There's no reason. I didn't even know the man. I ask you, why would I kill him?''

''We'll have the why soon enough, I'd wager,'' Provyn said. ''And then you'll hang.''

Liam blew hard, speechless in the face of the man's lies. Widow Saffian, seeing his face go red, decided it was time to reassert herself.

''Your chambers smelled of sulphur and lightning, a common sign that a demon has been summoned. How do you explain that?''

''I can't. Maybe Mother Aspatria arranged it. I don't know. But if I had summoned it, would I be so stupid as to do it in my own room?''

''You were arrogant,'' Provyn opined, looking down his nose at Liam. ''Overweening pride was your downfall.''

''And I'm going to be yours,'' Liam grated, the rage stronger now. He knew he was losing control, and could not help it. ''I'm going to kill you, Provyn. I'm going to prove you did this, and then I'm going to kill you.''

Widow Saffian recoiled. ''That is enough!''

''Bold words from a corpse,'' Provyn said at the same time.

''Bold words, you fat bastard?'' Liam demanded, his fists clenching so tightly that the muscles of his arms quivered like bowstrings. ''Bold words?'' He spun on his heel, facing away from them, not trusting himself to look at Provyn's face. ''Get him out of here,'' he grated. ''Get him away. I'll kill him if you don't.''

''You'll do no such thing!'' the judge declared. ''Y'are a prisoner of this court, Master Rhenford, and would do well to remember it!''

He turned back, the anger mastered now but still there, working through his body so that he trembled. Tasso moved directly in front of the Areopage, the uncertainty stronger on his face. He, at least, seemed to have been listening.

''Take him out of here,'' Liam told Widow Saffian. ''Come back without him and listen to me. Or not, as you please. But think about this: Provyn expected to be given the capital cases. Everyone expected him to get them. And there was only one way a position could open up on the court, wasn't there? Think about it!''

Provyn froze, suddenly wary; Widow Saffian's hands twitched once at her waist and were still.

''Think about it,'' Liam repeated at last, when the silence had gone on too long.

As if a spell had been broken, everyone spoke at once, Tasso warning Liam to stand back, Provyn yelping that this was the most monstrous lie of all, and Widow Saffian hissing at the both of them to be quiet.

''Be still!'' she shouted, holding up her hand. ''Be still! We'll leave the prisoner to himself, and return when he'll hear our questions and answer them. Come.'' She went up to the door without another word, Provyn at her heels. Tasso backed slowly up the steps, watching Liam as if he were a dangerous animal who might spring at any moment.

Liam's anger began to ebb when he saw how the young man regarded him. ''Tasso,'' he said, spurred by a sudden and desperate thought, ''Tasso, please—remember how much Gratian wanted to keep the details from Earl Raius? At dinner, you must remember! He didn't want Raius involved! Do you remember?''

Tasso reached the door and slipped through it, all the while watching him. His face was bewildered and frightened as he swung the door to.

''Tell the Duke!'' Liam called. ''Tell the Duke!''

The door clanged shut and he crumpled onto the cot, exhausted.

That could have gone better.

Kortenaer was not returned to the cell and Liam sat alone, trying to take some comfort from the fact. He wanted to believe that it was a sign that the conspirators considered him dangerous enough to isolate, that they had recognized their mistake in letting him learn what he had from the priest and were making a belated attempt to remedy the situation. It seemed more likely, however, that the soldiers had simply forgotten to bring the hierarch back. Fanuilh had found Raius's room and reported the earl sound asleep, while Provyn was calmly eating breakfast with Widow Saffian in her apartments.

Rather than brood on his troubles—or his aches: the cuffs and thumpings of his less-than-gentle captors had blossomed into a mottled collection of bruises, and his head throbbed—Liam concentrated on Fanuilh, his one link with the outside and, he knew, his main hope of escape should things get any worse. *As if they could get worse. . . .* He pushed the thought aside and projected: *Fanuilh!*

Yes, master?

Where are you? The dragon, it turned out, was horribly exposed, clinging to a window ledge outside Provyn's room. *If there's no one there, go inside and look around.*

Yes, master.

He closed his eyes and waited, humming to himself to pass the time, hoping the dragon would be careful. Careful and fast: waiting had never been his strong suit.

I am in Quaestor Provyn's bedroom, the dragon reported at last. *I do not see anything that might be useful. There is a strongbox in his sitting room, but it is locked and I do not see a key. There is a chest of clothing here and it is open, but I do not think I could go through it without disorganizing it. The clothes are very well packed.*

Liam blinked, surprised and pleased at its thoroughness. *You'd make a fine spy,* he told it. *Now, I want to see for just a minute.*

Yes, master.

Quickly, more quickly than he had ever done before, Liam forced himself into the necessary trance and commanded the silver cord to appear before him. The ease with which he did it surprised him, and for a moment he almost lost control of it. He mastered his surprise, however, and sent himself hurtling along the cord until he reached a knot in the cord. It vanished at his mental com-

mand and he dropped out of the trance, his eyes popping
open. *That was easy,* he marveled, then set himself to the
task at hand.

Seeing through his familiar's eyes was an experience
Liam disliked intensely, and he doubted that Fanuilh had
missed anything, but it would give him the illusion of
action, of doing something as opposed to sitting helpless
in a dungeon. He squeezed his eyes tight and imagined
putting on a helmet, a full metal bucket that covered his
head down to his neck. In his mental picture the visor of
the helmet was shaped like the snout of a dragon. He
flipped the visor down and opened his eyes.

His stomach lurched; his body knew that he was sitting
upright on the cot but his eyes looked up from close to
the floor, a distorted perspective showing a guest chamber much like his own, with a wardrobe, a bed, and three
doors. Sunlight streamed through a deep casement. A
chest loomed over him, a slashed green-and-red doublet
draped neatly over the open lid.

Did you look in the wardrobe?

It is empty.

Given the conspirators' experience with false evidence,
it was too much to hope that Provyn would be caught
with a sackful of chalk in his own chambers. *All right.
I'm switching back.* He closed his eyes, removed the
imaginary helmet, and looked out at his cell. Frowning,
he massaged his temples and tried to think how best to
use Fanuilh's freedom.

You say Raius is asleep?

Yes, master.

*Do you think you could scout around in there, very
quietly?*

*It would be risky. If he were to wake up and see me I
could certainly escape, but he would rouse the castle
against me. Thus far, no one seems to have given me any
thought.*

Liam knew the oversight would not last long, and
wanted to make the most to it. *Try anyway. If he wakes*

up, don't hurt him. You can put him back to sleep, can't you, with that cantrip?

Easily.

Once again he waited, praying to his Luck and to whatever gods would listen that the dragon would be careful, would be safe. With nothing except waiting to occupy his thoughts, he became aware of the fact that he ached all over. He filled the time by cataloguing his cuts and bruises.

Finally, Fanuilh announced that it was in Raius's room. *He is still asleep.*

Do you see anything?

He has a great deal of baggage. I doubt I could go through it—wait.

What? There was no reply. *What is it? Fanuilh?*

A servant has come in.

Liam jumped to his feet, cuts and bruises forgotten. *Get out of there! Get out now!*

I am hiding under the bed, the dragon told him, its thought cool and composed. He paced the cell, clenching his fists to ease the frustration he felt, digging his fingernails deep into his palms.

He is awake now, Fanuilh thought. *The servant is announcing someone to see him. The earl left orders not to be woken, and is very angry.* The matter-of-fact delivery of the messages only heightened Liam's suspense.

Get out of there as soon as you can!

The servant is apologizing. It is Quaestor Provyn.

Wait!

The earl says he will see him. Shall I—

Stay where you are! Can you hear them? He rolled his eyes at his own stupidity, bouncing eagerly on the balls of his feet. *Never mind, never mind. Tell me everything they say.*

The servant has let Quaestor Provyn in. Would you not rather listen for yourself?

Cursing his stupidity—where had his wits gone?—he closed his eyes tight and called up the image of the helmet. He had not mastered listening and seeing at the same

time, so instead of closing the visor, he imagined a peal
of thunder crashing around him, and when it cleared he
heard Provyn's voice, coming muffled through the bed
under which Fanuilh lay hidden.

". . . in upon your rest, Earl Raius, but the Areopage
would know whether the prisoner said aught of interest
last night."

There was a rustle of bedclothes, a stealthy padding,
and the sound of the door being pulled quietly shut. A
long moment of silence, and then Raius hissed, "What
would you here?"

"Your pardon, my lord," Provyn begged, and Liam
imagined that he could hear the fat quaestor nervously
drywashing his hands. "Rhenford's close on us, my lord,
close I tell you, he knows all—"

"Rhenford is naught," the earl interrupted, his voice
tight with anger. "Naught. I can scarce credit this fear in
you, Provyn. I thought you more a man. Will you quail,
with so much done?" The bed creaked as he spoke,
seemingly right above Liam's head. "It was foolish to
come, and you must leave me presently."

Provyn whined, "My lord, what of his creature? It is
at liberty, and a danger. Who knows what it might do?"

Liam held his breath, willing Fanuilh to do the same.

"I will not hear it! Rhenford's immured, his beast
wandering lost, masterless. He's no wizard, and his
dragon hardly worth the name. He'll not discover us to
anyone, and if he did, none would credit his tale. It is
too mad, too fantastical—and he has no proof. Our only
fear was Gratian, and that is past. The maid is yet in
Hounes, and I've sent men to see she never parts it. This
night we'll have the final rite; after that we may do as
we please, and none to stop us, nor Rhenford nor Saffian
nor the Duke himself. See you? *See you?*"

"Aye, aye," Provyn said hurriedly, worried at the way
the earl had raised his voice. "Your pardon, my lord—
but what shall I do this day? Rhenford'll talk! He told
the Areopage I'd taken off her husband! She's not so

clever as he was, nor so cold and suspicious, but she'll
have to listen!''

''Smile and wink with others,'' Raius counselled.
''Roll your eyes, as at a clown, a child puffed up with
fancies. Be above it all, deign not to answer. With Saffian, condole and hang your head, as at a questionable
jest. The book was in his room, was it not? The chalk
was his, was it not?''

Master, someone is coming into your cell.

While Liam heard through Fanuilh's ears, it used his.
He jumped, hastily imagining the helmet again, and the
thunder. The echoes faded and he turned to face the two
soldiers coming down the steps. One held a spear, the
other a tin cup of water and a loaf of bread.

''Your breakfast, master murderer.''

Liam nodded, wishing they would go so he could return to the conversation in Raius's bedchamber. Bread
and cup were deposited on the floor, but the soldiers did
not leave. They glared at him, as if they wished that he
would make an ill-considered move.

''Aedile Gratian was the best of men,'' the one with
the spear said at last.

''I know,'' Liam replied. *Go away!* ''I didn't kill
him.''

The soldier grunted his disbelief and would have said
something more, but his comrade touched him on the
shoulder and shook his head. With many a backward
glance they left the cell. The door was not even shut
before Liam was seeing the helmet in his head, hearing
the thunder and—nothing. Raius's room was silent.

Provyn left, Fanuilh thought. *The earl has gone to
bathe and dress.*

He opened his eyes and kicked at his breakfast with a
curse. Loaf and cup skittered across the cell without a
sound, and though he felt his lips move he did not hear
the curse.

They did not say anything of interest, Fanuilh reported.
*Provyn seemed to be trying to convince the earl to give
him more money, and the earl told him that after tonight*

*he would have all that he would ever want. Then he told
him to be ready for their visit to Mother Aspatria, and
dismissed him. He did not mention a time for their meeting.*

For the fourth time in as many minutes, Liam made
himself hear thunder, and returned all his senses to his
cell. *Nothing else?*

Nothing.

All right. When you can, get out of there and find yourself a safe place to hide.

Yes, master.

Liam paced his cell, furiously working over what he
had learned. In the end it seemed precious little, almost
too little when compared with the risk of Fanuilh's discovery. If anyone else had heard the conversation between Raius and Provyn it would have damned the two
men utterly, but no one would believe it coming from
him, and he doubted he could even get a single person
in the entire castle to listen.

More important than their past crimes was the meeting
they planned with the ghost witch, but the same strictures
applied. Who could he tell? Who would believe him?
Mother Aspatria's previous rites had required the deaths
of three children, and Raius clearly expected something
great from this last one, something that would put him
beyond even the Duke's power, which surely meant another human sacrifice.

Don't jump too far, he warned himself. *You don't
know that.* Nonetheless, sacrifice or not, the rite had to
be stopped, and his first impulse was to go to the grate
and shout until the soldiers were forced to listen. He restrained himself, though, knowing it would not work. No
one would listen to him, and if no one would listen to
him, he would have to take care of it himself. *Which
rather begs the question of how you're going to get out
of this cell,* a cynical voice at the back of his head pointed
out.

With Fanuilh's help he thought he could do that, although he had yet to figure out the details. Escape and flight he could manage; escape and a confrontation with a demon-summoning witch and her two henchmen was another thing entirely. A cot leg was good for taking a guard by surprise, not arresting practitioners of black magic.

Fanuilh, how far away can you cast your cantrips?

I must be within a few yards, master.

And how long do they last?

For Sleep and Laughter and Itch, perhaps five minutes. If I light a fire it will burn as long as a normal fire, provided there is fuel.

So for the dragon to be useful it would have to be inside the castle, in the dungeon with him. The meeting was scheduled for that night, which made things easier: Fanuilh could slip in under cover of darkness. *And it'll be late, too,* Liam decided. *They can't just get up from dinner and say, "If you'll excuse us, we're off to raise a demon."* He had time, time to think, to rest. Just looking at the cot set him yawning, and his bruises suddenly clamored for attention. He lay down on the cot, stretching and wincing at the same time.

Do you think you can get into the castle at night without being seen?

There are a great many windows. Finding my way to the dungeons would be more difficult.

If the dragon came in after sunset, Liam thought it would have at least an hour to get downstairs. *Would that be enough?*

Two would be better, but it should be possible. I will be very quiet. I wonder, however, if there is any purpose served in getting you out of the cell.

For a moment, Liam was speechless. *Isn't that the point of this little exercise?*

Fanuilh offered a long and complicated rationale with its usual pedantry, but Liam found its logic inescapable. To free him it needed the keys, which Liam had seen dangling from a ring on the belt of one of the soldiers. With the sleep cantrip it could get the keys and then free Liam, but the magically-induced slumber would not last longer than a few minutes, and in any case the keys would have to be returned for Provyn and Raius to enter Mother Aspatria's cell. Things would be different if there were a second set of keys, or if the guards were to put their set down for any space of time, but they could hardly rely on a chance like that. *I think the point of the exercise is not necessarily to free you, master, but rather to stop the rite, is it not? And to stop it in such a way as to prove the participants' guilt?*

Liam had to agree, already guessing what Fanuilh would suggest next and not liking it at all.

In that case, I should hide myself somewhere in the dungeons and wait until Quaestor Provyn and Earl Raius come down, then follow them in. If I need to put the guards to sleep, I will. Then, when they are in the middle of the rite, whatever it may be—but before they succeed in conjuring a Lord Daemon, which we may presume is their intention—I will cast the cantrip on them. I can continue to cast it until they are found, with all of their equipment around them. With a reasonable amount of luck my part will remain unknown, and thus there will be no question of your involvement. That should serve to prove your innocence, would it not?

It would. It was a strong plan, far stronger than any they could possibly devise that involved getting Liam out of his cell. The only weak spot he could see was Fanuilh's having to lurk around the dungeons until Provyn and Raius came, and even there he had to grant that the dragon could be a stealthy little creature when it wished.

Still, he did not like it. He did not like sending his familiar alone into danger, however well-understood and prepared for, and he did not like the idea of sitting idly by while events unfolded. Leading from the rear was not in his nature, and it galled him. Fanuilh waited patiently while he tried to work out a plan in which he could participate. He struggled with the pieces of the puzzle—the keys, the timing of the rite, the whereabouts of the soldiers—for half an hour, tossing and turning on the cot.

And finally gave up.

All right. That's what we'll do. What you'll *do. I'll sit here and worry. With any luck I'll sleep through the whole thing. Wake me when I'm innocent, will you?*

Yes, master.

That was a joke. You'll be careful, won't you?

Yes, master.

Are you tired? Can you find a place to get some sleep?

I am on the roof of the central tower. No one will bother me here.

Liam stretched out on the cot with a grudging sigh. It was the best plan they could devise, and if Fanuilh bore far more than the lion's share of the work, there was nothing he could do about it. Dissatisfied, he settled in for a nap, an unhappy frown on his face.

Sleep did not come, though he had not really expected it. Instead he wondered, a whirl of ideas and questions plaguing him but refusing to fall into any coherent shape.

What, for instance, did Raius expect from this final rite? Immortality? Infernal power? An army of demons to do his bidding? What had Mother Aspatria promised him, and what would he have to pay in return? Guessing was impossible—he knew too little—but that did not stop him from imagining the limitless possibilities, each more horrifying than the last.

Now all that stood between them and whatever it was they sought was Fanuilh. In the months they had been bound as master and familiar, Liam had come to rely more and more on the dragon, not as a servant but as a loyal presence, a friend. Lying on the cot, tired and sore but unable to sleep, he vowed to treat the dragon better, to be more patient with its pedantry and its lack of a sense of humor. *Not that I'm so vicious and cruel as it is,* he thought, *but I'll make fun of him less.*

As if in response to his promise, he heard a brief burst of chittering from beneath the cot, and then a strange scraping noise. He sat up, the cot creaked, and the scraping noise stopped; then, after a few seconds, it resumed. Slowly, striving for silence, he leaned over the edge of the cot and peered underneath, straight into the eyes of a large rat, its black fur slicked back and beaded with moisture.

Liam jerked back and the rat did the same, disappearing from sight. He rolled off the cot and knelt down but the rat was gone, along with the loaf of bread he had kicked there earlier. Suddenly excited, he yanked the cot away from the wall to reveal an open drain in the floor. Heedless of the fleeing rat, he reached down, feeling the walls of the drain. They were granite, too hard to chip away, and the hole was barely eight inches across, far too small for even an infant. From below he heard splashing, so faint and muted he might have imagined it.

Fanuilh! he projected. *Look at this!* He conjured the image of the helmet with unconscious ease, flipped down the visor, and staggered, reaching blindly for a wall that was not there. He looked down from an immense height, over the lip of a rain gutter at the very top of Deepenmoor's highest tower. Tiny people crawled about far below, and Liam gulped. *Do you see it?*

It is a hole.

Liam removed the visor, grateful to be back below the ground. *It's a drain, a sewer. Could you fit in it?*

Perhaps. Liam thought he detected a cautious note in the dragon's reply. *Why would I want to?*

Remembering his promise, he shrugged off the sarcastic answer that occurred to him. *You could get in that way, into the castle. If there's a drain in my cell, there must be one in Mother Aspatria's. Hiding there would be easier than hiding outside, where the guards might find you. And you could get in now, as opposed to waiting until dark.*

It is a sewer, master.

Since when were you so fastidious? A little muck won't hurt you.

What if I were to get lost? There must be drains all over the castle. I could wander for days and never find your cell.

To his surprise, Liam found the dragon's reluctance

amusing, not annoying. *Every time it branches, take the lower branch. There can't be much below here. And if you get really lost just follow the current.*

Are you sure there is a current?

I heard water. The castle's probably built over a spring or a well or something, and the water runs through or is pumped through to clear the drains and the pit garderobes and things like that. Look, I realize it won't be pleasant, but honestly, don't you think it would be safer to be there below than out in the hall, where any passing guard might spot you?

Fanuilh did not respond for a long while, and Liam was beginning to wonder if the creature had decided to just fly off and leave him when it finally thought, *It would be safer, assuming we can find where it empties out.*

That'll be easy, Liam replied. He had watched the foundation of a fortress being laid out once, and had studied the architecture of others. Mountains stood east of Deepenmoor, with the land sloping away south and west. *Look for the head of a spring to the south and west, more west than south, I should think, not far from the castle, at most a mile.*

The sound of footsteps echoed in the hallway outside his cell, and then keys jingled by his door.

Someone's coming. He lifted the cot and set it as quietly as possible back in position over the drain. *West of south, less than a mile. Take a look.*

I will look, the dragon thought.

As he turned to the door, Liam reflected that no one could blame Fanuilh for not looking very hard.

The Duke came into the cell.

CHAPTER 19

AT MOST LIAM had expected Widow Saffian, returned for another pointless interview; that the Duke himself had come spurred a momentary hope. *Gods bless Tasso,* he thought, then stifled the hope and swept a low bow.

Vespasianus came down the steps, his green eyes cold and impassive. Liam was tall, taller than most people in the Southern Tier, but the Duke seemed to tower over him. There was an interminable pause while the man simply stood, filling the silence with a gravity and a sense of imminent purpose that scattered Liam's thoughts and left him waiting, capable only of reaction. Only once before had he met a man with that sort of aura, a centuries-old wizard in the icy lands far to the north, steeped in ancient and evil power. The Duke's was a neutral power, impartial and indifferent—but power nonetheless.

"You make grave accusations, Master Rhenford," he said at last, as if the matter were more curious than important. "Galba is my intimate, a cousin of my blood, an ancient ally of my house."

"I know, my lord. And I have no direct proof—but I think I could get it, with your permission. Or, if it please you, I could prove it on the field of honor." He thought duels foolish and unproductive, but he knew the Duke believed in them as a test of innocence.

Vespasianus negated the idea with a slight movement of his head. "It has gone beyond that. You accuse Quaestor Provyn as well, and as my officer he is immune to such. Mother Aspatria, too—and you could not face a woman. No, this is a matter for the court, and the law. I would know your thoughts, Master Rhenford, and how you justify your charges."

Liam licked his lips and started to explain. He stumbled in his story, backtracking occasionally to reconcile events, but all in all he found it easier to tell the Duke than he had Widow Saffian. Vespasianus did not interrupt once, and he gave no reaction to anything Liam said.

He told about joining the Areopagus, Widow Saffian's unexpected assignment of the cases, Provyn's persistent hostility and his reluctance to hand over the reports. He touched briefly on his removal from the last capital case, the bandits on the road to Deepenmoor and his impressions from their first dinner at the castle. Finally, he recounted what Kortenaer had told him about Raius's illness and subsequent recovery, and then paused, wondering how to work in the conversation he had heard between Provyn and the earl.

Vespasianus noticed his hesitation. "Go to, there is more."

"I heard something this morning, my lord, but I cannot say how."

"Go to," the Duke growled. "This is no time for maidish dithering. Go to!"

Gulping, Liam blurted out what he had heard. "They plan to summon up a demon tonight," he finished. "The girl in Hounes must be why they killed Gratian. She must have seen something; I don't know what. But this rite has to be stopped, that's the important thing. I know it sounds unbelievable, there's no way I could know this, but you must believe me, my lord. I swear it's true."

After a pause the other man said, "Your familiar is at large." Liam nodded slowly, and the Duke closed his eyes for several seconds.

"I have a sword that is enchanted against demons, my lord. Let me have it and let me watch for them tonight. You can set as many guards on me as you like, so long as we can be hidden, and when they start we can catch them. Please, my lord." He tried to inject the urgency he felt into his voice without sounding like he was pleading;

he did not think begging would move the Duke.

As it was, when Vespasianus opened his eyes he seemed not to have heard what Liam said. He spoke quietly. "These twelve years past, I went to a Convocation of Lords in Torquay, to attend the crowning of our present king. There were two men, Midlanders, who presented a dispute before the Convocation, calling for settlement. A decision was taken, but the one did not heed it, and went back to the Midlands to prepare for war."

Liam froze, suddenly tense. It had been eleven years, actually, but he could still remember his father coming from the Convocation to take him from the university, his face a grim mask as he reported the judgement and Lord Diamond's determination to violate it.

"I'd returned to my seat ere the outcome was certain, but we had news of it. This Diamond made war on the other, sacked his keep and killed him. I was grieved to hear it, for that he was a man of parts, a goodly lord. I tell you this for that you share his name—he was Othniel, Lord Rhenford. Y'are a Midlander. Did you know him?"

What is he getting at? "The Rhen runs through most of the Midlands, my lord," he said cautiously, "and has many fords."

Vespasianus frowned, the corners of his lips quirking slightly. "Othniel's son avenged him, I heard later, slaying Diamond in his own home, beneath his very roof." He paused, fixing Liam's eyes with his own. "It was well done."

A wave of relief swept through Liam, but he did not relax. "I think now I remember the story, my lord. There was a price on the son's head, wasn't there?"

"Lifted a year past, in an amnesty from the latest Convocation, but the son was nowhere to be found. As his lands—and Diamond's—had long since been swallowed up in others' holdings, no restitution was considered possible, and the matter was dropped."

So he knows who I am. Now what? Would openly admitting it get him out of the cell? His comment about the length of the Rhen was true; Vespasianus could not be completely sure he was Othniel's son, and in any case it had no bearing on the present situation. However much the Duke might approve of his having killed Diamond, it did not prove that he had not killed Gratian. Before he could decide, the Duke spoke again.

"You'll stay here, Master Rhenford, and on the morrow will appear before the Areopagus. I charge you to stay silent on what y'have told me, silent as a tomb. You understand me? Say naught, and do naught. Call your familiar, and have him do as you—naught. You understand me? Upon your life, Master Rhenford."

"I understand, my lord," Liam said, turning his eyes from the Duke's, grateful the man had not made him swear.

Vespasianus left without another word.

Noon came and went, although Liam had only Fanuilh's word for it. The dragon searched the woods to the south and east, informing him of the time and its lack of progress with occasional thoughts. For his part, Liam lay on the cot and mulled over the Duke's visit, trying to decide if it made any difference to his plans.

Given their close relationship, it would be understandable for Vespasianus not to believe Raius guilty. Moreover, Liam's story had been just that, a story, without a shred of real proof. There was proof out there—with the girl in Hounes, and the two bandits, whom Liam was sure were the earl's men—but he could not get at it, and without it he could not convince the Duke.

As things stood, there was not enough evidence to convict any of the three prisoners. Nothing but her key implicated Mother Aspatria in the deaths of the three children; more substantial clues pointed to Kortenaer, but the fact that he had discovered the crime in such a public way argued strongly in his favor. Liam might be punished for possessing the *Daemonologia,* but even that and the chalk could not establish a reasonable motive for murdering Gratian.

It seemed likely that the Duke was hoping the cases might simply go away. Liam had seen the Areopage dismiss charges for lack of proof; perhaps Vespasianus expected the same to happen here. All three of the accused would be freed, and the mysteries declared insoluble. In time the furor over Gratian's death would die down, and the inconvenient rumors about Earl Raius would fade.

That's got to be what he's thinking. He doesn't want Raius's name—and his own, by association—dragged through the mud, and he doesn't want to execute me or Kortenaer as a scapegoat. If he just waits and does nothing, and everyone keeps their mouths shut, all will be well.

Except, of course, for the rite. It struck him that the Duke had not taken his warning seriously. If he had that would mean exposing Raius, his faithful vassal, and two of his officers as well, which in Liam's assessment he was unlikely to do.

So he would go ahead with his plan. He urged Fanuilh to look harder.

In one of the lull's between the dragon's negative reports, Liam dozed and had a familiar nightmare, one he used to have frequently but that had recurred less and less often as the years passed.

Rhenford Keep burned. He knew it was Rhenford Keep, though it looked like Deepenmoor in the dream's latest incarnation, and a stiff wind blew the fierce heat of the flames in his face. Diamond's soldiers—shadowy, monstrous forms—beat the fields around the keep, in search of him. He dodged and hid desperately, knowing it was futile but unable to stop, and all the while his father's body burned where it lay crumpled in the gate.

Liam woke sweating, astonished that the dream could still be as powerful. Scrubbing at his face, he wished he had not kicked the cup of water. His throat was dry.

Why don't I dream about killing Diamond? It had been two months later, when the lord was back in his own keep, lulled by victory and time. Disguised as a peasant,

Liam had slipped into the castle and into Diamond's chambers; when it was done, he had stolen a horse and ridden north. He only learned of the price on his head six months later, and by then the killing seemed so distant to him that it might have been the work of another man.

Diamond didn't beg, he remembered. *Didn't say anything.* He had woken the man, so he could see who was cutting his throat. Pinned and helpless, Diamond spat and thrust his neck forward, as if to help his murderer, but Liam held the man's head firmly, planning to draw the knife across at his leisure. The snarling hate in Diamond's eyes was too much for him, though, too much like his own, and he drove the dagger in quick, straight through. The blade snapped in the bones of the lord's neck. *There wasn't even much blood.*

The memory threatened to seem much less distant, and he roused himself both from his own thoughts and from the cot.

Any luck?

No, master.

He began to pace.

Toward midafternoon, Fanuilh found the entrance to the castle's drains. A very small stream rose from among a jumble of rocks, and the dragon had to squeeze its way among the stones to find the clay pipe.

Can you fit?

Yes, though I cannot fly. I will have to walk in the water.

How deep is it?

A few inches.

Liam wanted to switch eyesight, to see and judge for himself; instead, he held back. *Make sure it's safe. If the current is too strong, don't do it.*

It looks safe from here. I will go in.

At first the going was fairly easy. The pipe ran straight northwest, toward the castle, and Fanuilh simply waded up it. The current was weak, and the pipe did not branch. Pacing the cell, fuming at his own impotence, Liam fought the urge to pester his familiar for information. His relief was immense when, after half an hour, Fanuilh thought to tell him that it had reached a branching, above which the current was stronger. All too quickly they determined that the new pipe led to the village outside the castle walls, and the dragon moved on. If it found the current much harder to deal with it did not say, and Liam did not ask.

"I hate waiting," he muttered to himself, "I hate waiting." He said it again and again, hoping Fanuilh would reach another branching, that it would decide the current was too strong, that it would get bored with its lonely walk and decide to break the mental silence that lay so heavy on its master.

Soon, but not soon enough, it reached a branching.

I can go left or right.

Which is higher?

There was a long pause. Liam stood still in the middle of the cell, gritting his teeth.

The left pipe seems to slope upward.

He exhaled loudly. *Go to the right. Always stay as low as you can,* he projected, and almost instantly wished he had not. General instructions like that could be applied without consulting him. *Check in from time to time, will you?*

Yes, master.

Fanuilh had a very loose notion of "from time to time." An age passed before it thought to him again, and Liam had taken to plucking compulsively at the already-ragged blanket, muttering unhappily to himself.

I am under the castle now, it told him.

He jumped to his feet. *How do you know?*

I just passed beneath a garderobe.

"Ha!" Liam shouted, then winced. *No one was using it, were they?*

No, master. The water is a little thick, however.

He winced again, wishing they could have contrived a

better plan. *Ah. Fanuilh, you know if I could, I would do this myself.*

You would not fit in the pipe.

Now that they were both underground there was no way to tell the time. To Liam it felt as if the night must already have come and be half over, but he knew it could be no later than sundown, if that.

Unable to resist his impulse to pester the dragon, he systematized it. He counted to five hundred two times, and projected a question. Fanuilh replied, and he started counting again, trying not to think of all the things that might happen to his familiar. That it might get swept away, or wedged in some narrowing of the pipe, or drowned in the sewage of the castle, or overcome by the smell.

How is it coming?

Very well, master.

He counted.

You're not too tired? Rest once in a while, if you can.

I am not tired.

He counted, and started marking each set of one thousand with a long rip in the blanket.

How can you see down there?

There is some light from the garderobes and the drains. And my eyesight is very good.

He counted, and ripped.

There were nine long tears in the blanket when Fanuilh contacted him of its own accord.

Master, I think you should—

That was all. He sat tensed on the edge of the cot, waiting for more. *Fanuilh?* There was no reply. *Fanuilh!*

—moment—

Fanuilh! What is it? What's going on? He got to his feet, threw the cot away from the wall, and knelt by the pipe. *Fanuilh! Where are you?*

There was no reply.

Stricken, he hung over the pipe, glaring down into the

blackness. The sound of splashing reached him from a great distance. *FANUILH!*

The splashing noise faded imperceptibly.

Excuse me, master.

Liam whooped.

I was attacked by rats.

"Rats!" *Rats? Are you all right?*

I am fine, master. I was going to say that I think I am near you now, and that if you were to make some noise I might be able to find you more easily.

How many rats? Are you hurt?

Perhaps a dozen. I am fine. Could you make some noise? Sing, perhaps?

Liam started bawling out a song.

A few minutes later he plucked Fanuilh out of the drain and hugged the creature to his chest, grinning. "You are a beautiful thing, you know that? A dragon of parts, a passing dragon, the dragon of all the world, the best damned—" He held it away from his chest. "You're wet." The front of his tunic was foul. "You're dirty!"

It is a sewer, Fanuilh pointed out.

"So it is, so it is!" He used the torn blanket to clean the worst of the filth from Fanuilh's scales and wings. There was a small tear in one leathery wing. *What's this?*

It is from the rats. It is nothing.

Beaming with pride, he cleaned the dragon as best he could. It suffered his ministrations with ill grace, squirming and sneezing once or twice, but he would not be put off until it pointed out that the guards might have been attracted by his singing.

"Attracted?" Liam asked. "Scared off, probably." Still, he pushed the cot back against the wall and made Fanuilh a nest beneath it with the remains of the blanket. With the dragon safely hidden, he lay back on the cot, content. The prospect of the hours ahead, the wait they would have to endure before Provyn and Raius arrived for the rite, seemed a small thing.

Are you going to sleep? he asked.

No, master. I am not tired.

A passing dragon, I tell you. I'm going to take a nap. Wake me in an hour, would you?

Fanuilh promised that it would.

The guards woke him instead, to change his lantern and bring his dinner, another loaf of bread and a cup of water. He took the bread from the floor where they dropped it, and asked if they knew the time.

"Too late for you," said the one who had dropped the bread.

"Nigh on eight bells," said the other one, frowning at his comrade.

Liam thanked them, and when they were gone offered the meal to Fanuilh. It drank half of the water and a single bite of bread, then insisted it wanted no more. Liam took the rest, working his way through the loaf in small, thoughtful bites.

What do you suppose this rite is all about? I mean, what could be worth killing three children for?

The two are not necessarily connected. Sacrificing the children may have been a form of payment for Earl Raius's cure, with this new rite an entirely separate transaction. Lord Daemons, it went on to explain, were always anxious to enlarge their contacts with the material plane. Often enough a Lord was summoned for a specific task, usually as a desperate measure, and then through trickery and playing on the baser instincts of the summoner managed to broaden its role. *Needless to say, they are not to be trusted, though they will often promise what the listener most wishes to have.*

So Raius is cured, and the demon says, "Look what I did for you; wouldn't you like to know what else I can do?"

Precisely.

And what else could it do?

They will promise most anything, and in many cases they can do what they say. Immortality was beyond them, and they could not change the past, but they could grant

a long and healthy life, immense riches, political or magical power. The price, unfortunately, corresponded with
the magnitude of the gift. Fanuilh briefly recounted a
series of stories about deals with Lords and the exorbitant
prices they demanded, finishing with the grisly history of
a Suevi prince who was granted five hundred years of
life in return for the lives of five hundred of his subjects.

A single guard passed in the hallway outside the cell,
and Liam decided it was time for Fanuilh to go back into
the drains. *I think they've changed watches,* he projected.
Time to get to work.

Yes, master.

If the dragon was reluctant to go, Liam could not tell
from its thought, but then he was rarely able to judge the
creature's moods; in fact, he was not entirely sure it had
any. Before it went down into the drain, he elicited a
series of promises: that it would be careful, that it would
keep in touch with him frequently, that it would run at
the slightest hint of danger. Projecting back assurances,
it slipped into the drain.

Then, before he even had time to get impatient, the
thought came: *I am here, master.*

You're sure it's her cell?

She is sitting on her cot. I can see her feet.

Let me see. He imagined the helmet, closed the visor.

Mother Aspatria's feet swung back and forth within a
foot of his nose. She wore sandals. He caught his breath
and switched back.

More waiting.

It did not seem as long, however. Liam looked out
from Fanuilh's vantage from time to time, saw Mother
Aspatria swinging her legs, pacing, standing in the middle of her cell. She seemed as impatient as he had been
earlier, and the comparison made him smile grimly.

He heard a guard pass by once, then a second time.
On the third pass, Liam went to the grill and asked the
time. The guard was already beyond his cell, headed toward the far end of the corridor, a shadow among shad-

ows. If he heard Liam's question, he ignored it.

Another one who thinks I killed Gratian, Liam guessed, watching the tall soldier recede down the corridor. *He's a bold one, though—I wouldn't want to make rounds in a dungeon without a lantern.* The guard disappeared into the darkness further down the hall.

Liam went back to his cot and checked in with Fanuilh.

All is still well, master.

Just wanted to make sure.

He occupied himself by trying to remember as many songs as he could, humming them to himself and sharing the words with Fanuilh. In an hour he worked his way through seventeen verses of "The Lipless Flutist"—all he knew, though there were dozens more—and six shorter songs. Fanuilh dutifully repeated the lyrics back to him.

They were in the middle of "The Milkmaid and the Thief" when Liam realized that the guard had not returned from the far end of the hall. He went to the grill but the corridor was dark and he could see no sign of the man.

What's he doing? Liam wondered angrily. If the guard was still there when Provyn and Raius came, he would scare them off. "Come back, you idiot," he whispered. "Get out of here."

The guard did not come back.

Master, they are here.

Liam cursed and switched eyesight. Next to Mother Aspatria's sandaled feet he could see a pair of gleaming leather boots. He gave Fanuilh back its eyes and took its ears.

"—likes me not. Wherever are the guards?" It was Provyn.

Loitering at the end of the hall, Liam thought, and decided that the only thing he could do was keep a lookout, and try to distract the man if he returned.

"Asleep," Raius said, "or dead or drunk or flying to

the moon. What does it matter? Let's begin!'' He sounded eager.

Mother Aspatria spoke next, her voice thin and waspish. "Aye, let's to it. Y'are prepared?"

"Aye," Raius said. "Prepared and more."

The ghost witch demanded chalk, and there was the sound of shuffling feet followed by chalk squeaking on stone. *What's happening?*

She is drawing the pentagram.

When are you going to stop them?

It would be best to wait until they have made their sacrifice.

The squeaking went on, and Mother Aspatria began to mutter, strange liquid sounds without consonants that ran together.

Wait for the sacrifice? Are you mad? We don't want someone else killed!

In this case, they should need only to sacrifice an animal, something small. Presumably they are summoning the demon to bargain. The greater price would be paid later.

Liam watched the hall and listened to the ghost witch's moanings. *Are you sure?*

There is no one in the cell beside the three of them. I cannot see, but I assume either the earl or Quaestor Provyn is carrying the sacrifice.

All right, he projected. *But as soon as they've done it, put them to sleep.*

Yes, master.

Mother Aspatria chanted, her sandals shuffling over the stone, chalk squeaking. Her dress rustled. One of the men with her coughed, Liam could not tell which. He gripped the bars of the grill, praying to his Luck that the guard would not return in the next few minutes.

Everything stopped except for the eerie chanting.

The pentagram is finished.

The chanting stopped.

As soon as it's done, Fanuilh.

"Y'are ready?" Mother Aspatria asked, sounding breathless and excited.

"Aye," Raius said, and Liam heard a blade being unsheathed.

Master—

There was another cough, and Mother Aspatria said, "Not on the circle!" and then there was a crash that sounded as if it was directly over his head. Liam jumped.

What was THAT?

I believe it was Quaestor Provyn, Fanuilh replied. *He fell on the bed.*

Why?

He was the sacrifice.

The blood drained from Liam's face as he frantically switched Fanuilh's hearing for its sight.

Provyn's fall had forced the dragon back into the drain, and he was looking almost straight up. He saw the fat quaestor's face amid the wreckage of Mother Aspatria's cot, eyes wide and tongue protruding, blood smearing his jowls and chin like a beard. Beyond the dead man stood the ghost witch and Raius, and between them the demon that had killed Gratian, its horns knocking against the lantern hung from the ceiling.

It's here, he projected frantically. *It's here!*

It is not too late, Fanuilh told him. *Give me my eyes.*

For a long moment he could not think, only stare at the demon, at the milk-white muzzle and the gleaming horns. Mother Aspatria was talking but he could not hear her.

Master!

He closed his eyes and relinquished Fanuilh's sight. Shuddering, he opened them again and looked down the hall. The guard was there, moving silently toward him, a naked sword in his hand.

"Hey!" Liam called. "Hey! Come here! Stay here!"

It is done, Fanuilh reported.

The guard looked at him as he passed, but said nothing. He wore a heavy helmet with a full visor. His sword caught the light from Liam's lantern, the length of the blade gleaming silver.

"Don't go in there!" Liam shouted. The guard walked on toward Mother Aspatria's cell.

It is done, Fanuilh repeated. *They are asleep. The demon cannot pass outside the pentagram.*

Liam slumped against the door, suddenly exhausted. *Let me see.* Fanuilh made the exchange, and he was looking down from near the ceiling. Mother Aspatria and Raius lay collapsed on either side of the pentagram and the demon stood within, shaking its three-fingered fists in Fanuilh's direction. As he watched, it opened its muzzle and let out a bellow that Liam heard with his own ears.

Are you sure it can't get out of that circle?

Yes, master.

The demon pricked up its ears then, black tongue flicking out as if to taste the air, and slowly swivelled its head toward the cell door. One horn caught the lantern and tore it from its hook; the other dragged sparks from the ceiling.

In the doorway stood the guard, the silver sword in his hand, and even as Liam gave a warning shout heavily laden with relief, knowing the blade and the man who held it, the Duke strode down the steps to the floor of the cell.

Invisible bars pressed against Liam's face, the bars of the grill as he shouted, "My lord, stop! Stop! It can't get out of the circle!"

The Duke wasted no time with preliminaries: he swung the sword once in a high arc that sheared clean through the demon's upraised forearm. Even as the severed arm fell, bloodless, even as the creature lifted its muzzle to howl, Vespasianus thrust up on the backswing and drove the enchanted sword to the hilt in its chest. It staggered back a step, hung poised on one foot for a moment, and crashed to the ground.

"Ha! Yes!" Liam shouted. It felt as if he were in the room; he wanted to go to the Duke, to clap him on the back, to shake his hand, anything to celebrate. "Yes!" He gripped the bars he could not see and shook them, whooping.

In the other cell, the Duke threw off his helmet, and Liam's shouts of triumph died when he saw the man's expression. Grim-faced, Vespasianus glanced quickly around the cell, his eyes sliding past Fanuilh, the demon, Mother Aspatria, until they lit on the dagger in Raius's hand, dark with Provyn's blood. Kneeling beside the earl, he pried the blade from the sleeping man's fingers.

Fanuilh, get out of there, Liam ordered, but he was too shocked to return the dragon's eyesight.

What is going on, master?

With a single, deft stroke, the Duke cut Raius's throat, and crossed the pentagram to Mother Aspatria.

Get out! He closed his eyes, dredged up a sketchy image of the helmet, lifted the visor. *Go! Use the pipe!*

With his own eyes now he looked out into the hallway, and heard the sound of running feet far away, a hubbub of calling men. Then the Duke's voice rang out, "Stand where you are! Come no further! Stay out of the dungeon!"

Liam backed away from the door as a single set of heavy footsteps approached his cell.

CHAPTER 20

HIS BACK TO the rear wall of the cell, Liam dropped into a fighter's crouch as the door opened. He did not think he would have much of a chance if the man attacked—in addition to being bigger and far stronger, Vespasianus had retrieved the sword and wore a steel breastplate—but he wanted to have at least a chance.

He has to know I know, Liam decided. *He saw Fanuilh. He'll know.* The question was what he would do about it; a man who had just murdered a woman and his own cousin while they slept would hardly stick at removing the only witness.

The Duke scowled at his pose, his brows knitting together. "Come, Quaestor Rhenford, I mean you no harm." There was a wealth of disgust in his tone, as if he had caught Liam weeping over a skinned knee, but Liam did not relax.

"It is a reasonable suspicion, my lord," he said.

Grunting angrily, Vespasianus threw his sword to the floor. "Take it up," he commanded. "I mean you no harm. I've come to offer you a choice."

Liam snagged the sword with his foot, drew it close and picked it up. He felt better immediately. "A choice, my lord?"

"My coz was an innocent dupe," the other man said, "as was Quaestor Provyn, the both ensorcelled by Mother Aspatria. You yourself killed the beast she summoned—an honorable and glorious feat."

"I didn't kill it," Liam said slowly. "Earl Raius murdered those children. Provyn killed Acrasius Saffian.

They were both willing conspirators.'' He had been right about the Duke's purpose: to protect his duchy and his name, and that of his family's ancient ally. Few knew of Provyn's part, so that could be concealed, and since Mother Aspatria's involvement had been more public, she would take the blame, and it would end with her.

Thunder gathered in those remarkable green eyes. ''Only the witch went over to the Dark. Galba and the quaestor were ensorcelled. Saffian's death was by chance.''

Liam noted the anger, and decided there was only so far he could push. He was, after all, still on the wrong side of the cell door. ''The earl was ensorcelled,'' he agreed. Destroying Raius's name would not bring the children back to life. ''He came under her control while ill, and didn't have the strength to resist. Provyn, though, was a willing accomplice. And he killed Saffian.'' It was petty, he knew, but he refused to let the fat quaestor escape.

The Duke clenched his fists and sucked in a deep breath, struggling to control himself. ''A willing accomplice, then, but not Saffian's murderer. For Milia's sake.''

It took Liam a moment to remember Widow Saffian's first name, and then he could not understand how hiding the facts of her husband's death would help her in any way. Still, a look at the Duke's stern face convinced him he had injected as much truth into the story as would be allowed.

Nodding his acquiesence, he reversed the sword in his grip and went to the steps. ''Then that is what happened, my lord.'' He held out the hilt. ''Except that I didn't kill the demon. People will wonder how I got the sword, how I got out of my cell. You killed it.''

Their eyes met as Vespasianus took the sword, but there was no tacit agreement exchanged, no secret understanding. The Duke's eyes were clear and cold. ''You'll stay here this night, and on the morrow appear before the Areopagus to tell what happened,'' he said.

Something occurred to Liam. ''My lord, if Hierarch

Kortenaer is to appear as well, someone ought to speak to him beforehand.''

For a moment, Vespasianus considered the idea, then nodded curtly. ''It would be well.'' He paused, then added, ''I doubt not you'll both be found innocent.''

He spoke without the slightest trace of irony, and Liam made a low bow as the door shut.

Fanuilh's head poked from the drain, its claws braced on the rim.

You heard? Liam asked.

I did. He seeks to salvage his name.

Sighing, Liam lifted his familiar out of the hole and sank down on the cot. *I don't think it's quite that selfish. These are unsettled times. The king is a distant rumor, and his lords fight among themselves. If he thinks this will help keep the duchy stable, who are we to argue? Besides, I don't like the idea of an extended stay in this cell.*

They lay together, Fanuilh curled against his side, its warm presence and the steady rhythm of its breathing lulling him toward sleep.

Master? it thought after a while. *I am sorry I misjudged the rite.*

About Provyn, you mean? Forget it. You're the hero of the day, familiar mine. I was thinking about asking the Duke if he would let you hunt in his forests as a reward.

He had not been thinking about that at all, though he was proud of the dragon. He had been thinking that, after a week with the Areopagus, he had finally been bribed to lie about a case. Bribed with his own freedom, to be sure, and not explicitly, but bribed nonetheless. And whatever he may have told the dragon, he did not like it.

His father would not have lied about it. Othniel Rhenford had been his own court, riding his lands and holding sessions in barns and cottages, at crossroads and market fairs. There had been far less ceremony, Liam seemed to remember, and far more wisdom.

That's just nostalgia, he told himself. *The Duke is wise in his way.* He believed that, and he believed that the Duke's choice was a legitimate one, a practical response to the need to keep scandal to a minimum, and to ensure stability and faith in his rule. It was a legitimate choice—but not the best one, and he did not like being a part of it.

So thinking, he drifted off to a deep and dreamless sleep.

The guards were markedly more respectful when they woke him in the morning. His breakfast—hot porridge and fresh-baked bread—came on a platter, and the guard holding it waited patiently while Liam roused himself before setting it down on the cot. The other arranged a washstand with soap, linens, a razor and a basin of hot water.

When they asked him if there was anything else he needed, he laughed; it sounded nastier than he had intended. "Word has spread, eh?" Seeing the fearful look they exchanged, he relented. "Never mind. I'll need some clean clothes, that's all."

They hurried off, anxious to erase the memory of their bad behavior.

"It looks like we've been cleared," Liam told Fanuilh, as it nibbled reluctantly at a piece of bread.

They shared the breakfast, and when it was done Liam set about making them presentable. He shaved and then spent a few minutes trying to wash his familiar; by the time it was as clean as it would allow him to make it, the guards had returned with his things. He washed and dressed in his green tunic, then went through his bags. Everything was there except for his two swords and the *Daemonologia.* The swords he wanted back; the book they could burn.

And they will, too, he realized. It occurred to him that, while he would certainly be judged innocent of Gratian's murder, he was still charged with possession of a proscribed text.

"If they try to flog me for that . . ." he muttered defiantly, then shook his head and chuckled wryly at himself. *I'll be grateful the Duke didn't want a third corpse on his conscience.*

The court was held in Deepenmoor's main hall, a high and echoing room draped with old banners and faded standards. The Duke presided from the central table, with Widow Saffian at his side. The Areopage looked exhausted, her hands laid flat before her, her eyes half-lidded. Iorvram and his clerks sat at the only other table, Tasso among them. There was no separate table for quaestors, Liam noted grimly, because there were no other quaestors left. *And no Aedile, either. No ghost witch.*

A crowd filled the rear half of the hall, soldiers and castle servants, and he saw as he was brought in that many of their faces were blank with shock or wrinkled in confusion. A murmur accompanied his entrance, but the Duke silenced it by rapping his knuckles on the tabletop. The guards steered Liam into position and dropped back a few steps. Iorvram stood and stared off at the ceiling.

"This matter calls Liam Rhenford, of the Chartered City of Southwark. The charges are twofold: possession of a proscribed text of black magic, and use of the same for murderous purposes. Liam Rhenford, approach and be judged!"

The Duke spoke: "Master Rhenford, are these charges clear?"

"Yes, my lord."

"Are they true?"

"In part, my lord. I did have the book, but I did not use it to kill Aedile Gratian."

"The court agrees." Vespasianus's voice easily filled the hall. "Have you any justification for possession of a proscribed text?"

He's going to flog me, Liam thought. "I inherited it from a legitimate member of the Mages' Guild, and I did not know it was forbidden. Furthermore, it was extremely useful to me in my duties as quaestor with this court." *Choke on that.*

The Duke continued, unfazed. "The court has ordered the book destroyed, and will see it burned this afternoon. Ignorance of the law is no protection; nonetheless, in recognition of your services, the court will pardon you of the crime."

A wave of relief swept over him, but he refused to let it show. Through tight lips he said, "Thank you, my lord."

Vespasianus stood up then, and though he seemed to be addressing Liam, his words were meant for the gathered crowd. "In the matter of Aedile Gratian's death, it has been discovered to this court that the person responsible is Mother Aspatria of Deepenmoor, of late ghost witch in my service, and that she had the assistance since he came to Deepenmoor of Provyn of Southwark, of late quaestor of this court. The both were killed while attempting to summon a demon in this very seat."

Gasps started up here and there, and were silenced by a stern glance from the Duke. Beside him, Widow Saffian hung her head.

"Let it be noted that this court is satisfied of their guilt. Let it further be noted," he went on after a brief pause, "that also killed was Galba, Earl Raius. It has been discovered to this court that Earl Raius fell under the witch's power while ill some months past. It is our finding that Mother Aspatria did use black magic to ensorcel him, and that his death was unwarranted. His body will therefore be returned to his family. Let the proper punishments be visited on the bodies of Mother Aspatria and Provyn, and let them then be burned and the ashes scattered.

"I declare this session closed." He nodded once, turned on his heel, and left the hall.

And that, Liam thought, as a babble rose among the crowd, *is that.*

That evening the hall hosted a different gathering: a grand dinner, originally conceived in celebration of the end of the Areopagus's business but now purposeless, there being little about the just-completed circuit to celebrate.

At the lower tables Iorvram and his clerks made the best of it, drinking and eating their fill with the lesser officials permanently based at Deepenmoor: more clerks, scribes, tax assessors and land surveyors, the Duke's huntsman and his master of horse. If the score or so of men were not exactly wild with festive glee, they at least maintained a respectable level of talk, with the occasional bubble of restrained laughter. Liam wished he could have joined them.

No one talked at the head table. The Duke sat in the center, lifting food from his plate to his mouth without seeing it, his eyes sharply focused on the middle distance. On his right was Widow Saffian, her hands in her lap. She stared dully at her plate; her jaw worked from time to time as if she were chewing but she did not lift her fork once. To Liam she seemed to have aged a decade overnight: the flesh around her mouth and nose sagged heavily, and dark circles underlined her eyes. Beyond her, Tasso picked listlessly at his food.

Lady Lascelle alone seemed unperturbed. The girl ate gracefully, slicing tiny bites of meat from the bone and conveying them discreetly to her mouth, all the while surveying the hall with an interested and slightly superior expression. For a twelve-year-old, she showed more composure than any of the adults at the table.

There were no courses; everything was brought more or less at the same time, so there was not even the interruption of servants coming and going to break up the long stretch of silence. Liam was not hungry—the steward, Torquato, had arranged a large lunch for him when the session was over, after reinstalling him in his rooms—

but he doggedly worked his way through the plate. If he did not eat, he knew, he would drink, and end up calling over the boy with the wine pitcher far too many times.

An hour into dinner, her plate still full, Widow Saffian whispered something to the Duke and received his permission to withdraw. Lady Lascelle took advantage of the broken silence to turn to Liam and ask, "And where is your dragon, Quaestor Rhenford? I trust he eats as other creatures do?"

"Yes, but not at table, my lady." He had left the dragon in his rooms, asleep beside a half-eaten platter of raw mutton. "He has very poor manners."

She smiled, the serene smile of an accomplished hostess. "Is that so?"

"His conversation is also lacking," Liam went on, impressed by the girl's maturity, and grateful for any diversion.

"Still, I should think he would be useful for small things—lighting candles, for instance. He has fiery breath, does he not?"

"Lascelle!" the Duke said, his eyes still directed out over the hall. "You prattle. Do not try Quaestor Rhenford."

Liam thought better of a comment about her father's having done just that, and instead shook his head with mock regret. "I'm afraid not, my lady. He is only a very small dragon."

"But fearsome nonetheless," she responded. "My maids're quite afraid he'll tear the castle down about their ears."

"Lascelle!" the Duke commanded.

She said nothing more, accepting the rebuke with a regal air of indifference.

Suppressing a sigh, Liam beckoned to the wine boy. For half an hour he nursed the cup, glancing wistfully at the lower tables. He gave in a second time and had the cup refilled, and then, finally, the Duke spoke again.

"Quaestor Rhenford, the Areopagus parts Deepenmoor on the morrow. You'll with it?"

"No, my lord. I'll be leaving at the same time, but I'm planning to return to Southwark by way of the Cross-roads Fair." He had only decided not to go with the Areopagus that afternoon; he did not think he could ride with Widow Saffian for three days and keep the truth of what happened to himself.

"If you have no pressing business there, it would like me to have you stay a day with me. There are matters I would discuss with you."

The way the Duke said "pressing business" implied that it would have to be pressing indeed. Liam bowed his head. "It would be my pleasure to stay, my lord."

Vespasianus nodded imperceptibly and signalled to the waiting servants that he was done. They cleared the table in a flash and then he rose, precipitating a panicked ripple throughout the hall as everyone leapt to their feet for his departure.

"Stay on, stay on," he told them, more order than encouragement. "There is wine." He left with Lady Las-celle beside him, and Tasso followed them after a moment. Down at the lower tables the clerks and officials hesitated, then resumed their interrupted feast. Liam saw the jug boys hurry to fill a dozen lifted cups, and decided not to join Iorvram. He did not want his presence to put a damper on the clerks' evening. They had welcomed him once, but that was before his arrest. *Better to leave them to it,* he thought. *What would we have to talk about? "Glad you weren't a murderer, Quaestor Rhenford"?*

He drained his cup and left the hall.

Widow Saffian's maidservant was waiting outside Liam's apartments. She curtseyed as he approached, offered him the Areopage's compliments, and asked if he could spare the judge a moment. Shrugging, he let the woman lead the way. They followed the route he had run on the night Gratian was killed. *Only two nights ago,* he marvelled.

The Areopage sat by her fireplace, surrounded by a welter of chests and bags and clothing. She was stirring

a pile of clothes with her toe when Liam entered, and
rose to her feet to accept his bow.

"Quaestor Rhenford," she said, clasping her hands at
her waist. "I thank you for coming. I gather y'are staying
on with the Duke."

"Just for a day. I'm returning to Southwark by way
of the Fair."

She nodded absently, her gaze drifting over the mess
at her feet. Liam recognized a coat among the piles of
clothes, then another—both slashed—and realized she
was not packing her own things, but unpacking Provyn's.

"Areopage?"

Her head jerked up, as if he had intruded on a private
reverie. "Aye?"

"I don't think you'll find anything here."

She came back to herself, and he was relieved to see
the way her eyes focused, and to hear her sane tone of
voice. "Aye, I know—they were passing clever—there'll
be no trace. And yet I can't help wonder . . ." She threw
back her shoulders and faced him squarely. "Quaestor
Rhenford, I did you an injustice. Y'have been cleared,
but I would have you know I'm sensible of it."

He spread his hands to indicate that it did not matter.

"I'm sensible of it," she went on, her eyes wandering
away from his, "and so I've no right to ask what I would.
Yet I needs must. The Duke has said that Provyn did not
kill my husband. That it was but an opportunity for them.
That it may be they'd have done something like, but that
Acrasius's accident forestalled the necessity. And he has
forbid all further inquiry."

"I doubt it would yield anything," Liam said, and then
paused, unsure of what else to say. He had disagreed with
the Duke's story on this point, for the very reason that
he did not think it would satisfy the Areopage. On the
other hand, he really did not believe an investigation
would solve the matter. "In the end, it comes to the same
thing, wouldn't you say? If Provyn did—if Master Saffian was—well, Provyn's dead. He's not getting away
with anything." It sounded awkward to him, and she read

into it the interpretation he had feared she would.

"I don't seek vengeance, Quaestor. Only the truth. And for no reason I can say. Y'are right—Provyn's dead, and paid for whatever crimes may be his—and the Duke's made his meaning clear: no inquiry, no stir. But I would know. Can you understand?"

He shuffled his feet uncomfortably. "I can, and I'd like to know, too. But I don't think we can. We can only guess."

"And your guess?"

The image of Provyn's face came to him, the red fringe of blood along the jawline, the shock and surprise in the eyes, and he wondered if Acrasius Saffian had had the same look in his eyes when he died, the shock at being killed by someone he had trusted. Suddenly the whole situation seemed absurd.

"He killed him. I have no proof, but it makes no sense otherwise." What could the Duke do to him? Anyone who had even the vaguest notion of the details would come to the same conclusion.

Widow Saffian gave a nod, and then frowned sadly. "I would that you had made his acquaintance, Quaestor Rhenford. He would have taken to you."

"It is my loss, Areopage."

They were silent for a moment, and then she cleared her throat and called for her maidservant. "Clear these things away," she ordered, indicating Provyn's clothes and his baggage. "See that Torquato has them distributed to the poor." The maid hurried to do her bidding, and she held out her hand to Liam. "You see me sadly reduced, Quaestor, lacking husband, friends, and colleagues. When I return to Southwark I will have only Mistress Priscian for my friend. Yet it may be that when you return you may come to me some day, and sit with me for an hour. I am too old to be much alone."

Her smile was bleak as he bowed over her hand. "I will come," he promised.

• • •

The next morning she reminded him of his promise. He rose early to see the Areopagus off, and arrived at the inner courtyard just as she was climbing into her saddle. The rest of the column was already formed up.

"Good morrow to you, Quaestor Rhenford," she said when she was safely aloft. Dark circles ringed her eyes and the aging was permanent, etched into the lines around her nose and mouth. "Will I see you in Southwark?"

"You will," he assured her. She had more strength than he had given her credit for, and he looked forward to knowing her under different circumstances.

"Then I will take my leave of you. Fare well on your journey, and give my compliments to Aedile Tarpeia and all at the Fair." She raised her hand and signaled the Areopagus forward. It was strange for Liam to stand apart from the column, to watch it parade by amid the jingle and creak of harness and the clopping of hooves. Iorvram rode past at the head of his clerks; as a unit they waved to him, and he regretted not joining them the night before. Already the events of the previous days seemed far behind him, their impact diminished by a good night's sleep and the lifting of responsibilities. He was content to let the court leave without him, and satisfied that he had done all that was required of him—except for one thing.

The boy was riding a pony on the far side of the column; Liam caught up to him just outside the castle gate, and handed over the small purse of silver coins he had prepared.

Twisted backward in his saddle, the boy shouted thanks and waved furiously until the Areopagus rode out of sight.

Liam spent the rest of the morning in his rooms awaiting the Duke's summons, which came precisely at noon in the person of Torquato, who escorted him to Vespasianus's private study. It was sparely furnished—two chairs, a writing table piled high with papers, a single tapestry showing Deepenmoor and the mountains behind it—and the Duke seemed to fill the space. Over his plain tunic he wore an overlong brown vest that trailed and rustled behind him, so that when he moved it seemed as if he were raising his own dust cloud.

"Quaestor Rhenford," Torquato announced, and withdrew.

At a gesture Liam seated himself, though Vespasianus remained on his feet, striding about the study.

"Y'have business at the Fair, and then in Southwark," he said.

"Yes, my lord." Liam had to twist in his chair to follow the Duke's pacing.

"I would have you give them up. I would create you my Aedile here. Y'are a lord's son—trade is beneath you. In time, I could create you a lord again. Not of the rank your father held, it is true, but noble nonetheless." He stopped and glared down at Liam, expecting an immediate answer. "Well, what say you?"

Liam managed not to gape. "My lord, it is very kind of you," he stammered.

"Then you'll do it."

Squirming in his chair, Liam sought the right words. "It is kind, my lord, but surely there are better candidates?"

"There are others who could fill the office," Vespasianus agreed, "but I would it were you. Will you?"

"I'm afraid I must decline the honor, my lord." It was not even a question. He had seen what the post entailed, and wanted none of it. Coeccias worried night and day over Southwark, nagged by a thousand petty worries. How much more difficult would it be with the Duke looking over his shoulder all the time? The thought of working closely with Vespasianus frightened him more than anything he could imagine—and the man's reaction reinforced his fear.

"Will you never do as I say?" the Duke demanded, brows knitting in anger. "I tell you to sit in a cell, and you do not. I tell you I want you as my Aedile, and you refuse. There is a worm of perversity in you, Quaestor Rhenford—if you will keep even that title.''

Liam hung his head like a boy receiving a richly-deserved scolding. ''It is an honor I feel able to accept, my lord,'' he mumbled.

Vespasianus grunted. ''I offer you much more.''

''I appreciate that, my lord.'' Inspiration struck. ''It's just that I would hate to leave my business at the moment, and I think it will eventually prove to be of more value to the duchy than my occupying the post you have so kindly offered.''

''Y'have great confidence in your new trading routes.''

''I do, my lord. Your merchants will be the first to explore them, and the first to profit from them.''

''Bah!'' the Duke exploded, and trailed his dust cloud over to the writing desk. ''You offer me a feast in a year when I would have a loaf today.'' He sat. ''But I'll not force you. Y'are a free man. Leave me now—I must find a man to fill the office you refuse.''

Liam rose and bowed.

''You'll dine with me this night,'' Vespasianus said in the same angry tone. ''We'll have more on your business, and its value to the duchy.''

Liam bowed himself out, hoping that that would be the end of it—and it was, at least overtly. Over dinner the Duke spoke solely of his trading ventures, displaying a keen interest in an activity he had earlier deemed ungentlemanly, but his displeasure over being refused hung heavy in the air. The meal dragged on into the night; when Liam was finally released he practically fled to his chamber, offering a prayer of thanks for his escape.

Worn out, he crawled into bed quite sure he had made the right decision in declining the Aedileship. He had no doubt the Southern Tier was in capable hands—but every time he had looked at them during dinner, he had seen them holding a bloody dagger to Earl Raius's throat.

Early the next morning, as dawn was breaking over the mountains behind Deepenmoor, Liam stopped on the road. Determined to get a good start, he had already been riding for an hour, and the cold morning air had driven the sleep from his head. It felt good to leave the castle—and the overwhelming presence of the Duke—behind him. Diamond stood quietly, but the packhorse Vespasianus had given him for the trip whickered loudly.

"Hush," Liam told the horse, and it subsided, apathetically cropping the grass by the side of the road. The morning was still, apart from the sound of grass tearing, and then, as the first rays of the sun penetrated the forest, he heard a bird begin to sing, and then another, and another. Soon enough the woods were full of birdsong, and he lingered to hear it.

Savoring the feeling he had of being poised on the verge of escape, he waited for a few minutes and reflected on his time with the court. While the circuit could not be considered an unmitigated success—*How could it be,* he wondered, *when the court went home without either of the quaestors it started with?*—it was not a complete disaster, and he felt sure he had done the best he could. *Which, in the end, is all you can ask for.*

Nodding, satisfied, he set Diamond to an easy walk and began to whistle a travelling song. After a few bars, a thought occurred to him and he stopped.

"Fanuilh."

The dragon was perched on Diamond's withers, and snaked its head over its shoulder to face him. *Yes, master?*

"These woods are full of the Duke's rabbits. You haven't had a chance to hunt in a while. I would like to offer you one of his rabbits. Please help yourself."

But they are not yours.

Liam waved his hand airily. "If I can refuse the greatest offer ever made to a subject of the Duke of the Southern Tier," he asked with mock solemnity, "who is to gainsay me one of our lord's rabbits? Go to, familiar mine, go to, I say!" He shooed the dragon from its perch, and kept waving it away until it turned and flew into the forest. *And don't come back without a rabbit!*

Yes, master.

Alone, he decided that Diamond was going too slow, and urged the roan to a trot. He was eager to reach the Fair; there were avenues of business there he wished to explore, and he knew it would be better to do so early in the trading season. Besides, he was hoping that Cullum's musicians would still be there—and that he might have another dance with Casotte.

DANIEL HOOD

FANUILH   0-441-00055-X/$4.99

The wizard Tarquin valued the miniature dragon Fanuilh as his familiar—and the human Liam as his friend. And when Tarquin was murdered in bed one rainy night, both were left to grieve—and to seek justice.

WIZARD'S HEIR   0-441-00231-5/$4.99

Despite what people think, inheriting a wizard's familiar did not make Liam a wizard. But he is shaping up to be quite a detective. When his late friend Tarquin's magic artifacts are stolen, and then used to commit further crimes, Liam must solve a mystery that's already caused one death and threatens to start a holy war.

BEGGAR'S BANQUET   0-441-00434-2/$5.50

Liam agrees to help solve the theft of a priceless—and magical—family heirloom stolen from his business partner. And he recruits his dragon familiar, Fanuilh, to help. Because what's a little magic among friends?